SWEDISH BLOOD

For Kirsten,
All good wishes,
John Axford

SWEDISH BLOOD

John Amiard

Edson Press

Swedish Blood

This is a work of fiction. All characters, corporations, institutions, organizations, and events in this novel are products of the author's imagination, or if real, are used fictitiously.

For information, contact
Edson Press, 14 Glen Road South, Lexington MA 02420
www.edsonpress.com

ISBN- 978-0-578-01651-1

First Edition June 2009

Cover photograph: Katharine A. Mockett

In memory of Karl Hughes Oberteuffer (1969–1996)

Prologue

Lofsdalen, Sweden, 1939

IT WAS LATE AUGUST and the long twilight evenings of midsummer were over. That night a canopy of sharp, bright stars in a blue-black sky reflected in the lake below the lodge. But the serenity of that view did not ease Erik Svensson's distress. Pacing the small balcony outside the bedroom of his mountaintop lodge, Erik Svensson wrestled with a decision that challenged his conscience. The probability of war among the nations in Europe had increased to a certainty. And that reality created a dilemma for him as the owner of Gevarfabrik, the company that he had inherited, nearly forty years before.

When he had arrived a few days earlier, he had hoped that the solace that he always found at his country retreat would clear his mind and strengthen his resolve. But each night, after a few hours of fitful dozing, he would awaken tired but unable to sleep as he considered the advice that was being urged upon him to put his company on a new course.

The market for Gevarfabrik's firearms was no longer just game hunters. And Erik Svensson knew that converting his production to military weapons was an enormous business opportunity. But he had no desire to see his company grow beyond its current size and product lines. He greeted all his employees by name and managed the foremen himself. With careful planning and management, Gevarfabrik was successfully weathering the current depression. In fact, the business was prospering, thanks to strong exports of the company's world-class hunting rifles and shotguns.

Now, however, he was not sure he could withstand the insistence of some of his potential customers or the arguments of his colleagues. Among them was his trusted sales manager, Jon Anden, who had accompanied two men from Berlin to the lodge to persuade him to begin manufacturing military specification rifles. The Germans were dressed as civilians in dark suits, but from their bearing and aggressive confidence, it was likely that they were senior army officers. To his relief, they had left the day before, but the ominous quality of their visit remained in his mind.

During the past "Great War" that had engulfed Europe, Erik Svensson, with the strong support of his wife, had resisted the call for military weapons. But now he was older, a widower, and alone bore responsibility for Gevarfabrik.

He stopped pacing and stood for a moment looking out over the lake when a thought came to him.. It was time for his son and only child, Bjorn, to return home from the university and work with him. Eventually, Bjorn would take his place, just as he had taken his own father's place four decades before. Intelligent and thoughtful, Bjorn could help him come to the right decision.

He washed his face in cold water from the basin on the nightstand. Then, still in his nightclothes, Erik Svensson sat at a small oak desk by a window overlooking the lake and wrote out a short telegram to his son. His housekeeper, Anneke, could send it from the railroad station in the morning. It would be wonderful to see Bjorn again. He had come only for a short visit to the lodge over the Midsummer holiday in June and before that, briefly, at Christmastime to the family home in Sundsvall. Was something, or someone special, keeping his son in Germany? Perhaps, but at the moment, Bjorn was needed at home.

Slipping the note into an envelope, he dressed quickly for a walk outdoors. His housekeeper had suggested a rabbit stew a few days earlier. Perhaps she could be accommodated. Downstairs in the kitchen, he made some coffee and retrieved an old but well-maintained rifle from the rack over the stone fireplace in the main room of the lodge. While waiting for dawn to arrive, he carefully cleaned and oiled the small-caliber piece, drank his coffee, and ate a sweet roll. When it had grown light enough to walk safely in the woods, he pulled on a light wool jacket and left the telegram for Anneke on the kitchen table.

Walking out across the terrace and down toward the lake, the thought of Bjorn's return and the prospect of a morning tramp in the woods brightened his mood. The familiar feel of his favorite rifle resting lightly over his arm was reassuring. The air was cool and the leaves on the winding path down to the lake were slightly damp. He stepped carefully.

Skirting the top of a narrow ledge, he hesitated, thinking that someone had called his name. But he saw nothing in the brush above the path. Probably a crow, he thought, turning away.

The flash of an explosion erupted from the bushes. He felt something grasp his throat, throwing him backward out over the edge of the rocky outcrop. The pressure at his neck burst into a searing pain. Trees and sky revolved above him. Against the pale blue morning light, he saw a dark red spray. Erik Svensson realized for an instant that it was blood—his own.

* * *

Hamburg, Germany, 1939

STROLLING DOWN LINDENSTRASSE on a warm August afternoon with two tall, blond young men, Helen Wilson was briefly reminded of the disagreeable reality in the country where they were studying at university. They were approaching her friends' apartment building where the landlady had placed a large National Socialist flag in the window of her flat on the first floor. Its black swastika and red background was a common sight in Germany these days, but mostly on public buildings.

Helen climbed the steps with her friends and waited as they quietly opened the heavy front door for her. She hoped that the landlady would be taking a nap. They all preferred to avoid the scowling face that often showed itself behind the narrow crack of her door. Today, that door was completely closed. They walked past it toward the stairs with exaggerated caution, smiling at each other. Frau Freude, as they sarcastically referred to her, was glad to accept the rent which Bjorn gave her each week for the third-floor apartment that he shared with his friend Kjell. Otherwise, she seemed completely disapproving of them. But her darkest looks she reserved for Helen, whom she had sometimes caught creeping past her door in the early hours of the morning. Bjorn had told the landlady that they were planning to get married, but Helen thought that Frau Freude probably did not believe him.

On the first landing, Helen turned and poked Bjorn playfully, hoping to make him say something out loud, then dashed up the next flight. Bjorn let out a German slang word for prostitute they had just learned and gave chase, laughing. Behind them, Kjell walked up the stairs silently carrying what he had told Helen was a very interesting electrical device that he had bought for a few marks at a house sale.

In the living room of the apartment, Kjell set a lacquered wooden box with brass fittings down in front of him on the floor. Helen seated herself across from him on the thin, rust-brown carpet and watched. Kjell explained to her that it was a machine that could record their voices magnetically on an iron wire. He opened the cover of the box and showed her the wire that ran between two spools on the top of the device.

Bjorn sat down behind Helen with a bottle of wine. He handed her two glasses. With his arms wrapped around her, he poured the wine as she held them up. She handed a glass to Kjell, who took it without looking up. The other she kept for herself and Bjorn.

Kjell put his glass down and proceeded to connect a microphone and the loudspeaker from an old radio to the recorder. Then he moved a switch on the side of the box and told Helen and Bjorn that it was recording.

They were all suddenly silent. Finally, Helen said, "Hello, Kjell. How are you?" in German and giggled.

Kjell looked at Bjorn. Speaking in Swedish, Bjorn introduced himself and recited a short poem. Then he stopped, apparently unable to think of anything else to say. With exaggerated seriousness, Kjell said to Helen that since the recorder was made in Holland, it probably did not understand

Swedish. Helen turned her head and looked at Bjorn. He laughed and said Kjell just didn't know how to adjust the machine. Then Kjell and Bjorn proceeded to have a mock argument about the point. After that, they all began talking, and Helen realized that they had forgotten that the recorder was on. They spoke some German, the language of their studies in Hamburg. But mostly, they spoke Swedish, Bjorn and Kjell's native tongue. Helen preferred to speak Swedish, which Bjorn had told her she did almost without accent.

After about twenty minutes, the wire ran out. Kjell rewound the spool, and they listened to their voices. They each agreed that their own voice sounded quite unfamiliar but that the voices of the others were easily recognizable. Later, when the wine ran out, they discussed where they might go for dinner.

As they were getting ready to leave, there was an aggressive knocking at the door. Kjell opened it. Their landlady announced in a self-important voice that he had received a telegram. Behind her, almost completely blocked by her sturdy frame, stood a slight young man in a neat green uniform holding a yellow envelope. She moved slightly to allow him to get by her. The messenger clicked his heels as he handed Kjell the yellow envelope. Kjell looked at it and passed it to Bjorn.

Bjorn stared at the telegram for a long moment and then began absently digging in his pocket. Helen moved quickly to the door and reached into her purse. She handed the messenger several coins and, ignoring the curious stare of the landlady, closed the door in her face. She turned back to Bjorn and put her hand gently on his arm. He continued to look at the envelope then took a deep breath and opened it. He read the text and handed it to her. She read it as Kjell looked over her shoulder. She looked up at Bjorn and felt tears coming to her eyes.

Bjorn shook his head slowly. "I must return to Sweden."

Chapter 1

Cambridge, Massachusetts, 2005

A TELEPHONE BEGAN RINGING as Peter entered the stairwell. He paused, pulling up the large backpack that was slipping off his shoulder, and listened. He hoped it would be the phone in the third-floor apartment. But it sounded like his, on the fourth floor. Maybe it was a wrong number. That would be nice for a change, he thought. But more likely, it was one of the middle-of-the-night, click-buzz calls. Those had started after the first article on neo-Nazis that he had written.

Letting it ring was an option, but the memory of another late-night call three years before was always with him. He shrugged off the fatigue of a delayed flight from the West Coast and took the steps of the dark wood-paneled staircase two at a time.

Peter reached the fourth floor landing, grappling for his keys. By the end of the third ring, he was at the door of his apartment and jamming his key into the lock. But the lock was temperamental and resisted a direct assault. He forced himself to back the key out a fraction and twist it gently. The lock relented, and the door opened. He lunged at the phone on the hall table. But his voice mail had taken over, leaving him with only a dial tone.

He exhaled noisily in frustration. The caller ID was unhelpful. It read "Out of Area." Maybe whoever it was would leave a message if it was important. He crossed the hallway to his room and threw his backpack and jacket on the bed. As he started back toward the kitchen, the phone rang again.

He pushed the speakerphone button. "This is Peter."

"Hey, Frost, sorry to call so late, but your cell phone's been off."

Peter recognized the voice of his friend Bill Reilly. "I've been on a plane all day. Just got home. Did you just call?"

"No, why?"

"Never mind. Hey, what's up?" Peter asked. Reilly was a state police detective based on Cape Cod; his call at this hour was a bit unsettling.

"Your uncle Jed Barlow's gone missing."

"Missing? Like he didn't show up at the office?" Peter felt a wave of uneasiness.

"Something like that. He was scheduled to sail over to Nantucket on his boat to see a client on Wednesday morning and never showed up. His client called his office, and they called the Coast Guard. They sent a chopper out from the station at Otis Air Base covering the sound from Chatham to Nantucket yesterday. Didn't find anything."

"That's not good." Peter let out a long breath. Jed Barlow was his father's cousin and had always been "Uncle Jed" to Peter. "He's a good sailor. How was the weather on Wednesday?"

"Fine. Clear, light southwest winds. Good June weather."

"How'd you get involved in this? Is he a missing person?" Peter asked.

"Not officially. Maureen Darby, his law partner, called me yesterday afternoon. I know her from some public defender stuff she used to do. She called to ask if I could help, in case it wasn't a boating accident," Reilly explained.

"So you agreed to look into it?"

"Well, yeah, you know me. Tough cop, heart of gold. Maureen explained that your uncle is, like, a super-dependable, on-time, considerate kind of guy. And she's out of town." Reilly paused. "I told her it's likely just some misunderstanding. But I said I'd make some calls."

"What did my father say when you called him?"

"Well, I haven't been able to get hold of your father," Reilly said.

Peter felt his uneasiness turn into a chill of fear. Jed and his father often sailed together in the waters off Cape Cod. His father had also not returned his calls from the previous two days. Peter picked up the telephone receiver. "And you couldn't reach him? When did you try?"

"Since yesterday morning. Called, left messages. Swung by the house. Car was there; he wasn't."

Peter tapped the phone against his forehead and stared at the wall.

"Peter? You there?"

Peter brought the phone back to his ear. "Yes. Listen, let me call you back. I want to check something." Peter hung up without waiting for a reply.

He would give his father's next-door neighbor a call. He hated to do it at that hour. She was an elderly widow, but she kept good track of the goings and comings on his father's road. He depressed the button on the phone cradle and released it to dial her number. The stutter dial tone told him that there were voice messages. He hesitated and then called to retrieve them.

He had received five new messages since he had checked from California earlier in the day. He flashed through four of them listening briefly: his aunt Elena in Maine, a sports reporter he had a date with, a colleague at work, and Bill Reilly. The fifth call had been received at 2:09 Friday morning, the call he had just missed. It was his father.

"Peter, thought I'd catch you at home. I'm in Sweden. Left a few days early. Call you back when I have a chance. Off to sail on the Baltic this morning. Sorry we couldn't meet today. Have things to tell you when I get back. Love you, kiddo." End of call. It was a typical, short, Eric-Frost-style message.

Peter sighed in relief, but he was surprised by his father's early departure for Sweden. They had agreed to meet at the airport for a drink before his father's flight that evening. He was curious about his father's sudden change in plans. It was not like him. His father was an engineer and pretty methodical in his ways.

He called Reilly back. "My father's in Sweden. That's why you couldn't reach him. He called just before you did tonight. I just picked up the message."

"Really?" There was a pause. "D'you know he was going away?"

"Yes, but he was supposed to leave today, Friday," Peter said.

"So why'd he leave early?"

"No clue. We were planning to get together at the airport before he left. And I don't know how to get in touch with him. I thought I'd get that information when I saw him."

Reilly did not respond immediately. "According to Barlow's calendar, he was supposed to go for a sail with your father on Monday afternoon. Also, Jed's secretary, Marilyn, said they talked on the phone Tuesday morning. So that means your father might have been one of the last people he talked to. According to Marilyn, after the call, Jed left the office 'in a mood.' Could be he had something on his mind and might've said something to your dad."

Was Reilly suggesting that Jed's disappearance might be a suicide? Peter was reluctant to voice that disturbing possibility. "Well, maybe my uncle just needed some time away from everybody."

Reilly made a sound that indicated disagreement. "Whatever. Get some sleep, buddy. And when you talk to your dad, definitely have him give me a call."

Chapter 2

PETER HAD ARRIVED HOME tired but hungry. Now, as he wandered into the kitchen and contemplated the refrigerator, he realized that he still felt tired but less hungry. The possibility that something had happened to his uncle Jed was depressing. Jed was a few years older than his father and unmarried. He had lived on Cape Cod for as long as Peter had known him. He had retired early from what he said was an over-pressurized life in international corporate law to spend more time sailing. His general law practice in Chatham kept him "out of trouble" and near his boat, he liked to say. He was a gentle man who had always taken a great interest in Peter's work as a journalist.

More out of instinct than interest, Peter opened the refrigerator and rooted around inside. There was some sharp cheddar cheese showing spots of blue mold through the plastic wrapper, a package of sliced bagels of unknown age, and several cans of Labatt Blue. He opted for the beer.

On his way out to the living room, he opened the beer and took a swallow. But halfway to the couch, he changed his mind and turned back. In the kitchen, he retrieved the cheese and the bagels. He scraped the mold off the cheese and dropped a bagel slice in the toaster.

Peter returned to the living room balancing the bagel and slices of cheese on the can of beer and sat on the futon couch. He took a long gulp of beer and a bite of his sandwich. This snack was a definite improvement over the limp, greasy construction that had been offered to him in a cardboard box over Kansas several hours earlier.

Bill had said Jed's disappearance could be "just some misunderstanding." Peter wondered if Reilly was speaking from experience or just hope for his benefit. He had found that Bill Reilly, despite his career in law enforcement, was usually an optimist. It was probably what he liked about him. They had met several years before when Peter and his fiancée, Michelle, had come down from Maine to visit Peter's parents on the Cape. Bill and his wife, Joan, were sitting at the next table in a small bar in Hyannis that featured jazz combos. Between sets, Michelle and Joan had begun talking, eventually drawing in their men. Peter was impressed with Reilly's knowledge of jazz. In addition, the couples discovered a mutual interest in sailing. They kept in touch, getting together on the Cape or in Maine.

But since Michelle's death, Peter had seen less of the Reillys. He still went sailing with Bill and would occasionally accept Joan's invitation for dinner at their home in Harwich. But Peter had never shared any of his random dates with them.

Later in bed, Peter thought about his father's trip to Sweden. Had his own trip there sparked his father's interest in that country? Peter's research for an article on neo-Nazi activities had taken him to Sweden the previous fall. The neo-Nazi movement there was a dark corner in an otherwise tolerant, progressive, and peaceful country. When he returned, his father had talked to him about his trip. Peter remembered a conversation they had driving back from Aunt Elena's in Maine after Thanksgiving.

"Were you just in Stockholm or did you get out into the countryside, get to any other cities?" his father asked.

"Mostly Stockholm and a couple of towns in the south where there's been some significant neo-Nazi activity," Peter replied.

"Nothing north of Stockholm?"

"No, but I spent a weekend in the archipelago east of Stockholm. The guy I told you about, Claes, he and his wife have a summer place on one of the islands. It's like the Maine coast, only more. They must have ten thousand miles of shoreline. There are hundreds of islands. Lots of sailboats. You'd love it."

"What's your friend Claes like? I've heard some Swedes can be kind of cold, standoffish," Peter's father asked.

Peter laughed. "Maybe, but not Claes. Great sense of humor and pretty relaxed, especially for a cop."

"I've been thinking I might take a trip to that part of the world," his father said.

"Really?"

"Yes. You know I haven't been anywhere since ... since your mother died." He paused. "I was thinking maybe next summer I'd visit the Nordic countries, Norway, Sweden, Finland."

"Want some company?" Peter asked.

"Ah, sure, I guess. If you can get away," his father replied.

Peter remembered that he had been surprised his father had not sounded more enthusiastic about their going together.

He reached over and turned out his bedside light, trying to avoid seeing the red numbers on the clock radio. If he was going to get a little badly needed exercise in the morning with his running partner and editor, Gene Johanson, there would not be time for much more than a nap. But with that and a run, at least he could function for the rest of the day. But his concern about Jed and his curiosity about his father's trip to Sweden kept his mind from slipping into neutral and coasting smoothly into sleep.

Chapter 3

PETER'S ALARM SOUNDED AT six thirty. He had already been awake for ten minutes wondering if the day would bring good, bad, or no news about Jed. His body had suggested blowing off his run with Gene and getting another hour of sleep, but it was overruled. Ten minutes later, he was on the sidewalk in front of his building.

He loped down Magazine Street toward the Charles River about six blocks away. This part of Cambridge, once a lower-middle-class area of apartment buildings and familiar Boston three-deckers, was now a modestly gentrified neighborhood thanks to the continuing growth of Harvard and MIT. After a few blocks at an easy pace to warm up, Peter reached the corner where a tall, thin African-American in a long-sleeved yellow jersey and light brown shorts was waiting for him.

"Hey, man, you're dragging this morning. I've been jogging in place here for five minutes," Gene said, falling in beside Peter.

"Oh, right, I saw you running up to the corner to make sure ... I didn't get there first."

Gene smiled. "How'd you make out with the drug decriminalization crowd in Oregon?"

Thoughts of Jed's disappearance were still circling his consciousness. With a little effort, he brought himself back to his professional life. "Yes, well, now they're working ... on a long-shot ballot initiative to get the ... state to legalize marijuana and sell it ... in liquor stores."

"Think you've got enough to wrap up the piece you're doing for next month's issue?"

"Probably. But I may need a couple of days … in Ohio."

"Ohio?"

Peter huffed a "Yes" in the middle of a breath then went on, "Of the eleven states that have decrimmed grass … they seem to have the most liberal statute … but haven't legalized medical … uses like a bunch of other states … Plan to get out there next week … Should be able to make our Wednesday deadline."

Gene looked over at Peter, frowning slightly. "If you'd skipped going to Berkeley to talk about neo-Nazis … you could have hit Ohio on your way back. Can we get together on this after the staff meeting?"

"Definitely," Peter responded. Gene had been pushing him for the final draft of his drug reform article. His follow-up research on neo-Nazis had left him a little behind on his current assignment.

"Well, anyway, how was your time at Berkeley?"

"Useful. Spent an afternoon with a couple of people in political science. They're interested in comparing the neo-Nazi movement … here with what's going on in Europe. I asked a lot of questions. They picked my brain about Sweden," Peter said.

"Guess you're the man. How was the public lecture?"

"Good crowd. Along with three guys wearing swastika armbands. They started shouting and … the campus cops escorted two of them out. One guy didn't say anything. So they let him stay. Hope he enjoyed my talk on his Swedish cousins."

When they reached Memorial Drive, the four-lane roadway along the river, Peter lagged Gene jogging up the long sloping ramps of the pedestrian bridge. Normally, he sprinted ahead up the ramps or dashed across the roadway, if the traffic was light, and waited on the other side for his partner.

Gene looked over at Peter. "Actually, you do seem a little logy this morning. D'you pick up a date on the flight back last night?"

"As if. My flights were delayed. And I got a call when I got in … late, kept me up for a while," Peter said, his thoughts returning to Jed and his father.

The light changed, and Gene led the way across the street. "Another threat?"

"No. Bill Reilly called ... my uncle Jed is missing ... with his boat."

They joined some other early runners on the riverbank park that was known locally as Magazine Beach. An old-timer from the neighborhood had told him that sixty years earlier people swam in the river. Now there was talk about reviving swimming there. The Charles River was now somewhat cleaner than it had been thirty or forty years ago. A tetanus shot was no longer required in case of an accidental plunge.

"How long's your uncle been missing?" Gene asked.

"Couple of days. And it turns out Dad might've been one of the last people to see him. I found out last night that my dad left early for Sweden ... didn't give a reason. Bill would like to talk to him and get a read on Jed's state of mind."

"Seems reasonable. So how come your father took off early for Sweden?"

"No idea. We were supposed to get together for a drink tonight before he left."

When Peter and Gene reached the Eliot Bridge beyond Harvard Stadium, they turned back down the river.

Gene picked up the conversation. "You think maybe your uncle committed suicide?"

"I wouldn't think so, but I guess you never know. Could be some personal problems that I didn't know anything about."

When they reached the pedestrian light at Magazine Street, they walked to cool off. "But I still can't figure out why Dad would take off early for Sweden. It's a vacation he's been planning for a while."

"Isn't he still doing some consulting for his old company? Maybe he got a chance to do a little forensic voice analysis for the Swedish police and is writing off part of his trip," Gene offered.

Peter considered the possibility. His father had resigned recently from the small audio engineering company he had worked at since the early seventies. He had continued to work a few days a month for them. "That's possible, but I think he would have mentioned that in his message. Anyway, see you at the office," Peter said as they separated at Gene's cross street.

By eight o'clock, Peter had showered and produced breakfast from some yogurt and granola. He scanned the *Boston Globe* while he ate; there was no mention of his uncle's disappearance. In an e-mail to his father, he summarized what Reilly had told him about Jed's disappearance, not including his suggestion that it might be suicide, and relayed Reilly's urgent request to call him.

The offices of *VERITAS? Magazine* were located just outside Harvard Square on a narrow side street. Peter found a spot for his old Volvo station wagon in the next block. The magazine occupied a small traditional clapboard house painted light yellow with black shutters. It was similar to its neighbors, which were mostly early nineteenth century or Victorian houses on small lots bounded by uneven brick sidewalks. *VERITAS?* had been created by a large endowment from the former CEO of a company whose activities had significantly polluted a small third-world country. After retiring, he determined to repair some of the damage he felt he had done in his corporate life. A magazine dedicated to the idea of "speaking truth to power Left or Right" was his answer. Recent articles had included threats to the Freedom of Information Act and a Columbian drug/Middle Eastern terrorist connection.

Peter had joined the *VERITAS?* staff three years earlier after spending five years as an investigative reporter for the *Portland Journal* in Maine. He had been recruited by his college roommate, Gene Johanson, the editor and publisher of *VERITAS?*. After Michelle's funeral, Gene had told Peter that a position in Cambridge was open for him if he ever thought about leaving Portland. A month later, Peter was in Cambridge.

At *VERITAS?* he shared an office in a small front room on the second floor with his colleague Jill. "You stood me up again last night, Pietro dear," she said, as he walked in. She continued to type at her computer without looking up.

Jill was tall, dark-haired, and always stylishly and expensively dressed. Even after several years in Cambridge, Peter thought she still looked like New York. She told Peter that his

"L.L.Bean-casual-preppy" look was cute, but added that it bordered on "earth-crunchy."

"Where were you? Thought you'd be in early enough to come by the office," she continued.

"What can I tell you? I had other plans," Peter responded in a serious tone.

"I can imagine," she said, swiveling around in her chair to look at him.

"Actually, Delta Airlines had other plans. My flight was delayed. I got in around one."

"Poor boy."

"How about some dinner tonight?" Peter asked.

"Sounds good, if you think you can stay awake that long."

As Peter was trying to think of a smart comeback, Gene leaned into the room from the narrow hallway. "You guys ready for staff meeting?" he asked. "We're on in five minutes."

Peter and Jill joined Gene, along with two other staff writers, their fact-checker, the production manager, and the magazine's lawyer, downstairs to discuss the upcoming issue.

Gene waited until everyone was seated. "Okay, people, we've got four main articles for August: drug decriminalization, sobriety checkpoints, Web censorship, and mandatory gun ownership. Our usual good balance between the Far Left and the Far Right with an opportunity for some editorializing for the thoroughly unpopular middle. And we've got a photo essay on government-created pollution sites."

Most of the meeting was taken up by staff members' critiques of each other's articles with Gene supportively refereeing. After about an hour of spirited discussion, they reached the last item on the agenda, traditionally reserved for comments and cautions from the magazine's lawyer, Phil Jordan. Gene was coaxing him through his concerns on the pollution photo-essay when an intern signaled to Peter from the doorway that he had a phone call.

Peter started to wave her away then thought better of it. "Excuse me, folks." He extracted his tall frame from his chair by the window and edged around the conference table.

"It's a Lieutenant Reilly. He says it's important," the intern whispered as she handed Peter the phone.

"Bill, what's up?"

"A body was found on the beach on Monomoy. Some bird-watchers discovered it this morning. We think it might be your uncle."

Peter let out a quiet breath. Monomoy was an uninhabited sandy island off the Cape, not far from where Jed would have been on a course to Nantucket. "Are you sure?"

"No. There was no identification on the body."

"Any idea what happened? Did they find his boat?"

"We won't know until the autopsy. And no, his boat hasn't turned up." Bill sounded hurried. "We'd like to get an ID before we go ahead, preferably from a family member. Can you do it?"

Peter looked at his watch. "I'll be down by two."

Chapter 4

PETER RETURNED TO THE staff meeting just as Phil seemed to be summing up the final item on his list: a lawsuit against the magazine by a militant vegan group. They were apparently claiming damages as a result of an article Jill had written the previous year on the health risks of macrobiotic diets. When the staff meeting ended, Peter stayed behind to tell Gene that they would have to put off their meeting.

"Understand. First thing Monday morning then," Gene said, adding, "I don't envy your afternoon. Take care."

Peter returned to his office where he knew Jill would be curious to find out about the phone call. He was not disappointed.

Jill swiveled to face the door as he came in. "Your mysterious telephone call, anything serious?"

Peter provided a brief summary of Bill Reilly's calls and his father's message the previous night.

Jill interrupted frequently with expressions of concern and questions. "You must be upset. I remember you telling me about your uncle's teaching you to sail one summer when you were just in grade school. But do you think he really might've taken his own life? And your father, you've no idea where he is in Sweden?" She stood up and gave him a quick hug. "Well, do take care this afternoon. Must be a rather stressful prospect."

Peter picked up his jacket and laptop and moved toward the door. "Thanks. I'll be okay. Fill you in on everything this evening. Maybe I'll know a little more then."

"My turn to pay, so there's an extra incentive. As if you needed one to have dinner with me," Jill said, looking up at him with an exaggeratedly flirtatious look.

Peter had become fond of Jill in the year since she had joined *VERITAS?*. She had left a position at a national magazine in Manhattan, over editorial policy, she said. She and Peter had had some casual dates, mostly dinners after work. One dinner, after a long day on deadline, had evolved into a sleepover that, while technically successful, Peter thought, had not been very satisfying. Apparently, Jill had felt the same way, and by mutual agreement, their relationship had remained casual.

Peter headed out of Cambridge over the Charles River toward the Boston side of the Harvard campus. He turned east on Soldiers Field Road past the Business School toward the Southeast Expressway. Now that Boston's infamous Big Dig was completed, the new subterranean highway provided the fastest route south through the city to Cape Cod.

The early Friday afternoon traffic was light. His thoughts turned to his uncle. Jed was in his seventies, a little older than his father. Peter had been told that Jed had been married when he was young, but his uncle had always been single as long has Peter had known him. Although no one discussed it, Peter had figured out that he was probably gay. He lived alone in Chatham not far from Peter's father's house.

Outside of his work, Jed's major interest was sailing and a community theater group. He was an experienced sailor, relaxed and confident at the helm of his small cruising yacht. He seemed agile and strong for a man of his age, which was another reason to wonder how a sailing accident in light winds on a clear day could have happened.

As a lawyer, he was intense, super-straight, and anything but relaxed. Peter had consulted his uncle Jed a year earlier when he had been concerned about his personal liability in a lawsuit against *VERITAS?*. The lawsuit had been brought by the target of an article he had written. Jed had described every possible circumstance, however improbable, that could result in some risk for Peter. But he had finally conceded that Peter was probably 99 percent free of concern. However, Jed's review of all the unlikely circumstances of the remaining one percent had left Peter more, not less, anxious.

It took Peter about an hour to reach the Cape Cod Canal, which separated the crooked arm of the Cape from the mainland. Built in the early part of the twentieth century, it made the coastal shipping route significantly quicker and safer. Since the first Europeans had begun exploring the East Coast of America, hundreds of large and small boats had been shipwrecked on the sandbars off the outer Cape where it reached into the Atlantic Ocean. For modern travelers, the canal made Cape Cod an island, accessible only by two relatively narrow bridges that were notorious for long delays on summer weekends. However, on this preseason Friday, cars and trucks were approaching and crossing the bridge at close to the speed limit.

At ten minutes before two, Peter pulled into the parking lot of the Cape Cod Hospital in Hyannis. Hospitals brought back difficult memories for Peter. His mother had made several trips to the hospital in a protracted battle with stomach cancer. She had always left the hospital under her own power, and she had died at home in Cambridge. But the building reminded Peter of her in those days: her brave frailty and determined smile that was as much to reassure Peter and his father as it was for herself. It also reminded him of his fiancée, Michelle, who had spent three days in a hospital in Maine in an irreversible coma.

Bill Reilly was waiting for Peter outside the main entrance. He was sharing a bench with an elderly white-haired man who had a gauze patch over one eye. Reilly was sitting back, letting the late spring sun fend off a cool breeze from the sound. He got to his feet quickly as Peter walked up. Reilly had red, curly hair. He was shorter than Peter at five feet ten inches and broad-shouldered. His windbreaker was strained over his chest and arms. He was more muscle than fat except at his waist where his enjoyment of beer and his wife's good cooking undid his bodybuilding.

Reilly looked at his watch and grinned at Peter. "Right on time, true to your word."

"Naturally. Journalists know all about deadlines. We don't sit around eating doughnuts waiting for something to happen."

"Right, and if nothing's happening, you get some protesters together and persuade them to throw rocks so you can write a story about it."

The old man with the patch looked startled. Peter passed up another round of wisecracks, thinking how easily he and Reilly could lapse into irreverent banter. Perhaps it was their way of dealing with difficult emotions—at least that was what Jill would have said.

"Which way?" Peter asked as they walked through the automatic doors.

"The morgue's on the second basement level. Let's take the stairs. It'll be quicker."

The stairs held a heavy scent of disinfectant with hints of whatever it was that was being disinfected. The metal door banged behind them as they headed down the two short flights. The door to the second basement level opened onto a narrow corridor, which was well lit and painted a pale green.

Reilly led Peter down the hallway past several carts of idle electronic equipment and an empty gurney. They came to a counter with a sign that read, "Morgue, Please Check in Here." Two staff members were conferring behind the counter. One was a tall man in a white lab coat, the other a small, dark-haired woman in white pants and a smock top. The white lab coat was listening intently to the small woman.

As the visitors approached, the woman looked over her shoulder, revealing an attractive profile, and made a just-a-minute gesture with her hand.

Turning to Peter, Reilly said, "Jan Whitney is the medical examiner for Barnstable County. She's doing the postmortem."

The petite doctor signed something on a clipboard that her colleague was holding and turned toward Reilly and Peter. "Hi, Bill. You're looking well … fed, that is. But still sexy," she added, giving him a quick kiss on the cheek.

She turned and looked up at Peter while engaging his hand firmly. "Bill was right. You are better looking than he is, but not by much," she said, half turning back to look at Reilly.

Peter smiled and tried to think of something reasonably clever, or at least not dumb, to say. But Jan's expression turned serious before anything came to him.

"I'm sorry about your uncle, Peter. Thanks for coming down. You know we like to have at least a preliminary identification before we do a PM. And I know Bill is anxious to get moving on this." She smiled again briefly, keeping her focus on Peter. "Are you ready for this?"

"I've done some crime reporting," Peter responded.

"Well, that's good," Jan responded. "I hate having people barf; it makes me feel queasy." Reilly rolled his eyeballs and gave Peter a sympathetic half smile.

Jan led them past the counter and down the side corridor to a set of double doors. Peter adjusted his stride to keep up with her. The doors opened onto a large, well-lit autopsy room with two stainless steel worktables. There was a form under a white plastic sheet on one of the tables.

She moved quickly to the occupied table. "We've done some preliminary work: x-rays and drew blood for drug testing. But we held off on the slicing and dicing until you got here." Peter nodded as he faced her over the autopsy table. Despite Jan Whitney's attractiveness, he was a little put off by her humor.

"Okay, first the face." She drew back the sheet from the head with a quick, practiced motion.

Peter looked down at the gray-white face, which had a three-day salt-and-pepper stubble. The eyes were half-lidded, and the mouth was slightly agape. Longish, gray hair was matted down on one side of the head. He tried to match the face on the table to the one he knew as belonging to his uncle. But it didn't work. No way it was Jed.

"Ah …" Peter began.

"Take your time," Jan said, looking at Peter.

Peter shook his head. "No. For sure, this isn't Jed Barlow, but …"

"Okay. We probably should have guessed that. Your uncle's a pretty conservative lawyer, I hear. Our chum here— excuse the pun—has a ponytail," Jan said, reaching under the head and pulling a length of gray-blond hair held by a rubber band to one side. "Hello, what's this?" She drew her hand away and looked at the red stain on her latex glove. Then she leaned down and peered at the area under the ponytail. "Small entry wound, looks like."

Reilly tilted to one side and looked as Jan rotated the head to expose the small dark spot just above the neck. "Looks like I've got something else to worry about here. You're positive this isn't Jed?" Reilly asked turning toward Peter. "Guess we wasted your time coming down. But thanks."

Jan shrugged and pulled the sheet back over the head of the unidentified corpse. She moved toward the door and held it open. "Hey, you tried. Appreciate your coming down, Peter. Come back and see us. We'll do something else fun. Now I've got work to do, so you guys need to get your butts out of here."

Chapter 5

THEY WALKED DOWN THE corridor away from the morgue. When they reached the door to the stairwell, Reilly stopped with his hand on the door. "You started to say something back there when you saw the guy's face."

"I thought he looked like someone I'd seen around. But I can't place him. You know the problem: a face out of context. But somebody in Brewster or nearby."

"Well, lemme know if you remember," Reilly replied.

Bill and Peter did not speak again until they reached the sidewalk. Peter was glad to be outside the hospital. The sea breeze and sun represented a more agreeable reality. They moved away from the entrance to gain a little privacy.

"So, my uncle is still just missing? I guess that's good news. Sort of."

"Yeah, sort of. And all options are available."

"Which means what? Accident, personal escape, homicide, suicide?" Peter said.

"You forgot kidnapping," Reilly replied. "But I guess that covers it. Or it still could be a misunderstanding and he'll show up in a day or two. When his law partner, Ms. Darby, gets back, we'll see if she can tell us anything: drugs, money, love problems." Reilly pulled a roll of mints out of the pocket of his windbreaker and offered one to Peter. "Does your father hang out much with Jed?"

Peter declined the mint. "We do family stuff. They sail together, and they're both involved in a theatre group in Brewster."

"Still, it would be useful to talk to him," Reilly said, rolling the mint around with his tongue.

"I assume Dad'll call me again in a day or two, and I'll make sure he gives you a call."

Reilly looked at his watch. "I'd better get back to Jan. I told her I wanted to observe."

Peter looked surprised.

Reilly turned toward the main entrance of the hospital. "I just tell her I know she appreciates my company even if it's hard for her to say so."

Peter smiled. "Your Irish charm at work."

Leaving the hospital parking lot, Peter looked at his watch. It was just before three, plenty of time to get to Brewster and stop by his father's house to see if he had left any clue to his early departure and even more important, if there was anything that might provide an explanation for his uncle's disappearance—at least one that was more optimistic than what was currently being suggested.

From Hyannis, he drove a few miles east on the Mid-Cape Highway and turned north toward Brewster on Route 124. A large cranberry bog opened below the road on the left. At this time of year, the sunken field was grayish brown. There was just a suggestion of the brilliant color that it would be in October. Then, the bog would be flooded for the harvest and its surface would be a spectacular crimson carpet of floating cranberries.

The narrow road wound north to Brewster on Cape Cod Bay, passing mostly older, shingled homes of permanent residents. These gave Brewster a more rural character than other parts of the Cape where motels and strip malls often dominated the roadside. Somewhere, he had read that the town had been a favorite spot in the nineteenth century for retired sea captains. It offered the quiet water of the bay rather than the ocean surf on the outside of the Cape ...

Sea captains! That was where he had seen the face in the morgue, on a brochure for fishing charters. It was old Captain Somebody who took people out for the day or a morning to catch blues or stripers in his boat, the *Blue Something-or-Other*.

When he reached Route 6A, he stopped at the touristic Brewster General Store. Among the brochures for whale watching and real estate, he found one for Capt'n Haake's *BlueFinn* Fishing Charter. The Capt'n was definitely the man he had seen on the stainless steel table. He called Reilly as he left the store and left a message on his voice mail. In a few minutes, Peter turned off Brewster's main road onto Phillips Landing Road. It led down toward a small parking-sticker-required lot on the bay. His father's house was a short walk back from the water on a dirt road called Hannah's Way.

Peter crunched into the gravel driveway and parked behind his father's Audi. His father's two cats were sitting expectantly by the back door. As he was getting out of his Volvo, his father's neighbor Mary was walking towards him from her house further down Hannah's Way.

"Peter," she said, striding up to him. "I was just coming around to feed the cats, poor things. They came to my house this morning looking hungry. I guess your father's been away."

Mary Knight was the widow of a retired minister in Brewster. She was still gardening enthusiastically and active in her husband's parish at eighty-something.

"Thanks, Mary. They must be hungry. Dad left for Sweden a couple of days ago."

"Oh really? He told me last weekend he was leaving Friday, today." She paused for breath. "But I was curious since I haven't seen any lights on since Monday night."

Apparently, Mary had lost none of her powers of observation and her memory was in good working order. It seemed odd that his father's decision had been made on such short notice that he had not had time to tell Mary Knight. That made him slightly uneasy despite his father's explanatory phone message.

"Anyway, Peter," Mary said, trying to get his attention, "I'm happy to be on cat duty until he gets back."

They went inside using Mary's key. They determined there was enough food in the pantry for Ashes and Marmalade, two gentle, old male cats whose names accurately described their coloring. Mary knew her way around, and Peter left her in the kitchen making motherly noises.

The house had its normal casual look. Tuesday morning's newspaper was still on the dining room table. Peter had seen what looked like breakfast dishes, rinsed but left in the sink. There were several glasses in the living room. On the porch, there were cigarette butts in a teacup, which had been pressed into service as an ashtray. Peter wondered who the smoker was. Most of his father's friends had given it up years ago.

Peter returned to the kitchen where Mary was rinsing out the cat food cans. "So my dad didn't tell you he was leaving early for Sweden?"

"The last time I saw him was Monday. He was in front of the house saying good-bye to some men. Businessmen, I think."

"Businessmen?" Peter asked.

"Well, they were all wearing dark suits. Looked pretty dressed up for this neck of the woods." Mary seemed pleased to have some useful information to share and sat down at the breakfast nook. "I was just making my tea when I saw them out my kitchen window which, you know, is right over the sink."

"Right," Peter said, amused at Mary's need to give an explanation for her observations. "Were they here long?"

"Yes, I think so. They arrived at about two o'clock. Then I went out for my book club meeting. We always meet on the second and fourth Monday of the month unless it's a Monday holiday and ..." Mary went on.

It didn't sound like the theatre crowd, Peter thought. They sometimes had meetings at the house. It seemed more likely that it was a meeting involving some of his father's company's clients. But usually, those meetings were in Cambridge at the firm's offices. Perhaps his visitors were from a company on the Cape or possibly the government, agencies with three-letter initials. Peter knew his father sometimes did what his mother had called "hush-hush" work.

Peter decided he might as well take advantage of his father's neighbor's inquisitiveness. "Did you talk to my dad after they left?"

"No, I didn't. And I didn't see him the next day either. I don't know when he left. I guess somebody must have come to pick him up early."

Peter realized he had probably exhausted Mary's information about his father's recent activities. He was appreciative of her help but wanted the house to himself before poking around through his father's study. He waited as she spent a few more minutes in the kitchen tidying up and talking to the cats. When she had left, Peter climbed the steep stairs to the second floor. Perhaps there would be something like an itinerary or a hotel reservation, maybe a calendar entry relating to the meeting with the dark suits.

The study was in the front of the house facing the bay. Through the window over his father's desk, there were views across the water to the cliffs in Wellfleet farther out on the Cape.

Eric Frost's desk was in its usual state of "organized clutter," as he referred to it. Peter was reluctant to sift through the papers knowing how annoyed his father became if it appeared that anyone had rearranged things. Next to the telephone, there were some travel brochures for Sweden. Under the telephone was an American Airlines ticket folder. Looking inside, he found it contained flight coupons in the name of Eric Frost for a round-trip to Sweden. The first coupon was for the Boston to London leg for travel that day, Friday, on the six o'clock evening flight.

It was surprising that his father had left his original tickets even if he had changed his departure day. Buying a new set of tickets on short notice meant paying a large premium even on a coach fare. That was something else to puzzle over.

Peter's curiosity overcame his reluctance to rummage through his father's papers. He picked through the pile of technical articles. They appeared to cover several different topics in audio technology, including the effects of background speech on the recognition of speech by computers and a new method for identifying individuals by voice. There was some personal correspondence, including a couple of letters from Peter's aunt Elena in Maine. Other than the tickets, nothing seemed to be related to his father's trip to Sweden or his meeting on Monday afternoon.

Peter left his father's office and walked down the short hallway to the master bedroom. A pile of books and magazines crowded the bedside table. It was his father's usual mixture of mystery fiction and scientific nonfiction. He looked in the closet and saw that his father's roll-on suitcase and toilet kit were gone. On the bureau, there was a pad with the list of predeparture tasks:

> *stop* Times *delivery*
> *see Mary re cats*
> *call airport limo*
> *mail envelope to Jed*

Some of them were crossed off; others were not. The last item was circled and crossed off. "Mail envelope to Jed" means what? he wondered. Probably nothing to do with his leaving early. But could it have something to do with his uncle's disappearance?

The envelope was probably sitting in Jed's mailbox in Chatham. It would be easy to check, even if it wasn't strictly legal. It could also be a waste of time. His watch read a little before four. If he started back to Cambridge now, he'd hit rush-hour traffic.

Peter locked the house and drove back up Phillips Landing Road. At 6A, he turned right toward Boston but then almost immediately left onto Millstone Road toward his uncle's house in Chatham.

Chapter 6

CHATHAM WAS A SHORT drive south of Brewster on the Nantucket Sound side of Cape Cod. Peter parked in Jed's driveway and let himself in with a key that his uncle kept under a potted geranium by the back door. Several days' worth of mail was scattered in the front hall below the door. There were a few bills, a catalog, and several flyers from local businesses, but nothing from his father.

This was Friday. If his father had mailed the envelope on Tuesday before he left, it would certainly have arrived. But perhaps his father hadn't mailed it. Maybe Jed had stopped by the house in Brewster and picked it up.

Jed's study was off the hall to the right of the front door. A large desk in the middle of the room faced the door; behind it were two tables piled with manila folders and file storage boxes. Nothing there looked like a letter from his father. There was no "Good-Bye, World" letter either.

If Bill Reilly's explanation of Jed's disappearance as suicide was correct, then some sort of note in a fairly obvious place would be likely. Peter left the office and made a careful survey of the first floor, but found nothing.

He returned to the office for one more look. To the left of the desk, dark wood bookshelves lined the inside walls. Sets of formal-looking books on international statutes and case law occupied most of one wall. Jed had been a corporate lawyer for a Chicago-based multinational minerals company before semi-retiring to Cape Cod. Peter wondered how often his uncle consulted any of the volumes, which were tightly packed in place.

The other wall was filled up with a variety of nonfiction history titles and some fiction, mostly mysteries. Another shelf held a series of slim volumes labeled by year, apparently a full set of business diaries. The earliest was 1964, and the last was the previous year. But a small gap in the lineup caught Peter's eye. The 1970 volume was missing.

Peter turned back to the desk and saw it there. He flipped through several pages. The entries were mostly from a period when his uncle seemed to be spending a good deal of time overseas. Appointments were listed in a number of countries in Europe—including Sweden he noted—with the names of various companies and individuals. Would a closer reading of the entries reveal something related to Jed's disappearance? Peter decided that his uncle would forgive him, under the circumstances, for borrowing it—If he ever had to explain it at all.

It occurred to him that his father might have mailed the letter to his uncle's office in town. The nautical-looking brass clock on Jed's desk read four thirty. If the Barlow and Darby Law offices were still open, Jed's secretary, Marilyn, would probably let him into Jed's office to retrieve the letter.

Peter left his uncle's house and drove to downtown Chatham's winding main street, a short distance from Jed's house. A few early season tourists wandered in and out of the upscale clothing and gift shops, but otherwise, the town was quiet on this Friday afternoon. Peter turned up a side street to a big Victorian house that had been converted into professional offices and parked. The front door was open, but his uncle's law office on the second floor was locked. Peter knocked on the chance that someone might still be working late.

"They've all gone for the weekend," a voice behind him said.

Peter turned around and saw a slight woman in a dark pantsuit carrying a large computer bag on her shoulder. She was coming down the stairs from the third floor.

"I saw Marilyn locking up about ten minutes ago. You'll have to wait till Monday," she said, without stopping.

"Guess you're right," Peter said. And thanks for your sympathetic attitude, he thought.

The woman continued down the stairs, leaving Peter trying to think if there might be a way to get into the office. Bill had said that Maureen Darby was out of town, and he had no idea how to reach Marilyn. After he heard the heavy front door shut behind Ms. Attitude from upstairs, he took his Visa card out of his wallet. It slipped easily between the door and the jamb. When he felt the bolt click back, he pulled the door open.

Inside, the large central room was dimly lit from the windows of a conference room across from the door. Beyond a small reception area, which held a few chairs and a coffee table with magazines for waiting clients, there were several desks and a number of filing cabinets. Open doors to the left and right led to Maureen Darby's and Jed's offices.

Peter looked around on Jed's secretary's desk, but it was neatly cleared for the weekend. Jed's office contained more shelves of legal books and additional tables with piles of folders and bulging portfolios. Neatly stacked on the desk were two piles, one of various legal-looking papers, perhaps for Jed's review or signature, and another smaller pile of unopened mail. In the latter, Peter found a heavy manila mailing envelope addressed in his father's handwriting. He turned it over in his hands. It was incompletely sealed; the metal clasp did most of the work in holding the flap down. Peter carefully pulled up the tongues of the clasp and loosened the flap without tearing it.

Inside there were several items: two stapled, printed documents, a business-size envelope, and a padded envelope containing a CD. On the business-size envelope, "EWF Birth Certificate" was written. Why would his father send Jed his birth certificate? Peter wondered.

The envelope was unsealed, and Peter opened it. There were two papers inside. One was a birth certificate. It read:

Name: Erik Bjorn Svensson
Sex: male
Date of Birth: May 15, 1940
Place: Springfield, MA
Father: Bjorn Svensson
Mother: Helen Wilson

Who was Erik Bjorn Svensson? Peter wondered. Why did his father have this guy's birth certificate?

Peter unfolded a second official-looking piece of paper from the envelope. He had to read it twice before he could take in its contents. It was a notice of adoption changing Erik Bjorn Svensson's name to Eric Wilson Frost whose adoptive parents were Alan and Judith Frost of Munroe, Massachusetts, the people Peter had always known as his grandparents, his father's parents.

He stared at the papers. "Incredible. You were going to mention this to me sometime, right, Dad?" Peter said aloud to his uncle's empty office.

He started to put the birth certificate and the adoption papers back into the business envelope but stopped. He carefully reread both documents. There was no mistake. His grandparents—at least that was who he had always thought they were—had adopted his father.

He wandered out of Jed's office and into the conference room still holding the documents. He stood for a moment looking out over Main Street below and beyond it a narrow wedge of Oyster Pond. Who were Bjorn Svensson and Helen Wilson? Why had they given his father up for adoption? Had they been students at Munroe College where his grandfather taught? Back in Jed's office, he returned the documents to the large envelope and left it on the desk.

He walked out of Barlow and Darby's offices. As he turned away from the door, he saw the pantsuit lady hurrying up the stairs from the first floor.

"Forgot some papers," she said, looking slightly embarrassed. Then her expression turned into a puzzled frown, and she paused on the top step. "Oh, was somebody in the office?"

"Ah … well, Jed Barlow is my uncle," Peter said, realizing that now Jed probably wasn't. "I mean he might not be … but it's okay …" Peter nodded and tried to smile reassuringly but thinking, "Oh crap! So much for being unobtrusive."

The woman's frown deepened, and she walked quickly past Peter and on up the stairs. "I need to get something in my office."

Back in his Volvo, he wondered what Ms. Pantsuit would say to Marilyn on Monday morning.

Peter drove away from Chatham thinking Erik Bjorn with a "k" and "Svensson" all sounded pretty Swedish. Was the search for his birth parents the reason his father had gone to Sweden? He remembered his father's phone message: "Have some things to tell you when I get back." *Yeah! No kidding, Dad.*

After crossing over the Mid-Cape Highway, he missed the turn toward Boston and found himself back on Phillips Landing Road. He drove down to the beach and got out of the car. Clouds from the northwest had come in and blocked out the afternoon sun, although the sky was still blue to the east. It felt sharply cooler than earlier. It was low tide, and he was nearly alone. There was a couple with a dog way out on the flats that extended into the bay. He walked a little way down the beach and then returned and sat below a sand dune, which partly blocked the wind. Why hadn't his father told him about being adopted?

His first reaction had been amazement at what he had found; now there were angry thoughts spinning through his head. Maybe it was the sense that he had lost something, his Frost grandparents. His memories of them and his feelings were strong, even now, some years after they had passed away. He had always been the center of their attention and affection. He remembered happy weeklong stays with them when he was growing up and later when he was in college. The revelation that they were not his real grandparents was upsetting. It felt like another loss added to that of his mother and Michelle.

Michelle. He could accept the others in a way. But Michelle had been young and healthy, ready to live a life. He threw a handful of sand toward the water and watched the wind and gravity fight for it. A three-time convicted drunk driver had killed her, hitting her little Subaru broadside after blowing through a stop sign. How many times had that angry thought passed through his mind?

He left the beach and drove up to his father's house but didn't get out of the car. After a couple of minutes, he backed roughly out of the gravel driveway. Instead of answers, he was leaving with more questions—a lot more.

Chapter 7

BACK ON ROUTE 6 heading west in evening commuter traffic, Peter realized that he had only glanced at the two stapled, printed documents in the mailing envelope. They seemed to be transcriptions of dialogue among several people. Perhaps something related to the theatre group. One of them appeared to be in Swedish. Were they somehow related to his father's Swedish parents? He was annoyed at himself for not at least skimming the contents of the one in English. "Great investigative reporting, Peter," he said to himself, looking out at the stern of a trailered powerboat ahead whose transom read, "*OhMyCod*, Rock Harbor, MA." Peter called Jill and found her still in the office.

"Pedro, are you okay? Where are you? Did you ...?" She hesitated.

"No, the body wasn't my uncle's," Peter responded.

"That's good, I guess."

"I guess," Peter replied.

"Are we still good for dinner? Or will it be another night with my cat and Chinese take-out, watching a documentary on PBS about penguins in the Antarctic?"

Peter knew that this scenario was very unlikely. Jill had a wide circle of friends. "I don't know, Jill. I think that's supposed to be a very good documentary. Maybe you should skip dinner with me." He paused for effect and then went on, "I'll be there at eight. I'm on my way back now."

"Brilliant, see you then."

Peter hesitated. He needed to share his mind-rattling information with someone. He felt very comfortable with Jill.

After their brief attempt at something more serious, she had become something of a sister. "Actually, I found out something curious. My father was adopted."

"Really? And you never knew?"

"No, he never said anything. I found his birth certificate."

"Wow. Did you ever suspect?"

"No," Peter said. "No clue. Anyway, let's talk when I get there."

After they disconnected, Peter checked his voice mail. Perhaps there would be a message from his father letting him know where he could be reached. There was just one call that had gone to voice mail. The message was twenty seconds of what sounded like white power music or "hatecore" rock, probably courtesy of some member of the neo-Nazi community. They'll get tired of calling eventually, he thought.

Peter crossed the high arching Sagamore Bridge. Three sailboats far below were motoring south toward Buzzards Bay against the swirling tidal currents in the canal.

Five minutes on the phone with his absent father would certainly answer a lot of questions. Who else might know anything about his father's adoption? Peter's mother and his grandparents were gone. Peter, like his father, was an only child. He had an aunt and an uncle on his mother's side and some cousins who lived in New Mexico. They were real relatives. And, of course, there was Uncle Jed. But he was his father's cousin because he was the son of his grandmother Frost's sister. So now ... He realized that he was starting to divide his family into his real, biological relatives and his unreal, adoptive relatives.

Then there was Aunt Elena. She was a real-unreal relative. But Peter had always known that. She was what Peter's grandmother had told him was a courtesy aunt. When a family had a close friend, the children could address her as "Aunt first-name" instead of "Mrs." or "Miss last-name." It seemed a little old-fashioned, Peter thought.

Aunt Elena. Perhaps she would know something. Peter wondered why that hadn't occurred to him sooner. Aunt Elena, a spry New Englander now in her eighties, had lived in Boothbay Harbor ever since Peter had known her. She was a fixture at

Christmas with the family. While the older Frosts were alive, she and her husband usually stayed with them in Munroe.

Peter began to punch in her number and then stopped. As close as they were, he wasn't sure how to present this subject. He drove on for a few minutes. He finally decided to call her anyway and see how she was. Maybe he would think of how to put it when they were on the phone. Her message machine picked up. "Hi, Aunt Elena. It's Peter. How are things in Maine? I'm calling to …" He hesitated. "Anyway, I'll try you again in the morning. Love you."

At ten minutes before eight, Peter arrived at the Harvest Restaurant and found Jill at the bar. She was in an animated conversation with several people that Peter knew vaguely from parties at her condo. After a few minutes, Jill seemed to pick up on Peter's body language and excused herself and Peter, saying they had some work-related issues to discuss over dinner. Peter nodded good-byes and led the way to a quiet table in a back corner.

"So tell all," Jill said after their drinks had arrived.

"Cheers," said Peter, touching his glass of Irish whiskey to Jill's glass of Chardonnay. "Full report coming up as soon as I give my vocal chords a little lubrication."

They focused on their drinks for a moment in silence. Jill twisted the stem of her wine glass as Peter organized his thoughts.

"So where do you want me to begin?" he asked.

"Well, you went off to the Cape to identify what your friend Bill Reilly thought was your uncle's body. Start there."

Peter wondered how much he should tell her. He decided to make it simple. "The body wasn't my uncle Jed's."

"So he's still missing?" Jill said.

"Right."

"An accident?"

"Could be, but the most likely accident for someone alone in a sailboat would be falling overboard. If the boat was underway, it would sail off and you couldn't catch up to it swimming. But the boat wouldn't sink. And somebody probably would have spotted it before now," Peter explained.

"So that sounds more like suicide. Would he shoot a hole in his boat and then shoot himself?" Jill went on without waiting for answer. "But maybe he's just escaping, sailing away from his problems, literally and figuratively."

"The psychological explanation," Peter said with a half smile. "I think that's why Bill Reilly wants to talk to my dad. He and Jed were supposed to go sailing together Monday afternoon. Jed's secretary said they talked Tuesday morning, the day before Jed disappeared."

Jill nodded, smiling. Then she looked at Peter with a serious expression. "Do you sail alone?"

"Sometimes. Well, mostly." Peter took a last swallow of his whiskey. "But I always keep my remote control with me so I can get the boat to turn around and come back to get me."

Jill made a face and stuck out her tongue at Peter. She picked up her menu. "What are you going to have?"

After they had ordered, Jill was quiet. Peter took the hint. "So, I said I'd tell you about discovering that my dad was adopted. Kind of strange."

Jill nodded. "Mmm. So, how did you find out?"

"After I left the hospital, I thought I'd look around the house in Brewster. I guess I was hoping he might have left me a note or something about why he'd gone to Sweden a few days early. When I was down there looking around …" He paused. "Anyway, I ended up finding an envelope with his birth certificate and adoption papers."

"Quite a discovery." Jill sipped her wine. "And did you find out why he left early?"

"No. But I'm pretty sure I know the reason he was so interested in going to Sweden."

"Which is?"

"Dad's parents were Swedish, Bjorn and Helen Svensson, or at least his father was."

A waiter interrupted their conversation with their entrees. After a few minutes, Jill looked up at Peter. "So you must have a lot of questions."

"For sure. And Dad's in Sweden, incommunicado, more or less."

"Tracking down relatives?"

"Probably, but Svensson is a pretty common name in Sweden. How would he know where to start if he didn't have any other information?"

After several minutes of working on her seared tuna plate, which Peter had decided was more artistic than appetizing, Jill looked up. "So how do feel about your father never telling you anything about his being adopted?"

Peter picked up his drink and then held it in front of him, looking at the candle on the table refracted through the ice in the glass. "Surprised mostly, and a little annoyed."

"Only a little annoyed?" Jill said.

"Well ..." Peter continued to look at the glass, turning it to hit the light in different ways. "Anyway, I wonder if my father felt any different about his adoptive parents than I feel about him and my mother."

"You're not adopted, right?"

"Right. I saw my birth certificate when was I eight years old and got my first passport." Peter looked up. "But hey, it's just DNA, right? What counts is who you grow up with and accept as your parents."

"That's the nurture versus nature debate. Isn't it?"

Peter finished the last of his broiled swordfish before responding. "I suppose. Anyway, I may drive up to Maine tomorrow and see my aunt Elena. She's probably the only other person who might know something about it."

Jill made a quizzical face. "Don't you have a big date tomorrow night?"

"I don't know about 'big.'"

"Peter dear, for you, any date is big," Jill said gently.

"Don't worry. It'd just be a day trip. So dessert?"

"How about an after-dinner drink instead?" Jill responded. "Getting back to your father, you don't have any idea why he left early for Sweden?"

"No. And apparently in kind of a hurry. His neighbor Mary also thought he was leaving today. The last time she saw him was Monday. He was saying good-bye to some men that he had apparently been meeting with at the house, 'men in dark suits,' Mary said, who looked like they were from out of town."

"You make it sound a little sinister," Jill said.

"I don't know about sinister, but it is a little odd."

Jill excused herself to go to the ladies' room. Peter ordered their drinks: a Drambuie for Jill and a shot of his favorite Midleton Irish whiskey for himself. When Jill returned, she sipped her Scotch liqueur. "Mmm. Best thing to come out of the Isle of Skye since Bonnie Prince Charlie."

"Probably better. I think he had to leave disguised as a housemaid." Peter chuckled.

She ignored his comment. "So what's going on here?"

"You mean you think there are some connections?"

Jill sat forward with her arms on the table. "Let's go through this. You poke around your father's house and find out he was adopted and has a Swedish father, which probably explains why he wants to go to Sweden, *n'est-ce pas?*"

"Could be."

"But you said that when you talked to your father a week ago that you two had agreed to meet at the airport today for a drink before he got on the plane to go to Sweden. Sometime between then and … what … Tuesday morning, he changes his mind. Finally, early this morning, he calls you and says he's already in Sweden."

"True."

"But the day before he leaves, on Monday, he has some kind of a meeting at his house. The meeting that involved the 'Men in Black'—"

"Wait a minute …"

Jill ignored him again. "A.k.a., the FBI or worse …" Jill said, jumping to a conclusion that Peter had briefly considered.

"So when you channeled Hercule Poirot in the ladies' room, what scenario did he suggest to connect them?" Peter said with exaggerated emphasis.

Jill smiled and finished the last of her Drambuie. "Give me overnight, the reception in the ladies' room wasn't very good."

Peter smiled, but he was not all that amused.

Chapter 8

DESPITE HIS RELATIVELY SHORT sleep the previous night, Peter woke early. He was energized by the prospect of questioning his aunt Elena about his father's adoption.

He ran a fifty-minute circuit alone around the Charles River Basin. This route took him east and then across the Charles River Dam at the head of Boston Harbor. The dam, which was completed in the early part of the twentieth century, kept the expanse of water between the elegant Beacon Hill and Back Bay neighborhoods of Boston and the MIT campus in Cambridge from turning into acres of smelly mud flats at low tide.

By eight o'clock, he had finished reading the newspaper and eaten breakfast and was anxious for nine o'clock to arrive. He decided that was the earliest time it would be acceptable to call his elderly aunt, although he knew she was very probably up by seven.

He spent some time organizing his notes from his discussions at Berkeley on neo-Nazis, glancing at the clock above the desk in his study more than necessary. At five to nine, he dialed Aunt Elena's number. She picked up on the second ring. "Oh, Peter, I'm sorry I missed your call yesterday. Is everything all right?"

"Sure, yes. I was just calling to see how you were and … I was thinking of coming up."

"Well, you know you can come up anytime. Your Uncle George put the *Rhodes* in last week, so it's ready to sail. But he's giving a talk in Washington today and won't be home until tomorrow so you'll have to go sailing by yourself."

"Thanks. Maybe in a couple of weeks I can spend a long weekend. Anyway …" Peter decided to approach the main reason for his call indirectly. "I wondered if you had talked to Dad before he left for Sweden this week."

There was a pause. "Let's see, I talked to him last week."

"Did he say anything about maybe leaving early?"

"Hmm, yes." Another pause. "He … well, I'm sure it's all right."

"I was just surprised," Peter said. "But … you know my uncle Jed?"

"Yes?" she said in a cautious tone.

"I had a call from Bill Reilly. Jed has been missing with his boat since Wednesday. That's how I found out that Dad had left early. Bill called me to say he couldn't reach Dad. He wanted to ask him if he had any idea of where Jed might be."

"I see," she said. Peter waited for her to say more, but she said nothing. Peter heard her let out a breath. Peter wasn't really surprised at Aunt Elena's subdued response to the news about Jed. The few times they had been together at a family gathering, he had sensed some tension. Curious, he had asked his parents about it, but they said they didn't really know themselves.

"Anyway, there's something else I'd like to talk to you about. Today, actually."

"Oh, well all right." She sounded surprised but recovered quickly. "Will you be here for lunch?"

"Definitely. But I need to be back this evening." Peter knew his aunt would have enjoyed a longer visit with him. He had debated whether to spend the night. The round-trip drive would be about six hours plus a few hours to visit and talk. It was cutting it close, but he could be back by seven for his date with Diana, the sports reporter.

The familiar route to his aunt's house was one of his earliest memories. He had always measured it by all the bridges crossed. First, there was the bridge over the Merrimack River just south of the New Hampshire line, then the high bridge at Portsmouth, over the Piscataqua River, about an hour from Boston. That bridge offered spectacular views of the river, east toward Portsmouth Harbor and beyond to the Atlantic Ocean.

The next was a low bridge, which crossed a portion of Casco Bay in Portland, Maine, about two hours into the trip. There, Peter was not far from the apartment he and Michelle had lived in for two years. As he approached the bridge, he let the memory of their time together flood into his mind and then, with some effort, let it recede as he drove northeast away from Portland.

After about half an hour on Route 1, he crossed the bridge over the Kennebec River in Bath by the navy shipbuilding facility. Most of this road was now just two lanes bordered by stretches of pine forest that were steadily losing a battle with strip malls and outlet stores. Finally, ten miles down on the old coastal road, the bridge at Wiscasset spanned the Sheepscot River. At twelve thirty, Peter turned off Route 1 onto a side road that led down a long peninsula to Boothbay Harbor and Linekin Bay.

Aunt Elena was waiting on the porch as he parked his Volvo behind her green Subaru station wagon. Her tall, thin figure was silhouetted against the bright reflections of the noon sun on the bay. Peter mounted the steps of the long porch next to the driveway. He gave his aunt a hug that made her wobble a little.

"Be careful with this old lady, Peter." She laughed, and her eyes sparkled, but Peter thought she somehow looked frailer than the last time he had seen her.

"It's so good to see you," she said, giving him a kiss. "But I bet you're hungry. Lunch is ready."

Aunt Elena had prepared lobster salad and coleslaw, which they ate at a table in the living room overlooking the water. They talked about Peter's trip to California, Boothbay Harbor politics, and the state of repair and disrepair of her house. Peter was anxious to ask her what she might know about his father's adoption, but the conversation did not seem to offer him any easy opportunities. He politely responded to the topics that she chose. He even tried to generate some enthusiasm when she pried gently at what she called his social life. He knew she meant his love life. Aunt Elena had been very fond of Michelle, but she did not talk about Michelle now unless Peter mentioned her first.

After lunch, they took their tea out onto the porch, which was comfortable in the sun, at least with a sweater on. Peter broached his first question. "Did Dad tell you anything about his itinerary in Sweden?"

Aunt Elena sighed and looked down at the cup in her hand. "When we spoke on the phone, I didn't ask him where he was staying. I think he was planning to visit several places over there."

"Actually, it's sort of important for me to get hold of him."

"Oh, dear, well, I ..." She stopped and then went on, "I'm sure he'll call you in a day or two when he gets settled."

Peter had the impression that his aunt knew more about his father's trip than he did. He pressed on. "The reason that I need to talk to him is that Bill Reilly thinks it's possible that Jed committed suicide."

Aunt Elena drew back, her hand moving toward her chest. And then as though to conceal her reaction, she fussed with the top button of the blue cardigan she was wearing. She shook her head with her lips pressed together. "I would think a boating accident was more likely." Then her expression softened. "You must be quite concerned. I know you and he have been close."

Peter described what little was known about Jed's disappearance and the likelihood that his father had spoken to Jed a day or two before it occurred.

"Well, yes, I see why your friend Bill would want to talk to him," she said, getting up from the table. "There's more coleslaw and lobster salad."

Peter had the feeling that his aunt was trying to avoid talking about either Jed or his father. He decided to risk his aunt's discomfort and try one of his reportorial interview techniques. "So when did Dad make up his mind to go to Sweden early?"

Aunt Elena's mouth opened, and she looked away. "I ... I think it was a very last-minute sort of thing, you know." She looked concerned.

Peter continued, "Last minute, like Monday?" Perhaps Jill's intuition was right. Swedes were fond of dark suits. "So I guess it had something to do with the meeting he had on Monday afternoon?"

Aunt Elena looked down and put her hands together in her lap. She was quiet for a moment and seemed to be composing an answer. "He told me that he had been corresponding with some people in Sweden recently and that they were coming here to meet with him. I think that the meeting was with these people."

Bingo, Sweden! Peter thought.

"He told me that they have an American division of their company near Boston and that they come over from time to time."

A business meeting with Swedes seemed like too much of a coincidence. "Was it a meeting about work, his consulting? Or something else?" Like Swedish parentage?

Peter thought that Aunt Elena looked uncomfortable. "Well, I don't ... really know." She got up, bumping the low table between them, rattling the teacups. "I'm going to get the teapot. Would you like some more tea?"

"Yes, thanks," Peter said, following her into the kitchen. He wondered why she seemed so evasive. Had she been sworn to secrecy about his father's adoption and Swedish ancestry by his adoptive parents, the Frosts? But they were gone and his father must know. So why were these questions so difficult for her? Whatever. Apparently there was not going to be a simple way to ease into the question of his father's adoption.

Aunt Elena was standing with her back to Peter pouring more hot water from the kettle into the teapot.

"When I was at Dad's house yesterday, looking around ..." He plunged ahead. "I saw Dad's birth certificate." He paused. "I guess you knew he was adopted."

Aunt Elena stopped pouring. Peter heard her sigh. Then she put the kettle down quietly and turned to face Peter. "Yes, I did," she said, smiling slightly. Some of the tension Peter had seen in her seemed to go away. "I had an inkling that's what you had come up to ask me about. I guess you'd like to know about it. Let's go back out on the porch and sit down."

Peter nodded.

After they were seated again outside, Aunt Elena pulled her chair up closer to Peter. She leaned towards him and taking one of his hands into her hands, she said, "Peter, I know your father wanted to tell you this himself, but he isn't here, and I don't think it's fair not to tell you what I told him, now that you know about his adoption."

Peter noticed that there were tears in her eyes and her voice seemed slightly choked. He felt bad that he seemed to be causing her so much unhappiness. "So you know all about it? I hope you don't mind my asking you about it, but there isn't anyone else."

"No, there really isn't." She drew a deep breath. "It's a long story. But what I need to tell you is that I'm your grandmother and your father, Eric, is my son."

Chapter 9

PETER DREW BACK INVOLUNTARILY, but Elena held his hand tightly. Had he heard that right? "You're Dad's mother? But that's … " He almost said, "crazy." "…amazing." He wondered if his Aunt Elena could be fantasizing, making up a son she had never had? No, no way. That wouldn't be the Aunt Elena he knew. But then, this wasn't either.

He wanted to stand up and walk around to clear his head. But she kept a gentle grip on his hand, not letting him get away from this new reality.

After some moments, she spoke. "You must be wondering if I'm crazy. I know this must be a bit difficult for you to understand and to accept."

He nodded, his shock beginning to give way to curiosity. "So you're my grandmother, Helen Wilson," he said slowly.

"Yes, I am."

Elena looked away across the bay. She was still holding Peter's hand. He stood up and leaned over to her and gave her an awkward hug and a kiss. She looked up at him, gave his hand an extra squeeze, and let it go. "I'm sorry if it's more difficult, hearing all this from me. I know your father was going to tell you when he got back from Sweden." She paused. "I think he wanted to get it all straightened out before he talked to you."

"Yeah, I guess." His words rushed out. "But how long has he known about … this? Why was it a secret?" Peter realized that he sounded angry. He saw more distress in Elena's face and felt guilty for the pain he was causing her.

"Oh, Peter, I'm sorry. I know this is upsetting for you. But you mustn't blame your father. He was trying to do what he thought was best."

Peter took a deep breath and released it. "I'm sorry. It's just ..." He let the sentence trail off. He was still standing, and he looked down at the familiar, worn pine boards of the porch floor.

"I understand. And it's our fault too, your grandparents and I. We thought we were doing the right thing when we didn't tell your father all those years ago." She looked away, her hands working in her lap. "Perhaps when I tell you the whole story ... it will make more sense."

She returned her focus to Peter but then looked down. "Your father has known for some time that he was adopted, but not who his real parents were. He found out when he was about thirty after he sent away for his birth certificate."

"He must have been pretty surprised when he opened the envelope." Peter heard a little sarcasm in his voice. "I mean that was the first he knew, right?"

"Yes, he told me that he had never suspected."

"And when did he find out that you were his mother?"

"Last year, when he talked to me about it."

"But he must have asked his parents ... I mean ... Grandfather and Grandmother Frost when he found out."

"He did. But they seemed reluctant to talk about it, and I followed their lead. They were getting old, and I think they didn't feel up to disrupting the family as they had known it for so long."

"Didn't Uncle Jed know? Dad could have asked him about it," Peter said.

Elena's eyes narrowed slightly. "Yes, he knew. Out of respect for his aunt, your grandmother Frost, I suppose, he said nothing." She looked away; her expression had turned hard. "At least while the Frosts were alive."

Elena turned back to Peter and seemed to make an effort to change her mood. "You were very young. And in those days, your father was busy with his new family and his work. Last summer, when we talked, he told me that somehow it didn't seem so important to him then."

Peter sat back down in his chair and leaned over toward his aunt-now-grandmother. "So Dad found out you were his mother. But who was his father?"

Elena clasped her hands together in her lap. "Do you remember your grandmother Judy talking about my studying in Germany just before the war?" For Peter's parents and grandparents, "the war" always meant World War II.

"Yes, sure." There was a little bit of family lore about how Aunt Elena had come back from Europe just as things began to get really ugly there. His grandparents had been very relieved that their former student had managed to make the crossing from Europe before German submarines took everything in the North Atlantic as fair game for their torpedoes.

"I had gone to Germany in 1937 after college to study German history and literature at the university at Hamburg. Your grandfather Frost who had been my European history professor at Munroe had arranged for me to do graduate studies there.

"There were other students from outside Germany as well. After a couple of months, I met two fellows from Sweden. One of them was Bjorn Svensson whose name you saw on your father's birth certificate."

So this is the Swedish connection, Peter thought. "And your real name is Helen not Elena?"

"Bjorn always called me Elena, and I kept that. Anyway, he and I fell in love and we became a couple." A sailboat heading up the bay on a broad reach seemed to catch her eye, and she paused before going on. "It was a wonderful year."

"So Bjorn Svensson was or is my real grandfather? But you left Germany and Dad was born here in 1940, in May."

"Yes," she said softly. "In August of 1939, Bjorn's father died, and he was asked to go back to Sweden to run the family business."

"But you didn't go to Sweden with him?"

"No," she said quickly. "My family was very worried about my being in Europe. It was clear to them what the Nazis had in mind and that there was going to be a war." Elena paused and closed her eyes for a moment. "Bjorn and I were planning to get married when the telegram about his father arrived and we all left Germany. I left for the United States. Bjorn and I had agreed that when the war was over and it was safe to travel, I would join him in Sweden."

Peter wanted to ask a question, but Elena went on without pausing. "I was very seasick, or so I thought, on the voyage back to the U.S. That seemed strange to me because I hadn't been seasick at all on the way over. After I had been back for a month or so and was still seasick, I understood why. I was here in Maine, in Wiscasset, where my parents lived. I found out then that I was pregnant with your father."

Peter's questions raced ahead of Elena's narrative. "But the birth certificate said Dad was born in Massachusetts."

"Yes, and that's another happy and sad part of this too, Peter." Elena sighed again and seemed to force a smile. "I need to explain that in 1939, respectable young women didn't come home from Europe pregnant and not married. I never told my parents. At the time, I didn't think they would forgive me. My father was very Victorian, you know, lots of rules for proper behavior. Now as I look back, perhaps I could have told them. They were very loving for all their belief in decorum.

"Anyway, when I really couldn't hide my pregnancy any longer, I wrote to your ... ah, other grandparents, the Frosts. They had been very good to me when I was in college at Munroe, and I knew they were very modern in their thinking.

"They immediately understood my situation and offered to take me in and let me stay with them for as long as I wanted to before and after the baby was born."

Peter stood to stretch his legs and leaned against the porch railing facing his newly discovered grandmother. "Did Bjorn know about the baby?"

Elena looked away and seemed distracted for a moment. "Yes, he knew. We wrote each other often, many letters." Her eyes filled with tears again. "He was happy about the baby and glad that I was safe in the United States away from the war, but he was very concerned that he wasn't with me."

She went on, but her voice was unsteady with emotion. "After your father was born, I had one more letter from Bjorn. He was very pleased that I had named your father after his

Swedish grandfather, and he ..." Elena hesitated. "And he said he was getting very busy." Her eyes filled with tears, and she didn't speak for several moments.

Peter felt very uncomfortable about his grandmother's pain. He moved next to her and took her hand. "Maybe we should talk about this later."

She smiled up at him blinking. "No." She sighed. "It's all right." She went on, but her voice had lost some of its animation. "I continued to write to him but I don't know if the letters got through. England was being bombed, and by then, the war was really on."

"So you didn't hear from him after that last letter?"

"No, there were no more letters." Elena let out a long breath. "Anyway, I had time to think about what I should do. You know, Peter, that was a different time."

"So the Frosts adopted Dad. But that ..." Peter began, trying to imagine how hard that must have been for her.

"Yes," she said, seeming to anticipate his thought. "It was a very difficult decision. I nursed your father until he was about eighteen months old, and during that time, Judith Frost and I were sort of joint mothers."

"When did you move to Maine?"

"After I stopped nursing, I decided I needed to make the break and let the Frosts really be Eric's parents, so I went to Maine and lived with my parents again. That was probably the worst time of my life." Elena looked away from Peter. After a long moment, she looked back at him and took a deep breath. "So that's the story."

Peter hesitated but then said, "And did you ever hear from Bjorn, after the war?"

She shook her head and looked away again. Peter was afraid that perhaps he had asked too painful a question.

Eventually, Elena turned to Peter, her eyes narrowed slightly and her jaw set. "Bjorn Svensson wrote to me after the war. He said he was busy running the family business and married. He made no mention of the baby. I wrote him back, but he never replied." She got up out of her chair. "I'm going to have that cup of tea."

Peter followed Elena into the house. "When did Dad ask you if you knew about his adoption?"

Elena filled the teakettle with fresh water from the tap at the gray soapstone sink that had seemed so old-fashioned when Peter was a child and now was fashionably retro.

She turned to face him. "It was last year. He came up and stayed for a week." She sighed. "Quite an emotional time for us, as you can imagine."

Peter carried the tray with their tea back out onto the porch. The pines behind the house cast long shadows into the bay. They sipped the tea in silence for several minutes before Peter ventured back into his father's secret.

"So what about Dad's meeting with his father? Is that going to happen in Sweden?" Or had it already happened in Brewster last week? Peter wondered.

Elena's expression changed, and her tone of voice became uncharacteristically hard. "I wrote to Bjorn last year after I talked to your father. I told him that Eric wanted to see him. It was the first time I had written to him since just after the war. I got a rather cool reply. Bjorn wrote back that he had divorced his first wife, had remarried and had a daughter, and that he had been a widower for many years. He said he thought that not much would be gained by making contact with Eric.

"When I told your father about Bjorn's response, he seemed to lose his enthusiasm for looking him up. But then, after you came back from Sweden last fall, he told me that he was going to write to Bjorn. I warned him he might be disappointed."

"So did Bjorn write him back?"

"Yes, he received a reply from Bjorn. Your father said it was polite but not very encouraging. But this time, your father wasn't going to be put off." Elena smiled slightly. "So this spring, he made his reservations for Sweden and wrote to Bjorn that he was coming to see him."

"You said that Dad's meeting on Monday afternoon in Brewster was with people from Sweden that he had been corresponding with. Was that anything to do with Bjorn?" Peter squinted at Elena with a mock "gotcha" expression and then smiled.

"Yes. Bjorn called him about two weeks ago and suggested they meet here in the United States. When I talked to your father last weekend, he said they were going to get together in Brewster. I didn't tell you that when you first asked me. Forgive me, I was still thinking that if you didn't know about the adoption, your father should tell you."

"It's okay, Aunt ... I guess I mean Grandmother Elena. You were just covering for Dad."

"Peter, you know it's all right to keep calling me Aunt Elena if it seems more natural." She leaned over and patted his hand. "But, oh my," she said looking at her watch. "I need to get into the kitchen. It's nearly dinnertime."

Dinnertime! Peter looked at his watch. He realized that their family history discussion had overtaken his plans to get back to Boston and his Saturday night date with the sports reporter. Another attractive and eligible young lady blown off! He could expect to hear from Jill about that.

Chapter 10

PETER LEFT HIS GRANDMOTHER to her dinner preparations. He walked up the hill from the house thumbing a number into his cell phone. It was only six thirty, so perhaps he could reach his wouldn't-be-date Diana, the sports reporter, before she left for the restaurant. At least he could spare her the embarrassment of sitting alone when he didn't show up. She answered her phone at home but did not sound very appreciative of his efforts.

The road from the shore led up past a number of brown-shingled summer homes, most of which had been built in the early 1900s, a few more recently. At the top of the hill, Peter turned around and looked back across the bay. Fishhawk and Cabbage Islands, close in, were sharply defined but the horizon was blurred by offshore summer fog. And how did Bjorn feel about meeting his son Eric after deserting Elena? Was that why he had come all the way over to the U.S. to see Peter's father instead of just waiting a few days before his father got to Sweden? Had it been perhaps to try to persuade his father not to come to Sweden?

When Peter returned to the house, Elena shooed him out of the kitchen. At dinner they sat overlooking the bay. The lights from a few houses and the headlights of an occasional automobile delineated the opposite shore.

"Do you mind my asking about Bjorn and his friend and what it was like in Germany just before World War II?"

"No, of course not." Some of Elena's usual energy seemed to have returned. "You should know something about that time. Those were special days for me." Elena described her

voyage to Germany in 1937. It had been an exciting opportunity
for her to study there for two years and return with a master's
degree in nineteenth-century German history and literature at the
university in Hamburg.

"One day, in my history lecture class, two Swedish
students were sitting nearby. They were making some witty
remarks about 'Herr Professor' in Swedish. I was amused and
thought they were cute. So after class, I said something to them
because I knew a little Swedish from my grandmother ... not
enough to talk politics but enough to chatter in the kitchen. They
realized that I had understood their comments. So that's how I
met Bjorn Svensson and his friend Kjell."

She pronounced their names as "B'yorn" and "Chell."

"I didn't know that you had a Swedish grandmother,"
said Peter. "You never said anything about it even when I went
there last year."

"No, I didn't. I guess that seemed like a part of this
family secret too. How silly!" She sighed.

"I think they were impressed that I was an American who
spoke Swedish. We began to spend more time together. They
were both very Nordic-looking, blond and blue-eyed. At first, I
was more attracted to Kjell who was studying art history. Kjell
was charming and outgoing. But eventually, I was drawn to Bjorn
who was quieter and more thoughtful. He was studying
engineering. Kjell was very bright but less interested in his studies
than Bjorn. He used his knowledge of German art to support
himself by buying and selling antiques and paintings. Bjorn came
from a wealthy family and could afford to spend all his time
studying."

"This was 1937, right? Didn't the Nazi activities bother
you?" Peter asked.

"Not at first. Although looking back, they should have.
But, you know, in spite of Hitler who had already been in power
for several years, Germany, for me, was still a respected country
with a long tradition of important literature and philosophy.

"But after Kristallnacht, at the beginning of my second
year there, when all the Jewish shops were vandalized, we realized
how awful it was. Before that, we had debated fascism,

communism, and democracy as though they were just different approaches to government. After that, we began to think about what we believed was right. Bjorn and Kjell discussed what they would do. They talked about going to Spain to fight against the fascists who were being helped by the Nazis. But it all still seemed a bit theoretical. We were foreign students. We were from countries that were not really involved, at that point."

Elena stopped and gestured to Peter to start in on the chowder. "It won't be good cold." For a few minutes, they ate in silence, enjoying the New England fish soup, a traditional thin milk chowder. "Not all filled with cornstarch—making it like library paste—like you get in Boston restaurants with chefs from Texas," Elena always said. Elena's chowder was buttery with large chunks of haddock, onions, and potatoes. It also included some wonderfully sweet scraps of politically incorrect fried salt pork.

After she had confirmed that Peter was paying enough attention to his dinner, Elena resumed her narrative. "Bjorn and I had fallen very much in love, and somehow, the rest of the world didn't seem to matter," she said, her eyes dancing.

Peter tried to imagine Elena and her friends in their early twenties. "Do you have any pictures of all of you then?"

"No. Unfortunately when my parents moved into the nursing home, my photograph album from that time was thrown out."

"So, there's nothing ..."

"No," she said slowly. "There are no photographs."

Peter sensed again that Elena was holding something back. Perhaps there were photographs, but looking at them would be too difficult. They ate for a while in silence, and then Peter's questions resumed. "You said that when you all left Germany in the summer of 1939, that Bjorn had to go back to Sweden to run his father's company."

"That's right."

"Did Kjell go back too?"

Elena looked away and seemed lost again in the recollection of her last days in Germany. "No, after it was clear that England would go to war with Germany, Kjell decided he would go there and find a way to fight the Nazis. It would not

have been possible from Sweden, which was neutral. He
eventually returned to Germany to work in the small resistance
movement there." She anticipated Peter's next question. "He was
killed there early in the war."

"Pretty dangerous work," Peter responded. "Were you
surprised that he went to fight the Nazis?"

"Oh, Peter, it was a time when we all made difficult,
strange choices." She paused and shook her head slowly. "I often
thought I should have persuaded Bjorn just to take me back to
Sweden with him." She let out a long breath. "But I didn't."

After dinner, Peter helped Elena with the dishes and then
went outside. He walked down the road and onto the float on the
public dock. He sat on a small bench as the ocean waves,
attenuated by the length of the bay, gently rocked the float. A few
yards off the dock was Elena's sailboat, the rigging clinking
against its aluminum mast. With a piece of broken oar, he stirred
the water to produce sparkles of phosphorescence. The effect
looked like the cartoon of a comet tail. The dock at night was a
favorite place for him: a beautiful, quiet spot in the faint light of
the houses behind him and the stars above, a place to think about
the unknowability of life.

So Peter and Eric Frost were really Peter and Eric
Svensson ... Well sort of, he thought. Now suddenly, he had a
Swedish family connection in his life and a grandmother again. It
was something curious for him, but for Elena, it was a great
sadness returned from the past. He could relate to that, losing
someone who might have been his life partner. She had lost
Bjorn and what might have been a very different life. But that
very different life probably wouldn't have included him. Talk
about unknowability!

Chapter 11

PETER WOKE UP IN a familiar room with its dormer window looking out on the bay. The room faced east and admitted a stream of foggy sunlight that morning. As he was getting dressed, he realized that he had not pursued the question of what Elena might know about his father's meeting in Brewster with Bjorn. His grandfather Svensson was apparently a wealthy man. Was he concerned that his father was going to demand some inheritance? That was not likely, he thought, knowing his father.

Elena was already up when Peter got downstairs. He found eggs and bacon with blueberry muffins waiting for him on the kitchen table. She joined him there with her coffee.

"Last night, you said that Bjorn came to the U.S. and met with Dad in Brewster last Monday. I've been wondering why. Dad was going to be in Sweden in just a few days," Peter began. As he spoke, he saw a look of concern come across Elena's face.

She put her coffee mug down on the table carefully and looked up at him. Her expression was sympathetic, but her mouth was set. "Peter, I think I would like your father to take up the story from here. I hope you understand."

"Yes, I guess ... sure," Peter replied. He was not really surprised. It was probably reasonable that Elena would not want to talk about today's Bjorn Svensson any more than necessary. But he felt a renewed sense of irritation that his father was still unavailable to answer his growing list of questions.

"Anyway," he said, changing the subject. "Is it okay if I take the *Rhodes* out for a sail?"

"Of course. You don't have to ask," Elena replied smiling broadly.

After breakfast, Peter rowed out to the small sailboat at its mooring off the dock. He sailed over to the familiar shore of Cabbage Island and then decided to head south out of the bay.

As he tacked down the bay, he thought about why his father would have sent Jed his birth certificate and adoption notice. Was he trying to establish that he was an heir of Bjorn Svensson? And the transcripts in Swedish and English, what were they all about? He wished he had read the one in English. As he rounded Spruce Point at the mouth of the bay, Squirrel Island came into view ahead about half a mile away. He hadn't sailed all the way around it for some time, and the wind was good today.

But why would his father send Jed a transcript of a conversation in Swedish? Perhaps Elena would know, but would she stonewall him on this too?

He made a decision. Looking around, he saw there were no other boats close by, and he pushed the tiller all the way over. The *Rhodes* came about, its sails flapping and then filling in the following wind, as it headed back up the bay to Elena's mooring.

His grandmother was sitting on the porch reading. "That wasn't a very long sail. Did you get hungry?"

"Ah ... no, but I got thinking ..." Peter began. "When I was at Dad's house, I found what looked like a conversation in English, and maybe a translation in Swedish."

Elena seemed to tense slightly but said nothing.

"I wondered if it had anything to do with Dad and Bjorn or why Dad might have wanted Uncle Jed to look at it." Peter hoped this wasn't forbidden territory too, like the meeting.

"Well, I guess I shouldn't be surprised," Elena said. She snapped her book closed and stood up quickly. Nearly losing her balance, she reached out for Peter's arm. Then she turned away and walked to the porch rail and looked down the bay.

"Aunt Elena, are you okay?" Peter wondered at her reaction.

She turned back holding the rail with one hand. "Yes. It's just that ..." She stopped and said nothing for several moments. Then she took a large breath and appeared to force a smile onto her face. "Well ..." Elena hesitated. "I told you last night that I didn't have any photographs of Bjorn and Kjell and myself, but I did have something else ... a recording that we made one night in Germany. I gave it to your father." Then she added almost to herself, "Which was probably a mistake."

"A recording? Like a tape recording?"

"I don't think they had tape recorders back then, but Kjell had found this recorder that used some kind of wire instead of tape. I gave the recording, just a spool of this special wire, to your father when he was here last fall. I thought with his knowledge of that sort of thing, he might be able to find a machine to play it on."

"So the transcript was of something you recorded that night in Germany? But why would—?"

Elena interrupted him. "You need to ask your father about the transcript. I really don't know ..." Then with a change in her tone of voice, she said, "And it's nearly lunchtime."

She got up and went into the house leaving Peter wondering why Elena thought it was a "mistake" to give the recording to his father? Was there something in it that would help him to understand what his father was doing in Sweden and why he had left early? Getting back to Chatham to have another look at the document suddenly seemed like a priority.

Peter went into the kitchen. "Listen, I think I should get back to Boston. I'm going to leave right after lunch and beat the weekend traffic," he said trying to ignore the guilt he felt about leaving so abruptly and offering only a weak excuse.

She looked at him with a questioning expression and turned back to the counter where she was preparing lunch. "Well, that's too bad. The weather is so good for sailing, and George won't be back until later. But you do what you have to."

They ate lunch on the porch without a lot of conversation. When they finished lunch, Elena brought out some coffee. "Peter, I've been thinking about your father's meeting with Bjorn Svensson and his trip to Sweden." She hesitated a moment. "I'm a little worried."

"Why ... oh, that he may be disappointed?"

"Yes, and ..." she said. "I don't know. I wish there was someone he knew in Sweden."

"Well, he's already met Bjorn, and he still decided to go to Sweden. That seems like a good sign," Peter said.

Elena's expression continued to indicate concern. "Yes, but still ..." She paused. "What if it doesn't work out or is unpleasant or something?"

"I guess that's always a possibility when you try to connect with your biological parents," Peter said and caught himself. "Present company excepted, of course," he added.

Chapter 12

ARRIVING BACK IN CAMBRIDGE at about four, Peter made a quick stop at his apartment to check his e-mail before going on to the Cape. There were no messages from his father, just a nasty-gram from his blown-off date Diana. More guilt. He wondered how to apologize appropriately without leaving the impression he was sorrier than he really was. A good question for Jill, he decided.

It was about six thirty when Peter parked on Main Street in Chatham. He left his Volvo some way beyond the side street where his uncle's office was located. Most of the shops were closed, and the weekend tourists were on their way home. He heard the sounds of a social gathering in progress as he mounted the steps of the old Victorian building. The front door was open. The real estate office on the first floor was serving wine and cheese for some occasion. Peter passed by the open door of the office unnoticed. Upstairs, his credit card did the trick again on the door at Barlow and Darby's.

Peter went directly to his uncle's office and took the large mailing envelope off the desk. Having it in hand would allow him to read through it carefully and perhaps discover its significance.

He exited the office and left the building without encountering any partygoers or others. From Chatham Center, he drove back toward Brewster. As he was approaching the town field where a well-attended Little League baseball game was in progress, a police car appeared in his rearview mirror. He began to pull over to let it pass, but it remained behind him and switched on its strobing blue lights, which were accompanied by

64 John Amiard

a short siren burst. He cussed himself out quietly as he pulled off and stopped by the home plate backstop fence. Had someone seen him today or had the lady with the attitude taken his license number on Friday?

Peter knew the drill and stayed in his car, while the officer presumably computer-checked his license plate number. Reaching toward the glove compartment for his registration, he glanced over and saw that all eyes on the field: players, parents, and even the umpire had turned to catch a moment of *Cops*. The officer left the police car, speaking into his shoulder-mounted microphone and appeared at his window.

Peter rolled down his window. "Officer, I'm—" he said before he was cut off.

"Please put both hands on the steering wheel, sir." The officer was young and sounded as though he was trying to push his voice down a little below its natural range.

"Okay. But—" Peter began again but was interrupted again.

"Please remain in your vehicle with your hands in sight." The young officer stood slightly behind Peter by the car window.

After a few minutes, another Chatham police cruiser arrived from the direction of the town center. Its lights were in full flash mode. The baseball game, which had resumed in the interim, stopped again, as the players ignored directives from the umpire. The officer in the second cruiser, which pulled in nose-to-nose with Peter's Volvo, was older. Obviously, this was not a routine traffic stop.

The older officer conferred briefly with his younger colleague, and Peter was ordered out of the car. "Please place your hands on the roof of the car and move your feet apart, sir," the younger officer said.

As Peter looked over the roof of the Volvo, he could see that the whole infield and both benches had rushed over to look through the backstop at the action. The umpire had given up and was staring up from home plate with his mask off.

As the younger officer moved his hands expertly around Peter's upper body, the older officer's radio came to life. There was a brief discussion. When it ended, the younger officer had just run his hands down Peter's left leg and was moving to his right leg.

"Okay, that'll do, Bob," the older officer said. Bob hesitated then stood up and moved back.

"You may get back in your vehicle, sir, but please remain here," the older officer said. His tone of voice seemed friendlier than before.

Peter got back in his Volvo, and the two men moved off out of earshot. In his side mirror, Peter could see the older officer explaining something to Officer Bob. Peter wondered what was coming next, maybe just a case of mistaken identity, but he didn't think so. He looked over at the baseball game. The players had begun to drift back to their benches and positions in the field. After a few minutes and some encouragement from the parents, play resumed. Just as the pitcher was throwing his second pitch of the restarted game, Peter heard a siren and saw a cruiser with the familiar gray and blue markings of the state police with its emergency and headlights flashing impressively. It pulled up behind the second officer's car. A uniformed state trooper got out and walked toward Peter's car.

It took Peter a moment to recognize his friend, Bill Reilly, with a crooked smile on his face. Reilly looked over at the ball field, where a batter had apparently hit a pitch into center field. He was running around the bases in the empty infield as the players were once again focused on the road behind the backstop. Bill Reilly's police lights reflected off their sunglasses.

Bill leaned into the passenger window of the Volvo. "Give me a minute, and then we'll go somewhere I can chew your ass out," he said smiling.

Reilly walked to the backstop. "Hey, guys, hope you enjoyed the chance to watch a police training exercise. What's the score?" Two different totals were shouted out. "Okay, well, listen …" He paused for effect. "Time to go back and play ball."

He stood for a moment waiting for his words and the power of his uniform to take hold. He turned and walked up to the Chatham police officers for a brief discussion. Peter overheard him thanking them and explaining that Peter was a relative of the missing man and authorized to visit the office. The officers got into their respective police cars and left without making eye contact with Peter.

After they had pulled away, Bill Reilly came over to the window on the driver's side of the Volvo. "You can buy me a cup of coffee in town and tell me about your B and E at your uncle's office."

"Just E, I didn't break anything."

"Whatever," Reilly said over his shoulder as he walked back to his state police cruiser.

In Chatham Center, they found a quiet booth at the back of the Village Grill. Reilly laid his visored hat on the bench and twisted his neck in the tight collar of his uniform.

"You're all dressed up today. What's the occasion," Peter asked as they sat down.

"Flag Day ceremony in Harwich. My turn to represent the force. You're lucky I was so close; otherwise, you'd be drinking three-day-old coffee in a holding cell." He paused to catch the waitress's attention. "So tell me why one of Barlow and Darby's fellow tenants reported a suspicious male in a Volvo station wagon, with a license plate number that matches yours, was coming out of B and D's locked offices on Friday evening. And why that same Volvo was noted by Chatham's finest parked on Main Street this afternoon." Bill looked as though he was enjoying himself at Peter's expense, but his tone of voice was not entirely playful.

"Well, it's a long story."

Their waitress arrived and took their orders for coffee.

"Is there a short version?" Bill asked.

"Sort of. On Friday, I went to Jed's house to see if I could find an envelope that Dad had sent to him before he went to Sweden." Peter paused. "But, more important, is there anything new on Jed?"

"Nothing, nada, zip. No Jed, no boat. But thanks for your tip about the body. That was Captain Haake all right. Haven't figured what happened with him. In addition to the bullet in the head that killed him, we know he was legally drunk. And his boat is missing. So getting back to your story." Reilly tipped his head slightly to one side and narrowed his eyes. "Of course, if what you found would tell us anything about Jed, you would have let me know?"

Peter smiled. "Of course. But what I found out was that Dad was adopted."

Reilly looked surprised. "Okaaay," he said slowly. "And you never knew that?"

Peter shook his head. "Nope." He went on to explain about going to his father's house in Brewster, finding out from Mary Knight that his father had probably left for Sweden on the previous Tuesday, and discovering the unused airline tickets. Peter described his father's list of things to do before he left, which included sending an envelope to Jed. "I was curious and thought that maybe it would tell us something about what happened to Jed or why Dad left early. Anyway, just on the spur of the moment, I decided to check it out and went to Jed's house … and didn't find anything, basically."

"Basically?" Reilly asked.

Peter ignored the question. "So I went to Jed's office. I figured if my uncle's secretary was still there …"

"But she wasn't. So you did what any reasonable investigative journalist would do," Reilly said, smiling.

Peter returned Reilly's shot. "Naturally, Investigative Reporting 101. And I found the envelope. Dad's birth certificate and adoption papers were in it. So at least I know why he went to Sweden."

"I'm not sure I get the connection or why you went back again today. But, listen, I have some news for you about him going to Sweden. He left the U.S. and flew there Tuesday in a private jet."

So that was the explanation for his father's early departure for Sweden. He had hitched a ride with his biological father Bjorn Svensson. Still, it was a surprisingly spontaneous decision for his father, Peter thought. "How did you find out?"

"I did a routine check. The INS, except it isn't the INS anymore, it's a Department of Homeland Security, Something-or-Other Division, anyway, they have a database we can tap into that lists everybody in and out of the country every day," Reilly continued. He pulled out a small black notebook. "Let's see.

Three passengers: B. Svensson, R. Stengren, E. Frost. Left at 10:00 AM Tuesday from Boston, Logan Airport, on a Gulfstream G150 jet. Nice bird. Registered to a company in Sweden called Gevarfabrik AB." He spelled out the name. "Flight plan called for one stop in Keflavik, Iceland, and then a final destination in Stockholm, Arlanda Airport."

The waitress returned with their coffees and a plate with three doughnuts. "On the house," she said, smiling. Reilly started to say something. She put her hand on his arm. "They're yesterday's."

Peter stirred the contents of a packet of sugar into his coffee. Well, that explained the unused tickets that he had found. "So the telephone call between Dad and Jed must have been just before Dad and the others left for Sweden," he said.

"Apparently. But what's the connection between his adoption and Sweden?" Reilly asked.

Peter told him about the names on the birth certificate. He described his trip to Maine and his aunt/grandmother Elena's information, including his father's meeting on Monday with Peter's newfound biological grandfather.

"So I guess they hit it off and Mr. ... What was it? ... Svensson offered him a lift back to the old country."

"Yes, I guess so," Peter said, thinking that it was a reasonable scenario. He wondered if it would allay Elena's fears about Bjorn Svensson and his father getting along. It didn't entirely ease his own concerns about his father's early departure.

"That's a lot of news for one weekend, huh?" Reilly said. "But why'd you go back to Jed's office this afternoon?"

Peter explained about the recording and the transcripts. "I wondered if they had anything to do with the meeting and maybe with inheritance issues."

Reilly sat back in his seat and gave his chin a small massage. "Yeah, I can see where you'd be curious. I guess I'd like to have a look at that transcript too. Where's it now?"

Peter retrieved the envelope from his car and returned to the Village Grill. While Reilly examined the birth certificate and adoption papers, Peter began to look through the transcripts. Comparing the Swedish and the English texts, even with his limited knowledge of Swedish, it seemed clear that the English was a translation of the Swedish.

"Adoption looks legit. You finding anything in the transcripts?" Reilly asked.

"It just seems to be a kind of conversation between my grandmother and grandfather and a friend when they were in Germany."

Bill looked puzzled. Peter explained about the wire recording. He gave Reilly the English translation to read. "I thought there might be something about my grandfather making a commitment to my grandmother or ... I don't know. But there isn't anything like that, just a lot of joking around and playing with the recorder."

Reilly looked up from reading the transcript. "So why would your uncle be interested in this?"

"No clue," Peter said, returning the contents to the envelope.

They drove back to where Peter had left his car. "Make sure you tell your dad to call me when you hear from him."

"I sent Dad an e-mail asking him to call you. Have you had any contact with him?"

"Not directly. He left me a message. Called in the middle of the night. Probably morning for him. Said he got your e-mail. He left a call-back number, which I've tried a couple of times. Left him a message to call my cell phone anytime. I'm still waiting. I assume you haven't heard from him or you would have called me, right?"

"I've been checking messages. Dad hasn't called me. Maybe he's just gotten very involved in this whole process of meeting his biological father," Peter said, hoping it was true.

"Gotcha. It sounds like I might be able to get in touch with him through his Swedish father at the 'Gev-whatever' company. Meantime, you work on it too."

It was eight thirty and getting dark as Peter left Chatham driving north toward Route 6. He suddenly felt very tired and not up for driving a couple of hours back to Cambridge in a convoy of returning weekend traffic. He crossed over the trail of red taillights on the Mid-Cape Highway and continued toward his father's house in Brewster.

Back at his father's house, Peter sat on the couch in the living room and booted up his laptop. He was curious to know more about Gevarfabrik. Google produced about a hundred hits, most in Swedish. Gevarfabrik was a manufacturer of hunting and military arms. Gevarfabrik's own Web site offered a choice of languages including English and Arabic. Most of the pages on the site were devoted to the company's high-quality hunting arms. The company was located north of Stockholm on the Baltic Sea in a town called Sundsvall. The name seemed familiar to Peter, but he was not sure where he had seen it before. Much of the Web site was password protected, apparently intended for serious, registered customers of the company's military-grade weapons. The open pages on the Web site gave only very brief descriptions of these mostly small-caliber automatic weapons.

After shutting down his computer, Peter stretched himself out on the couch. Just as he was drifting off to sleep, he remembered where he had seen the name Sundsvall. He recovered his uncle's 1970 business diary from his backpack. Among the detailed entries for September of 1970, he found a four-day period marked only "Sundsvall" with a telephone number. No company name or other contact information was listed.

Chapter 13

AT A FEW MINUTES before six, the sun lanced through the window in the guest room of his father's house. Peter woke up from a vaguely disturbing dream that he could not remember and decided to go for a run.

The tide was a little past high so there was a good strip of packed wet sand at the water's edge. He joined a couple of early walkers and several flocks of seagulls in the cool, sunny morning. He thought about the transcripts and wondered why his father sent them to Jed along with the obviously significant birth and adoption documents. If Jed was involved because of some legal paternity issue, had he been investigating that possibility since 1970? The letters that Elena said that Bjorn had written to her in the United States would seem like better evidence. She hadn't said whether she still had them.

Back at his father's house, he showered, gave the cats some food, and left a note for Mary Knight who would certainly notice that someone had been in the house. He was about to leave when he realized that there was one room in the house that he had not looked into the previous Friday: his father's lab in the cellar. Maybe the wire recording itself would be there and, perhaps, some indication of why it was important.

He walked down the narrow, uneven stairs off the kitchen to the cellar. When his father had retired and moved down to the Cape, he had walled off a good-sized area in the cellar and added soundproofing and laboratory benches. He had explained to Peter that he had virtually recreated his former audio lab in Brewster with electronic hardware and computers for sound analysis of audio recordings.

The key to the lab door was always left under a can of nails on the workbench near the stairs. But when Peter picked up the can, he was surprised to see the key was missing. He crossed the cellar to the door of lab. It was closed, but the padlock with the key in it dangled from one side of the open hasp. It was not at all like his father to have forgotten to lock the door and put the key back in its place.

Peter opened the door and saw a dark landscape of electronic devices dotted with green and red power lights. Everything seemed normal. The lab was in its usual completely orderly state, in contrast to his father's office. The two lab benches were clear except for an antique-looking wooden chest about the size of a toaster oven. Wires from the front of the well-made oak box were connected to one of the modern instruments behind it on the bench. Probably the wire recorder, Peter thought. It seemed to belong to another technological age. His father occasionally bought ancient microphones, telephones, or recording devices, which he enjoyed repairing and testing out.

The wooden chest on the bench seemed to qualify as one of these specimens. It had a lid, which Peter cautiously unlatched and raised. On the inside was a metal label with the inscription "Telegramophone" and "Hamburg" and some other notation in German, which Peter could not understand.

Under the lid, there was something that looked like an old reel-to-reel tape recorder. There were two spindles. On one of the spindles was a spool somewhat different from the tape reels that Peter had seen. It was smaller in diameter but thicker than a tape reel. He assumed it was the take-up spool. He looked around but saw nothing like another spool with wire that might be the recording his grandmother had described. A quick search of the shelves and drawers in the lab produced a similar negative result. So the lab was left open, and the wire recording was not where Peter expected it would be. They seemed like additional indications that his father had been somewhat distracted by his meeting with Bjorn Svensson and his hasty departure with Bjorn to Sweden. That realization added to the creeping uneasiness that had begun with Bill Reilly's late-night call a few days before.

By eight thirty, Peter was part of the commuter traffic moving slowly along the Mid-Cape Highway toward the Sagamore Bridge. He called his editor Gene to let him know he would be late for their ten o'clock meeting.

"Are you avoiding me? Second time in three days," Gene said in a kidding voice.

"No, I'll just be a little late. It's been kind of weird the last few days since I got back from California."

"Understand, but I want to make sure you can get the drug piece wrapped up before the end of the week—"

"Sure, no prob," Peter interrupted.

"... before you tell me you want to go back to Sweden and work on the neo-Nazi piece again," Gene continued.

Peter grunted in response. Catching up with his father in Sweden was becoming an increasingly appealing idea. He wondered how he could make the neo-Nazi follow-up seem urgent enough to get Gene to change his mind.

"So Jill said something about your finding out that your dad was adopted and you were going to Maine to get the story from your aunt?"

"That's right. Long story short: I'm partly Swedish. My father's father was Swedish, named Svensson."

"So we're probably related," Gene said.

Peter could hear the grin in Gene's voice. Gene enjoyed surprising people when they met in person after talking on the telephone. After two generations in a small town in Vermont, his voice, like his name, carried no hint of his African-American heritage. If people looked surprised when they saw him, he would reintroduce himself smiling good-naturedly. "I'm Gene Johanson, the Swede you talked to on the phone."

The warmth of Gene's smile and manner allowed him to offer this mild ribbing without offending people for their mistaken assumption. It was his gentle reminder of everyone's built-in racial unconsciousness. Gene had actually traced his Swedish ancestor through colonial Philadelphia back to Southern Sweden in the 1600s.

"Later, cousin." Gene disconnected.

Peter reflected on his aunt-now-grandmother's revelations of the previous day. It changed so much of what he had taken for granted and what he had taken as his parents' words and others' silences for his own family's history. But did it really change his own life? Not much, he imagined.

Peter punched the speed dial code for Jill's number.

"Where are you?" Jill answered.

"Just on my way back from the Cape."

"The Cape? I thought you were going to Maine. Any news of your uncle?"

"No news. I was in Maine. Drove back down to Brewster yesterday. It's complicated."

"Sounds interesting. And you'll fill me in, of course?" she said.

"Naturally," Peter said, smiling to himself.

"Did you find out anything from your aunt Elena about your father's being adopted?"

"I did. For starters, she's not my aunt."

"I knew that. She's a courtesy aunt."

"No, she's actually my grandmother."

"No way!"

"Way."

"Oh wow. So she's your father's birth mother. That's a trip. Listen, Peter, I'm just on my way out and I want to hear all about this."

At eleven twenty, Peter found a parking space in a restricted area on Brattle Street and put a "Press" card on his dashboard. This was a ploy he used sparingly, figuring that the neighborhood meter maids would catch on if he tried it too often.

Gene was waiting for him in his office behind a desk no less cluttered than Peter's father's. "Give me a five-minute summary of your genealogical researches, and then we'll talk business. You can give me the long version over a beer." Gene leaned back in his chair and put his sandaled feet up on the edge of his desk.

Peter summarized what he had found out about his father's Swedish connection. He decided not to confuse things with a discussion of his concerns about his father's reuniting with Bjorn.

"Interesting, a whole new history of your family. It's amazing how compelling it can be to find out things about people you don't know, maybe never could know, just because you share a little DNA."

"Well, in this case, for my father, maybe more than just a little DNA."

"True," Gene replied. "So, about the drug piece. Do you have your trip to Ohio set up so you can wrap it up by Friday?"

"Well … actually, I think I've got enough without going out there."

"Really? Good. Last week you seemed …"

"I know, but I've been thinking that … this would be a good time to get back to my Swedish neo-Nazi article. We promised some follow-up and dangled the question of where these groups got their money. I want to get on that," Peter said.

"After the call you got a couple of months ago from your buddy in Sweden—what's his name? Claes?—I thought we decided it would be a good idea to wait on that and let the skinheads over there cool off a little," Gene said.

"Well, it's been over three months and …"

"And now do I wonder why you might want to go to Sweden?" Gene said with a half smile and raised eyebrows. "Well, if you book three weeks ahead, you should be able to get a cheap flight, make it your summer vacation. Right?"

"Actually, my friend Claes and his wife invited me to come over for the Midsummer celebration and stay with them in their place on an island near Stockholm and …"

Gene was nodding with his lips pursed. "So when is this Midsummer celebration?" He glanced over at his wall calendar. "Isn't it this weekend?"

"Yes, I'd have to leave this week," Peter said quickly. "But I think I can get one of those cheap last-minute deals on a flight."

Gene pulled his heels off the desk and brought his chair forward. He consulted his diary, flipping several pages ahead. After a moment, he looked up at Peter. "Okay, but here's the deal: cheap flight, drug decrim article, fact-checked and proofed in my e-mail inbox before you leave."

"Sure," Peter said, thinking it was always possible. "I'll see what Pam can dig up for flights on short notice."

"Good man," Gene said, swiveling around to open a file drawer behind his desk. "Stay in touch."

Peter left to speak to Pam, Gene's very attractive and happily married Eurasian assistant, about his travel plans.

"Ah so, you need a fright to Stockholm," she said doing her Oriental accent. Like Gene's, her real voice was totally Northeastern American suburban.

Peter acknowledged her pun with a grimace.

Upstairs, Jill was typing furiously into her computer when Peter came into the office. She spoke without looking up. "Done already?" She typed a final burst of words. "Let's get some lunch. I'm ready for a break," she said hitting *Save* and swinging out of her chair in one motion.

They left the office and walked down Brattle Street into Harvard Square toward the Casablanca. The Casa B, as it was known, was a long-standing Cambridge restaurant and one-time nightclub. The food was Middle-East-inspired; the wall murals were Rick's-Café-inspired. Peter and Jill were early for lunch and found a quiet table in the back. They gave their orders to a waitress who seemed to have exhausted all the possible sites above her neck for piercings. Peter did not want to think about the sites below.

When their well-perforated server had left, Jill leaned forward and looked intently at Peter. "Okay, I want hear all about Aunt Elena, who isn't, and so forth."

By the time they had finished lunch and their coffee had arrived, Peter had provided Jill with a very complete account of his conversation with Elena.

"How did she seem, telling you all this? It must have brought back a lot of tough memories for her," Jill said.

"It did, certainly," Peter responded. "I guess that's why she seemed to be kind of concerned about Dad's getting in touch with Bjorn."

"That seems pretty reasonable. Your grandmother probably doesn't really know much about today's Bjorn Svensson and maybe doesn't want to."

"Yes, there were definitely areas she didn't want to get into. Like why he would come over here to see Dad when they could meet in Sweden. I'm wondering if he might have some worries about Dad's claiming some inheritance or something?"

"Could be. And I would imagine this Bjorn would be pretty defensive on the emotional issues. There's the son he knew about but later wouldn't acknowledge. And your father's feelings about the way Bjorn treated Elena, his mother."

"That was a long time ago but maybe that's why she thought I ought to go to Sweden to be with him."

"Why not? So now you've got two reasons to go to Sweden," Jill said.

"Actually three, I told you Bill Reilly's been trying to reach Dad to ask him about Jed Barlow's state of mind. Bill's getting a little ticked that Dad is out of touch. I'm sure he'd like me to go to Sweden and track Dad down."

"There you go," Jill responded as her cell phone played a couple of familiar bars from Beethoven's "Ode to Joy."

"Hello ... Hi, Pam ... Yes, he's right here. Did you find a flight? No, he needs to leave tonight."

Peter started to protest, but Jill waved him off.

"That's all that's available tonight? Yes, do it. I'll talk to Gene. He needs to get there sooner rather than later. Okay, thanks." Jill closed the phone. "You're all set on American tonight through London to Stockholm in the splendid comfort of business class."

Peter whistled softly. "Gene's going to go ballistic when he sees that."

"No, he'll just take it out of your paycheck."

"Thanks, I guess. You think it's that urgent?" Peter didn't want to admit he was concerned enough to be relieved that he was going to be able to leave that day.

Jill put on her mother-knows-best face. "Peter, you need to complete a significant follow-up article. Your father may have important information about a missing person." Peter started to object but Jill ignored him. "He also seems to be missing." She looked at Peter as though she expected some confirmation. "And, he is visiting his real father who may be a real SOB. I think he could use your support in person. So that's why you need to go home right now and start packing."

"Right," Peter said nodding patiently.

"So I suppose you think I'm over dramatizing the normal confusions and uncertainties of everyday life again?"

"I'd never say anything like that," Peter replied.

Chapter 14

ARRIVING AT HIS APARTMENT, Peter retrieved his combo roll-on/backpack. Within a few minutes, he had stuffed it with a selection of sufficiently all-purpose khakis, shorts, shirts, running gear, and a windbreaker for what he expected would be fairly benign June weather in Sweden.

He tried the telephone number in Sweden that his father had left Bill Reilly. A British-accented woman's voice on a recorded message in English informed him the offices were closed, but he was invited to leave a message. He declined, and instead plugged in his laptop and sent his father an e-mail. Peter wrote that he had seen the envelope sent to Jed with his father's birth certificate and then talked to Aunt Elena who had given him the basic facts. He looked forward to hearing the details from his father. And, now coincidentally, he was coming back to Sweden on a follow-up assignment. He needed some excuse, he thought, for jumping into the middle of his father's hush-hush family research. He also said he was looking forward to meeting Bjorn Svensson and hoped that would be okay. He also he reminded his father that Bill Reilly was anxious to talk to him about Jed Barlow's disappearance.

Next, he made a call to a man he called Anders in Sweden. He punched in the long international number. After a few clicks, the call seemed to go through but with a distinctly non-U.S. ringtone. After two warbles, an answering machine picked up. The long outgoing message in Swedish made him suspect that its content went beyond "Sorry we're not here, leave a message." But his rudimentary Swedish was not good enough to make out anything useful.

Anders was middle-aged, the manager of a small tourist shop in central Stockholm. Peter had met him at a neo-Nazi rally in a small town southwest of the city. He had tried to give the impression that he was a journalist sympathetic to the white power movement. After a few moments, Anders had seen through the pretense. He suggested that others might as well, putting Peter in danger. He told Peter he should leave the rally but that he would contact him. When they met later in Stockholm, Anders told him that he had become disenchanted with the movement. In several subsequent meetings, Anders had provided considerable and, Peter believed, accurate information on the organization of the neo-Nazis in Sweden.

Normally, Peter preferred to speak directly to Anders but because of his immediate departure, he decided to leave a brief message in the code they had worked out. It was a request to leave word for him at the Wallin Hotel in Stockholm suggesting a time and a place to meet in the next three days. At the beep tone, he said, "I'm not sure I have the right number. If this is Sven Hausman, please call me at home." Sven Hausman was a made-up name. He didn't know Anders's last name.

Peter's flight was at 6:00 PM. It was now just three in the afternoon, so he judged that he had plenty of time to get to the airport by public transportation. It was a small cost saving over a taxi, his usual mode of travel to Logan Airport. It wouldn't really mollify Gene when he saw the business class airfare on Peter's expense report, but he thought it would show good intentions. Peter race-walked to Central Square with his bag in backpack mode. The short walk to the "T" subway station was the only exercise he would get for the next fifteen hours.

He negotiated the security screening smoothly. Occasionally, if he forgot a pen or a piece of foil-wrapped chocolate in his shirt pocket, he joined those infrequent flyers, who walked through metal detectors talking on their mobile phones or wearing three-pound Harley-Davidson belt buckles, in the Full Body Search Club. All a part of life in the depraved new world of suicide bombings, he mused.

By four o'clock, Peter was in the American Airlines club with an hour and a half before boarding. He found a quiet cubicle and plugged in his laptop to review the notes from his previous trip to Sweden. He wanted to plan a strategy for the follow-up article and give his subconscious some time to work on the task during the flight.

In his first article, Peter had related Anders's description of several loosely federated neo-Nazi groups in larger Swedish cities that were well organized and secretive. They generated hate literature and pressured local politicians and civic leaders with implied threats of violence. They organized rallies against immigration. Although their public statements and activities remained within the law, there were always suggestions of actions outside the law. The more visible members of the movement were mostly young, lower-middle-class men. They sported shaved heads and tattoos with neo-Nazi motifs and formed the bulk of the crowds at rallies. Arson and mugging designed to intimidate immigrant communities were often traced to the faces in these crowds. But the solidly respectable and often prosperous-looking group leaders managed to avoid any open connection with these thugs.

Peter had also interviewed three other individuals who were willing to be identified as neo-Nazis supporters. They claimed that although they occasionally participated in demonstrations, they were not active organizers. Other information, including that from Anders, indicated otherwise. Two of the individuals did not have full-time jobs. They told Peter they had government pensions, but it was unclear why. They were younger than the legal retirement age and appeared to be in good health. The third individual ran a small printing business, which he said he did not own. All three, Peter noted, seemed to be living pretty comfortably in large houses and driving expensive Mercedes sedans.

Peter had also discovered that a number of the less-reputable-looking persons, mostly skinheads, some of whom were involved in white power rock bands, also seemed to have limited means of income. Yet they also drove good cars and, according to his informant, often traveled to other parts of

Europe and even Australia to meet fellow supporters of the neo-Nazi movement.

Peter's informant indicated that there were two main sources of funds. The first was the contributions in cash from white power music record and merchandise sales. This was distributed mostly to skinhead types who were associated with the bands. The other source of support was larger and more clandestine in origin. Anders said he knew little about this second source of funds. This money appeared to be allotted to the more senior individuals, local leaders of the movement in five or six larger cities and towns across Sweden.

Tracking down the larger source of the funds was Peter's objective for the follow-up article. His informant had agreed to see if he could make some inquiries without arousing too much suspicion. There seemed to be several possibilities, which ranged from foreign terrorist groups like Al Qaeda to wealthy Argentinean businessmen whose Nazi fathers and grandfathers had escaped the Allies after the Second World War.

At five fifteen, Peter checked his e-mail a final time for a response from his father and found none. He sent Bill Reilly a short message letting him know about his own sudden departure for Sweden. He assured Reilly that he would have his father call him as soon as he caught up with him. He closed down his computer just as the boarding was announced for his London flight.

Eager tourists and students, already on summer break, crowded into the economy section of the Boeing 767, and business class was nearly full. Happily, Peter noticed that the window seat next to his was empty; he moved over to enjoy the view of Boston Harbor on takeoff. After the seat-belt light went off, he spread out over the two seats and turned on his laptop. He spent an hour working his West Coast notes into the draft of his drug article.

When he was satisfied that he could do a quick polish the next day in Stockholm, he decided to take advantage of his travel upgrade. He put away his laptop and stretched out on the wide reclining seat. His call button brought a flight attendant to take his request for a beer. In the future, he would be sure to have Jill make all his travel arrangements. After dinner, he found earplugs and sleep-shades in his complimentary flight kit. With his seat adjusted to a nearly horizontal position, he fell asleep. The jolt of wheels-down woke him on landing at Heathrow.

After a sleepwalking transfer on people-movers, escalators, stairs, and a crowded inter-terminal bus, Peter boarded the British Air connection to Stockholm. Scrambled eggs, two large sausages, and the required grilled tomato of an English breakfast revived him. It compensated for the breakfast he had missed on the American flight. The early morning flight to Stockholm was full, mostly businessmen on day trips chatting among themselves or reading the *London Times*. They wore what looked like expensive suits, blue dress shirts with white collars and French cuffs, and silk ties. Peter felt very American in his jeans, comfortable boat mocs, and open-collared oxford shirt.

The flight touched down at Arlanda Airport about twenty miles north of Stockholm at eleven thirty in the morning local time. By one in the afternoon, Peter had checked into the Wallin Hotel on Wallingatan Street where he had stayed on his previous trip. It was a modest, comfortable hotel on a quiet street not far from the center of Stockholm. Drottninggatan, a bustling pedestrian street, was half a block away. It offered a variety of small restaurants, *konditori*, or pastry shops, and other boutiques.

Peter's room was Swedish modern simple, all blond wood in the bedroom and steel and glass in the bathroom. He looked forward to a couple of hours of real bed sleep before trying to do anything useful. But first, he plugged in his laptop to check for an e-mail from his father. His in-box contained messages from Jill and Gene but none from his father.

Peter stripped to his shorts and happily slid under the duvet, that Swedish all-purpose combination upper sheet and quilt. He put on his sleep shades again and settled in for a short nap. Just as he was drifting off, there was a tentative knock at his door.

"Mr. Frost?" It was the receptionist with an accent that was more British than Swedish. "We have an envelope that was left for you to the front desk. I am very sorry that we have forgot to give it to you when you checked in. May I slide it under the door for you?"

"Yes, thanks," Peter said groggily.

"*Varsågod,*" was the polite reply.

Probably one of those smarmy letters from the hotel management "wishing you a pleasant stay. If there is anything we can do for you blah, blah," Peter thought. But then, he wondered if the desk clerk would make a trip up to his room just to deliver some hotel propaganda. Curiosity overcame sleepiness, and he retrieved the letter.

The envelope was light gray, good quality paper, and said simply, "Peter Frost." Inside were two sheets of matching paper. On one, he recognized his father's handwriting and usual elliptical style:

Peter, welcome to Sweden. Sorry not to get back to your e-mails. Lots to talk about. Guess you know most from Elena. With Bjorn, sailing in the Baltic this week. He suggests we get together on his island for Midsummer this weekend. Work for you? Directions enclosed. Love, Dad.

On the second sheet were typewritten instructions for getting to Smavik, an island in the Stockholm Archipelago. There was no return address, no phone number and no indication that his father would or could respond by e-mail.

Peter considered that "sailing with Bjorn on the Baltic" sounded like father and son were getting along. But the questions for his father would have to wait.. He dropped back into the bed, annoyed but too sleepy for the moment to care.

Chapter 15

THE MID-AFTERNOON WAKE-UP CALL, which Peter had left at the front desk, ended his two-hour recuperative nap. He had slept soundly but woke with a sense of uneasiness at not being able to talk to his father directly. He decided a run would help his mood and along with his nap would reset his jet-lag-disturbed circadian rhythm. He dressed quickly in shorts and a sweatshirt and left the hotel.

Peter headed south toward Gamla Stan, the old town, located on an island in the center of Stockholm overlooking the inner harbor. It was one of several islands between the Baltic Sea to the east and Lake Malaren to the west, on which most of Stockholm was built. He ran south down Drottninggatan and then across the Riksbron Bridge, which led to the west end of the royal palace on Gamla Stan. In addition to the palace, several churches shared the island with small restaurants, clothing boutiques, bookstores, and tourist shops. Most of the buildings were centuries old, crowding the sides of the narrow streets on the hill, which occupied the center of the island.

Peter looped around the palace, an imposing and stolid, rectangular block of a building. He headed back north again by another bridge just east of the Riksbron Bridge over the Norrstrom waterway. He turned and ran along Stromkajen, the wide quay in front of the Grand Hotel. There, numerous ferries began their routes to different parts of the archipelago. Several medium-size passenger ferries were currently taking on passengers. The directions in the note from his father had specified which ferry Peter should take to Smavik, his grandfather's island, on Friday afternoon.

Although he was disappointed that the note had not offered any way to contact his father, it was mostly reassuring. His father loved sailing; he probably wouldn't spend a week with Bjorn on a boat if there were any significant tensions between them. Perhaps they were catching up on a lifetime of missed experiences. How would his father feel about that lifetime? Would he be angry at what he had missed or grateful for a small opportunity to make up for it? Most likely some of both.

His run was a route he had taken several times the previous fall around the inner harbor. Beyond the Grand Hotel, he passed the National Museum and crossed over another bridge onto Skeppsholmen Island, which sat across the harbor from Gamla Stan. It was a pleasant circuit on paved surfaces but with few cars and constantly changing views of Stockholm's waterfront.

By four thirty, Peter was back in his hotel room, showered and feeling refreshed. Hoping to stave off serious hunger pangs until a reasonable dinner hour, he found a small café with tables outside in the sun on Drottninggatan. He ordered a beer and an open-faced prawn sandwich.

Peter was enjoying the last of his after-lunch coffee when two figures in sleeveless black T-shirts appeared in the stream of pedestrians on the street. Their shaved heads and skin-piercing hardware separated them from the other walkers. As they approached, one of them looked directly at Peter with what might have been a slight smile or a smirk or neither. A serious scar from his left cheek to his upper lip made it impossible to tell. Peter looked away to avoid a challenging stare. After they passed, he watched and noticed that they turned down Wallinggatan. He recalled Claes Vikstrom's phone call earlier in the year and wondered if their route was anything more than coincidental.

When he walked to his hotel a few minutes later, the skinheads were not in sight. Back in his room, he called Claes, reasoning that at a little before five, he might still be in his office at the National Police Headquarters.

His friend answered on the first rang. "Peter! How are you? You are coming to Sweden soon, I hope?"

Peter explained that he was already in Sweden, on an unplanned visit, to follow up on his article and on some personal business.

"Wonderful, it is nearly time to be leaving from work. I propose we should take a beer together."

They agreed to meet at a café near Claes's office. The police headquarters building was in a neighborhood on an island just west of Norrmalm, within walking distance of Peter's hotel.

When Peter arrived at the café, Claes was sitting at a table in the back. He stood and greeted Peter with a warm handshake and a wide smile that crinkled his round, tanned face. Claes was tall and slightly stooped, the result of an on-duty injury that had left him, as he said, "a little crooked myself." His dark brown hair was just graying at the edges where it lapped around his ears. It was longer, Peter had remarked, than regulations or custom would have dictated in America. Claes wore a light-colored tie and a dark blue shirt. A brown leather jacket, which looked formal enough for his position but practical enough for fieldwork, hung over the back of his chair.

"So, Peter, I think we should celebrate your arrival with a whiskey, yes?"

Peter agreed to let Claes buy the first round insisting the next would be on him. Scotch was an expensive treat in Sweden. Taxes on liquor were supposedly designed to address what was perceived as a potentially alcoholic population depressed by long, dark winters. Claes, whose politics were slightly right of center, contended that the taxes had more to do with paying for the extensive social services than saving Swedes from drinking themselves to death.

When their whiskeys arrived, Claes toasted Peter in the traditional Swedish fashion, raising his glass while looking at Peter, drinking, and again raising his glass to Peter. Peter responded a short time later in a similar fashion.

"Tell me what is bringing you to Sweden again so soon."

Peter explained that the original article he had written on the neo-Nazis had been well received and that he had come to research the promised follow-up article. "I decided that now was a good time to do it." Peter paused to take a sip of his Scotch before going on. "And actually, I have another couple of reasons for coming over. It turns out that my father was adopted and that his biological father was, or is, Swedish. In fact, my father is here now in Sweden with him."

"But you did not know about your Swedish family when you were here last year?"

"No, I just found out last week, in fact."

"Ah yah," Claes said generating the syllables in a strong incoming breath. It seemed to be a linguistically unique vocalization used by Swedes to emphasize the affirmative "yes."

"Well, *det är bra,*" Claes said lapsing into Swedish. "That's wonderful. Welcome to being a Swede. That explains why you enjoy your whiskey so much."

Peter went on to give a short version of his recently discovered genealogy.

"Bjorn Svensson. Well, I am sure I know him," Claes said with a serious expression.

"Really?"

"Yes, I should think I know at least three of him." Claes laughed. "A very common name here. Where does he live?"

"He apparently has a weapons manufacturing business in Sundsvall, according to their Web site. It's a good one, I guess. He has a corporate jet."

"Ah yah. Perhaps then I really do know him. Or I know who he is. Bjorn Svensson is the owner of a company called Gevarfabrik, a wealthy man," Claes said nodding. "And you said your father was going to visit him?"

"Yes, he and my father are sailing together somewhere in the Baltic this week. And I'm afraid if you were thinking about my coming to spend Midsummer with you and Kristina, I have to apologize. I have been asked to join them this weekend on the island that Bjorn Svensson owns in the archipelago."

"Well, I am glad you have plans for the weekend. We will make a Midsummer celebration another year, I hope," Claes said.

"Yes, definitely. But this year, I'm really curious to meet my grandfather Svensson."

"Of course." Claes was thoughtful and looked as though he was going to say something, changed his mind, and instead smiled and repeated his toast with Peter. "So, now you will have to learn some Swedish, Peter. We will sign you up for some government-sponsored classes."

"Yah," Peter replied. "You mean *'Var är toaletten'* isn't enough?"

They drank quietly for a moment, and Claes excused himself to find the *toaletten*. When he returned, Peter inquired about his wife, Kristina, and their grown-up children. Claes responded with a few details and assured him that once Kristina knew he was in Stockholm, she would want him to come to dinner one night.

"Now, Peter, may I return to the first subject we were discussing, your article?"

Claes paused, perhaps organizing his thoughts in English. "When we spoke by telephone in March, I told you we had arrested three young men for setting fire to a rooming house in Linköping, a large town south of Stockholm. One of them had a copy of your article in his apartment. He boasted to us, 'If Peter Frost ever comes back to Sweden, we have some plans for him.'"

"Yes, I remember," Peter said, thinking about his encounter on Drottninggatan but deciding not to mention it. "Thanks. I'll try to watch out for myself."

"I hope you will be careful, Peter, in your researches and interviews. Will you be seeing your informant again?"

"Probably. I'd also like to spend some working time with you when you can spare me an hour."

"Tomorrow morning at my office at eleven o'clock, and then we take some lunch afterward?"

They left the café and prepared to depart in different directions, Peter toward his hotel and Claes to the central station to catch a train to his home in the suburb of Bromma. As they shook hands, Claes looked hard at Peter. "Remember, my friend, we have very little serious violence in Sweden, but sometimes even government ministers are not safe."

Chapter 16

PETER WALKED BACK TOWARD Wallingatan. The sky had clouded over, and the air was cooler than when he had left the hotel. He felt comfortable, warmed by the Scotch and his reunion with Claes. But he thought about his friend's warning. As a journalist, he had occasionally faced hostile newsmakers both in the United States and abroad. He considered himself reasonably cautious and alert to individuals or groups that might be a threat. Claes's concern wasn't unreasonable, but at least for the moment, the chances of being recognized on the street as the author of a critical article in a relatively obscure American publication by some random neo-Nazi types were probably pretty low.

In addition to the two skinheads who had walked past him on Drottninggatan earlier in the day, he had passed a couple of groups of similar types during his run. One bunch had been loitering near the ferry docks, another drinking at an outdoor café in Gamla Stan. Most of their hostile-by-design appearances looked more like affectation than aggression. On his previous trip to Sweden, he had talked to a number of them. Many seemed to be just somewhat alienated young men who could be found in many countries. Most were more different in style than in substance from the spike-haired punks with whom they shared a common interest in skin-piercing jewelry. However, there was a hard core whose disaffection had evolved into hate that generated violence. These few acted out their anger rather than just dressing the part. But he admitted it was not always easy to tell which they were by appearances.

When Peter collected his room key from the desk clerk at the hotel, he was also handed an envelope with the imprint of the Grand Hotel. His name appeared on the front in block letters. He waited until he had reached his room before opening it. Inside was a piece of yellow lined paper with a short hand-printed note: *The restaurant at 1900 today.* Apparently, his informant had received his telephone message.

"The restaurant" was the Röda Fisket, or Red Fish, in Gamla Stan where they had met before. His informant, Anders, knew the staff and was able to arrange for a table in a private corner. It was short notice, but Peter was pleased to be able to start on his research so quickly.

Peter checked his e-mail and read the messages from Gene and Jill. Gene in his usual e-mail style, which ignored the shift and punctuation keys except for rare occasions, wrote:

peter what is your eta on the drug decrim article for jill understand you had a COMFORTABLE flight gene

Jill wrote:

Dear Peder,

When do you expect to be able to send me your draft of the drug decriminalization article? Gene found out about your business class flight. I said that you told me that you always fly first or business class ... (joke!).

Enjoy Sweden!

Jill

Peter hit the reply button on each e-mail, telling both Jill and Gene he expected to send them his draft within a day or two. In a short e-mail to Bill Reilly, he said that he had heard from his father and would see him on the weekend. He would call later with details.

He left the hotel at six thirty. A ten-minute walk brought him to the Norrstrom, the narrow waterway that separated Gamla Stan from the northern half of Stockholm. The Strombron Bridge, at the east end of the royal palace, was busy with automobile traffic and pedestrians, a mixture of tourists and locals. A Volvo police station wagon was parked on the near side of the bridge. A single uniformed officer was standing by the car giving directions, it appeared, to a destination in Gamla Stan.

From the bridge, Peter looked up at the palace on the hill across the channel. Its yellow sandstone walls glowed in the late-day sun. He crossed the bridge and walked on past the palace, turning onto a steep, narrow street, away from the water. It led up to Osterlanggatan, a cobbled street that ran north to south on the east side of Gamla Stan. It was lined with buildings more than four hundred years old with portions that might be twice that age.

The Röda Fisket restaurant was a short distance along Osterlanggatan. Peter entered through an ancient wooden door. Early diners occupied most of the white linen-covered tables in several small, interconnected rooms. Bits of cheerful, animated conversations in American English and German voices and some more subdued Swedish voices filled the rooms. Peter told the tall, balding maître d' that he was meeting a friend with a blue scarf. The maître d' seemed to recognize Peter immediately so the use of the code phrase, which Peter and Anders had agreed on, seemed a little silly.

"Yah. Please follow me," the maître d' said pleasantly but without smiling. He led Peter down a set of stone steps to a basement level. Like a number of the restaurants in old buildings in Gamla Stan, the Röda Fisket had dining rooms in a low vaulted cellar. What had probably once been storage areas were now chic, candlelit stone chambers of various sizes. Thick foundation walls separating them allowed for considerable privacy for partying groups or intimate couples. Peter and his informant, though not partying or intimate, made use of a quiet niche near the kitchen. The maître d' led Peter past several empty rooms off the passageway to a small room where they had met before. The arched entrance was low enough so that Peter had to stoop slightly as he entered.

"I believe your companion will be joining you shortly," the maître d' said quietly.

Peter noticed the table was not set. Apparently, dinner was not on the menu. He asked for a beer as the maître d' turned to leave.

"Of course. *Pils* or *lager?*"

"Pilsner," Peter replied.

The maître d' ducked out of the room and disappeared through a door off the passageway. The beer arrived quickly in a tall, graceful glass. Peter took a drink and pulled out his notebook.

Anders appeared suddenly and silently at the table. He sat quickly, facing Peter with his back to the passageway. His fleshy face was shiny with perspiration and dark circles showed under his eyes. Thinning reddish hair was plastered on his forehead from a baseball cap he taken off when he came in. He hunched over the table and put out his hand to Peter. It was damp and soft, and he withdrew it a little too quickly.

He looked intently at Peter. "I have new information for you," he said without offering his usual pleasantries. The relaxed manner Peter had observed in him when they met in the fall was gone.

"That's good," Peter replied sitting back slightly, hoping to put his informant more at ease. "So, how have you been?"

Anders ignored the question. "I think this information is very valuable for you."

Peter sat up slightly trying to match his informant's mood a little better. "Yes, I'm sure it will be. I appreciate what you were able to tell me before." The previous fall, Anders had described a clandestine organization of outwardly respectable citizens who supported and directed the more visible skinheads and older active members of the neo-Nazi movement. Although Anders was not a member of the elite group, he had acted as a courier between it and the more visible groups and individuals.

"This information is valuable," he repeated. "I mean it is worth money, *kronor.*" Anders looked uncomfortable and hunched lower. "I need you to pay me for it," he said in a low, intense voice. "Fifty thousand *kronor,*" he said in a tone that sounded more questioning than demanding.

For a moment, Peter did not respond. In their previous meetings, Anders had seemed happy to supply what information he had. It appeared his reward was relieving his conscience. Or perhaps he was exacting revenge for not being accepted into the inner circles of the leadership. Anders had explained that he had begun to feel the acts of violence against immigrant families were unjustified and wrong. He told Peter that he was afraid to go directly to the police because he would be exposed and in danger. He had said that he planned to continue to work with the neo-Nazis but that he would reduce participation slowly over time so as not to arouse suspicion.

"We haven't worked that way in the past," Peter replied neutrally, hoping that Anders was just testing him.

"But now we must." Anders brought his head up and looked around. Then he leaned down across the table toward Peter again. "I need money to leave Sweden, probably for some time. I think they know that I talked to you last year."

Peter tried not to show his concern by remaining still. "How do you know?"

"There were informations in the article you wrote. I told you about a murder. You remember? I told you some particular facts. I thought they were in the newspapers. But they were not. I believe only a few people knew about them."

"Okay," Peter said slowly. The implications were not good for Anders or himself. "Do they know we meet here?"

"No. A friend of mine in the organization warned me. He said they suspected me but he did not know anything else. But if I tell you more they will ..." Anders sucked in a breath through closed teeth. "Question me."

Peter looked at Anders for a long moment and then spoke. Paying sources was strictly *verboten*, to use Gene's favorite German expression, whenever the issue came up. "Well, I don't think we can pay you," Peter said quietly.

Anders let out a long breath through his mouth. He stretched his hands out on the table as though he was going to try to pull Peter toward him. "But I have learned some important facts. I can tell you how the money is coming. I know the names of big people who are doing this. This is valuable to you, yah?"

Peter nodded. He did not want to let this opportunity go, but he needed some time to see what he could arrange—perhaps something with Claes. "Let me see what I can do."

Anders sighed, and his shoulders sagged slightly. "I need to do this soon. When can we meet again?"

Peter estimated the earliest he could get an answer and the cash would be a couple of days. "How about Thursday?"

"*Ja, okay. Torsdag. Här,*" Anders confirmed.

"Yes, but not here," Peter said, reaching down to get his diary off the chair beside him. When he looked up, Anders was gone. The door to the kitchen was swinging back into the passageway.

Chapter 17

IF ANDERS'S ROLE AS an informant was suspected, Peter decided it would probably not be a good idea to hang around the restaurant on Osterlanggatan. He left fifty *kronor* on the table for his unfinished beer and made his way back to the street. A short walk brought him to a square behind the palace where he had seen a small restaurant with outdoor tables. There were some in front on the sidewalk; others nestled under the side of a church across the pedestrian street.

Peter was directed to a table by the church. He ordered an appetizer with several types of marinated herring and smoked salmon as a main course. After dinner and another beer, Peter passed up dessert and coffee. Not feeling ready for bed, he decided to walk to the far end of Gamla Stan before heading back toward his hotel. The exercise would be relaxing before the full night's sleep that he was looking forward to.

He left the restaurant and headed up the hill toward the palace, turning south on Vasterlanggatan. It ran the length of Gamla Stan on the west side of the island, curving gently around the contour of the island's hill. At nine thirty, the sun was lurking above the skyline in the northwest providing a soft summer evening light. The older tourists had been mostly replaced by a younger crowd that included Stockholm natives in pursuit of drinks and music in the small cafés and clubs of the quarter. The music in these establishments did not hold much interest for Peter. It was mostly hard rock and heavy metal, but with a little less than the usual amplification in the U.S. Looking through the window of one club, Peter saw a number of shaved heads. It might have been a hate rock or white power music band, but the lyrics were in Swedish. At another large café, the sound of something like a broken washing machine on spin-dry cycle spread into the street indicating that an industrial rock band was hard at work.

The tourist shops that seemed to account for about every second storefront held the usual mixture of T-shirts, Swedish pins and stickers, and the required display of traditional wooden horses. These were painted in either orange or blue and were available in all sizes. They ranged from less than an inch tall to large enough to be ridden by a small adult. The latter, Peter had discovered, cost more than a round-trip business fare from the United States to Sweden.

At the end of Vasterlanggatan, there was a small square. Several cafés with tables both inside and outside offered a mixture of live and recorded rock music. Just off the square on a quiet side street, he saw a small café with several tables on the sidewalk. As Peter came closer, he heard the sound of live jazz. Inside, just to the right of the door, a combo was playing to a very small, crowded room. Through the cigarette smoke, he could see a single waitress negotiating her full but attractive form through the narrow spaces between the tables. She saw Peter immediately and caught his eye. After delivering her tray of overflowing beer mugs to a group in the center of the room, she motioned for him to come in and pointed out a single seat in the back at a rectangular table across from the bar.

Peter wanted to hear some of the set but hoped that he could sit near the door and make his exit easily. However, that did not seem to be an option. He followed the waitress to the seat she had indicated and ordered a beer. She returned quickly with the beer and a friendly *"Varsågod,"* that Swedish combination of "here you are and thanks for being our customer." By then, Peter was already immersed in the music of a Dave-Brubeck-like arrangement of "Take the 'A' Train."

His seat was on a bench but it was in a corner, so he leaned back, supported by the two walls behind him, and closed his eyes. The set ended after one more number, and he decided to stay for at least part of the next set. His tablemates were two couples who seemed as serious about the music as he was. Between sets, they nodded to him in greeting but returned to conversations with their partners, leaving Peter to his own thoughts. Before the next set began, he had finished most of his beer. When the music started up again, he leaned back into his corner and closed his eyes.

Peter felt a gentle hand on his shoulder and thought perhaps one of the couples was leaving and were politely saying good-bye. He realized the music had stopped, and the room seemed strangely quiet. When he opened his eyes, he saw the café was almost empty, and his table companions as well as the rest of the patrons were gone. The band was packing up, and the waitress was clearing tables. The hand on his shoulder was that of the barman.

"I am sorry, but we must wake up you now. We are closing."

"What time is it?" Peter asked.

"About half after one. I hope you had a chance to listen to some music before you fell asleep."

Peter nodded and stretched, a little stiff from sitting asleep for so long. He settled up for his beer and found his way to the door.

"Enjoyed your numbers," he said to the combo.

"Yah, vee noticed, especially the last set," the bass player said, smiling.

Outside, it was nearly dark; a few of the brightest stars were visible against a dull gray sky. The streets of Gamla Stan were almost deserted. Occasional groups of mostly twenty- to thirty-ish types stood talking, smoking, and calculating how to continue the evening. Having made up for a lot of his lost sleep of the previous night, Peter felt revived. The air was pleasantly cool. He retraced his route along Vasterlanggatan toward the palace. The walk back to the Wallin Hotel would take him about twenty minutes.

The cafés were closed. In front, the chairs were set on the tables to make the morning sweeping easier. The shops were dark. Somewhere behind him, probably in Södermalm, a large island just to the south, the "hoo-hee, hoo-hee" warning signal of

European police vehicles sounded briefly. Otherwise, the streets seemed very quiet for a large city.

When Peter reached the end of Vasterlanggatan, he turned right toward the harbor. On the south side of the palace, there were guards stationed at intervals along the walls. Some distance behind him two men were walking; one seemed to be involved in a long call on his mobile phone.

Peter came out onto Skeppsbron, the thoroughfare that bordered the east side of Gamla Stan on the waterfront. From experience, he knew that getting back to sleep now would be difficult and slowed his pace to enjoy the view across the water. It was an opportunity to appreciate Stockholm's nightscape. He crossed to the sidewalk on the harbor side and walked toward the Strombron Bridge. The police car that he had noticed earlier on the far side of the bridge had left. Traffic was light both on the bridge and beyond on Stromgatan. Alone on the bridge, he looked out across at the ferries in front of the Grand Hotel, tied up and waiting for their first early morning runs into the archipelago.

When he looked again toward the far end of the bridge away from the palace, he saw two men approaching. The streetlights glinted off their shaved heads and picked up reflections from bits of metal on their clothes. Skinheads. A ripple of apprehension put his senses on alert. The pair was about fifty yards away, walking side by side. They seemed slightly drunk. Peter made a quick, city-dweller decision to cross the roadway. As he crossed, he wondered if he would have done the same thing if the two men had just looked drunk, but not punk. Probably not, he decided.

As he reached the sidewalk on the other side, he saw the two shaved heads also cross the roadway. They reached the sidewalk about twenty yards in front of him. Peter decided they probably intended to give him a bump and perhaps an insult. He resigned himself to stepping into the roadway and skirting around them when they met. Otherwise, he would have to test his conditioning, shove his way past them, and run if they followed. He didn't doubt that he could outrun them. But their intrusion into his pleasant evening was annoying.

One of the skinheads was thin and slightly bowlegged; the other was heavyset. Peter judged they both were a couple inches shorter than he was. They separated slightly as they walked, effectively blocking the sidewalk. Their hands were loosely hooked in their black, studded belts. Bowlegs was on the railing side; Heavyset, on the roadway side.

Peter considered his moves. If it wasn't safe to step into the roadway when he reached them, then he could fake a rush toward Heavyset. Heavyset would probably plant himself to resist the hit. At the last moment, Peter would turn toward Bowlegs and shove him back toward the railing, duck between them, and get by with minimal contact. It seemed like a plan.

Just as the distance between Peter and the skinheads had narrowed to about ten yards, Peter heard running steps behind him. He turned back to see the two men who had been behind him in Gamla Stan running toward him on the bridge.

Good Swedish citizens, Peter thought. Seeing a potential confrontation with these thugs, they have come to help. He started to relax slightly. He looked for the skinheads to move to the side to let him and his newly acquired bodyguards past. But the skinheads continued to advance toward him, showing no reaction to the men who were coming up behind him. Were they drunk, or just really nasty?

Peter stopped for a moment to let the men behind him catch up, so they could confront the skinheads together. As he stopped, he noticed a car on the bridge. A black Mercedes was approaching from behind the skinheads and slowing. It was a limousine, an extra door's width longer than the standard four-door. Perhaps the driver had also guessed there was a problem developing and was stopping to lend a hand ...

Yeah, right! Suddenly, Peter realized this wasn't an unpleasant situation getting better but a bad situation getting seriously worse. Peter's adrenalin rushed to help. He had let the men behind him get too close, but he kept his eyes on the skinheads. He made a run at Heavyset with his head down slightly, right arm in straight-arm position. He hoped it would look impressive. But he remembered that the one time he had tried it in freshman football at college, a stronger, smarter defenseman had grabbed his arm and spun him down easily. Heavyset's face registered surprise, but he set himself for the impact. Heavyset ignored the Mercedes, which had pulled up by his side, and kept his eyes on Peter.

A yard away from Heavyset, Peter swerved toward Bowlegs, his left elbow connected with Bowlegs's chest and produced a painful hollow noise. Bowlegs backed into the bridge railing and collapsed. But before Peter could squeeze past Heavyset, he felt large hands gripping his arms from behind. There was the smell of a leather coat. Its owner was pulling him toward the black Mercedes. Heavyset grinned and opened the rear door of the car. Leathercoat grabbed the top of the door with his right hand, still holding Peter with his left.

Then a second set of hands, belonging to someone who was wheezing noisily, grabbed Peter by the neck and shoulder. Wheezer joined his companion in trying to propel Peter toward the car. Peter put his hand on the door and tried to push it closed. Leathercoat's right hand held the top of the door to keep it open. He yelled something in Swedish to Wheezer. Wheezer twisted Peter away from the door and tried to angle him into the car. The twisting momentarily put all Peter's weight on his left foot. He kicked back hard with his right foot connecting with Wheezer's shin. Wheezer grunted in pain and let go of Peter's neck.

Peter surged toward the car and put all his weight against the door with his free hand. The door shut and latched. Leathercoat screamed in pain, the top half of his right hand trapped in the door. His grip on Peter weakened.

Heavyset looked confused. Leathercoat screamed at him. Heavyset reached for the door handle and pulled but could not open it. Wheezer released Peter and reached past him for the door handle. Both he and Heavyset pulled at it uselessly. Wheezer leaned down and shouted at the driver.

With his assailants distracted, Peter yanked himself away from Leathercoat's grasp. He stumbled over Bowlegs who was down on his knees by the railing. He turned to run back toward the palace but he saw the driver of the Mercedes coming around the front of the car towards him. Peter turned away from the palace, but Heavyset had stationed himself at the back end of the Mercedes. He was in the middle of the sidewalk with what looked like a hunting knife in his hand. Wheezer gave up trying to free Leathercoat for the moment and turned back to face Peter. Peter felt behind him for the railing on the side of the bridge. Without thinking further, he turned and vaulted over the railing toward the dark water of the Norrstrom channel below.

Chapter 18

THE DROP INTO THE Norrstrom channel took longer than Peter had imagined. There was time for the awful thought of a hard, crippling landing on the edge of a boat or a piling to flash through his mind. But he hit the water cleanly, back first. He came up quickly, with a nose and mouth full of the Norrstrom.

He kicked hard, treading water, and moved his arms, fighting the increasing weight of his wet clothes. There was a long, urgent whistle from somewhere behind and above him. When he looked up, he couldn't see the bridge. He felt completely disoriented. He stayed afloat but realized that a strong current was moving him backwards. His head hit something hard, and he saw flashes of light, then it was suddenly dark. Above him, he heard voices and screaming. A car door slammed, and there was a screech of tires on pavement and more screaming. The noises seemed to fade as he was pulled along, unsure of where he was and pumping his arms and treading water with his legs to keep from going under.

Suddenly, it became lighter, and he realized that he had been under the bridge and was looking back at it. He was drifting out into the harbor. The palace was on his left and the quay where the ferries docked was on his right. For the first time since being in the water, he realized how cold it was. He began trying to swim toward the ferry docks. He was a strong swimmer, but the current and his clothes made his progress slow.

He could see several people on the quay and yelled for help. It was lucky, Peter remembered ironically, that the word for *help* was the same in English and Swedish. The figures on the quay seemed to be able to hear him, but he wasn't sure they could see him in the dark waters. Then people on the quay began yelling and pointing. Peter looked back toward the bridge and saw that someone had thrown a life preserver ring into the water, but it landed too far away to reach.

After what seemed like a long time and not getting much closer to the ferry docks, Peter saw a beam of light flashing across the water. In a moment, it came to rest on him, casting a long shadow of his head toward the shore. He heard the sound of a motorboat behind him. He turned and raised his arms to make sure he could be seen. He opened his mouth and started to call out. Instead, he caught a small wave in the face. A moment later, the boat was beside him and he was being hauled aboard. Two friendly sets of hands pulled him up as he coughed and choked on another mouthful of Baltic water.

One of the blue-vested harbor policemen who had pulled Peter into the small police boat bundled him in a large wool blanket. The boat turned and headed for the ferry quay. One policeman dabbed at a spot on Peter's head, which felt tender and stung. The other asked Peter's name and where he lived. Peter was shivering hard enough to make talking difficult. He started to explain that he was an American visiting Sweden.

"Yah, okay. You tell me on the way to the hospital," he said, as he and the other policeman helped Peter off the boat. When he stepped onto the dock, he was greeted by several camera flashes.

The small group of onlookers who had gathered stood respectfully back from the boat. They moved to make way for a paramedic crew that materialized from the roadway with a stretcher. Peter waved the stretcher away and walked with the support of one of the policeman to the brightly lit emergency vehicle. He was barefoot; his boat mocs had come off in the water. The policeman and one of the paramedics rode with him in the back.

Peter sat up but was still shaking from the cold as the paramedic tried to take his blood pressure. The paramedic shined a light in each of Peter's eyes and made a note of the result. He asked Peter to blow into a device with a white plastic tube. As

Peter took the tube in his mouth, he felt a wave of nausea and tried to suppress the urge to vomit. He did not succeed and blew the device out of the paramedic's hand. The paramedic sighed and proceeded to mop himself and the floor of the vehicle up.

"Your name, please?" the policeman began again.

"Peter Frost. I am an American. I'm staying at the Wallin Hotel. I was—"

"Okay, a little slower please," asked the policeman whose nameplate read Lieutenant Bengt Olson. His tone was friendly but serious.

Peter repeated the information more slowly. He added that his passport was in his hotel room for confirmation. His shaking had lessened, but he still spoke through chattering teeth.

"Please, how did you fall into the water, Mr. Frost?"

Peter answered without thinking. "I didn't fall. I jumped." Then he realized that would sound like a suicide attempt. "I mean I jumped to get away from some ..." He hesitated, unsure how to characterize the group of men who had attacked him on the bridge. He knew there was no way he could easily and convincingly explain the possible neo-Nazi connection. Like the possibility of suicide, that explanation might land him in a mental hospital for several days. "They were some muggers," he decided.

Lieutenant Olson wrote on a small handheld computer. "And can you tell me what these ... ah 'muggers' looked like?"

"Yes," Peter started. "No, not very well. There were ... several."

Lieutenant Olson's head came up from his computer. "Ah yah, more than two?"

Peter heard the polite skepticism in the policeman's response. Remembering he was a journalist, he decided to ask Lieutenant Olson if he could just report what happened after his stop at the Jazz Café. The policeman put away his handheld computer and produced a small recording device, which he held between them.

"Okay," he said. "Please tell me your what happened."

Peter described his evening in Gamla Stan and what had happened on the bridge, leaving out his stop at the Röda Fisket restaurant. He explained that he had jumped off the bridge to get away from his attackers, which was why he had to be fished out of the Norrstrom channel by Olson and his partner. They were interrupted several times during Peter's narrative, first by the arrival of the emergency vehicle at the hospital, then by Peter's examination in the emergency room, then by the x-rays of his head, and finally by his transport on a gurney to a very small but private room. Olson asked questions occasionally but mostly listened, recording Peter's account.

Olson finally completed his interview. "Okay, good. Thank you, Mr. Frost. While you were having x-rays, I reported some preliminary information to my superior. I understand you will have another visitor in a little while."

"More questions?" Peter asked.

"Probably, but don't worry. Now you should rest a bit. I will be outside."

Peter lay back in the hospital bed finally warm. He kept going over what had happened in the last couple of hours. Were his assailants neo-Nazis? Hard to imagine anything else, he thought, especially considering Claes's warning. But how had they found him? Had they followed him from the Röda Fisket restaurant? Probably. Had Anders been wrong to think that the organization was not completely on to him, or had he set Peter up? And even if Anders had not betrayed him intentionally, would he still be able to get the information that Anders had offered him? Eventually, he closed his eyes with the events still churning through his mind.

He realized he had been sleeping when he heard a familiar voice call his name. He was surprised to see Claes at the foot of his bed. Looking out the window, Peter saw the sun was up. "Did I miss our eleven o'clock meeting?"

Claes looked amused. "No, Peter, we have some hours yet. It is about four o'clock in the morning."

Peter looked out the window again and remembered that the sun rose at about three o'clock at this time of the year in Stockholm.

Claes explained that he was on call as the senior duty officer after midnight. He had called in about two o'clock to see if anything needed his attention, although he had not been paged.

He was told that there had been a little excitement at the Strombron Bridge, involving some sort of fight. An American had ended up the water and been rescued. Claes had asked if they had a name for the American, and he was told it was "Peter Frost."

"Naturally," Claes said smiling, "it was a difficult decision whether to stay in bed or come in to see if you were all right."

Peter smiled weakly. "Thanks, Claes. Hey, sorry to get you out of bed. I think I'm fine, but they told me they wanted to keep me overnight," he said, pointing to the side of his head.

"I have the statement you made to Lieutenant Olson. But I would like to hear all the details from you; perhaps you may remember some additional facts when we talk. Let us meet this afternoon at 1400 hours. The doctor says you may leave after they do a final checkup."

Peter was grateful that Claes had not pushed him for details. He needed some time to think through how much to tell Claes. He fell back asleep as soon as Claes left.

He was awakened at seven by the same doctor that he had seen the night before. He was a short, plump man with thinning reddish hair. He looked to be about Peter's age. From his accent, Peter assumed he was English. He introduced himself as Dr. Roberts.

"Nasty bruise on the side of your head. Thought you might have a concussion when they brought you in last night. Vomiting on the medic's breathalyzer in the emergency vehicle and all."

"Breathalyzer?" said Peter.

"Oh yes, quite standard here. Very strict about being tipsy. Anybody falls in the drink, they get checked out. Hefty fines."

"But I wasn't drunk," Peter insisted.

"Well, we'll never know. The Breathalyzer test was useless. When your friend the inspector showed up, he said no need for a blood test."

"I think it was the water I swallowed."

"Yes, quite. That's what I put in the report, and slight hypothermia, no indication of alcohol, patient very damp." Dr.

Roberts went on to explain that after a quick exam, Peter could check out.

"Are you going to give me a tetanus shot?" Peter inquired.

"Whatever for? Oh. The bruise on your head hardly broke the skin. Water in the harbor is clean enough to drink, except for the salt, of course. Swedes are quite proud of that. Rather unusual for a big city anywhere in the world."

"Oh, right," said Peter remembering something he had read about pollution control in Sweden. "What about my clothes and wallet?" Peter asked. After his hot shower, he had been given a hospital gown to wear.

"Still wet, in a plastic bag with the nurse at the desk. We have a set of scrubs and slippers for you. Should be enough to get you back to your hotel. Just leave quickly and don't walk back through the emergency room or somebody may press you into service," Roberts said cheerfully.

Chapter 19

OUTSIDE THE HOSPITAL, PETER found a taxi waiting for him. As he got in, he noticed a Volvo *Polis* car pull out from the curb across the driveway. It followed them as they left the hospital.

In the taxi, Peter retrieved his watch and wallet from the plastic bag of soggy clothes at his feet. The glass on his watch was fogged, but it seemed to be working. It read eight fifteen. His wallet was wet but otherwise intact. At the hotel, his driver accepted two very limp and damp fifty krona notes to cover the fare. Seeing the look on his face, Peter gave him another damp fifty krona note. Tipping was rare in Sweden, but the driver took the bill without comment.

The police car pulled up behind the taxi at the hotel. An officer got out and followed Peter into the lobby. He introduced himself as Sergeant Gunnarsson and offered Peter a hand that felt as large as an outfielder's mitt. Gunnarsson was a half a head taller than Peter and broad-shouldered.

"Good morning, Mr. Frost. Inspector Vikstrom suggested I stay here and be available to you if you need to go anywhere before your meeting with him this afternoon." He was very polite, but Peter understood that this was probably an order, not an offer.

That morning, accompanied discreetly by Sergeant Gunnarsson, Peter arranged to have his clothes laundered and bought a new wallet. He invited Gunnarsson to have lunch with him on the small terrace of the hotel restaurant. The sergeant reluctantly agreed to join but seemed to enjoy himself once he sat down. At one thirty, they left the hotel for Claes's office. Peter felt nearly recovered from the previous night's adventures.

The National Police Headquarters buildings occupied a large city block in the Kungsholm neighborhood where Peter had met Claes the previous afternoon. They entered the lobby and passed through security. Sergeant Gunnarsson was relieved by a very attractive, tall young woman. Her identity badge indicated she was a police *kadett*. And perfect for a role in a TV series about the Swedish police, Peter thought. She escorted Peter up to Claes's office on the seventh floor, acknowledging him with a smile but with a formality that seemed designed to discourage Peter's attempt at conversation. They made their way toward Claes's corner office and then waited briefly as Claes finished a telephone call.

"Thank you, Astrid. Peter, you look well enough. How is your head?"

"Fine, no headache, just a little tender on the side."

"Good, have a seat." Peter sat facing Claes in the small, neat office.

Behind the large blond wood desk, Claes swiveled in his chair and looked out over the small park across the street for a moment. "I think you had some luck," he said turning back to face Peter. "The men who attacked you last night were pretty bad characters. Not muggers, as you call them, but professionals, we believe."

Peter thought perhaps he was going to get a lecture from Claes about being more careful after his warning the night before. Claes went on, "Before I tell you what we know, I would like to hear your account of the attack last night."

Peter had considered how much to tell Claes about the connections that he saw between the attack and his earlier meeting with Anders. In order to protect Anders from possible prosecution, he had never discussed the details of his meetings or given any description of Anders to Claes. Claes said that he could accept this as long as Peter was willing to share the information from Anders with him before publishing it. But now the situation had changed. Anders appeared to be in trouble and might need police protection. And if Anders refused to talk without money, he might have to rely on Claes to supply the funds.

"There's more to last night's story than I told Lieutenant Olson."

"Of course. So you should tell me everything." Claes paused. "The attack at the bridge, it changes our agreement on your information sources." His voice had a hard edge that Peter had not heard before.

"I understand what you're saying, but you know I need to protect my source," Peter replied.

"Peter, the information you provided to us last year was useful. So I was able to defend our quiet agreement about your source with my superiors but now ..." Claes reached down beside his chair and retrieved a newspaper. "Do you recognize anyone?" he asked, handing it to Peter.

The photograph on the left side of the front page showed Peter wrapped in a blanket being helped off the police boat onto the dock in the glare of a photoflash. There was a caption and a short article. Peter could only understand two words as he glanced at it: *Amerikansk turist*. His negotiating position with Claes was rapidly diminishing.

"What does the article say?" Peter asked.

"It says that a young American visitor was trying to impress some friends by balancing on a bridge railing. When he fell in the water, his friends ran away." Peter looked puzzled. "I wrote that myself after I saw you at the hospital. We occasionally ask our journalist friends for a favor. But, of course, it costs us something. And I must tell you I have lost my bargaining power here for allowing our secrecy agreement."

Despite Peter's desire to retain his friendly relationship with Claes, he believed that he had both a professional and a humanitarian responsibility to Anders. "My informant is in danger already. Can you promise me that what I tell you will not put him at more risk?"

"No promises, Peter." Claes stood and supported himself on the desk, leaning forward toward Peter. "This is police business. The attack last night was serious. You do not run the Swedish Security Police, and neither do I."

Peter brought his head back to look directly up at Claes looming over his desk but said nothing. After several moments, Claes stood up and turned away. "I think we have the same interest to keep your informant in good health." He turned back to Peter. "I can give you my word for that."

Peter decided that was probably as good as he could get. "Okay," he said slowly. "I can accept that. Basically what I told Lieutenant Olson is correct. What I didn't tell him was that I had a meeting with my informant in Gamla Stan around seven. I think I was followed from there."

"Ah yah, so your informant has turned against you."

"Possibly. But I don't think so. He told me that he thought he might be under suspicion by the organization. He seemed genuinely scared, not like the times I met him last fall," Peter said.

"Perhaps he is a good actor."

"Maybe. Anyway, if the point was just to get me to the meeting so I could be followed, he didn't need to put on an act or even show up." Claes looked skeptical but said nothing, and Peter continued, "He asked for money, for new information on the funding sources. I told him *VERITAS?* didn't do that. And we don't. But I didn't want to lose him so I told him I would think about it. He says he needs the money to leave Sweden and get away from the organization. I think he's in trouble."

Claes was standing looking out the window. "Yes, I see. But before we discuss the next step, please describe for me everything that happened after we said good-bye yesterday afternoon." Claes placed a small recorder on the desk between them.

Peter related his return to the hotel, the note from Anders, and their meeting at the restaurant. He described the rest of his evening before the events on the bridge.

"So you noticed nothing to alert your concerns before you reached the bridge?"

"I was aware of the two men behind me sometime after I left the Jazz Café. But they didn't seem threatening until they grabbed me," he admitted.

Peter explained how the confrontation on the bridge had developed, his struggle with Leathercoat and Wheezer, and finally his leap off the bridge.

"Yah, so. It appears now that your jump was a good decision. But you are a very trusting fellow. First, you trust Mr. Anders that his meeting place is secret, then you trust the men behind you to help you, and then you trust the Norrstrom to save you." Claes smiled for the first time that afternoon. "It was a very risky decision to jump into the water."

"I didn't think it was all that risky when I did it. The bridge was higher than I thought, but better than getting into the black Mercedes with those guys."

"Yes, definitely." Claes nodded thoughtfully. "Did you recognize any of the men from your last trip here, anyone you might have had an interview with?"

"No. I did get a good look at the skinheads, but I only had a quick impression of the other men. But nobody looked familiar. After I jumped in, I ended up facing away from the bridge in the water. I guess I heard what might have been the black Mercedes tearing away and someone screaming."

"Yah, we think we know about that now."

"Did you catch any of them?" Peter asked.

"Maybe yes, maybe no."

Peter looked puzzled.

"I will explain in a bit. I think we can agree that these men were probably related to your research into the neo-Nazis?" Peter nodded in response, and Claes continued, "They appear to have been trying to abduct you."

"I imagine they wanted to give me a good scare, rough me up, and dump me in the woods," Peter said, hoping that was all they did have in mind.

"Yes, that is possible." Claes did not sound convinced. "So, do you still believe that you will be able to meet this Anders person again?"

"That depends. Assuming Anders wasn't in on the mugging and assuming that the guys who were haven't decided to take Anders out, then they might try to use him again to get at me. That gives me another chance to meet with him."

Claes stood up and turned to look out the window. "That is a rather risky proposition for you, my friend."

"Well, I wouldn't meet him at the Röda Fisket, for sure. It would have to be in some public area during the day where they wouldn't be able to try anything."

Claes turned back to Peter. "You put me into a difficult position. Officially, I should ask you to leave Sweden while we look for your informant and your attackers and the group that employs them." He paused. "But unofficially, I know you are a journalist and perhaps this danger is part of your work. Also unofficially, you have been able to penetrate an organization in a way that is useful to us. I think the information that Anders has promised you would allow us to arrest some of their senior people. So I would like you to continue."

"Now that I know that they're looking for me, that gives me some advantage. I can be more cautious."

Claes puffed some air out between his lips. "Perhaps so, but these fellows are very serious, Peter, and I cannot authorize police protection for you."

"By the way, thanks for sending Sergeant Gunnarsson to the hospital, but I really think I'm okay." Claes looked skeptical, and Peter went on, "I'll try to make my meeting with Anders on Thursday at the Vasa Museum in the middle of the day. If he doesn't show up, we can assume he's been discovered, and I'll give you all the contact information I have. Meanwhile, I'll keep a low profile."

Peter stood to stretch his legs for a moment and faced Claes. "But I have another problem: the money that Anders says he needs. Can the Swedish police help with that? I'll be in touch with my editor, but I'm not hopeful."

Claes grimaced and made a grunting noise. "I have been thinking about that. I will talk to my bureau chief and see what we can do. But you will have to arrange your meeting at the *Vasamuseet* for next week."

"Next week?"

"Yes, I will need more than one day to arrange something … if I can do anything," Claes added. "And you can tell Mr.

Anders that we will provide protection for him if he gives you the information."

"Deal," Peter said.

Claes looked puzzled for a moment and then said, "Yah, okay. Shall we have a coffee then?"

They walked down the hall to a small kitchen area equipped with an automatic coffeemaker. It dispensed small cups in various combinations: milk, no milk, sugar, no sugar, caf, decaf, cappuccino. The coffee was remarkably good considering the automation, but probably not a threat to Starbucks. When they returned to Claes's office, Peter reminded Claes that he was going to tell him something about his attackers.

"I will tell you what we know. The whistle you heard when you were in the water was from a guard at the northeast corner of the palace. He had a good view of the bridge. When he noticed the Mercedes stop, he took out his binoculars. He saw something he thought was some criminal activity. His signal brought some additional guards out, but they were too far away to help. But the sound of the whistle did seem to panic your assailants. You were now out of reach, so they were very concerned to get away before the police arrived.

"The guard with the binoculars reported that the Mercedes drove away very fast into Gamla Stan. One of the skinheads appeared to be hurt, but the other one got him up. They walked together to the north end of the bridge. There, they separated. One disappeared in the direction of Central Station. The other man went toward the ferry docks. The guards lost sight of him in the midst of the people who were looking at you in the water."

"So the bastard was probably watching while they put me in the rescue truck," Peter said.

"Quite possibly. Anyway, the Mercedes limousine continued over the bridge and turned right at the palace. Then it headed west and then back north over the Vasabron Bridge, which leads away from the center of Stockholm. We recovered the car this morning in a shopping center parking lot. It had been stolen earlier in the evening yesterday."

"The guy in the leather coat, who got his hand caught in the door, what happened to him?"

"Oh, yes. The fellow did not do so well. The palace guard said he could not open the door. He held on to the door handle with his other hand and was dragged along when the Mercedes drove away. I think the scream you heard was from him. When the car was below the palace, it appears someone inside the car finally unlocked the door. Your leather-coated friend was released, but the car kept on going."

"So were you able to catch him?"

"Yah, we got him." Claes sighed. "But he's not doing well. The Mercedes was making probably about fifty kilometers per hour when he fell off. Your Mr. Leathercoat rolled along the roadway and was stopped by a very hard lamppost. I don't think we will get much information from him."

"Poor guy."

"Ah yah," Claes said with a soft intake of breath.

Claes and Peter talked for a few more minutes about Peter's attackers. Claes was pessimistic that without any good eyewitnesses they would be able to find the perpetrators. There was a possibility that some of the onlookers at the quay whose names had been taken by the police would be able to tell them something. He reminded Peter that he might need to be available to identify them.

"So you will be in the archipelago over Midsummer, with your father and Mr. Svensson. Yes?" Peter nodded.

"And what about your low profile? I could arrange for you to stay in another hotel under a different name until the weekend. Or perhaps you could go outside Stockholm for a few days," Claes said.

"Getting out of Stockholm sounds good to me," Peter replied. Perhaps he could use the next two days before the Midsummer weekend to do a little exploration of his Swedish roots on his own. "I might fly up to Sundsvall where Bjorn Svensson's company Gevarfabrik is located. Come back to Stockholm in time to take the ferry out to the archipelago on Friday."

"Yah, you should be safe in Sundsvall. But I suggest that we make sure you are not followed from the hotel." Peter protested that he thought he could lose any skinheads who might be watching his hotel, but Claes insisted. "I will have your clothes picked up at the hotel by a plainclothes officer and brought here. Then he can drive you in a van to the airport where he will bring you quietly into the terminal for the flight to Sundsvall." Claes rose and held out his hand to Peter. "Deal?"

Chapter 20

WITHIN AN HOUR, PETER was sitting in the back of an unmarked police van with his backpack on the way to Arlanda Airport. He was able to get a seat on the five o'clock SAS commuter jet to Sundsvall. He called Anders from the departure lounge to reschedule their meeting. When the answering machine picked up, he left a message and took the risk of leaving his cell phone number. Within ten minutes, Anders called back. Peter explained that he could not meet him again until Monday. "If we got together on Thursday, I wouldn't have anything to give you. If I can do it, it's going take a few days."

"But you agreed to meet on Thursday ... You are a bastard ... I have risked my life to give ... ahh." Anders made a guttural sound, followed by several words in Swedish that Peter did not understand, and hung up.

Peter thought he sounded more desperate than angry and wasn't surprised when Anders called back within a minute. "Okay, so you will have the money? On Monday?"

"I'll do my best, Anders. I'll be at the Vasa Ship Museum on Monday at ten o'clock. When I see you go in, I'll follow you upstairs to the balcony area overlooking the bow."

"Yah, yah. Okay," Anders muttered and hung up again. Peter wondered if he would show up.

The fifty-minute flight to Sundsvall tracked Sweden's east coast north from Stockholm. The airline magazine at his seat described the city as a robust commercial center of about a hundred thousand people and dated its existence to Viking times.

The flight arrived at six fifteen. When Peter tried to rent a car, he discovered that neither of the agencies at the airport had any cars available. One had cars at their location in the city. They said he could pick up one there now or the next morning. Peter decided to wait until morning and take a taxi to the Sodra Berget Hotel. Claes had arranged for him to be registered there under a different name. The hotel was located on a hill south of the city and, according to his guidebook, offered commanding views of the city, the harbor, and the sea. Despite these amenities, it was listed as a moderately priced hotel.

Sundsvall was in a narrow valley that ran from east to west and opened into the Baltic. As they approached the city, the taxi driver pointed out his hotel across the valley. They descended into Sundsvall and drove along the short waterfront. Soon, they were on a winding road up to the hotel. As advertised, Peter's room looked northeast across the harbor toward Sundsvall Bay and the island of Alnö.

Without a car and looking forward to finally spending a night in a real bed, Peter ate in the hotel dining room. Like his room, it offered panoramic views of the city. After dinner, he approached one of the hotel receptionists, a cute blonde with her hair cut short. She was neatly outfitted in the corporate uniform, a tailored gray-blue suit with a blouse and scarf. Peter asked her if she had heard of a Bjorn Svensson who owned a company in Sundsvall, wondering what a typical Sundsvall resident would know about him.

"Bjorn Svensson? Oh, yes," she responded. "He is a wealthy man. His family have owned Gevarfabrik AB for many years. The company was started by his great-grandfather."

"Does he live here in Sundsvall, with his family?" Peter asked.

"Yes, he owns a large house which overlooks the city. I believe if you look north and a little to the west from here, that you can see the top of his house." She took Peter back into the dining room and pointed out the red roof of what appeared to be a substantial house across the valley. Peter guessed it was three or four miles away.

"Sometimes, we can see a helicopter leave from his factory in the valley and fly up to the house. I suppose it picks him up and flies to Stockholm."

"Are there other Svenssons in Sundsvall?" Peter asked.

"Of course, but I do not think they are closely related. Mr. Svensson has one daughter who is grown-up. She lives in Stockholm."

So she'd be Dad's half-sister, he mused. It all takes some getting used to.

"Are you a journalist?" she asked, interrupting his thoughts.

Peter said yes without thinking. He hoped that his assumed name would keep him out of trouble.

"And are you writing about Gevarfabrik?" she asked.

That seemed like a reasonable explanation for his interest. "Yes, I'm thinking about writing a magazine article on important and wealthy Swedish industrialists." It occurred to him that that might actually be a worthwhile piece. Sweden's relatively few, very wealthy capitalists kept a low profile. It was a country where standing out from the crowd was considered bad manners.

The receptionist seemed happy to continue their conversation. "Gevarfabrik is a very important company in Sundsvall. They have many visitors from other countries who come and stay with us. Some of them are ... interesting."

"Interesting?" Peter said. "Like how?"

"Yes, well ..." She looked a little uncomfortable as though perhaps she had shared a little too much information. She lowered her voice slightly. "Some of them come with other people to protect them."

"You mean bodyguards?" Peter asked.

"Yes, that is it," she said quickly. She switched to a more formal tone, ending their discussion of Gevarfabrik. "How else can I help you this evening?"

Peter asked about getting a rental car. She told him that her colleague would be glad to call the agency and arrange it for him in the morning. When he returned to his room, he sent Gene a long e-mail explaining the need for providing his informant, Anders, with some cash. He also related his conversation with

Claes about whether the Swedish police could help out financially but urged Gene to bend *VERITAS?* rules for his informant. He asked Gene to wire it to a bank in Stockholm where he could convert it to *kronor* for his meeting on Monday and to call him if there was a problem. He was not optimistic about Gene's response, but he decided the best strategy was to sound like this particular case for breaking precedent was so overwhelming that, of course, Gene would agree.

* * *

Peter awoke at seven the next morning. Using a map provided by the hotel, he took a forty-five-minute run on a system of woodland trails that began next to the parking lot. They wound around the hill and looped down to the south and west. As he returned to the main entrance of the hotel, he noticed the sports center rental shop located on a lower level of the building. They offered kayaks and bicycles in the summer and cross-country skis in the winter.

Peter found the idea of renting a bicycle instead of a car appealing. He could probably see more of the city and get some exercise as well. He made arrangements to take a bike for two days. After breakfast, Peter took his day pack and picked up his bicycle. He coasted down the long hill to the city center. There, he found a bookstore and bought a detailed local map. The clerk at the bookstore had only recently moved to Sundsvall and was not very helpful in determining where Bjorn Svensson's house might be on the map. Peter found a café near the bookstore. He sat at a table outside and ordered coffee and a pastry. From the map, it appeared that the house would be on one of two roads leading up the north side of the valley west of the city. He decided to ride up to the house and have a look around.

A main road led west from the center of the city. He rode through an area of low-rise apartments and shops and then a section of single-family houses. After about a mile, he came to an industrial zone. There were mostly modern, single-story buildings for light industry. He recognized the name of a medical products company on one. After another mile, there was a large complex of buildings located behind a serious chain-link fence. At the entrance, a motorized gate and a guardhouse controlled access to the driveway into the plant. A small sign in front of the guardhouse read "Gevarfabrik AB."

Peter considered stopping and asking the guard if they had plant tours. But he knew from past experience that such activities had to be arranged in advance. Beyond the plant, the landscape gave way to fields and occasional herds of sheep. At the next main intersection, he turned north. After about a mile, the road began to climb out of the valley. Consulting the map, he found a road about a quarter of a mile ahead that looked as though it might lead him to the Svenssons' property. Woods alternated with small, cleared fields at first and then gave way to all woods.

He almost missed the driveway. There was a small sign close to the ground that said simply, "Svensson." After a short distance, the driveway became paved. It led up the hill for about a hundred yards and then leveled off. A little way ahead, there was a wooden gatehouse next to an open iron gate. Beyond it, the driveway curved up to the right. An elderly uniformed guard sat in front of the gatehouse. He was smoking a cigarette in the sun with his cap on his knees.

Peter pedaled up toward the gate trying to decide what he could say to get past the guard and have a look at the house. Perhaps that he was writing an article about large Swedish country houses? The guard stood up and put his cap on as Peter approached. He said something in Swedish, which Peter didn't understand. But from the intonation, he decided the guard had asked a question that required an affirmative response. Peter said, "Yah, hey." That seemed to satisfy the guard who waved him through with a nod and sat back down.

About a hundred yards beyond the gate, the woods gave way to a large expanse of lawn planted with bushes and trees. There were several stands of birch and some impressive rhododendrons. Closer to the house were a number of flowerbeds arranged in a semi-circular pattern. Several gardeners were at work. Two were clipping a hedge that surrounded the house; another was working in a flowerbed.

The house was Mediterranean style: yellow stucco with a red-tiled roof. It was large, but not by the standards set by CEOs in corporate America. To the left of the house, a terrace offered a view across the valley to the southwest. Peter got off his bike; he was glad to give his bottom and bicycle leg muscles a break.

The gardener working in the flowerbed on her knees was a woman. She turned and said something to Peter in Swedish. He walked his bike over to her, thinking about his mansions-in-Sweden cover. As he approached, she stood up. Athletic shorts and a light-colored blouse tied above her waist accentuated her attractive figure. Peter's eyes reluctantly moved up to her face but were not disappointed there either. She brushed some blond hair away, which had come out from under her blue kerchief. The gesture left a small smudge on her forehead. She spoke again, another question in Swedish that seemed to have some of the same words the guard had spoken.

"I'm sorry. I don't speak Swedish. I'm, ah, I guess I am looking for Mr. Svensson," Peter said.

"Oh, are you here to help with the gardening?" she replied in perfect, lightly accented English. She looked slightly puzzled as she pulled her bandana off and used it to wipe her hands.

"Ah, no. I'm not," he said, suddenly confused and losing confidence in spinning a line about researching Swedish houses. He realized he had been looking at her figure and face a little too intently and a little too long. She had large blue eyes, and her high cheekbones gave her a slightly exotic look.

"I ... I'm actually a relative of Mr. Svensson," he said, wondering what this very striking gardener would do with that information.

She looked surprised for a moment, and then her face broke into a wide smile, which made her eyes crinkle up. "Are you Peter?"

His surprise at being recognized only added to his confusion. He nodded and said something that he hoped sounded like "Yes."

"Well, I am your Aunt Anna. Half-aunt, anyway," she said stepping forward and taking his hand with a warm, firm grip.

Chapter 21

THE BEAUTIFUL YOUNG WOMAN standing in front of him did not fit Peter's image of Bjorn Svensson's daughter. Both his aunt-now-grandmother Elena and the receptionist at the Sodra Berget Hotel had mentioned a daughter. He had reasonably assumed that Bjorn's daughter would be roughly his father's age, maybe a little younger but not, what ... thirty-something?

"You're not very old," Peter said, realizing immediately how stupid that sounded and compounding his loss of composure.

Anna looked at him quizzically and then smiled. "Not so very old. My mother was much younger than my father," she added in explanation.

"I see, yeah ... okay." Peter realized he was blushing, something that happened to him only rarely. He moved back slightly, and his bicycle, which had been leaning up against his hip, began to slip down. He grabbed at the handlebars to keep it upright. "Right," he said quickly. "I guess I thought ..."

"Oh, yes, of course," she said pleasantly. "My mother was my father's second wife." She hesitated. "I guess I mean his third wife, in a way." Now it was her turn to blush. She looked at Peter half smiling, her lips pressed together, and raised her eyebrows.

"This all this takes a little getting used to." He was relieved to find something reasonably intelligent to say.

"It does," she agreed. "I'm surprised to see you here in Sundsvall. We didn't expect you until this weekend on Smavik."

"It turns out I had some free time," he said hoping no additional explanation would be necessary. He said his father had

left a message that he would be off with Bjorn sailing. So he
thought he would see what his grandfather's hometown looked
like. "I didn't think anybody would be here. I hope you don't
mind that ..."

"No, of course not. You are very welcome here. I am
here from Stockholm for a few days of vacation. But you look
quite warm. Did you cycle all the way up to here from
downtown?"

"From the Sodra Berget Hotel actually."

"Would you like an iced tea or a cold beer, maybe a
Swedish light beer?" She touched his arm and started toward the
house without waiting for his answer.

Peter followed her along a flagstone path to the raised
terrace on the left side of the house. She slipped off her clogs and
opened French doors leading to a large sitting room. Sofas and
armchairs covered with a warm orange-and-yellow-striped fabric
surrounded a heavy teak coffee table. A large glass cabinet was
built into one wall. It held an impressive display of rifles and
shotguns. Some were ancient-looking; others, very modern. They
passed through a hallway and into a bright kitchen full of blue
and white tiles. The tiles matched those on a large antique
cylindrical stove, which sat in a corner of the room.

"Classy kitchen," Peter said, trying to sound more casual
than he felt.

"Yes. My mother found the stove in an old farmhouse
and had it rebuilt here. Then she designed the kitchen to go with
it."

"Is she a professional designer?"

"No. She just enjoyed projects like this." Anna paused.
"It was her last project. She was killed in an automobile accident
just after we moved in here," she said, opening the refrigerator.

"I'm sorry." The thought of the automobile accident that
had taken his fiancée away three years earlier was never far from
the edge of his consciousness. But the intrusion of Michelle's
memory at that moment was disconcerting. "That's very hard, I
know."

"It was a long time ago, but it was hard. I was thirteen. My mother and I were very close." Anna held up a glass pitcher of iced tea. Peter nodded in response.

Peter started to say something about Michelle but decided not to. "Yes, I was close to my mother too. If she had died when I was thirteen, I would've been very upset."

"So your mother is not living now?"

"No. She died of cancer two years ago."

"I'm sorry, Peter. It's such a terrible disease. When I see it in children, it's so cruel. We do what we can, but it is usually not enough. Did your mother suffer much?"

"I think so, but she said very little. She was being brave for my father and me, I guess. So are you a doctor?"

"Yes, I'm a pediatrician."

She poured the iced tea into two glasses and led Peter back through the sitting room to the terrace where they settled onto colorfully painted wooden furniture. Peter chose an armchair; Anna sat facing him, cross-legged on the end of a lounge chair.

He asked Anna about her work. She described her specialty in neonatology at a clinic at the Karolinska Institute in Stockholm. She also consulted at several hospitals around Stockholm. Occasionally, she went to other parts of Sweden to determine whether some special cases should be brought to the institute for treatment.

"That sounds like a big responsibility," Peter said.

Anna smiled and nodded. "I worry a lot about making the wrong decision. Speaking of medicine," she said with a slight laugh in her voice, "I hope you had that bruise on your head looked at. How did it happen?"

Peter instinctively reached up to touch it just as Anna's hand moved toward it brushing his as she pushed a bit of hair away to get a better look. Peter started to pull his head back and then changed his mind, turning slightly toward her and enjoying the touch of her fingertips. "Bar fight," he said, trying to look exaggeratedly serious.

"No, really." She laughed.

It was a moment when the truth seemed inappropriate. "I was walking—running really—in Stockholm and looking out over the harbor. It was stupid. I ran right into a street sign. Looks worse than it is."

"No headache?" Peter shook his head.

Anna seemed satisfied and sat back. "What about your work? I understand you are a writer."

"I'm a journalist. I work for a small publication called *VERITAS?*."

"Yah hah," she said with a sharp intake of breath, suddenly sounding very Swedish. "So you are the Peter Frost who wrote the article about neo-Nazis in Sweden last year?" She smiled, looking at him intently. "That created a bit of discussion here, you know. I remember talking to my friends about it. My father had even heard about it. He said he thought it was exaggerated. He says those young men with their Iron Crosses and swastika tattoos are just playacting Nazis."

Peter had hoped to keep his work separate from his father's pursuit of his Swedish roots and his meeting with the Swedish side of their family. When he tried to change the subject, Anna chided him about being modest.

"Anyway, I only learned last week that my father had been adopted and that he had a Swedish father. Did you know that he didn't find out he was adopted until he was about my age?"

"Really? That must have been something of a surprise for your father, at the time."

"I guess. But I haven't even had a chance to talk to him about it."

"You sound a little ..." Anna seemed to search briefly for the right word "... *disturbed* by that."

"No," he said. "... Well, maybe a little. So what about you? Did you know you had an American brother?"

Anna shook her head. "No, like you, I only found out recently, about a month ago. My father came down to Stockholm and told me about your grandmother and their child, your father."

Peter guessed that must have been about the time that his father had written to Bjorn asking to meet with him. "So you didn't know either. Family secrets all around, I guess."

"I always thought my father had just been married twice. His first marriage, I was told, was to a woman called Karen, during the Second World War after he came back from Germany and took over the family business. She and my father never had any children. They were divorced a long time ago. Later, he married my mother. She was much younger than he was. Like you, she was a writer. She met him when she was preparing an article about old family businesses in Sweden for *Dagensbladet*, the big daily newspaper in Stockholm."

"So she would've been about the same age as my parents," Peter said.

"Yes, probably." She paused. "I've often wondered why she married my father. They are … or were very different. My mother was … I think *spontaneous* is the right word. She worked hard at her writing, I remember, but she was always ready to go on a trip or an adventure with me. My father was always too busy with something to join us, and he still is."

"But he is off all this week sailing with my father," Peter remarked.

"Yes, but I think perhaps …" Anna left the thought unfinished. "Anyway, after my mother died, I went to live in England with my godmother who was a close friend of my mother's. I went to school there and visited my father on vacations. He was glad to see me, but I think he was not unhappy that he didn't have to take care of me. His work is his life; there's really not room for anything else."

They sat on the terrace, looking down the valley, having run out of things to say for a moment. The sun was warm, and Peter felt very comfortable with Anna. Blood is thicker than water, he thought. But he had a strange mixture of feelings. He found Anna very attractive in a way that wasn't appropriate for a close relative. Their family relationship was a disappointment but also something of a relief. It put her in the category of women to whom he didn't feel the need to present himself as a competing male in the universal game of sex.

Jill will love this one, he thought. Drawing on her years of psychotherapy, Jill would probably accuse him of once again making sure that someone he found attractive was also unavailable. "Approach avoidance," she would say, "you're at it again."

Anna broke the silence. "So you are an only child, too." Peter nodded. "Well, I think we should consider ourselves like a brother and sister. I always wanted to have a brother. Being your aunt just doesn't seem right."

"That would be great." Peter tried to sound enthusiastic.

Anna went on, "Anyway, you must stay here tonight; there is lots of room. I can't let my brother stay in a hotel. We will pick up your things after lunch." She reached over and touched his arm. "I am so glad you came up to Sundsvall."

Chapter 22

ANNA PREPARED A LIGHT lunch of bread and cheeses, some *gravad lax*, and Swedish light beer. After lunch, she changed out of her gardening clothes into a pair of Bermuda-length blue shorts, a white linen blouse, and sandals. With Peter's rental bicycle in the back of her Volvo station wagon, they retraced his route back to the Sodra Berget. Anna came into the hotel with Peter to admire the view and glimpse her father's house across the valley.

The cute blond receptionist who had pointed out the Svenssons' house to Peter the evening before was back on duty. She checked him out of his room while Anna stood behind Peter holding his backpack. He had the impression that the receptionist was amused at his arrival with Anna and his sudden change in plans. Did she wink conspiratorially at Anna when he reached down to get his wallet? If she only knew.

"Hey, thanks for your directions last night," Peter said feeling a little self-conscious.

"You are most welcome. We hope you'll come back and stay with us again sometime, Mr. Williams," the receptionist responded using the alias Claes had provided to the hotel. As Peter turned away from the counter, he saw a quizzical expression on Anna's face but she said nothing.

In the car, Anna suggested they might go for a swim at the house, "in our little lake." Peter readily agreed.

As they passed the Gevarfabrik plant, he told Anna he was curious about the family business. "Do you think I could get a tour?"

"I should think so. I have seen groups of schoolchildren sometimes. I am sure Rolf can arrange something for us."

"Who's Rolf?" Peter asked.

"Oh, he is my father's executive assistant. Let me call him and see if we can go over this afternoon. You men and guns. It must be genetic." She laughed.

Anna used her mobile phone to call Rolf. The conversation was in Swedish, but Peter was able to get a sense of what Anna was saying and to infer Rolf's responses. A number of words in Swedish were close to those in English like *come* and *here*, along with *yah* and *nay*. She seemed to be telling Rolf about Peter's unexpected arrival at the house and his interest in seeing Gevarfabrik with some enthusiasm. From her expression and the tone of her voice as the conversation progressed, Peter inferred there was some problem with Rolf's response. When she hung up, she let out a long breath.

She turned to Peter and seemed to make a conscious effort to brighten her expression. "Okay, so Rolf apologizes. He says he is very busy with some important customers today so this is not a good time to visit the plant. But he will have some time tomorrow morning." She paused. "He also apologizes that it will not be possible for him to have dinner with us. So it appears that we will be on our own tonight. Rolf has clients he needs to entertain this evening."

When Peter looked slightly puzzled, Anna explained, "Rolf and I are—how do you say in America—seeing each other. We had planned to go out this evening for dinner so I thought that it would be the three of us." A brief frown crossed her features and then she continued, "Anyway, sometimes Rolf forgets to let me know when things come up. He works very hard; my father is quite dependent on him," she added.

"Right. I guess I'll get to meet him tomorrow morning then." Peter tried to sound a little disappointed at the prospect of not having Rolf join them for dinner.

"Also," Anna went on as they drove back down into the valley toward the city, "unless we can persuade him to leave early tomorrow, you and I will be traveling together to Smavik. Rolf and I had planned to fly down in his plane, but now he says he has some affairs that need his attention and cannot leave until Saturday morning. So I told him I would try to get a reservation on a commercial flight tomorrow."

"So you and Rolf are an item, Sis?"

"An 'itemsis'? What is that?" Anna asked.

"Oh, sorry. An 'item' means you and Rolf are going out together. 'Sis' is just short for 'sister.'"

"I see. Yes, we are an item, I guess."

On the way back to the house, Peter asked Anna if she knew the story of his father's adoption. She replied she knew very little about Eric's life, only the brief account her father had given her earlier in the spring. Bjorn had called her in Stockholm to say he was coming down to take her out to dinner to discuss some "family business." She realized it was something important. It was only the second time in four years that he had come to see her in Stockholm. He had sounded a little agitated. She thought that perhaps her father had learned he was terminally ill and wanted to discuss his will. She had been very surprised to learn what the "family business" was.

"My father explained that he had been contacted by someone in the United States who claimed to be his son. I asked him if he was, and he said, 'Yes, probably.' He told me that before the Second World War he had met and had a relationship with a young American woman in Germany where he was studying. She had left to return to the United States. He said he had never heard from her again."

"Really?" Peter started to say more but decided to just listen.

"When I asked him if they had been married, he said they had intended to be, but he had returned to Sweden to take over Gevarfabrik when my grandfather Erik died suddenly and the American woman ..."

"My aunt, I mean my grandmother Elena."

"Yes, Elena. She had gone back to the United States. When I asked my father why he never tried to find your grandmother after the war, he became a bit annoyed and defensive. He said it was all old history, and he was just concerned now that his son might try to claim some inheritance.

This, he said, would threaten my well-being and what he assumed would be the succession of Gevarfabrik to me and Rolf, assuming, of course, that we will marry."

"So I guess you're pretty serious about Rolf," Peter said, suddenly more curious about the present than the past.

"Yes ... I suppose so. We met two years ago when I was visiting my father here in Sundsvall." She smiled and gave a short laugh. "I think my father was playing matchmaker. We haven't spent a lot of time together. But I come up from Stockholm on weekends ... when I can," she added.

"I see," Peter said. "So what does Rolf do at Gevarfabrik?"

"He is really the managing director although my father still officially holds that title. He has been working for my father for several years. My father is very impressed with his business sense and his efforts to develop new products. He thinks Rolf could probably run the company very well."

"And what do you think?"

"Are you looking out for your little sister already?" She laughed and turned to look at Peter. "I think Rolf is very intelligent and would manage Gevarfabrik quite successfully. In fact, I think he really does now."

They came to the intersection of a main road, and Anna stopped talking and watched the traffic for an opening to pull out. They turned onto the main road and drove west toward the Svensson house. "Anyway, like me, he is very busy with his work and has very little time for a social life. So we are a good match, I guess."

"Sounds like it," Peter replied.

"He can be very charming and is very clever. You know, when we met for the first time, he had read several of my papers on neonatal conditions and could discuss them with me with quite good understanding for someone who was not a doctor." She paused. "I met him just after a rather long relationship, which I had been in, had ended.

"But I was telling you about my father's visit with me in Stockholm. He said that when he heard from Eric this spring, it was the first he knew that his relationship with the American ...

with your grandmother, Elena … that she had a child, which was his."

Peter forced a professionally neutral expression and made no comment. He wondered when he might tell her what he thought was more likely the truth.

"I suggested that there might be some doubt especially if she had left before they knew she was pregnant. I suggested a DNA test. He said that was probably not necessary; the date of Eric's birth seemed to confirm that he was the father. I was surprised, but I thought that maybe the idea that he had a son was perhaps appealing to him, in spite of his concern."

"Yes. I guess that kind of makes sense," Peter responded, glad to be able to give his grandfather and Anna's father some bit of credit for humanity.

"He told me that Eric wanted to meet him. I asked if Eric had made any demands, and he said no, not yet. He said that your father was going to come to Sweden around Midsummer, and he would probably offer him some sort of settlement then."

"I don't believe Dad had anything like that in mind. I'm sure he's just curious about who his biological father was, or is," he said. But would that explain why Dad had sent Jed the information on his birth parents and adoption? Peter wondered. Maybe he didn't know his father as well as he thought he did.

"Yes, when I met him here last weekend, that was what he said to me, and I am sure that is true." She smiled. "He seemed very kind and honest, a good half-brother, although he felt more like an uncle." She laughed.

Anna's casual reference to his father was reassuring, a lot more than the short, cryptic messages he had received over the last week. It also reminded him that Bill Reilly was anxious to ask him about Jed. "So Dad was here?"

"Yes. Just for a few days before they left to sail on my father's boat down to Smavik," she said.

"Is it possible to call him on the boat?" It would be good to confirm that his father had been able to talk to Bill directly. Peter explained to Anna about Jed's disappearance and the possibility that his father might know something about Jed's plans or state of mind that would be helpful.

"That is very distressing about your uncle Jed. Your father mentioned that he had received a call from your police friend. He said that he had called him back and left a message. And yes, we can call the boat. But at this time of year, the ship-to-shore channels get very busy; e-mail is generally more reliable."

When they reached the Svenssons' house, Anna parked in front of the three-bay garage, which extended from the right side of the house. Peter shouldered his backpack and followed Anna to the front entrance. The heavy front door lock used an electronic keypad. Behind the door was an entrance hall leading to a large foyer paneled in dark wood. A wide staircase at the back angled up to a mezzanine on the second floor. A multitiered chandelier hung down from the timbered cathedral ceiling. On the right, a wide doorway opened into a large formal sitting room. Another doorway led to what looked like a library lined with floor-to-ceiling bookshelves.

Anna seemed to anticipate Peter's question. "My father lives here by himself. He just rattles around in this big house with a cook and a housekeeper and his driver, Lars."

"Sounds lonely."

"Yes, and it seems the older he gets, the less he sees of friends. He spends almost all of his time at work. In the summer, he goes out on his boat with Lars, who is also his bodyguard."

"Bodyguard?" Peter asked.

"That is a recent development. He explained to me that with all the terrorists in the world and possibly even in Sweden these days and being a weapons manufacturer, Rolf thought it would be wise."

Peter remembered Claes's admonition about even government ministers not being safe, but he didn't want to confirm Bjorn's fears to his daughter. "Well, maybe Lars is also a good companion," Peter offered.

Anna said nothing but made a face that indicated considerable skepticism.

At the top of the stairs, Anna showed Peter his room on the front side of the house looking out over the city. "There are towels in the bathhouse, so come along when you are ready. I will see you downstairs," she said from the hall.

"Okay. Hey, do you think I could borrow some swim trunks of your father's? I didn't bring any with me."

Anna looked amused. "Peter, this is Sweden, and our little lake is very private. You won't need a bathing suit."

"Ah ... sure," he said.

In a few minutes, Peter met Anna on the terrace. She told him that she had been able to get a seat on the same flight as Peter's the next afternoon.

From the terrace, they followed a mowed grassy path through some woods. After about hundred yards, the path opened out onto what Peter thought would be called a farm pond in New England. An earthen dam held the water in on the left side where the natural contour of the land sloped down toward the valley. The woods had been cleared back from the pond making the setting open and sunny. The bathhouse was a typical Swedish cabin with batten siding painted a bright brick red. There was a small deck in front with chairs overlooking the pond.

Anna disappeared into the cabin and emerged barefoot wearing a short, light blue terrycloth robe. She handed Peter a large yellow towel. "See you in the water." He thought he saw some impishness in her smile.

He wasn't exactly sure what the protocol for skinny-dipping with his Swedish half-aunt should be. He watched her walk to the edge of the pond and out onto a diving board that had been constructed at the near edge of the pond. She sat cross-legged facing away from him. She shrugged off her robe and tilted her head up toward the sun. Peter wondered if she was waiting politely for him before going in.

Peter went into the cabin. There was a front room with a couch and a kitchen area. In the back were two smaller rooms, a bathroom and a room with bunk beds where Anna had left her clothes. He stripped down quickly and left his clothes in the bathroom. He wrapped the large yellow towel around his waist and walked out to join Anna. He approached the pond, trying to decide on the strategic moment to drop his towel and jump in.

Anna turned her head and looked over her shoulder. "All ready, Peter?"

"All set," he replied.

She stood up with the robe still around her waist. Peter looked down to loosen his towel and heard the diving board creak. When he looked up, he saw Anna's robe on the diving board and two perfect legs disappearing with a very small splash into the smooth surface of the pond.

Chapter 23

THE POND WATER WAS not as cold as Peter had expected. It felt refreshing on what had turned out to be a rather warm day. Anna swam laps across the pond, about fifty yards. Peter followed her lead. After about ten minutes, he tired of going back and forth and began exploring around the edge of the pond. Just to the right of the diving board, a large load of sand had apparently been brought in to create a sort of beach extending into the water. Even at a depth of five feet, Peter could easily see the bottom. Anna joined him in swimming around the pond, keeping a discrete few yards between them, much to Peter's relief.

"Great place to swim," Peter called out. "Water's super clear, not like a lot of the ponds where I come from."

"Yes, Sundsvall has a reputation for the good natural water. Maybe we should be in the business of bottling it. That seems to be very profitable these days. Unfortunately, so are guns," she added.

Peter didn't know quite how to respond. "So how long has Gevarfabrik been in business?"

"It was started by my great-great-grandfather about 1850, I think. Originally, they just made hunting rifles and shotguns. Swedes love to hunt, and it was a good small business. But during the Second World War, my father began making rifles for the military. Since then, the company has grown very rapidly."

They talked for a while, treading water. Peter kept his eyes on Anna's face but from time to time, his gaze would drop to the surface of the pond in front of Anna where the swell of her breasts would become briefly visible and then disappear again as the water lapped around her shoulders.

"It sounds like you have some misgivings about the weapons business. Does it bother you that …" Peter was uncertain of how to put it.

"Yes, I suppose it does bother me. We sometimes get children who come to Stockholm for treatment from wounds they suffered in wars like Iraq. Then I wish very much my family was involved in the water-bottling business."

Anna told Peter that she was going to get out of the water. She apologized that she had work to do that afternoon. She told him to swim as long as he wished and invited him to feel free to explore around the house and the grounds. She said she needed about two hours in her study before they went to dinner.

Peter agreed that he could keep himself busy with his own work for the rest of the afternoon. He swam off slowly to the far end of the pond. When he turned to come back, Anna was headed toward the cabin with her blue robe on.

Peter swam by himself for a while longer, floating on his back and enjoying a cloudless blue sky and the view down the valley. After Anna had dressed and left for the house, Peter decided to try out the diving board. He managed to get some good height from the diving board and executed a reasonably smooth dive. But he wasn't prepared for the unusual and slightly unnerving sensation of his uncovered private parts hitting the water.

After drying off in the sun, he dressed and found his way back to the house. The crew of gardeners that had been working there when he arrived had left for the day. The lawn around the house extended to a low retaining wall and beyond to the woods. He walked down some steps in the wall and away from the house. As he reached the tree line, he could see a tall chain-link fence, which apparently encircled the grounds including the pond. Goes with the territory when you're in the gun business, he thought.

Back in the kitchen, Peter found a light beer in the refrigerator and a container with some leftovers from their lunch. He sat at the table near the tile stove. He mulled over what Anna had told him about her father wanting to come to a "settlement" with his father. He thought he knew his father well enough to know that he would not even have considered the possibility of what ... a payoff? Was Bjorn worried about a paternity suit or was it just guilt? If anyone deserved something, it was his grandmother Elena. But he was certain she would have no interest in money from Bjorn Svensson either. Although they were certainly not rich like the Svenssons, no one in his family had been financially deprived.

But Peter knew that very wealthy people, like Bjorn Svensson, often feared bounty hunters or blackmailers, probably not without reason. Wealthy celebrities or successful businessman like Bjorn were fair game. It wouldn't matter whether a supposed heir was legitimately illegitimate or illegitimately illegitimate. Peter assumed that Bjorn Svensson was probably just following his lawyer's advice and acting to protect the assets of Gevarfabrik, which had increased so substantially in the sixty years that he had been in charge. But how had his father responded to Bjorn's proposing a settlement? Was that the reason that Bjorn had wanted the meeting in his father's house in Brewster? Was that why his father had sent his birth certificate and adoption papers to Jed? But why the transcripts? More questions.

Beyond the question of a settlement, maybe his father's decision to fly to Sweden with Bjorn and to sail with him were indications that their acquaintance was evolving into a warm, personal relationship. Perhaps what had begun as curiosity on his father's part and a cynical defensive strategy on Bjorn's had evolved into a happy reunion. His father would gain a close relative, a new father, after the loss of his adoptive parents and then his wife. For Bjorn, a son whom he had given up, for reasons good or bad, would be regained in his final years. Would Bjorn ask his father to become his male heir and change his name to Svensson? Peter sat up suddenly, realizing that his thoughts had drifted into fantasy. Maybe the *lätt öl*, that Swedish light ale, actually had a higher alcohol content than advertised. He shook off his reverie and headed upstairs to unpack his laptop and spend some time working on his drug decriminalization article.

At six o'clock, Anna stopped by his room and announced that they should begin to think about getting ready for dinner. Peter asked if he needed to dress up, explaining that he had a jacket and a tie, if necessary, but only his running shoes.

"That's no problem," Anna said. "But you don't mind if I put on a dress?" Peter assured her he didn't.

Before shutting down his computer, Peter sent his father a note via the e-mail address for Lars onboard Bjorn Svensson's sailboat. He found a slightly wrinkled but clean shirt for his dinner out with Anna.

They drove into Sundsvall and parked on a side street near the waterfront. When they arrived at the restaurant, the manager greeted Anna by name and directed them to a table by the windows overlooking a marina. The restaurant's decor was typical waterfront style: pieces of heavy nautical rope, pulleys, ships' wheels on the walls, and reproduction ships' lanterns for lighting. The restaurant was only about half full so their table was relatively private.

After they were seated and had ordered drinks, Anna reviewed the menu. "I never asked you if you wanted to eat Swedish food tonight. There is a very good Italian restaurant also on the water."

Peter was looking over the top of his menu at Anna. She was wearing a white dress with a low-cut, tight-fitting V-neck. It was made of some clinging, silky looking material, which revealed the contour of her breasts, apparently unencumbered by a bra.

"Peter, do you see something that appeals to you?" Anna asked, looking up.

"Ah ... yes ... it all looks pretty good. I really like Swedish food." Anna looked back down at her menu with a half smile on her face.

When they had decided on *Toast Skagen*, a salad with tiny shrimp on toast, as an appetizer, Peter asked Anna why she decided to become a pediatrician.

"Do you mean why I chose to become a doctor or as a doctor why I chose to become a children's doctor?"

"Both, I guess," Peter said, happy to be taking his more familiar and comfortable role as a journalist and making some recovery from his involuntary ogling.

Anna explained that her mother's father had been a doctor. "I was very fond of my grandfather and admired him. He was ... there is a long word in Swedish for it ... He was not a specialist."

"A general practitioner?"

"Yes, that is it. He treated everybody for everything, children and adults for emergencies and routine examinations."

"So why a pediatrician in critical care?"

"Well, again because of my grandfather. He told me once that many pediatricians are often not able to deal very well with really sick children. That is because children generally are so healthy. He thought it was an important specialty that needed more doctors. So I guess that is why."

Peter pictured Anna leaning over a very sick child gently speaking to the child while its parents stood by anxiously. "It must be difficult to deal with children who may die and sometimes do."

"Yes, but for those we can save, it is very rewarding. In any case, we are there for the children and their parents."

Their main courses arrived. Peter had chosen the halibut and smoked salmon; Anna, the venison with lingonberries. Conversation stopped while they sampled their choices. After a few minutes, Anna asked if she could have a taste of Peter's fish.

"Sure, if I can try a piece of the venison, probably brought to us courtesy of a Gevarfabrik hunting rifle," he said smiling.

Anna made a face at him, cut off a piece of the steak, and piled some of the lingonberry jam on for him. "Do you think I should x-ray it and make sure there are no pieces of lead in it before you taste it?" she said as she held her fork across the table for him. He completed the exchange carefully balancing his white fish and salmon for her and hoping that it would reach her mouth and not her lap.

They ate in silence for a bit, and then Anna took her wine glass and toasted Peter as Claes had done. "Welcome to Sweden and into your new Swedish family," she said touching Peter's glass lightly with hers. Peter returned the toast.

"So, Peter, I have told you about Rolf, so now you must tell me about the ladies ..." She looked impish again. "... in your life. I only know from your father that you are not married."

Peter grimaced inwardly. "Well, I'm not attached to anybody at the moment." He wondered why he hadn't seen this coming.

"Really, I would think in Boston, you would have a lot of women admirers or ..." She stopped and looked a little uncertain. "Or am I moving in the wrong direction?"

Peter thought he knew what she meant. "No, no, I'm definitely hetero. It's just ..." He always tried to avoid talking about Michelle in relation to the present status of his social life. But that evening, with Anna, he was surprised to find that he didn't mind. "Three years ago, my fiancée died in a car accident, and I'm ..."

"Oh, Peter, I'm so sorry," Anna said, reaching across the table and touching his arm. "I was being rather flip."

"That's okay. I need to deal with it. Jill says I'm avoiding reality."

"Jill, who is Jill?"

"Oh, she's a colleague at work; we talk a lot. But we're not ... you know ..."

"I see. But tell me about your fiancée. What was she like?"

Peter let out a long breath. "Ah, okay. She was ..." then he had to stop until the tightness in his throat began to go away. He told Anna how he and Michelle had met and began living together, their common interests in left-wing causes, sailing, and jazz. He then explained how she had died, killed by a drunken driver who ran a stop sign at an intersection on a country road. "And I feel a lot of guilt about that."

"Is that because you are here and she is not? Or something else?" Anna asked quietly looking directly at Peter.

"Something more, I guess," he said slowly. "Michelle and I had had a fight, not a major thing, but she was pretty mad. I don't blame her. I was being kind of dumb, so she left to spend the night at her parents', but then she decided to come back to our apartment late that night." Peter stopped, unable to go on for a moment. "That's when she was killed. If we hadn't fought, if I hadn't made her mad …" Peter's voice trailed off.

"I see," Anna said quietly. "I think emotionally, that it is very reasonable. You would be very callous not to feel that way … for a time."

Peter nodded. They were silent for a while. The waiter cleared their dishes and brought dessert menus.

"May I ask you a question, Peter?" Anna said reaching across the table again holding his arm lightly. "If you had been the one in the car and Michelle had been at the apartment, would you not have wanted her to find someone else?" Peter looked at Anna, but he said nothing. Anna went on, "I am sure Michelle loved you. What do you think she would want for you?"

Peter looked away for a time and then replied slowly, "Yes, you're right. She probably would want that."

Anna excused herself to go to the ladies' room, touching Peter's shoulder as she moved past him. Peter sat back down and turned to look out at the harbor in the soft Midsummer evening light.

When Anna returned, they decided to pass up dessert. Peter suggested that they walk around Sundsvall. As they left the restaurant, Anna moved to Peter's side and took his arm. He realized that it had been a while since he had felt that pleasant pressure.

They wandered around the city center. In a large open square, they stopped to listen to an energetic but distinctly amateurish disco-rock band, playing for a small but elaborately punk teenage crowd. Anna pointed out some of the famous stone buildings constructed after a devastating fire in the late 1800s that had destroyed the original wooden structures in the city.

On the way back to the car, they passed a hotel where the infectious notes of ABBA's "Waterloo" were coming through the lobby and out onto the street. Peter had never outgrown his enjoyment of the seventies' Swedish band of his preteen years, and he suffered the good-natured ribbing of his friends when they discovered his ABBA CDs. This, despite the presence in his collection of bands like the way cool Dresden Dolls.

Peter held Anna back, curious about the source of the music.

"Thursday night dance at the Sundsvall Stats Hotel," Anna explained.

"Really?"

"Yes, it's a custom at some hotels in Sweden, especially in small towns, to have a dance one night a week for anyone who wants to come, hotel guests, people from the town. Everybody dances with everybody."

"What do you think? Want to dance?" Peter asked, pulling her along into the hotel without waiting for an answer.

Chapter 24

PETER AND ANNA MADE their way through the lobby to the source of the music in the hotel dining room. It was a large room with a high ceiling and a suggestion of 1930s modern décor. Beyond the tables that occupied about half of the room were a good-sized dance floor and a small stage for the DJ.

The dance floor was reassuringly full with couples that ranged in age from mid-thirties to sixties. Women in dresses and men in ties but without their jackets danced with moderate enthusiasm. The group was a study in contrasts to the fifteen- to twenty-five-year-olds, who made up the spiked-hair and blue-jean-clad crowds in the square outside.

Anna left her small purse on a free table while Peter followed the lead of the other men and removed his jacket. They made their way to the dance floor just as ABBA's "Voulez-Vous" began. They danced without contact, coming together occasionally for a spin or a bump. Peter enjoyed dancing but considered his ability not much better than just socially acceptable. He watched Anna's fluid and seemingly effortless response to ABBA's disco melodies. She was caught up in the music and seemed unaware of Peter's attention to her graceful figure in motion.

Following "Dancing Queen," the DJ said something in Swedish, and everybody laughed. Peter started to ask Anna to translate, but a new record had already begun, switching to the slow beat of Frank Sinatra's "Night and Day." Peter asked Anna if she wanted something to drink.

"No, let's dance," she said, moving up to Peter. Peter put his right arm around her back and his left hand out to hold her right hand, in his best dancing school position. His left hand grabbed air as she put her right hand on his shoulder. Peter followed her lead and moved his hand to her shoulder. Anna looked past him, somewhere in her own thoughts.

They moved closer as they made easy turns on the floor. Then Peter felt Anna's head on his shoulder. It was a good feeling, but he stiffened just slightly in surprise.

Anna's head came up off his shoulder, and she turned her face toward him. Peter tried to read her expression, but in an instant, her mouth was on his. Her kiss was soft, and her mouth was slightly open but it lasted only a second or two. Her head returned to his shoulder, leaving Peter thrilled and confused. After a minute or so, he began to wonder if it had happened or if he had just imagined it. When the song ended, they stood for a moment still holding each other. The DJ said something, and other couples began to move off the floor. Anna smiled at Peter, giving him a little squeeze before releasing herself.

She turned to walk back to their table. "Perhaps we should have a drink," she said looking over her shoulder.

Peter left Anna seated at the table and went to the bar, glad for a chance to replay in his mind the brief moment on the dance floor without having to think what to say next.

"Perhaps two more dances and then we should go," Anna said when he returned with two glasses of beer. "I didn't completely finish my report."

Peter drank his beer without saying anything. He wondered why Anna seemed to have suddenly switched to a more serious mode.

"Did you take ballroom dancing lessons when you were growing up?" she asked, maintaining their conversation.

"A long time ago, when I was about twelve. Did it show?" Peter responded.

"Oh no. You are a very good dancer."

"Not really, but thanks. You're terrific. I liked watching you," he said.

She gave him a warm smile. Anna asked about his childhood in Boston, continuing their safely neutral conversation about being only children. Before they finished their beers, ABBA's "Does Your Mother Know" brought them back to the dance floor. After two more fast numbers, the DJ began to spin another Frank Sinatra record. Peter looked at Anna, but she had already begun to walk back to their table.

As they walked back to her car, Anna again held Peter's arm. "You are very different from Rolf, you know," she said laughing softly. "He always has the evening planned; he would never suggest doing something so … impulsive."

Peter drove back to the Svenssons' house. Anna had reclined her seat and lay back, her eyes closed. He thought about the moment with her on the dance floor and wondered, how could something that feels so good not be quite right?

At the house, Anna told Peter she was going to have some tea. "I need a little caffeine if I am going do some writing. Will you have some?"

Peter agreed. He was happy to keep the evening with Anna going. He wandered into the sitting room and examined the guns in the glass case he had seen before. His thoughts came back to Bjorn. He was still curious to know what Anna thought about her father's intentions and his motives with respect to his father. But tonight was not the time to talk about it and risk spoiling a day and evening that had been such an unexpected pleasure.

Anna brought in a tray with two mugs and some cookies. She put them on a low table in front of the couch and sat down. Peter took a mug and hesitated a moment before sitting down next to her on the couch. He noticed that she did not move away to make room for him but instead leaned back and turned toward him. She drank a little of her tea and then put the mug on the table. Peter took a sip of his but found it was too hot to drink. He put the mug down, and when he turned back, he saw that Anna was looking at him. He leaned toward her reaching his arm around her and drawing her to him. She seemed to melt into him, and their mouths connected for a longer and deeper kiss than before. Peter's other hand found the side of her face. It slipped down her neck and then under the fold of her dress. It found her breast, and she breathed in sharply as his hand moved over her nipple.

After a long moment, Anna reached for Peter's hand and gently drew it away putting it in his lap. She moved away slowly against the back of the couch. Her face was flushed, but her features were calm. Peter started to say something, but she put her finger against his lips. Anna looked at him and then leaned back so that her head was resting against his other hand.

After a time that seemed both too long and too short, Anna sat up and reached for her mug. "I imagine the tea has cooled off." Peter nodded, and they drank in silence.

Peter carried the tea tray back to the kitchen and followed Anna upstairs. At the top of the stairs, Anna reminded Peter of the date they had made for a run in the morning. "Seven o'clock, okay? We will run my little one-mile loop."

"Only a mile?" Peter asked.

"That's a Swedish mile." She laughed. "About six English miles. And hills," she added.

Anna gave Peter a kiss on the cheek. "Thank you for a … special evening, Peter." She turned away and walked back toward her room.

He watched her until she closed her door and then turned toward his own room. In bed, the thought of Anna's body against his as they danced and her mouth soft and open on his, his hand around her breast, stayed with him, even as other thoughts intruded. Would Michelle be happy for him or only forgive him? What was Anna thinking? What would Rolf think? For that matter, what was he thinking? Whatever. It felt awfully good. And still, there were unanswered questions about his father and Bjorn. It was eleven o'clock, but it still seemed too light outside to go to bed. He retrieved his sleep mask and slipped it on. It provided a calming darkness as he let the day's events and questions cycle though his mind.

Chapter 25

A SOFT, BUT DETERMINED knocking woke Peter. He pushed up his sleep mask and wondered for a moment where he was.

"Peter, are you awake?" Anna's voice came beyond the door.

Then he remembered. "No, come in and wake me up." There was silence. He wasn't really surprised, but part of him had hoped for some other response.

Anna called again through the door, "It's about a quarter till seven."

"Okay, I'll be right down," Peter said, launching himself out of bed and grabbing his shorts and a T-shirt.

They met in front of the house. Anna looked terrific, like an ad for the blue sports bra she was wearing with her white running shorts and light tan in the morning sun. Her blond hair was secured with a blue and yellow sweatband.

"Did you sleep well?" she asked kneeling down to retie her running shoes.

"Yes. You?" Peter said, looking down at her, hoping for a hint of the intimacy they had shared the night before in her voice or expression.

"Ready to go?" she asked looking up at him with a smile that did not seem to communicate anything in particular. She bounced to her feet, touching his arm lightly as she jogged past him down the driveway.

They began Anna's Swedish-mile loop at an easy pace, running past the guardhouse and on down the driveway. They started up a gentle grade on the main road. At first, the route was mostly uphill on roads and paths through fields and woods with occasional long views of Sundsvall and beyond. Eventually, their run turned into a gentle downhill jog as they completed the circuit. When they reached the Svenssons' driveway, they walked to cool off. The guard, who had assumed Peter's gardener status the day before, seemed to recognize him and looked surprised, but said nothing. He tipped his hat to Anna.

"Is there a guard here twenty-four hours a day?" Peter asked.

"Yes, I'm afraid so. It seems a bit more than necessary to me. Before, we just locked the gate at night. And when I was growing up, we had no gate at all."

"You said 'before.' Before what?"

"Oh, one night about a year ago, some neo-Nazi types— we think they were—came up the driveway and painted swastikas and white power slogans here on the guardhouse and pavement."

Neo-Nazis. Peter felt a sudden chill in his sweat-damp T-shirt. And wasn't this the place to get away from the skinheads?

"The police thought it was just some random vandalism, but my father was very upset."

After Peter had showered and dressed, he found Anna in the kitchen laying out the components of a Swedish breakfast: slices of sweet bread, rye crisp, several types of cheese, two types of herring, and three soft boiled eggs. An insulated carafe of rich, dark coffee and a pitcher of orange juice completed the buffet. They filled their plates and ate on the terrace in the sun. Peter wanted to say something about what had passed between them the night before, but could not think how to begin.

After breakfast, they gathered their things for the weekend on Smavik and left for Peter's promised tour of Gevarfabrik. He was still curious to visit the plant but felt uneasy about meeting Rolf. Anna seemed to have adopted an it-never-happened attitude about the previous evening. That seemed logical to Peter under the circumstances but still somehow disappointing.

When they drove up to the Gevarfabrik entrance, the guard recognized Anna's Volvo. He came out of the gatehouse and greeted her by name. He still went back inside and followed the protocol of calling in. After a few moments, he activated the motor-driven gate and waved them through. They drove a short distance to a parking area where a sign in several languages indicated it was reserved for visitors. The adjacent entrance to the plant was a low, modern addition to a much older, multistory brick building. Large, tinted plate-glass windows overlooked the parking lot.

An automated sliding door led into a reception area. Three uniformed attendants staffed a wide counter facing the door. Behind them, there was a sitting area with Swedish modern furniture, all glass, steel, and black leather. A set of stainless steel doors with small safety windows in the center of the back wall apparently led to the main building.

Peter and Anna signed in at the reception counter. They traded Peter's passport and Anna's identity card for clip-on visitors' badges. Just as they walked around the counter to the sitting area, the double stainless steel doors opened. A tall, dark-haired woman in a gray pantsuit entered. She crossed the room briskly and greeted Anna with familiarity but without warmth. Anna introduced her as Olga, Rolf's secretary. She shook hands with Peter and tried to smile but didn't succeed. Olga turned and directed them through the double doors, which opened as they approached.

Inside the doors was the high-ceilinged entrance hall of the older building. Directly in front of them was an elevator with open grillwork that had been built into the center of the original staircase. They took the elevator to the second floor and exited onto a mezzanine. From there, they could see the entire ground floor of the building, an area about the size of a large gymnasium, which was filled with low walled cubicles. Casually dressed men and women were busy at computers or on telephones. The few empty places seemed more than accounted for by workers walking in the aisles between the blocks of cubicles.

"Our accounting, marketing, and personnel resources are all located in this building on the ground floor. The executive offices are located on this level," Olga said in response to a question by Peter. The overlook was an impressive way to show off the healthy activity of the company to customers or bankers, but it reminded Peter of the ant farm in his fourth-grade classroom.

They followed Olga down a corridor along the front of the building that provided access to the offices. The dark wood doors and paneling looked original. The walls above the wainscoting were hung with 1930s vintage photographs of hunting expeditions. The big-game trophies of toothy lions and sad-eyed moose displayed in the photographs were presumably the result of the accuracy and power of the firearms from Gevarfabrik. Olga led them into her office about halfway down the corridor, which also seemed to serve as the waiting room for Rolf's office. She knocked on the connecting door to Rolf's office and then opened it, standing aside to let Anna and Peter enter.

Rolf's office, like the hall, had dark wood trim and paneling. As they entered, Rolf was sitting at a large desk facing them. The only source of light appeared to be the large window directly behind him, which looked out on the administrative floor below. Rolf's face was in shadow. He remained engaged by something on his desk and looked up only after Olga had retreated, shutting the inter-office door behind her.

"Rolf," Anna said moving across the room to his desk and switching on his desk lamp. "You keep it so dark in here all the time. This is my new ... what shall we say?" She looked at Peter with a smile but it was too dark to see if there was any special expression in her eyes. "... nephew, Peter."

With the desk light on, Peter could see Rolf's face. He had very light, thinning blond hair and Robert-Redford good looks.

"Yes, I keep it a bit dark in here. It's better for my night vision when I fly," Rolf said, taking a last look at something on his desk. "Yah, so Peter, we didn't expect you here in Sundsvall." And then after a moment, he looked up, smiling, and said, "But welcome to Gevarfabrik." He stood up and came around from behind his desk, exchanged a quick cheek-to-cheek kiss with Anna, and extended his hand to Peter. He was tall and thin. He wore a dark suit and an expensive-looking tie.

"It is a pleasure to meet Anna's new relation," he said smiling and nodding. His handshake was friendly firm, lingering for a moment as he looked at Peter.

Peter did his best to smile back and ignore the memories of the previous evening, which kept jumping up and down in the back of his mind. "I'm glad to have a chance to meet you … all, too," he said. "I didn't expect to be in Sundsvall either. But I had a couple of days before the weekend. Anyway, thanks for taking some time to show me the plant," Peter said.

"I must apologize. As Anna has probably told you, I am rather busy today and yesterday. We have clients from abroad, and then we close today for two weeks summer · holiday for everyone. That is why I could not join you for dinner last night. And so I'm afraid the plant tour will be a little short."

Peter glanced at Anna standing just behind Rolf. Her expression was a slight smile that was perhaps masking more complex thoughts. "No problem, Rolf. I appreciate your taking the time. We will be getting together this weekend, anyway."

"Yes, we will." He paused. "But let me give you a short history of Gevarfabrik before we set out. Please," Rolf said, indicating a group of chairs and a couch on either side of the coffee table across from the door to the office. Peter sat in one of chairs while Anna perched on the arm of the couch where Rolf sat. Momentarily, Olga appeared with coffee on a tray, which she served silently while Rolf began his narrative.

Rolf described the origins of Gevarfabrik. The original Gevarfabrik workshop, nearer to the center of Sundsvall had been established by the first Erik Svensson, Anna's great-great-grandfather in 1852. The original factory had twelve workers and employed very limited mass production techniques. The rifles and shotguns were assembled and hand-finished at the rate of two or three per day. The original workshop had burned down in the great fire that swept the center of Sundsvall in 1888. Erik Svensson had wisely taken out fire insurance and was able to rebuild a larger, newer plant on the present site away from the center of Sundsvall. In 1890, Erik's son Johann took over the running of the business. Gevarfabrik grew with exports to other European countries, particularly Germany, where the

Gevarfabrik shotgun was considered a prestigious item. Johann had built the building in which they were sitting. In 1909, Anna's grandfather, also named Erik Svensson, replaced his father Johann.

"The business was profitable, but a big opportunity to grow was missed, during the First World War and afterwards, by failing to begin manufacturing rifles for the military." Rolf paused and looked at Anna. "That was a mistake that Anna's father, Bjorn, did not make when he took over the business after Erik's death in 1939. Bjorn began immediately to develop a line of military weapons. He hired outside experts and exploited Gevarfabrik's strong reputation for quality."

Rolf was leaning forward over the coffee table, focusing his attention on Peter. His enthusiasm for the business and his admiration of Bjorn's role in its success seemed evident. Anna looked less and less enthusiastic as Rolf's narrative approached the present.

"So I guess now the hunting rifles and shotguns are a small part of the whole business?" Peter asked.

"Definitely. We are still known for high-quality sports arms. But the real revenues of Gevarfabrik come from our automatic weapons, assault rifles and handguns, and from some related armaments. We still emphasize quality over quantity, which means we sell smaller lots of very reliable weapons, intended for small tactical groups."

"Not including terrorists in the category of small tactical groups, I hope," Peter said lightly, assuming the answer would be affirmative.

Rolf stiffened and sat back slightly. "I cannot disclose our client base, but in the arms business, one does not ask too many questions."

Including visiting relatives, Peter thought.

Anna, who had been looking down at the carpet, put her coffee cup on the table and then stood up. Looking at Peter, she said, "Rolf, you have clients, and we have to catch a plane. Shall we begin the tour?"

Chapter 26

ROLF LOOKED SURPRISED AT Anna's sudden assertiveness but recovered quickly. "Of course, we will go now." He led them through a door from his office, through a small conference room, and into Bjorn Svensson's corner office. Like Rolf's, Bjorn's office also had a large inside window which looked out on the administrative staff on the ground floor. Windows on the two outside walls overlooked the Gevarfabrik complex.

Rolf pointed out the other major buildings of the plant. "On the left is the machining facility. We finish rough-forged components there which we buy from outside suppliers for many of our products." He went on to indicate the other buildings, all connected by covered walkways that housed the assembly, test, and research and development facilities.

"On the other side of the parking lot is the Jaktgevar Verks, or sportarms facility. There is a small company museum there as well," Anna volunteered, pointing out a small, older building.

A private staircase from Bjorn's office brought them to ground level and into the walkway to the finish machining facility. A hallway along the outer wall of the building with observation windows allowed visitors to look into the facility without actually stepping onto the production floor. Peter could see what looked like a large number of automated machine tools. The grinding, cutting, and drilling noise of the machines was muffled in the visitor's corridor. Workers in bright blue smocks were adjusting the controls of some of the machines and monitoring the output of those in operation. None of the machines was close enough to see any detail of the parts being made.

Rolf walked them quickly along the corridor, launching into what sounded like the tour lecture he had given often. He pointed out several large machines that, he said, were the latest and most expensive models in a line of computer-controlled tools from Japan. Despite the somewhat mechanical quality of the presentation, Rolf seemed to enjoy the opportunity to tout the capabilities of Gevarfabrik. He directed his presentation at Peter, virtually ignoring Anna who had undoubtedly been on the tour many times. She gave the impression of following Rolf's remarks, but Peter sensed that her thoughts were elsewhere.

The next building on the tour was the assembly facility. Again, as in the machining plant, a corridor along the outside wall provided a limited view of people and equipment. Peter could see some fully automated assembly systems. There were also workbenches where women in blue work smocks were assembling components by hand.

In the test facility, there were a number of machines whose purpose was not immediately apparent. Occasional thumps and a series of drumming noises indicated test firing somewhere in the building. Rolf explained that there were firing ranges located underground in one of several subbasements.

"Peter, I am sure you have toured other manufacturing plants, do you not find that we have a world-class facility here?" Rolf asked.

The question seemed odd to Peter like a request for affirmation from Rolf. "I'm not really up on manufacturing processes, but it seems impressive," he responded politely. As a journalist, he felt more comfortable asking questions, and his curiosity about Gevarfabrik was personal rather than professional.

"Perhaps, I assumed you had more experience in industrial matters. Anyway, you may be aware that some new lightweight materials have been developed as substitutes for metals in some applications?" Rolf seemed anxious to offer Peter something that he might be impressed by.

"Yes. Aren't there some research efforts to develop both new kinds of ceramics and plastic for internal combustion engines? And for guns, maybe?" Peter added.

"Correct. So you can appreciate that we have constructed prototypes of automatic handguns and rifles that are composed entirely of nonmetals," said Rolf, pleased that he had finally found something that Peter could appreciate.

"Really?" said Peter slowly. "And you expect to be selling these soon?"

"Oh yes, we have a number of very interested customers. Why ..." Rolf hesitated as though some new thought had intercepted his next utterance. "Anyway, we expect it to be a successful and profitable line."

"Yes, I guess it would be," Peter said neutrally, but now his professional instincts were aroused. Perhaps a piece on the development of hard-to-detect weapons and explosives would be of interest to *VERITAS?* readers. He looked ahead along the passageway at Anna, who seemed to have given up all pretense of interest in the tour and was walking several yards beyond them.

As they approached the doors to the walkway that led to the next building, Rolf touched Peter's elbow holding him back while Anna continued through. "Peter," Rolf said in a low voice and turned to face him. "You are probably aware that your father and Mr. Svensson have been discussing an arrangement with regard to your father's position as Mr. Svensson's ..." he hesitated, "natural son." Peter nodded, surprised that Rolf would raise this issue and not sure where he was going with it.

"Mr. Svensson is naturally anxious for Anna. He would like to ensure her interests in Gevarfabrik but, of course, your father must be recognized as well." Rolf glanced back to the doors that Anna had exited. "I wonder if I can ask you to help me—all of us really. I will try to persuade Mr. Svensson to offer your father a very fair settlement if you will talk to your father."

Peter was sure his surprise must have shown on his face. "I don't think ..." he began. As he had told Anna, he found it hard to imagine that his father would have any designs on Gevarfabrik and the Svensson family fortune. But was this something else about his father he didn't know? "Do you know what it is that my father is asking for?" It seemed very strange to be having such an intensely family-business conversation with someone he had just met minutes before.

Rolf put his hand on Peter's arm and moved slightly closer. "Your father wants …" Rolf stopped as he heard doors behind him open.

Anna appeared. "Rolf, are you trying to convince Peter to come help you run the family business?" she asked with a laugh in her voice.

Rolf turned to her. "Not yet, Anna," he said matching her light tone. Then he turned back to Peter and said quietly, "Will you talk to him about Mr. Svensson's intentions? And I will talk to Mr. Svensson," he added quickly. "I will see what I can do with him." Rolf caught Peter's eye and held it, smiling slightly.

As they joined Anna and proceeded with the tour, Peter wondered how much fun his father could be having sailing on a small boat with Bjorn Svensson for a week if they were in serious disagreement about this issue.

The research and development facility was next. It appeared to be mostly cubicles that Peter guessed were for programmers or computer-aided-design specialists. Rolf pointed out an area beyond the cubicles that he said was a prototype construction facility. However, nothing more than the shapes of various machines and workbenches could be seen from the observation corridor.

As if sensing his thought, Rolf said, "Now we are going to walk through the Jaktgevar assembly facility where you will see our high-quality arms assembly close up."

Instead of a glassed-in observation corridor, the Jaktgevar facility offered a painted yellow pathway, which led through the middle of the plant floor. Visitors were apparently expected to stay on the designated route, but there was nothing to prevent a side excursion for a closer look at the components and assembling of the completed rifles and shotguns. The assemblers and other workers in the facility looked up and smiled as they passed. Occasionally, one would greet Anna by name. Most nodded deferentially to Rolf.

The sports arms facility seemed very modest in comparison to the rest of the operations of Gevarfabrik. Peter guessed the production might be a few tens of rifles per day. When they reached the far end of the room, Anna pointed out a rack of finished shotguns. They were cleaned and polished, waiting to be packed in expensive-looking individual wooden cases. Her interest in the tour seemed revived by their entry into the recreational arms building. "This model is very much like the original Gevarfabrik shotgun designed by my great-great-grandfather," she explained.

She asked the foreman standing nearby if they could pick up one of the shotguns. He smiled and nodded his assent. She lifted the gun off the rack, weighing it in her hands but not raising it to her shoulder.

"Peter, see how light it feels," she said handing it to him. "But it's actually quite solid and comfortable to shoot, with very little kickback. It's all in the balance."

Peter hefted the gun carefully, politely agreeing with Anna since he had no experience with shotguns, well balanced or not.

Rolf stood by looking at Anna; his eyes narrowed slightly. Peter wondered about Anna's enthusiasm for the Jaktgevar facility considering her apathy, which seemed to border on disapproval, for the really profitable part of the business.

Peter replaced the shotgun in the rack and thanked the foreman. They passed through a door into the small museum, which Anna had mentioned earlier. This was obviously the end of the tour. The parking lot was visible through the windows at the end of the room. *What, no gift shop?* Peter thought about remarking but decided neither Anna nor Rolf would appreciate his humor.

The museum included display cases with rifles and shotguns from each of the historical periods since the founding of Gevarfabrik from the 1850s to the present era including the two world wars. The basic design of the sport rifles and shotguns seemed not to have changed greatly since the mid-1800s. Highly polished expensive-looking hardwoods were used for the rifle and shotgun stocks. There were no plastic or ceramic parts on display.

Enlarged photographs of Gevarfabrik, as it had evolved from a small workshop in central Sundsvall to the multi-building complex on the present site were mounted on the walls. Sepia-toned prints of workers at machine tools driven by overhead belts gave way to color prints of blue-coated technicians at computer terminals and numerically controlled milling machines. Gevarfabrik's owners, Peter and Anna's grandfathers of various degrees, were depicted in formal portraits. So this is my heritage, Peter thought, a lot of new information to absorb in a week.

A walkway led from the museum back to the administration building. When they reached the central hallway, Rolf said, "Okay, Peter, so I hope you have enjoyed our little tour of Gevarfabrik." He looked at Peter with a quick movement of one eyebrow that seemed to be a reference to his brief aside to Peter during the tour. "And I look forward to seeing you again this weekend. Please excuse me now to get back to my customers."

Peter thanked Rolf as they shook hands. Rolf turned and kissed Anna on the cheek. "I will fly down tomorrow morning and see you at lunch."

"Are you sure you can't get away this afternoon? Then we could all fly down together," Anna said, her hand on Rolf's arm. "Last chance before we leave."

"No. Impossible. I am sorry. We have major customers here today. I am concerned that I have left them this long. I will see you tomorrow." Rolf turned away and went up the stairs, easily taking them two at a time with his long legs.

Back to business, Peter thought. A clock mounted above the elevator door indicated they had spent just thirty minutes with Rolf in his office and on the tour. Peter looked at Anna; her expression was hard to read.

When they had left the plant gate behind, Anna turned to Peter. "Well, we have a little extra time; we can take the longer route to the airport along the coast."

"Sure. Well, Rolf seems pretty intense. What's his business background? Technical or marketing?"

"Marketing. He worked for a record company," Anna said.

"So from musical heavy metal to military heavy metal, sort of."

"Yes, I guess so." Anna seemed to be making an effort to be positive. Peter wondered if it was something about Rolf or Gevarfabrik that was bothering her. There were certainly things about Gevarfabrik that were bothering him. Rolf's answers to his questions seemed to indicate the likelihood that the company was selling highly effective weapons to terrorist groups. And these might include weapons made of non-metallic materials that could avoid easy detection at security checkpoints. He wasn't sure Anna fully appreciated or wanted to admit to herself that she was an heir to such an enterprise. What was the Frost family getting into?

"I can understand your mixed feelings about Gevarfabrik," Peter said cautiously. "Rifles and shotguns for hunting are one thing, but automatic weapons are another."

"Yes, I do have very mixed feelings. Perhaps once my father passes away, I will change the direction of Gevarfabrik, back to my grandfather's original business."

"That would be a big step," Peter said. "Would you sell the military weapons business or just dissolve it? What would Rolf say to that?"

"I don't know," Anna said. "And Rolf …?" She let out a long breath. "Life isn't simple, is it?"

"For sure," Peter replied.

"Even the *jaktgevär*, the hunting rifle business … you know, when you really think about it." She paused. "As a doctor, I try to save lives. Guns, whether they are military or hunting, are designed for one purpose: to kill living things."

Chapter 27

PETER AND ANNA ARRIVED at the airport in plenty of time for their flight to Stockholm. The small airport was busy with families traveling out of town for Midsummer. They ate lunch in a small cafeteria above the main floor of the attractive modern terminal. When their flight was called, they walked a short distance to the gate. It looked like a full flight, but they boarded easily and without delay.

As the plane pushed back from the gate, Peter turned to Anna. "I just realized there was no security check. We just walked on the plane, like when I was a little kid."

"Yes, I guess we are lucky here in Sweden. We haven't caught up with the rest of the world yet in that area," Anna replied.

Their taxi from Arlanda dropped Anna at the Karolinska Institute on the outskirts of Stockholm, where she had a meeting with a colleague. Peter continued into central Stockholm, so that he could get tickets for the ferry, which Anna expected would be full on this Friday.

The taxi let Peter off at the Stromkajen ferry docks. The ticket office was in the middle of the wide quay, between the roadway and the harbor. Peter stood in a short line and bought two round-trip tickets on the five o'clock ferry to Moja Island, as specified in the directions he had received earlier in the week. He also picked up a brochure with schedules and routes. At this time of year, there were six or seven ferries a day to multiple destinations in the central part of the archipelago. Theirs was the *Cinderella I*.

When Peter turned away from the ticket office on the quay, he saw the spot by Strombron Bridge where he had come off the police boat earlier in the week, wet and shivering. Today was definitely an improvement. The afternoon sun was warm, and he was looking forward to the weekend on Smavik. Across the street from the quay in Kungstradgarden Park, he found a table at a small outdoor café. Hoping the city of Stockholm had thought to provide wireless Internet in the park as an obvious social benefit, he took the laptop out of his backpack. While it was booting up, he realized that he had never followed up on his short e-mail to Bill Reilly. Jet lag, jumping off bridges, and meeting new and interesting family members were reasonable excuses, he thought. He dialed Bill's number at his office in Hyannis.

"Peter who?" Reilly said. "Nice of you to call."

Reilly was often sarcastic. Today, he also sounded really annoyed.

"Bill, listen, I've been kind of … busy."

"I guess. Have you caught up with your father yet?"

"No, but there was a message from him at the hotel when I arrived like I e-mailed you. I'm going to see him this weekend, later today, actually. He's been on a boat all week."

"Hey, this is the twenty-first century. Cell phones, e-mail, boats with radio telephones. You really haven't been able talk to him?"

"Bill, I'm sorry. I e-mailed him again yesterday on the boat."

Peter heard Reilly take a deep breath before he spoke. "Yeah, OK. I'm sorry. I just got off the phone with Maureen Darby, Jed's law partner. She's upset, got clients who are upset."

"Is there anything new on Jed?"

"No. He's still missing and so is his boat. And my guess is still suicide, but we haven't found a note. Could be on the boat or in the stomach of some haddock out there. But meantime, I like to keep my sources untainted, so just keep that to yourself until I have a chance to talk to your dad."

"Gotcha. By the way, did you try to get hold of Dad through Gevarfabrik, the company that owns the jet that he flew to Sweden in? Because that's Dad's father's company."

"I tried. Got some chief assistant to the assistant chief. It was a 'her.' Spoke perfect English. Told me that info about the company president and his family and friends was confidential. She didn't seem impressed with my position as an officer of the law in the U.S. of A.

"My next stop woulda been to go through channels which involve the State Department, the Swedish embassy, and writing up requests in triplicate, filling out forms, and so forth. You get the idea. Also, they'll want to know if your father is a suspect."

"A suspect of what?" Peter asked.

"Let's just say that if I tell them he's a suspect of something, the desk jockeys in DC will move their butts a little faster. I was hoping you could make it easier for me by finding him and getting him to call me."

"I'll do it," Peter responded. "He'll give you a call either tonight or tomorrow ... that is, depending on the phone situation. We're going to be on a private island this weekend."

"Nice. Well, work it out with your dad." Reilly sounded more relaxed; his summer squall of anger had passed. "By the way, the body you took a look at last week, the fishing boat charter captain, we're still trying to figure out how he ended up floating in the sound. His boat showed up at somebody else's mooring in Hyannis last Monday. Or at least that's when the somebody-elses came back. They tried to pick up their mooring and found a forty-five-foot flying-bridge charter boat tied up to it. And their zodiac inflatable was missing. The harbormaster called the Coast Guard and determined it was a fishing boat, the *BlueFinn* out of Harwich."

"Any theories? Any connection to Jed's disappearing?"

"Nothing we can come up with so far," Reilly replied.

"Timing?"

"There is that. Anyway, we're treating the boat as a crime scene. Forensics is still working on prints and a little bit of blood near the wheel. Captain Haake was something of a loner, not married, not many friends, but obviously at least one enemy."

"Drug deal gone bad?" Peter offered.

"Possibly, although alcohol was his psychoactive substance of choice. Been warned by the Coast Guard a couple of times for running his boat under the influence. Once he was coming back from a charter and was too smashed to make it from his dingy to the dock. Had to be fished out by some of his clients at the public dock in Harwich. But he never had anything more serious than that before. So, we're trying to figure out who might have been with him and when it all happened. Anyway, what's happening with you in the land of herring and aquavit?"

Peter wasn't sure he really wanted to talk to Bill about either of his two memorable events of the last few days. Reilly would want more details on his mugging in Stockholm than his cell phone battery could afford. His scrape in Stockholm could wait for an evening over a beer. That would make it easier to endure what was sure to be Reilly's critique of his personal defense tactics. He also had mixed feelings about telling him about Anna. Unlike Jill, Reilly had never asked directly about his social life, although Reilly dropped inquiring hints from time to time, probably at the suggestion of his wife. Peter knew they were prompted by friendly concern, so he decided to share the irony of his meeting Anna. "Well, I met an interesting woman," he said, knowing that would get a reaction from Reilly.

"Oh, yeah? You better give me the details for Joan."

"There's good news and bad news. The good news is she is a really likable, smart, and beautiful Swedish woman."

"And the bad news is, she's married," Reilly responded.

"Well, she is kind of attached, but it turns out that she's my aunt, at least half-aunt, Anna Svensson. She's my father's half-sister."

"Yeah. Well, I guess that would be a problem. But it sounds like she made an impression on you."

"Definitely." Peter went on to give Reilly a short, heavily edited description of his two days in Sundsvall with Anna.

"Anyway, I learned something about the family business."

"Geevare Fabrication, Inc.?"

"Right. Got a plant tour from Anna's squeeze who's the number two guy there. Started as a company making hunting rifles, but now they're into specialty light arms for SWAT teams and ... other groups."

There was a grunt from the other end of the line. "Profitable business, I imagine. So have your father give me a call," he reminded Peter again. "And see if you can find somebody who isn't a relative to watch the sun not go down with."

They disconnected, and Peter walked over to a refreshment stand. He ordered a coffee and a pastry and watched some workmen who were setting up a stage in the center of the park. It was in a sunken, paved area. The previous fall, when he had walked through the park, it had been flooded and was being used as a skating rink. Now, from the oversized loudspeakers flanking the platform, it looked as though rock music was scheduled for the holiday weekend.

Back at his table, Peter opened up his laptop and did a final polish on his drug decriminalization story to send to Jill. He was happy to confirm that there was in fact an open WiFi network in the park. With his draft off to Jill, he felt relieved that he could take the weekend off without guilt. He could also call Gene Johanson to follow up on his request for money for his informant without preparing some demeaning excuses about his article. After several rings, Gene's voice mail picked up, and Peter left a short, urgent message.

He called Jill to alert her that he had sent in his story. She answered on the first ring. "So, Pierre, how is Sweden?"

"Well ... some surprises." He went on to tell her about his mugging knowing that as a true-crime addict she would enjoy the story. He told her he had visited Sundsvall but avoided any mention of Anna. He knew Jill had his best interests at heart but didn't want a psychobabble lecture on her theories about his social life.

Jill oohed and aahed at appropriate times during his narrative of the bridge incident in Stockholm. When he was finished, she added, "If you had just looked up that attractive policewoman you told me that you met the last time you were in Sweden and had dinner with her, that would never have happened." Despite his best efforts, Jill always found a way to introduce her favorite topic. She told him she had just received his article, and she would make sure that Gene called after she had briefed him on his escapade in Stockholm.

Peter started to object when he heard Gene's voice in the background. "What's this about an escapade?"

"Sorry, Peter, Gene's been lurking around my office again listening to my private telephone calls. I'll hand you over to him. Take care of yourself."

"Hey, dude. I heard the tail end of something about an adventure in Sweden, but I'll let Jill tell me the story later." Gene paused, and when he resumed, his voice had become serious. "I got your e-mail about the money for Anders. I sent it on to Bar Harbor for an opinion." That was Gene's way of saying that he had concluded the decision should be made by the director and founder of *VERITAS?* who spent his summers on the family vacation estate in that exclusive part of the Maine coast. "If the decision is positive, we can make arrangements to get you the cash by Monday."

"Thanks," Peter responded, but he was disappointed that Gene wasn't willing to make the decision himself—not a good indication.

"Sure. Hey, I've been doing a little research on your family."

"What? Like genealogy? Peter asked."

"No, more like the family business. Gevarfabrik's come up in a couple of stories in the European press on weapons sales to unsavory groups."

"Yes?" Peter said cautiously.

"You don't sound surprised."

"No, not exactly. I got a plant tour at Gevarfabrik today in Sundsvall. I picked up some hints that that they weren't too particular who they sold to, like some individuals and organizations on the State Department's who's-been-naughty list."

"You're in Sundsvall?" Gene asked.

"Was. That's part of a long story. My assistant there will fill you in," Peter said, hoping Jill was listening in.

Gene chuckled. "Okay, I guess. Anyway, there is also another angle on Gevarfabrik. There was a report in a Swedish newspaper *Expressen* about tax problems, underreporting of taxable income."

"No idea about that. But that sounds like the usual garden-variety corporate misbehavior."

"Yes, I suppose. But you know in Sweden, they take tax issues very seriously since they have to pay for all of those socialist welfare womb-to-tomb benefits for everyone. Anyway, Peter, maybe there's a story there. Of course we'll have Jill do it since it would be a bit of a conflict of interest for you."

Gene's kidding was normal, but Peter felt slightly uncomfortable. Being the close relative of the subject of a possible story was a new experience. He switched to a safer topic. "Jill says she just got my drug decriminalization article and everything is under control."

Peter endured a couple of additional zings from Gene and signed off. His watch said four fifteen; he had time for one more call. He punched in Claes's office number. It rang once and went into a recorded message in Swedish. Peter was about to hang up when it rang again with a different tone. Claes picked up. It sounded like a cell phone.

"Claes, this is Peter. Are you on your way out of town?"

"No, unfortunately. It happens that this is my weekend on call. But perhaps my last Midsummer weekend on duty, if I can retire this winter as I am planning."

"Well, at least you're not at the office."

"No, but still on duty." Claes didn't elaborate.

"I've set up a meeting with my informant for Monday at the Vasa Museum. Is there any word on what you can do for him?"

"No." Claes paused. "I have made the case with my director, but I would not depend on SAPO for this. Unfortunately, Swedish Security Police protocol makes it difficult for us to work with journalists in this way."

Peter wondered what Anders would do if he arrived at their meeting on Monday empty-handed.

Claes's tone softened. "But please keep me informed. So, how was your visit to Sundsvall?"

Peter provided a short description of finding the Svensson house and his unexpected meeting with Anna. He also mentioned his visit to the Svenssons' plant.

"Ah, yah," Claes responded. "So did you find the tour of Gevarfabrik interesting?"

Peter wondered if he was just being polite or whether the issues that Gene Johanson had raised were on his mind. "Yes, it was interesting," Peter said cautiously. "I guess the arms business is a little tricky."

"Tricky," Claes repeated.

"Yes, you know, selling devices intended to kill … things," Peter said deciding that raising the "tricky" remark to a philosophical level might head off a more detailed discussion.

"Ah yes, of course," Claes replied. "So now you are going to the islands for Midsummer, yes?"

"I'm on my way, walking to the ferries right now," Peter said, gathering his things and leaving the café.

"Well, have a good time and be careful."

"Be careful?"

"You know, dancing around the *Majstang* after too much beer. You could break your leg."

Peter wondered what a *Majstang* was, but Claes had already hung up.

Chapter 28

PETER CROSSED FROM THE Kungstradgarden Park back to the Stromkajen. Five or six of the Vaxholm Bolaget Line's archipelago ferries were waiting to take on passengers. The boats were docked nose-in, allowing loading and unloading over gangways that sloped down to their bows. Queues had formed at three of the ferries.

Peter was relieved that there was only a short line at the *Cinderella I*: several families and two couples with backpacks. Anna had asked Peter to hold a place in line so they could get seats on the upper deck. They had agreed they preferred sitting outside if the weather was anything short of a hurricane. At ten to five, Anna appeared at Peter's side, just as the deckhands were moving the narrow gangway into place. The line behind them had grown and reached nearly back to the ticket office.

"You have the tickets?" she asked.

"Tickets?" he said feigning a blank look.

"Peter, they may have sold out." Then seeing his expression, she laughed and poked him gently in the side.

At a minute after five, the *Cinderella I* gave three blasts from its horn, backed out into the harbor, and turned slowly away from its berth. Peter and Anna sat in the stern facing back toward the crowded quay. The upper deck, like the rest of the boat, was filled with jolly-spirited Midsummer vacationers.

Leaving the inner harbor, they passed Gamla Stan on the right and Skeppsholmen Island on the left where Peter had run on his first afternoon in Stockholm. At the end of Kastellholmen Island, the *Cinderella I* turned east toward the Baltic. Anna pointed out Djurgarden on the left, a large island east of the center of Stockholm. Formerly a game reserve for the kings of Sweden, it now provided gentle pine-covered hills and fields for walking as well as museums and a small amusement park.

"The large gray building right on the water is the *Vasamuseet.* Have you been there?"

"Yes, briefly when I was here in the fall," Peter replied thinking about his scheduled meeting with Anders there.

"You should really go again and spend a little more time." Peter nodded.

"Do you know the story of the *Vasa?*" she asked, putting her hand on Peter's arm as they stood at the rail looking out.

He did, but he let her go on, enjoying her enjoyment at relating an anecdote of Swedish history. "Isn't it an old warship that they fished out of the harbor a few years ago?"

"Yes, in the 1970s. It was very well preserved. It had just been built in 1628 and had never seen any combat. It was slid down into the water, sailed a few meters, turned over, and sank."

"Not sabotage?"

"No, just ... what is the word ... hubris ... and miscalculation. At that time, in the seventeenth century, Sweden ruled the world, at least this part of it."

"Some things never change," Peter replied.

Past Djurgarden, the waterway widened and then narrowed again. To the right, just beyond the shore, were the high cliffs of a suburb of Stockholm surmounted by large apartment blocks. The ferry stopped briefly at a dock there. A fountain near the landing shot a stream of water about fifty feet into the air. It was an exuberant salute to the ferries, freighters, tankers, and passenger liners coming in and out of Stockholm Harbor from other ports in the Baltic and beyond.

Anna seemed content to sit and enjoy the sun, reading reports and articles from the briefcase full of papers, which she had brought with her. Peter playfully accused her of being a workaholic.

"I get it from my father," she said. "I did not get very much done yesterday, you know," she said looking up from the papers on her lap.

Peter hoped that it might be an opening to touch on their interaction on the previous day, but before he could think of something to say, she went on.

"Working a lot, I mean. About the only time my father doesn't work is these two weeks at Midsummer. More like you Americans, not like most of us good Swedes who take five weeks vacation."

Peter decided to go with the flow of the conversation. "Have you always come out to Smavik for summer vacations?"

"Yes, my father loves the island. So we always came here at Midsummer. Then my father would go back to Sundsvall and my mother and I would stay through August."

"Has the island been in your family for a long time?" Peter asked, thinking about summer colonies he knew of in Maine. Families had bought cottages and land there in the late nineteenth century and several generations of these families had grown up vacationing together.

"Oh, no," Anna replied. "My father bought the island just after the Second World War. But some of the other people we know on islands nearby have been coming here for many years. The Svenssons' old family vacation house is in the mountains west of Sundsvall. I think my father intends to take your father there next week."

"Really?"

"Yes, with Rolf and a lawyer from Gevarfabrik. More discussions, I guess."

"Right." Peter wondered if he would be asked to participate. Would Rolf encourage that this weekend?

"I haven't been there very much, but it's quite pleasant. It is not far from a town called Lofsdalen. Great-great-grandfather Erik came from a town nearby. When he became wealthy, he bought the land and built the original hunting lodge."

Peter had a sudden vision of sitting in front of a stone fireplace beside Anna with snow falling outside in the woods. "What's it like up there?"

"Lots of mountains and lakes. The lodge is on the top of a small mountain overlooking a lake. The road winds up around the hill, which is very steep in places. I remember when I was a little girl and my mother took me there. I was afraid the car might go off the road and into the lake."

"But you spent your vacations on Smavik?"

"Yes, my father always said he didn't like it in the mountains. I always thought that was strange because he loves to hunt. And when he was a child, they went there every summer. He said there were lots of children his age nearby, and they sailed and fished in the lake. I thought that sounded wonderful. When I pressed him for an answer, he said that it was his because father had ... died there and so he had a bad association with it."

"Was there something about his death?" Peter asked.

Anna nodded. "It was a hunting accident, but my mother told me once that there was a question about it ... because it might have been suicide, she thought. Something about the way some of the longtime employees at Gevarfabrik spoke about it.

"But my father kept the hunting lodge and paid someone to maintain it for many years. About five years ago, that changed. He began to go back. Now he often takes customers there as my grandfather used to do for hunting."

"Give them a chance to try out some of Gevarfabrik's products," Peter said. But why would his great-grandfather have committed suicide? Or Jed for that matter? He stood up. "So, time for a beer?"

"A light beer for me, please," she responded.

He went below to the bar. When he returned with two cups, the *Cinderella* was slowing and turning into a small harbor and toward a wide pier. Beyond it a large building proclaimed itself the "Vaxholms Hotel."

The *Cinderella I* butted gently up to the wharf, discharged a few passengers, and took on more. Leaving Vaxholm, they stood by the rail of the upper deck, their shoulders touching lightly. Anna pointed out a fort across the narrow channel from the town. As she began to explain that it was built to guard one of the major entrances to Stockholm's inner waterways, Peter put his arm around her.

She drew back and turned to face him. "Peter, I'm ..." She closed her eyes and took a breath. "I think I have confused you because I am a little confused too. You are a wonderful, and handsome, and intelligent man. And if ... if ... if ... but it's not," she said, pressing her lips together, her eyebrows raised.

"But why?" Peter started to say. But Anna put her finger against his lips. "It's me. Please let it go at that," and she drew her fingers away.

Peter opened his mouth but just looked at Anna for a long moment as the *Cinderella* made a wide turn to thread its way into a narrow channel between two islands. Finally, he took her hands in his and said, "Okay, but I have to say this: I think I'm in love with you. That was so incredible last night. And ... I don't know ... why don't we just run away and find a place where nobody knows we're related."

Anna looked at him. "Oh, Peter." She shook her head laughing lightly. "What a wonderful, crazy idea. You are so sweet. But we're brother and sister, remember? And I need to finish this article," she said, moving back to where they had been sitting.

Peter smiled as best he could and then turned back to the rail and watched the shore move by wondering whether he should be relieved or crushed.

Over the next hour and a half, their ferry sailed further east into the archipelago, stopping every ten or fifteen minutes to let off one or several people at small docks. Most landings were just a concrete pier with a dirt road leading back into pine woods. The departing passengers were usually greeted by friends or family who loaded their belongings onto various conveyances of island travel: pushcarts, bicycles, or ATVs pulling small wagons.

Peter tried to follow their route on the water with the map on the back of the ferry brochure. But there were many more stops than were indicated on the small map. A more detailed chart would be required to navigate these islands, which seemed to range in size from an acre or two with a single brick red cottage and dock to islands several miles in length. Anna finally closed her briefcase and joined Peter at the rail again.

"My guidebook says there are twenty-four thousand islands in the archipelago," he said.

"Depending on who you ask, there are anywhere between twenty to thirty thousand skerries in the Archipelago," Anna said.

"How big does a skerry have to be to qualify?"

"Oh, probably about a square meter," Anna replied.

Their intermediate destination was the island of Moja. There, a launch from Smavik would pick them up. Moja, which Anna pronounced "Moyah" with the stress on the second syllable, was a large island about thirty-five miles from Stockholm with a few hundred year-round inhabitants. They approached the landing on Moja through a channel between it and its sister island to the south, Moja Sodra. Peter wondered if his father would be there or if he would just meet them on Smavik, continuing his seeming remoteness.

The *Cinderella* rounded the southern end of the island and approached Berg's *brygga*, the dock at the small settlement of Berg. Anna and Peter moved down to the lower level just behind the bow and retrieved their luggage from the informal jumble of baggage. They were joined by a majority of the remaining passengers.

The dock was crowded with enthusiastic greeters. Among them was Peter's father. Peter was surprised at the sudden sense of relief he felt at actually seeing him. Eric Frost was leaning casually against a pile of crates on the dock. His long face was framed by several days' worth of salt-and-pepper beard and his full head of gray hair. He wore a plaid cotton shirt and beige cargo shorts. He looked fit and tanned from his sail with Bjorn. Peter decided he could almost pass for a native. He waved to his father as they moved up the gangway behind a family struggling with bicycles, suitcases, and a three-year-old too tired to walk. Eric stood to one side to allow the other passengers coming up on the pier to get by. He smiled broadly when he caught sight of Peter and Anna and waved back.

On the dock, Peter and his father gave each other a quick hug. Eric then reached out for Anna and pulled her into a hug and gave her a kiss on the cheek, which she returned. "So I understand you two got acquainted when Peter dropped into Sundsvall unexpectedly. Bjorn talked to Rolf this morning."

"Yes, so you know he's not coming down until tomorrow?" Anna asked. "He had some important customers. Actually with Rolf's being so busy, I have had a chance to get to know my new nephew." She smiled at Peter.

"Nephew!" Eric said, chuckling. "That never occurred to me. Anyway, Lars is right over there with the launch." He pointed to a small cabin cruiser tied up further along the dock. He grabbed Anna's suitcase and put a hand on Peter's back as they walked up the dock.

On the cabin cruiser, Lars acknowledged Peter with just a quick, firm handshake and a smile, which briefly creased his suntanned face. He wore a long-sleeved T-shirt, running shorts, and Nike trainers without socks. Peter thought he seemed to better fit the role of crewmember for Bjorn's yacht than bodyguard.

Lars exchanged a *"Hej"* and a nod with Anna and then reversed the boat into the channel. Anna went into the cabin while Peter and Eric sat on the cushioned benches in the open stern. The question of Jed Barlow's disappearance moved up to the front of Peter's mind. "Have you had a chance to call Bill Reilly this afternoon?"

Eric looked confused. "This afternoon? Was I supposed to? I called Bill last Saturday after I got your e-mail and left him a voice message."

"You didn't get Bill's second message? Did you get the e-mails that I sent you?" Like Bill, Peter wondered how, with all the communication options in a first-world country like Sweden, their messages had been lost or misread.

Eric looked puzzled. "No. But more important—is Jed okay? When I didn't hear anything, I assumed he turned up."

Peter shook his head. "I talked to Bill today. He hasn't turned up. And Bill would really like to talk to you."

Eric looked down and then back at Peter. "It's been what, ten days? That's awhile. If he was sailing alone … there's always a chance the boom can swing around in a light wind …"

"Well, they don't really know. Anyway, please give Bill a call."

"I will," Eric said.

Peter's feeling of relief at seeing his father was fading and being replaced by a restiveness to finally get to a long-awaited conversation with him.

Eric spoke first, putting his hand on Peter's knee. "I'm very glad you came to Sweden. And I know I owe you an apology for not telling you about Aunt Elena and being adopted and all."

"Right. It was kind of a major surprise. I guess I'm not sure why …" Peter left the sentence half-finished.

"Of course, and I don't have a good answer. It always seemed like there was a reason to put off talking about it."

"That must have been what Grandpa and Grandma thought too, when they didn't tell you. I'm sorry that sounded a little angry. I'm really just curious," Peter said.

"And I didn't have all the answers so that's why I wanted to get it all sorted out before we talked. But now you're here."

"Sorted out?" Peter wondered if that meant the agreement with Bjorn. "I understand you been having some discussions with Bjorn … ah, Grandfather Bjorn."

"Yes, a grandfather Bjorn. Strange, isn't it?" Eric smiled, turning to Peter and nodding. Then looking up toward the cabin, he said, "Let's talk about that when we have some time together alone." His expression had turned serious.

"Okay," Peter said, wondering when that might be.

"So you and Bjorn have been getting to know each other this week?"

"Yes, we have." He paused and looked away from Peter and into the cabin where Anna was talking to Lars. "It's a little complicated." He turned back toward Peter. "I didn't know you had any plans to come to Sweden."

Peter was not sure how to respond. "Well, you know, I'd actually been thinking about a follow-up article to the piece I did on neo-Nazis in Sweden last fall. And then when I found out about … anyway, I've got a lot questions for you."

"But at least you know why I suddenly got very interested in Sweden," Eric said, smiling.

"For sure. But I really want to find some time to talk this weekend."

"We can, and we will. We need enough time so I can explain the whole thing to you. As I said my—or I guess—*our* relationship with Bjorn is complicated."

"I would think it would be after sixty-plus years. And I guess there are some issues about whether you get to inherit part of the gun factory." Peter enjoyed the irony knowing his father's left-of-center opinions on gun control.

Eric looked pained rather than amused. "Well, it's a little more than that." He started to say something and stopped when Anna stepped out of the cabin.

"May I join you gentlemen?" Peter and Eric moved apart, and Anna sat on the seat between them. They were cruising at fifteen to twenty knots across a wide stretch of water between several islands.

Peter looked back but couldn't find the point on Moja that they had left from. "How do you navigate here if you're not familiar with the area? I've hardly seen any buoys and the ones I have seen don't seem to be numbered," he said.

"When I'm not sailing near Smavik or not on a course I'm familiar with, I use my GPS a lot. It is confusing with so many islands," Anna said.

"That's true about the buoys," Eric offered. "I was telling Bjorn about sailing in New England and how much we depend on our navigation markers. But then, in New England, we have six- to ten foot tides, fogs, and a lot of reefs to watch out for."

"Which we don't have here in the archipelago, thanks to Njord," said Anna.

"Who's Njord?" Peter asked.

"He is the Norse sea god in charge of such things, if I remember my mythology correctly," Anna said.

They were now speeding through a relatively narrow passage between two islands. Anna looked annoyed, got up, and put her head in the cabin. Lars slowed the boat down to a no-wake speed. Just before the channel opened out again, it narrowed to just a few yards across. Peter wondered if Lars would have at least slowed there if Anna hadn't spoken to him.

"That's Smavik," Anna said, pointing ahead and a little to the left, about a half a mile away. "The dock is on the other side, so we'll go around to the north."

As they approached, Peter noticed a channel between Smavik and another island on their left. From what he remembered from the chart that Anna had shown him on the ferryboat, he guessed their landing on Smavik was just beyond the channel on the backside of the island. "Couldn't we take that channel ahead instead of going around the island?" Peter asked.

"It looks wide enough, but it's actually quite narrow and not deep enough for this boat. I'm not sure I would take a small outboard through there, even carefully," Anna said.

Smavik Island looked like its many cousins in the archipelago. It was about half a mile long, covered with pine trees and surrounded by a rocky shore. They passed a dock with a small house behind it close to the shore. It was yellow with blue shutters and a small vegetable garden in front. Uphill from the house was a large tool shed, nearly the size of the house. A clothesline between the buildings held a load of wash.

"That is the Pederssons' house. He and his wife take care of the island and our house," Anna said.

They rounded the northern end of the island and turned into the yellow-red sun, which was drifting at a low angle toward the northern horizon. Late in the evening, it would dip into the water and then emerge after a couple of hours of twilight in the north-northeast. They turned south on the far side of the island, and in a few moments, a dock came into view.

As they approached the dock, a cove opened on their left where two sailboats were tied up on either side of another smaller dock. Eric pointed out the larger boat, on which he and Bjorn had sailed. The other was Anna's thirty-foot sloop.

Lars brought the cabin cruiser into the inner side of the main dock. Before it touched the bumpers, Anna was out of the boat fastening a stern line to the dock. A wide, smooth rock sloped up from the dock toward a large two-story house and several cabins. All were painted in the traditional style, brick red with white trim. At the top of the slope stood a tall, slightly stooped figure in shorts and a blue denim shirt. He was holding the back of a deck chair with both hands, peering down at them. Eric waved, and Anna called to him, but Bjorn Svensson continued to stare at them without acknowledging their greetings or offering one of his own.

Chapter 29

WHEN ANNA REACHED THE edge of the flagstone terrace in front of the house, Bjorn smiled at her and seemed to snap out of his reverie. He embraced Anna in a fatherly hug. She kissed him on both cheeks and then moved to his side. He stood, slightly off balance, to greet Peter while leaning on Anna's arm.

"Peter, I am pleased to meet you. How nice you could join your father to be with us. A pleasant surprise." His English, like Anna's, was more British than American, but with a heavier Swedish accent. His previous self-absorbed stare was replaced by a penetrating look from his watery but bright blue eyes as he shook Peter's hand and held it.

"I'm glad I can be here and have a chance to meet you," Peter said. "I hope you didn't mind that I went to Sundsvall on my own. I was curious."

"Of course. And you had the opportunity to meet my Anna." Bjorn turned toward her with an affectionate look. "So you are welcome to Smavik. Perhaps you would like to leave your things in your cabin," he said letting go of Peter's hand and gesturing up the slope behind them. "I will make some martinis for us. Then dinner, yes?"

Bjorn called to Lars who had been standing off to one side to show Peter where he would be staying. Then Bjorn turned and walked toward the terrace in front of the house. He moved surprisingly quickly despite a slight hitch and a significant stoop in his large frame.

Lars led Peter up a path to one of several cabins on the side of the hill across from the main house. His father was staying in the first one, across from the main house. The cabin, like the one by the pond in Sundsvall, had one large, all-purpose room with a couch, a table and chairs, and a small refrigerator and stove. There was also a bedroom and a bathroom. The bathroom offered a shower and a sink but no toilet. Peter guessed that a path leading around the back of the cabin ended at an outhouse. Even wealthy Swedes, it seemed, enjoyed roughing it slightly. He dropped his backpack in the front room and washed up quickly for dinner.

Peter joined his father walking down to the large terrace where Bjorn and Anna were sitting. As they approached the others, Peter held his father back briefly. "I promised I'd have you call Bill Reilly as soon as possible," he said.

"I'd like to use my phone card and a payphone for that," Eric said. "There's one on the island we're going to be on tomorrow."

"I have my cell phone you can use."

"No, thanks. They don't work very well out here."

Peter suspected his father's aversion to cell phones rather than the strength of the signal was behind his preference.

Bjorn greeted them and offered martinis or other drinks as they wished. Bjorn seemed to enjoy his role as host leading Peter and Eric to the bar where Lars stood in attendance. Bjorn was drinking a martini; Anna had a glass of white wine. Eric agreed to a martini; Peter opted for a beer.

When they were seated and Bjorn had toasted Eric and Peter's visit to Smavik, he asked about Peter's work. Remembering Anna's comment about her father's concerns about neo-Nazis, Peter talked in general terms about writing for VERITAS? and his experience as a newspaper reporter. Bjorn did not ask about his current assignment in Sweden, although he seemed to know that Peter's trip was not entirely personal. Bjorn then shifted the conversation to Peter's visit to Sundsvall and Gevarfabrik. "A different factory from the first Erik Svensson's gun shop," he said smiling with a question in his voice that seemed designed to elicit affirmation. Eric nodded as did Anna who reached across and found her father's arm.

"Yes," Peter said responding to Bjorn. "I enjoyed looking at the old photographs of the first factory in the 1850s. But Rolf said that your main sales now were for small tactical groups. How do you keep those weapons from ending up in the hands of terrorist groups?" Peter thought that by not framing the question as an accusation, he could satisfy his investigative reporting curiosity without risking his grandfather's hostility.

Bjorn narrowed his eyes for an instant then relaxed his face into a gentle smile. "Gevarfabrik is very careful to comply with all of Sweden's very strict rules relating to the sales of weapons systems." The tone and cadence of his response signaled that he did not want to continue the discussion. He held Peter's attention for a moment, still smiling, and turned to Eric. "Shall we move to the table for dinner?"

Peter decided that Bjorn's response was a stock answer to a question he'd been asked before by the press. A look of alarm crossed Anna's face then was replaced by a quick frown at Peter. Eric looked slightly embarrassed and got up quickly to move toward the table.

A table on the terrace had been set for five. Mrs. Pedersson emerged from the house carrying a large pot of soup and was introduced to Peter. Lars sat with them at dinner responding to occasional questions or remarks by Bjorn but offering none of his own.

Bjorn spiritedly explained to Eric and Peter that the broccoli and potato soup, being served by Mrs. Pedersson, was a traditional, rich Swedish vegetarian chowder. It was followed by smoked salmon with a mustard and dill dressing and small boiled potatoes garnished with more dill. Peter wondered if dill was listed as a vegetable in Swedish nutrition charts.

The food was accompanied by a full spectrum of alcohols including white and red wine, beer, and schnapps. Bjorn insisted on separate schnapps toasts for Eric and Peter. Eric politely returned the toast to Bjorn. Peter looked at Anna, thinking of offering a toast to her. She smiled at him but moved her eyes in a way that Peter interpreted as meaning that they had had enough toasts with strong spirits.

The dinner conversation focused mainly on the food and drink with some discussion of Eric and Bjorn's sail from Sundsvall to Smavik during the week. Bjorn, at eighty-seven, had competently captained his fifty-foot sailboat with help from Lars and Eric. Bjorn toasted Lars, describing him as his invaluable first mate. Lars responded politely but without much enthusiasm to his boss's praise.

It was odd, Peter thought, to again be in the company of his father and grandfather, especially one he had never known. Peter looked at Bjorn at the head of the table and to his father on his right. He tried to see the family resemblance. Both had similar coloring and long faces. His father's was more angular and thinner while Bjorn, with age and more weight, was fleshier and rounder. Both were tall, however, and Peter thought that on a football team, his father would have been an end and Bjorn a tackle. But Bjorn's outgoing personality was more of a contrast to his father's generally retiring nature than any differences in their physiques.

Peter had wondered if Bjorn would raise the issue of the settlement or make some reference to the issue of parentage and grand-parentage. But Bjorn seemed careful to keep the conversation away from these areas. Before dessert, Lars had excused himself to "lock down the island for the night," as he put it.

As dinner progressed, Bjorn grew quieter leaving Eric, Peter, and Anna to carry the conversation. Peter thought that perhaps the alcohol, which his grandfather seemed to be able to consume in significant quantities, was taking effect. But after they had finished a dessert of vanilla ice cream with cloudberry sauce, Bjorn brought the table to attention by putting down his spoon and announcing that he wanted to speak about a subject that was important to all of them.

Bjorn looked at each of them in turn and spoke their names, "Anna, Eric, Peter, you are my family in one way or another, so I would like to tell you some family history to help you understand how all this came about."

Peter leaned forward, anxious to hear the story of his father's Swedish origins from Bjorn. It was ironic that he had yet to hear anything from his father and was hearing it first from his grandparents.

Bjorn looked at Eric. "Eric, you and I have had some discussions and you know my concerns about Anna's financial security.

"Anna, you did not know very much about my early life and, until very recently, nothing about what resulted from my time in Germany before I returned to Sweden.

"Peter, what I have to say will begin to help you to understand and support your father's decision in these matters and protect Anna as well, I hope."

Eric nodded in acknowledgment of Bjorn's remarks but did not smile. Anna looked both concerned and slightly mystified. Peter could read nothing from his father's expression.

"Peter, I understand from your father that you learned something about our time in Germany before the Second World War from your grandmother. So for you and, of course Eric, I will be repeating some of what you already know. Anna, some of this will be new to you."

"Father, it's all right," Anna said gently. "I don't need to know this. What happened a long time ago is not important now."

"It is, Anna. Please, I want to tell you." Bjorn's voice was strong, but his eyes seemed to plead for Anna's understanding.

"Of course, Father." Anna looked at Eric and Peter; her expression seemed to ask them to humor Bjorn as well.

Bjorn continued, "I met Eric's mother, Elena, in Germany in 1938." He paused, straightening himself up in his chair. "My childhood friend Kjell Hendrikson and I had gone to study in Germany the previous year. We met Elena in a German history class. We were very impressed that she was an American but spoke Swedish. At first, we were just three friends: Bjorn, Anna, and Kjell. Kjell and I lived together in an apartment. Elena had a room in a boarding house not far away. Then after a bit, Kjell and Anna became more than just friends. But that did not last very long. And then, it was Bjorn and Anna who were special friends."

Mrs. Pedersson appeared to clear the remaining dishes, and Bjorn paused in his narrative. The others waited quietly until Mrs. Pedersson had left. Bjorn went on, "We were still all good friends. That was not surprising because Kjell and I were almost like brothers. Kjell was the son of a worker who had been killed at the factory in an accident. My father, Erik, helped Kjell's family financially. When Kjell's mother died, about a year after his father, Kjell came to live with us. We were both about eleven years then." Bjorn spoke slowly and deliberately, with some effort, it seemed. Perhaps it was the nostalgia of his childhood with Kjell that made it difficult for him to talk about these distant events. "When my father decided that I should go to Germany to study, I insisted that Kjell should go as well. My father agreed, and he supported both of us.

"Then, in August of 1939, Erik Svensson, my father, died suddenly. The telegram arrived with the news; it requested that I return home immediately to take over the family business. We had to make a decision very quickly. I returned to Sweden, and a few days later, Elena sailed back to America. I didn't know and she didn't know that she was pregnant with Eric here." Bjorn looked up at Eric and seemed to be studying his face. "Perhaps if we had known, a different decision might have been taken." He paused again, briefly closing his eyes as if to revisit a crucial time sixty years before.

"Kjell decided to go to England. He had decided that he wanted to support the English and fight with them against the Nazis." Bjorn paused again, apparently struggling with an emotion. "And eventually, that cost him his life."

Peter wasn't sure how to question Bjorn's account without sounding as though he was accusing him of deserting Elena. Finally, he said, "Did you expect to get together again after the war was over when you all decided to go in separate directions?"

"Yes, that is what we imagined," Bjorn said. He seemed lost in thought for a moment, looking out over the terrace and beyond across the water into the continuing sunset. The others were silent.

At last, and still looking away, he said, "I think that Kjell did not want to go back to Sweden to the circumstances he had been in before."

"I think that he would have been resentful at having to return to Sundsvall and probably begin working for his wealthy friend," Anna said. "Because their relationship would have changed."

Bjorn turned and looked at Anna. "Yes, that is true. You have good insight, my dear. It took me many years to understand that."

The exchange with Anna encouraged Peter to ask his questions. "And did you want to be with Elena again, especially when you knew she had your child?"

Eric and Anna stiffened slightly at the directness of Peter's question.

"I didn't know of the child, of Eric, until recently." Bjorn sounded defensive. "But I did want to be with Elena. It just wasn't possible. By the time the war was over, we had begun separate lives." Bjorn sighed and sat back in his chair, apparently signaling that he wanted the conversation to conclude.

Peter was amazed at Bjorn's account. It contradicted what Elena had said: that Bjorn knew all about the birth of his son Eric. Peter looked at his father, but Eric said nothing and looked down at the last of the wine in his glass and then finished it.

Anna leaned forward and put her hand on her father's arm. "Father, you look tired. Shall we go to bed and leave Peter and Eric to have some time together?"

He nodded slowly and pulled himself up unsteadily. She rose to help him. He spoke to her briefly in Swedish.

"Of course," she said, "my father wants to talk to me so I'll say good night." She kissed Peter and Eric each lightly on the cheek. Bjorn wished them *sova gott* and turned toward the house.

"What does that mean?" Peter asked his father.

"It means sleep well."

"No," Peter said whispering forcefully as Anna and Bjorn retreated into the house. "I meant Bjorn telling a totally different story about him and Elena and not knowing about you."

Chapter 30

PETER WAS BURNING WITH curiosity to understand why Bjorn's narrative differed so greatly from his grandmother's and why his father seemed to show so little reaction to the discrepancy. "Dad, can we go somewhere and talk?"

"Sure. Let's take a walk. There's a trail that follows the shoreline around the island, and there's still plenty of light even though it's—what—nearly ten thirty? Neat, huh?" Eric said.

They walked up the hill between Eric's cabin and the water. The trail began at the top of the rise behind the cabins and followed the edge of the woods and the rocky shore. The path was wide and well tended, allowing Peter and his father to walk side by side in the long summer evening light.

Peter was quiet until he was sure they were out of earshot of the house. "Why is Bjorn lying about not knowing about you before this year? Elena said that—"

His father interrupted. "I know, I know. He told me that he was still trying to decide how to tell Anna the whole story in a way that he was comfortable with."

"Well, I'd like to know the whole story too," Peter said, hearing a little irritation in his voice. But how could that explain two such different accounts?

"Okay, let me start from the beginning."

Peter groaned inwardly, knowing his father's habit of explaining things with facts and events that progressed in an orderly way toward a conclusion. More like a mathematical proof than a journalist's report with a the highlights first, he thought.

Eric turned toward Peter. "By the way, it really is good to have you here," he said putting his hand on his son's shoulder as they started along the path.

"For me too, Dad," Peter replied. "So, anyway, I know most of the beginning if you mean Elena's going to Germany and meeting Bjorn. I told you I went to Maine and talked to her after I found your birth certificate. And now this evening, I've heard Bjorn's side of the story, and it doesn't add up."

"Well, there's more to the first part of the story, but let me start with what I knew or didn't know when I was a kid because I know you were wondering about that too."

"Okay." Peter sighed inwardly. "Well, I have been a little curious about that too. You had no clue growing up?"

"Right. Your grandparents, Alan and Judith Frost, were my parents—Mom and Dad—as far as I knew." Eric went on to explain that he thought he remembered Elena living with them and taking care of him when he was two or three years old before she had moved away. "When I was older and thought about it, I assumed that she had just been babysitting for my parents. But I always remembered her as very special." He paused. "Then I found out why."

"I had a friend in high school who was adopted. He knew about it and told me. I mentioned it to my parents, but they didn't volunteer anything about me. If anybody in the town of Munroe knew, they didn't say anything, at least not to me."

"How about your cousins? Did they know?" Peter asked.

"Maybe. I guess they were told not to talk about it. They lived in the Midwest, and we didn't see them very often."

"What about Uncle Jed, your cousin ... well, now your adopted cousin?" Peter asked.

"Yes, he knew but he respected your grandmother Frost's—his aunt's—feelings. He never said anything to me, until recently, when I told him that I had discovered that Elena was my mother," Eric said.

Peter wondered if that had anything to do with the tension between Jed and Elena. Perhaps Jed thought that his father should have been told about his adoption instead of finding out about it on his own. "Elena said that you found out when you applied for a government security clearance, when you were about twenty-seven."

"That's right. I had to produce a birth certificate. I sent away to Springfield where I had been born, in the hospital there. When I opened up the letter, I saw that Mom and Dad were not my real parents—not my biological parents anyway. And I had no idea who Helen Wilson and Bjorn Svensson were."

"Weren't you blown away?"

Eric turned to look at Peter and nodded. "I was surprised, yes. But not thrown for a loop, if that's what you mean. Mostly curious. But you had just been born, and we were moving out of an apartment into a new house. Somehow, it didn't seem as important as all the other things that were going on in my life at that point. Naturally, I asked your grandparents about it the next time we got together, face to face."

Peter tried to imagine how difficult that discussion must have been. "What happened? And what did they say?"

"Actually not much. They sort of apologized for not telling me. They asked me if it bothered me, and I told them no. They didn't offer any more information. They seemed kind of uncomfortable talking about it. So I just let it drop."

Peter had trouble understanding how his father could have been so relaxed about the discovery of his adoption. But it was consistent with his generally calm, rational technologist's temperament. "Really, and you never asked them again?"

"I tried once or twice and so did your mother on her own. But all we ever found out was that they wanted to have children but couldn't, so they decided to adopt me. As you know, Elena had been living with them when I was born. But they never mentioned anything about her."

"I thought it was strange that Aunt Elena gave you up for adoption, but she told me being a single mother wasn't very normal in those days."

"It does seem kind of strange now, but I think Elena wanted me to have a home with a father and mother. So when she knew she wasn't going to be with Bjorn, my father, she made the decision."

"Did you ever figure out that Helen Wilson was Aunt Elena?"

"That thought went through my mind at one point after I found out about being adopted, but I never said anything. Finally, last summer, I decided to ask Elena about my adoption. I visited her in Maine. We went for a long sail together, and she told me who my biological parents were. I was pretty blown away then."

Eric stopped and turned to Peter. "Imagine, suddenly I found my real mother was sitting in a sailboat with me in the middle of the bay. It was like doing a science experiment and getting a totally unexpected result. Here I was in a place I thought I knew everything about. Now it was all sort of different. Not bad, just different."

Peter remembered sitting at the table overlooking that bay and his own discovery that Elena was his grandmother.

As they approached the south end of the island, the shoreline curved into a wide channel, which separated Smavik from Sodra Smavik. A number of sailboats were moored near the opposite shore. Their path turned eastward along the shore of the channel.

"And you never told me about your being adopted. So history repeated itself. Ay, Dad?" Peter said looking at his father and putting his hand on the older man's shoulder.

Eric smiled slightly. "Yes, I'm guilty. I'm not sure just why. Your mother and I did talk about it. But when I first found out, you were a baby. Later, when you were older, I was afraid of hurting Mom and Dad if you knew and asked them about it. I just kept putting it off."

As they approached the east side of Smavik along the path, the width of the channel decreased. Eventually, they came to the narrow gap that Peter had noticed earlier in the day. There, the path turned north toward the Pederssons' house. It went behind the house and then back along the shore.

Eric went on, "Anyway, last fall, I talked to Elena again to see if I could find my birth father in Sweden, if he was still alive. Then I thought I'd wait until I knew more to tell you."

Peter thought that was both typical of his father's logical mind and irritating. "So do you have the whole story now?" And what does that have to do with the discussion about the agreement? he wondered.

"I think so. Anyway, that brings us up to the present or really to my contact this spring with Bjorn, which ..."

Eric was interrupted by the snap of a branch on the ground in the path behind them. They turned to see Lars's wiry figure striding up to them. "Good evening," he said formally. "I am making my last check around the island. Can you find your way back?"

Peter and Eric assured him that they could. Lars passed them and walked a little way ahead, studying the shoreline. Peter and Eric continued their walk. But with Lars remaining within earshot, Eric seemed reluctant to talk about Bjorn; he asked about Peter's trip to California. After a few minutes, they came to the cove where Bjorn and Anna's boats were tied up. The boats swayed gently at the dock, tugging on their lines.

"Tomorrow, apparently, we have been invited to lunch on Grenvik Island. It's not far from here," Eric said. "I imagine Bjorn will want to take the launch, but perhaps we can persuade Anna to sail us over in her boat."

After they passed the dock, Lars took a path up to the back of the main house. Peter and Eric continued across the terrace and up to their cabins.

Peter followed his father inside his cabin. "So you were saying that you contacted Bjorn this spring."

"Can we go on tomorrow? There's somewhat more of this story to tell you but it will take some time, and I think I'm ready for bed now," Eric replied. "Let's try for tomorrow afternoon when we can get away for a little while. Is that okay?"

"I guess," Peter replied. "But tell me, what's Bjorn really like? You had a number of days in the boat with him. Did he seem more like your father than Grandpa Frost?"

"The short answer to your first question is that Bjorn is a complicated guy. The long and the short answer to your second question is 'no,'" his father responded.

"So nurture trumps nature."

"Well, of course, that's always debatable. *Sova gott.*"

Chapter 31

BY SIX O'CLOCK IN the morning, even the fully drawn shades could not pretend to keep the Midsummer daylight out of the bedroom in the cabin. Peter rose and found some orange juice in the small refrigerator. He dressed in shorts and a T-shirt for a morning run. A couple of circuits around the island would give him his preferred start to the day.

Peter ran down past his father's cabin and up the path that started south around Smavik, the same way they had walked the previous evening. The temperature was comfortable, about seventy degrees, he guessed. The sky overhead was clear blue. Peter started slowly, warming up. By the time he had reached the south end of the island, he was running smoothly at his usual pace. Just as he turned into a long straight stretch of the path that bordered the channel, he spotted Anna running toward him. He realized he had forgotten to ask her the evening before if she wanted to run with him and felt bad. Anna saw him, seemed startled, and slowed her pace. Peter slowed also, expecting one or the other of them would turn around so they could continue their run together. But as Anna approached Peter, she gave him a quick wave and resumed her normal running speed. She met his eyes briefly as she passed.

Peter stopped completely and looked back at her trim figure receding down the path. Was she annoyed he hadn't asked her to run with him? Not likely, he decided. Perhaps she just wanted to run alone that morning. It was something he could appreciate. He often liked to use his running time to think through projects or concerns in a quiet, uninterrupted way. Was

it the previous evening's discussion at dinner or something her
father had said to her later that evening?

Peter continued around the south end of the island
passing the Pederssons' house and then up to the north end of
the island. Eventually, he came to the little cove and the
Svenssons' compound beyond it and began a second loop. He
did not pass Anna again.

Despite his rationalization about Anna's avoiding him, he
felt a little rejected. It was probably just as well since she was his
half-aunt. But he was attracted to her—aunt or not. Lucky Rolf.
What did she see in him anyway? Successful business executive,
good-looking, flies his own plane, probably drives an expensive
Mercedes. And Bjorn must think it was a great match:
Gevarfabrik stays in the family, run by his handpicked successor
and son-in-law. But would Anna sell Gevarfabrik, if she could,
and build an orphanage? It would be for children left without
parents by the guns that Gevarfabrik and other weapons-makers
were sending around the world. She would travel around the
world raising more money for these orphans. The campaign
would bring her to the United States. And they might meet in
some city where no one knew they were related and ... wow!
Peter realized his meditation had totally morphed into fantasy.
He would begin to feel very uncomfortable in Anna and Rolf's
company if he continued that line of thought.

His mind turned to what Bjorn had said at dinner the
evening before about protecting Anna. From what? he wondered.
Was his father holding Bjorn up for some huge financial
settlement on his and Elena's behalf? That didn't seem to make
sense. But maybe that's why Uncle Jed, a lawyer, had gotten
involved. He'd try to confirm that today. Anyway, Bjorn didn't
seem to be treating his son like someone who might be trying to
blackmail him.

When Peter reached the cove on his second loop, he
walked the rest of the way back to his cabin. He looked briefly at
the water, thinking about a quick swim, but he remembered how
cold his dip earlier in the week in Stockholm had been. He
guessed it wouldn't be any warmer this far out into the Baltic and
opted for a warm shower in his cabin.

At eight o'clock, Peter left his cabin and saw that breakfast had been laid out on the terrace. Anna and her father were sitting on deck chairs, eating and talking. Bjorn greeted Peter with a pleasant gruffness. Anna looked at Peter and smiled. But she provided no explanation in her expression or greeting of her behavior on the trail. While Peter was helping himself to a couple of soft-boiled eggs, smoked salmon, and toast, Eric joined them.

Bjorn explained the plans for the day at the Midsummer festivities. They had all been invited to lunch with friends on a neighboring island a few miles away. Rolf was due to arrive about mid-morning.

"Any chance we could go for a sail this morning?" Peter asked looking at Anna.

She seemed uncomfortable and looked at Eric. "Perhaps, tomorrow we could go out. I think Rolf and I will sail over to Grenvik and meet you there."

"We will come over in the launch," Bjorn said looking at Peter and Eric. "After lunch, you younger people can stay on Grenvik for the *Majstang* dancing. They have a traditional Midsummer celebration there."

"Mystung?" Peter said.

"That is Swedish for maypole," Anna said giving Peter a quick smile.

"So Lars will bring me back to Smavik and the rest of you can sail back on Anna's boat, provided one of you is still sober," he added winking at Anna.

When Anna announced she had some work to do and got up to bring her breakfast plate into the house, Peter followed her. "Can we take a little walk before your date with your laptop?" He tried to sound casual.

Anna half turned to look back at him with an uneasy frown. "Later, Peter … there will be some time." She paused. "Maybe, I don't know." She turned to face him fully. She was smiling although her lips were closed. "Anyway, I do have some work to do," she said, her expression becoming serious.

Suddenly, she was back to doctor mode, Peter thought. "Okay," he said, letting the door shut between them and turning

back to the terrace. Something seemed to have changed since
yesterday. What? he wondered. Something Bjorn said to her last
night? He returned to the terrace to finish his breakfast, more
confused by Anna than ever.

After breakfast, Eric and Bjorn left the terrace for a
discussion in Bjorn's study. Peter didn't feel he was specifically
excluded, but somehow, he was not specifically included either.
He wandered down to the dock where Lars was washing down
the launch. He greeted Lars and tried to engage him in a
discussion of his work for Bjorn. He gave up after it was
apparent that Lars's "yah" or "nay" answers indicated that either
he was not a gifted conversationalist or that his job precluded
disclosing or confirming any information that was not already
obvious. Peter left Lars and walked back up the hill toward his
cabin. As he walked past the terrace, he saw Bjorn sitting with his
shirt off, his hairy gray chest toward the sun.

"Grandfather Bjorn," Peter said trying out that new
salutation.

Bjorn seemed surprised but said, "Ah yes. But you have
spoken to your father of course?" He motioned for Peter to sit
down. "He's a good man. And I have spoken to my Anna. I think
they both understand the situation. There should not be a
problem."

Peter pulled up a canvas deck chair next to Bjorn's.

"You agree?" He smiled nodding at Peter.

"This is about the agreement, you mean?" Peter replied.

Bjorn looked slightly surprised again. "Yes, of course."
Then his eyes narrowed slightly as he looked at Peter. "I'm sure
you understand how things are and what happened so long ago.
And we are all of us now where we are."

That's true, Peter thought, but it really didn't explain why
Bjorn couldn't just own up to leaving his grandmother Elena if it
was true that she had borne his son. What could Bjorn say that
would change that? He decided to plunge in and find out. "But
you knew about Dad. Didn't you write to Grandmother Elena
after he was born? But last night, you said—"

Bjorn's face registered surprise as he interrupted, "Peter,
surely you understand now why I ..." He stopped as Eric came

up behind him to where they were sitting. Bjorn turned toward him. "Eric, I assumed that you had spoken to Peter last night. Is that not correct?"

Erik looked distressed. "No, no, we didn't, actually …" He seemed annoyed, looking at Peter but speaking to Bjorn. "I wanted to have time to lay out the whole thing. We'll probably have time later today."

Bjorn made an irritated huffing sound but nodded in assent. "But, Eric, you and I are in full agreement, yes?" Bjorn said sitting up reaching out for Eric's arm.

"Yes, yes." Eric turned toward Bjorn. "We're good, I think."

There was obviously something Peter didn't know, which was maddening in itself, but his father's withholding whatever the information was and releasing it on a schedule was even more infuriating.

"So later, right, Dad?" Peter said getting up and walking off the terrace. What the hell was going on? Whatever it was, he guessed that Rolf's concern about convincing his father and Bjorn to come to an agreement was unnecessary. He wondered which one had caved in or for that matter what the disagreement might have been anyway.

He went down toward the docks in the cove thinking he would have a look at Anna's and Bjorn's sailboats in the cove when he heard the drone of a small plane. He saw Lars looking up from the deck of the launch, scanning the sky to the west. Eventually, by following the direction of Lars's binoculars, he spotted a plane approaching from the northwest. It came in low and made a pass close to the water. Peter guessed Rolf was assessing the waves and the wind for the best landing direction. He then circled around and landed with a short spurt of spray from the plane's pontoons, about a hundred yards off the dock. Rolf killed the engine and waited while Lars took a small outboard out to the plane to tow it back to the dock.

In a few minutes, Rolf was climbing onto the end of the dock. He smiled and held out his hand. "Good morning, Peter. I see you two arrived safely." He moved past Peter and up the dock to embrace Anna who had come down to meet him.

Peter stood awkwardly for a moment watching Anna and Rolf. He felt even more awkward when he caught Anna's eye over Rolf's shoulder. He thought he saw a fleeting look of confusion in her face, or perhaps hoped he did. Peter turned and walked down to the end of the dock where the outboard was tied up and tried to look interested in the details of its construction.

After Rolf and Anna had gone to the main house, Peter walked back up hoping to catch his father for a continuation of their previous evening's conversation. He found his father reading on the terrace. Rolf and Anna were in the living room with Bjorn. Their conversation in Swedish was animated and sounded argumentative. Anna seemed to be asking questions. Rolf was responding in a firm and calm tone. Bjorn's interjections seemed to be directed at Anna and carried a slightly plaintive tone. After a minute or two of additional discussion, Peter saw through the large picture window that Bjorn and Rolf were going into Bjorn's office leaving Anna who turned and strode into the kitchen.

A moment later, Anna emerged on the terrace, her expression set in a defiant smile. "Okay, boys, shall we go for a sail then?" Anna explained to Peter and Eric that Rolf needed an hour with Bjorn to discuss some business. Her attempt at good-humored resignation was not entirely successful. When Peter offered a word of sympathy, she responded sarcastically, "Oh, but this never happens!"

Chapter 32

PETER WALKED DOWN TO the sailboat dock and arrived before his father and Anna. He used the time to admire the Svenssons' yachts. Anna's boat, like her father's, was a Swedish-made Hallberg-Rassy. Peter knew the make by reputation, but had never seen one up close. He had heard that they were designed for comfort but without a loss of performance. His brief inspection of the cockpits seemed to confirm the former. He envied his father's sail down the coast from Sundsvall in Bjorn's 62. Eric had told Peter that his only complaint about the boat was what Hallberg-Rassy called "push-button" sailing. Despite its size, its multiple large sails could all be easily raised and adjusted by electric winches controlled from the cockpit. Eric enjoyed being a hands-on sailor. He delighted in crawling out on the deck in a stiff breeze to free a snagged jib line. When he was not at the wheel of Bjorn's boat, he said, there was really nothing to do.

Anna's thirty-four-foot boat, the *Sjöflicka*, looked like a smaller version Bjorn's. It had a large, deep cockpit, well protected for sailing in off-season weather. The teak decking and seats were features of an expensive boat.

After a few minutes, Peter looked up and saw Anna and his father coming down toward the cove dock. At that distance, their conversation seemed somewhat serious. He wondered if he would be able to hold his father's attention long enough that afternoon to get the "whole story." It was pretty damned annoying to be the last to know what was going on.

When they were all assembled on the dock, Anna went onboard and started the engine of the *Sjöflicka*. Peter put aside his irritation and helped Eric cast off the mooring lines. Anna reversed the boat out into the cove. She maneuvered carefully around Rolf's seaplane but with an expression that seemed to say she wouldn't be unhappy if she knocked a wing off. When they were out of the cove in open water, she turned the boat into the wind and Peter and Eric raised the sails. Anna bore off to the northwest, letting the prevailing southwest breeze fill the sails. Soon, they were heeled over and making good way across the mile or so of open water between Smavik and a neighboring island to the west. She called out to Peter to ease the main sail slightly and to Eric to trim the jib accordingly. They responded with nautical "Aye, ayes."

Eric perched on the windward edge of the cockpit watching the sails for any need of further adjustments. Peter sat opposite him, his legs stretched out across the cockpit, watching Anna at the wheel through half-closed eyes. Being at the helm of her boat seemed to erase Anna's irritation at Rolf. The tension he had seen in her body at the house had disappeared. The sail also eased Peter's vexation. He was enjoying just being on the water and watching Anna at the wheel confidently handling the boat, as the shore of Smavik quickly receded. Even behind her sunglasses and the shade of her visor, the attractive lines of her face were evident. She wore a blue bikini top under an open blouse that billowed behind her. Below her narrow waist, a short wraparound skirt also responded to the wind, occasionally revealing the top of her long legs.

When he glanced away, he saw that his father had been watching him watching Anna. Peter gave a sheepish half smile that his father returned with a grin and a slight lift of his eyebrows. Perhaps his father was glad that his son was showing more than casual interest in a woman again. He knew his father had been fond of Michelle but concerned that Peter had not seemed to be able to make peace with her loss. Well, he's probably right, Peter thought, and here was more proof, falling in love with his aunt.

They sailed over close to the opposite shore where Anna executed a careful jibing turn and headed northeast on a quiet run before the wind. She offered the helm to Eric and Peter. They took turns at the wheel and sailed around several small islands north of Smavik. Peter followed their course on a chart he had found in the cabin.

Eventually, Anna suggested they set a course toward Grenvik, as it was approaching noon. They headed back south, tacking into the wind. With Anna at the wheel, they threaded their way back through several island passages. As they approached the eastern shore of Grenvik, Anna pointed to an inlet ahead to their right. Peter and Eric let down the sails, and Anna motored toward it.

Near the mouth of the inlet, a large performance powerboat was anchored. It was the sort of watercraft that Eric disparagingly called a "muscleboat." It was red with black detailing and the name *AkvaVitt* stenciled in angular letters on the stern. It seemed out of place in waters that mostly accommodated boats of a more traditional design. The *AkvaVitt* was moored in the typical fashion of the archipelago: a bowline was tied to a tree with another line off the stern to an anchor. Peter started to ask Anna what the name meant, but she was busy guiding the *Sjöflicka* around the *AkvaVitt's* stern line, which stretched more than halfway out into the relatively narrow channel. Not a great place to leave your boat, Peter thought.

Beyond the power cruiser at the far end of the inlet, several sailboats were tied up at a dock. The Svenssons' cabin cruiser, which had brought Bjorn and Rolf over was tied up on the far side of the dock. On the near side, three sailboats, all somewhat larger than Anna's boat, were rafted together. Anna brought her boat alongside, and Peter and Eric tied it to the outermost boat, extending the raft. They clambered carefully over the other boats and made their way onto the dock.

The section of the dock that reached into the channel was joined to a longer, wider section built along the shore. A long table had been set up there for lunch. Several families were already in the midst of eating and drinking and lively conversations. Behind them, a flagstone path led up a short slope from the dock to a large version of the red vacation cabins found on the islands. Early summer flowers, grass, and small boulders shared the informal front yard. To the left of the house was a

8888888

pasture, separated from the house by a fence that ran down to the water near the dock. A black-and-white cow stood chewing and observing the festivities from behind the fence. Peter smiled inwardly at what seemed like the studied Swedish casualness of a lunch party with a cow on one side of the dock and a clutch of several very expensive yachts on the other.

Anna, Peter, and Eric joined about fifteen adults and children at the table. Bjorn and Rolf stood to greet them. Anna made a general introduction to their hosts, the Karlssons, and the other guests, calling Eric and Peter "our long-lost American cousins." Their Swedish friends laughed and called out informal hellos. Eric and Peter waved and sat down. Anna exchanged hugs and kisses with several women and men before sitting down next to Rolf with a fixed smile on her face. Bjorn pointed out a selection of herring dishes in various marinades, smoked salmon, cheeses, and, inevitably, small boiled potatoes and dill. He then renewed his conversation with a man about his age, sitting to his left.

Lunch was very informal with the participants getting up to bring more food onto the table and changing seats to speak to different people. Bjorn included Eric in his conversation with his older friend. Peter and Anna talked about sailing. Rolf offered an occasional comment, but he seemed satisfied to let others carry the conversation.

When Peter went to get coffee and some dessert at a separate table, a professorial-looking man in his forties with a neat beard introduced himself. "I am Goran Lindskog. Are you the Peter Frost who has written about the neo-Nazis in Sweden?" Pleasantly surprised, Peter confirmed that he was and shook hands with him.

"I am interested because I teach political science at the university in Lund. I have written some articles, more academic than yours, I should say, on the movement. I very much enjoyed your article."

"Thank you. It would be good to have a chance to talk," Peter responded.

"Well, I don't want to take you away from the Svenssons now, but perhaps later in the day?"

"We can try. Maybe sometime after the maypole dancing," Peter said, thinking there might be an opportunity after the time that he was anxious to spend with his father, so they could continue their conversation of the previous night.

After lunch was over, Bjorn excused himself and said he would ask Lars to take him back to Smavik. Peter saw Anna look at Rolf as though she expected he might leave with Bjorn. But he said nothing. Anna took Rolf's arm, and with Eric and Peter and other members of the lunch party, left the dock to walk to the field where the maypole was being set up.

The narrow dirt road passed several other summerhouses of various sizes in the rocky, wooded terrain. The area looked very much like the coast of Maine around Elena's house. After about a half a mile, the road came to a large field on the far shore of the island. The field sloped gently away from the road. In its center, the maypole had been erected, and a large area around it had been left open. Around the edges, people had spread blankets on the ground and were finishing up picnic lunches. In between the blankets and drink coolers, children chased each other in happy anticipation of the games and dancing. Rolf laid out a large blanket. Eric and Peter set down a cooler that Lars had produced from the cabin cruiser before departing with Bjorn.

In the center of the field, several men and two women were working on the maypole. They were securing it against the breeze off the water that rocked it back and forth. It was a tall pole wrapped in garlands of green leaves. About fifteen feet from the ground was a long crosspiece that was also wrapped in leaves. At each end of the crosspiece, two circular garlands hung down. Above the crosspiece, the pole continued another six or seven feet and was topped with a small Swedish flag.

When the maypole was secured, one of the women in a peasant dress returned with an accordion and began to play. A man also in a traditional costume began calling the dancers to the center of the field. Children and adults gathered in a loose circle around the maypole and the dance leaders.

"So now you will learn some Swedish folk dancing," said Anna grabbing Peter's and Eric's hands and pulling them up.

"Rolf, you coming?" Peter called. Rolf shook his head and leaned back with his hands behind his head on the blanket.

"No, Rolf doesn't dance. But I forgive him," Anna said. Rolf smiled appreciatively. Peter thought perhaps Rolf had managed to make amends for not sailing with Anna that morning.

Dancing between Peter and Eric, Anna did her best to translate the caller's instructions on the steps and names of the dances and games. In one game, the dancers pretended to be various animals, turning and crouching and making antlers with their hands or bleating like sheep while circling the *Majstang*.

After several sets of dances, they sat down for a respite with beer from the cooler and watched others dance for a while. Anna sat next to Rolf. He seemed to have little to say when he was outside of his professional environment. Anna told Peter and Eric about the origin of the Midsummer celebration as a fertility rite. Even when Rolf excused himself to take a call on his mobile phone, she avoided any reference to the previous evening's discussion. Since dinner, Peter had hardly exchanged a word with her directly. This, after spending nearly two days almost constantly alone with her, he thought.

Just as Anna had gotten up to urge Peter and Eric to rejoin the dancing, she reached for her waistband. Until then, Peter hadn't noticed the small black pager there. She pulled it off and studied it for a moment.

"Oh no," she said. "I hope this is not an emergency consult for me." She sighed. "Well, perhaps I can do it by telephone. Rolf, can I have your mobile?"

Rolf handed her his cell phone. Anna walked up to the road. Peter watched as she made the call. He guessed by the way her posture changed after several moments that she was going to leave. By the time she returned, her professional persona had taken over. She explained that she was very sorry but that she would have to go to Lulea, about six hundred miles away in the north of Sweden for the case. She said there was a very sick child, who might need treatment in Stockholm. Her expression was neutral, but she had lost the animation in her voice and movements after receiving the page.

If Rolf was very disappointed about losing Anna for the weekend, he didn't say anything. Peter thought to himself that at least Rolf didn't tell Anna that she had now evened the score for that morning. Rolf said simply, "I will sail back with you to Smavik, and we will call a water taxi to take you back to Stockholm. I assume you can get a flight up to Lulea tonight or early tomorrow."

"Thank you, Rolf. My turn to let business interfere with pleasure. Peter, Eric, I am so sorry to have to leave. I will try to join you at the lodge in Lofsdalen, perhaps on Tuesday."

Eric gave Anna a hug and reassured her that they understood her responsibilities. Anna hugged Peter, and as she drew away, she looked directly into his eyes. Her smile was fixed, but he felt, or thought he felt, her give his arm an extra squeeze. However, Peter also sensed in her a hint of relief at leaving them. He wondered if he would see her again.

Rolf said that Lars could come back for Peter and Eric later, assuming they wished to stay. They said they would. After Rolf and Anna had left at a fast walk back up the road to the dock where they had eaten lunch, Peter reminded his father about the call to Bill Reilly.

"Oh yes. The public telephone is right nearby at the ferryboat landing on this side of the island. I'll do it now," Eric said.

They left the field and started down the road toward the ferry dock.

"So now we get to spend the weekend with Rolf but not Anna. That's a bummer," Peter said.

"It doesn't sound like you think much of him."

"That's about right. And I wonder what Anna sees in him," Peter responded.

"Do I detect a little rivalry here?"

"Dad, come on. Anna is my aunt. Right?"

"Wrong, actually," Eric replied.

Chapter 33

PETER TURNED BACK TO look at his father, wondering if he was kidding. "Wrong? Really, Dad? Is she adopted too? If that's true, she doesn't know it."

"No, I don't believe she was adopted. But that's not the point," Eric said standing up. "First, let me make this call to Bill Reilly, and then I'll explain. You need to understand the part of the story that we didn't get to last night."

Peter wondered if his father realized that his combination of short communications, cryptic hints, and methodical narrative style were so frustrating. So he and Anna were not related? Did she know too? Had she already known? He resigned himself again to waiting until his father had called Reilly.

"Sure, Dad, whenever you're ready," Peter said, making no attempt to hide the sarcasm in his voice. His father appeared not to notice.

They left the field and walked down the road. In a short distance, they came to a small settlement on the water. A sign on the porch of one of the houses announced it was *Bageri* and below, in English, pastries and sandwiches. Several outdoor tables and chairs were set up on the lawn. Further on, there was an island-sized supermarket, and beyond it, the road led down to a sturdy cement pier. To the right of the pier, a restaurant overlooked the water. A public telephone in a clear plastic half-shell was mounted on the side of the building.

Peter left Eric with Bill Reilly's cell phone number and wandered down to the pier. It was deserted; everyone seemed to be at the maypole dancing. Several small motorboats were tied up along one side. A wooden dock running along the shore to the left of the pier hosted a number of cruising sailboats about the same size as Anna's. Beyond this dock, an even larger number of boats, both sail and motor, were tied up archipelago-island style along the shore. He assumed most of the boats had brought visitors from other islands for the maypole celebrations.

Peter was watching two boats offshore whose occupants had apparently opted for sailing over dancing, when he heard his father's footsteps behind him.

"Peter, you didn't tell me that Bill thinks Jed may have committed suicide."

"Sorry. He asked me not to go into detail until he had a chance to talk to you himself."

"Okay. Anyway, he asked if Jed mentioned anything that would make me think he was depressed or troubled. How did he seem the last time I talked to him? Also, he wasn't very happy that I took so long to get back to him."

Peter remembered his conversation with Bill the day before. "Right. And I guess they still haven't found anything?"

"No, Bill just said they were continuing to follow up some leads. I didn't press him. But I wonder about Jed committing suicide," Eric said as they walked out on the pier.

"Don't you think it's possible? People sometimes keep stuff pretty well hidden," Peter said.

"Well, I suppose, but I told Bill I didn't think it was likely. When I saw Jed before I left, he seemed fine. Bill asked me about the conversation that Jed and I had on Tuesday before I left. I told him that Jed was upset with me. It wasn't about him."

Peter was reminded of the envelope his father had sent to Jed. "When I was at the house, I noticed a list you made. There was something about sending an envelope to Jed." Peter decided not to get into how he had discovered its contents.

"That's right, but I'll get into that in a minute," Eric replied.

Peter turned away from his father and made a here-we-go-again face to himself. "Monday was the day when you met with Bjorn at the house in Brewster, right?" he said hoping to move his father along.

"Yes. So, I guess you know about the meeting."

"Elena told me about it," Peter said.

"Also, Bill Reilly wanted to know if I knew anything about Jed's meeting on Nantucket on Wednesday, which I didn't," Eric said.

"So about your meeting with Bjorn in Brewster, how come he flew over to see you? Why didn't he just wait until you got to Sweden?" Peter asked.

"Well, that's part of the story. But let me give you the background; it's quite interesting."

Peter sighed quietly. He hoped there wouldn't be too much background. When they reached the end of the pier, Eric sat down and leaned back against a piling. Peter sat cross-legged facing him.

"Last fall, after you came home from Sweden and told me about your trip, I got to thinking that it would be interesting to find out more about my Swedish father. Actually meet him, if he was still alive. So, as I told you last night, I went up to visit Elena and asked her to tell me more about him. Did she know how I could get in touch with him? She suggested that might be difficult. He might not still be alive, and if he were, he might not be pleased to have his illegitimate son show up.

"I told her I'd take that chance. I thought Elena was trying to discourage me from looking up Bjorn, perhaps because of how she felt about him. She told me that she had written to Bjorn during the war and had heard nothing back and then finally heard that he was married. So she had been effectively abandoned by him."

"That's what she told me, which makes Bjorn a real bastard," Peter said.

"Well, wait," Eric said. "There's more." Peter sighed again, audibly this time.

"Finally, after I went up to Maine a second time, I told her I was really curious and it wasn't right of her to hold back information about my real father, and she agreed. She said she did have an address. She told me she would write to him, and she also gave me his address.

"I found out that my father, Bjorn Svensson, had inherited a company that made hunting rifles, Gevarfabrik AB, in Sundsvall, Sweden. She said that she had corresponded with him a few times in the sixty years since they had last seen each other. She didn't elaborate on these contacts, and I didn't pursue it. I was just grateful to have the information."

That was all pretty different from the story that Bjorn had told them at dinner the night before. It even differed somewhat from what Elena had told him, Peter thought.

Eric continued, "But despite Elena's misgivings about having me contact Bjorn, she did seem willing to talk more about their days together in Germany. She told me she had wonderful memories of Bjorn, and if things had worked out, she would've been very happy to move to Sweden to be with him. We talked a lot that evening about Bjorn. Apparently, he had been very idealistic and was very concerned about Nazism."

"I guess he must have lost his idealism when he found out that he was the CEO of a gun factory," Peter commented. "According to Rolf, soon after he took over, they started making rifles for the military, and, I assume, selling them to the Germans."

Eric ignored Peter's comments and went on, "She told me that she didn't have any pictures of Bjorn, but that she did have an old recording the three friends had made in Germany."

"Right." Peter sat up and looked at his father. "Elena told me about that. She said she gave it to you, figuring if anybody could find a way to play it back, you could." Peter decided not to tell his father about his snooping around the house or ask why his lab in Brewster had been left unlocked. That would only delay the narrative while he explained what he had found.

Eric sat forward, smiling. "It was a very interesting project." He explained how he had managed to locate an antique wire recorder and put it in working order. "The quality of the recording was pretty poor, about like listening to an old 78-rpm record over a bad telephone line. The range of frequencies was restricted and distorted where the wire had stretched in places."

Peter wondered what this had to do with the rest of the story. Was it just interesting, or was it a piece of the puzzle his father seemed to be tediously fitting together for him?

"And of course they were speaking in Swedish, mostly," Eric said. "There were a few English words here and there and maybe some German. I didn't know what they were saying, but it was really exciting to think that I was listening to these voices out of the past. I could hear the voice of Elena, my mother, as a young woman. Even with her speaking Swedish, I thought it sounded like her. And I was thrilled to think I could hear my real father's voice."

"Sure, that's cool," Peter said, trying to share some of his father's enthusiasm.

"But I wanted know which voice was my father's. So I digitized the recording and copied it onto a CD. I asked around and found somebody who could transcribe the Swedish and translate it for me. I figured if I could understand what they were saying, I could determine which one of the men was Bjorn and which was Kjell from what they were saying."

"And?" said Peter.

"And I did. I found a librarian right in Brewster who had grown up in Sweden. She was happy to do it and wouldn't let me pay her. It turns out they weren't saying anything very interesting. You know how people are when you turn on a recorder. There was a lot of 'Elena, say something' and then remarks like 'That didn't sound like me' after they had played it back and started recording again. They recited some poetry. But finally, I guess, they sort of forgot it was on and started talking more naturally and casually. They talked about where Kjell had found the wire recorder. Apparently, he was into buying and selling antiques and paintings and sometimes radios and things."

"That's great. But when did you contact Bjorn?" Peter asked trying to move the conversation ahead.

"Actually, he contacted me first. Elena had given him my address. He wrote a polite, sort of formal letter saying if I ever came to Sweden to please contact him and we could meet. He didn't acknowledge that he was my father. He said something like, 'I would be happy to meet with the son of my old friend Elena.'"

"So he wasn't admitting to anything at that point?"

"Right. That was in February this year. When I decided in March to make the trip over here, I wrote to him and said I was planning to come over for Midsummer. I didn't hear back for over a month, and I figured he was going to blow me off, but then he called. I wasn't home, so he left a message on my answering machine, apologizing for not getting back to me. He invited me to stay with him in Sundsvall when I came."

"But he didn't tell you he was going to fly over in the company jet and pick you up?"

"No. I don't think he knew then he was going to. That was a decision he made later." Eric was speaking rapidly; his eyes were focused intently on Peter. "But let me tell you what I discovered."

Peter felt like a straight man in some old comedy routine. "What did you discover, Dad?"

"I'll tell you. Remember, I said that Elena's voice on the old wire recording sounded like the Elena, only younger. So I got to thinking it would be interesting to do some voice identification analysis on Elena and Bjorn, which I have all the software for. I had a message on my machine that Elena had left me a week before, and I also had Bjorn's message."

Peter stretched out full-length on the pier with his eyes closed sensing a long technical discussion was in the offing. One of his father's areas of expertise was forensic voice identification. "Okay, Dad, so I bet you fed all this information into your computers and analyzed the voices."

"That's right. Now ideally when you're trying to match recorded voice samples, the words and the language should be the same in both. Also, the samples should be good quality, with low noise and no tonal distortion. And, of course, you wouldn't expect that the person you're trying to identify would have aged significantly between the time that the samples were recorded," Eric said, gesturing with his hands to his audience of one, his voice rising. "So those were the challenges."

"Right," said Peter opening his eyes and squinting at a seagull that looped over the pier.

"I'll spare you the gory details of the voice analysis, but I really got into it. Even had some of the guys at my old company involved. It took us about a month to make sure we had it right. The bottom line was that Elena's voice matched up very well, taking into account the aging of her vocal tract. But ..."

Suddenly, Peter realized where this was going and sat up facing his father. "But?"

"But the Bjorn voice on the wire recording, which I could figure out from the transcripts, was not at all the Bjorn voice on my telephone answering machine," Eric said. "It was—"

Peter interrupted. "Kjell? Far out! And you're sure?" Peter said automatically, but he knew his father, ever the cautious engineer, would have added some condition if he were not certain. "But Bjorn ... or at least whoever we had dinner with last night said that Kjell was killed in the Second World War. And so did Elena."

"That's right. That's what they said." Eric emphasized the point with his hands held up in front of him as if to ward off any doubt. "Until I did the voice analysis, that's what I thought too. But after I ran all the data and checked my numbers, I convinced myself that I had it right: Kjell's voice on the wire recorder was Bjorn's on the answering machine. Then I called Elena."

"What did she say?" Peter asked.

"She just said I must be mistaken. She said it wasn't possible. But somehow, she didn't sound very convincing. And she sounded upset. She wanted to know if I was still going to go to Sweden to see Bjorn. I told her I was."

"Did you call Bjorn and ask him about it?" Peter asked.

"No, not then. I decided that I'd wait until I got to Sweden and sort it out when I saw him there."

"So the reason that Anna is not my aunt," Peter said, trying to cut to the chase, "is because this guy Bjorn is her father, but not yours. And—"

"Yes, but hold on. Let me finish." Eric stood up and stretched his back. "About three weeks ago, Bjorn called from Sweden and said he was coming to the United States on business.

Could we meet? I was surprised, but I said sure, if he wanted to. I told him I was still planning to go to Sweden. Then when I called Elena back to tell her that Bjorn was coming over, she said she probably knew the reason why."

Eric paused, and Peter jumped in, playing the straight man again. "Which was?"

Eric responded, "She told me that she had written and told Bjorn that I had found out that he was actually Kjell. But she said that he would have to explain it to me himself."

Peter's mind flew away from his father's narrative and back to his evening with Anna. Had some mysterious mutual intuition about their actual relationship been at work?

Peter and Eric were both quiet for a moment. A breeze brought a gust of music from the maypole field and rippled the blue and yellow Swedish flag at the head of the pier.

"Elena wouldn't talk about it," Eric went on, "But when I told Jed what I'd found out, he said he had always suspected that Bjorn and Kjell had changed places. When I asked him why he thought so, he just said he'd done a little research on his own."

Peter nodded. It was pretty likely that research was what Jed had been doing in 1970 on his trip to Sundsvall. "But then Bjorn, or really Kjell, came to Brewster last week," Peter said.

"Yes. He called from the Barnstable Airport a week ago last Sunday," Eric continued. "We met at a restaurant in Hyannis that evening. Rolf was there and also Lars, who was their driver. Bjorn and Rolf and I had dinner—I'm going to refer to him as 'Bjorn' since he's been Bjorn for sixty-odd years. The dinner was a little formal and awkward. Bjorn introduced me, as the son of an old friend, to Rolf. But I had the impression that Rolf knew more about me than that."

Peter was on his feet walking back and forth in front of his father trying to guess what was ahead. Something his father had just said bothered him, but he couldn't quite bring it into focus. And in addition, he was having trouble keeping Anna out of his mind.

Eric explained that the conversation at dinner was mostly an exchange of biographies. "Bjorn told me about his life from the time he returned to Sweden in 1939, his two marriages, his daughter Anna, and the growth of Gevarfabrik under his management. I told him about growing up thinking that the Frosts were my real parents, and said that I had found out, only as an adult, that I was adopted. Bjorn asked me about my work. I told him about what I did in audio engineering and forensic sound analysis. He wanted to know about voice identification. He didn't ask me directly about how I had found out about his being Kjell, but I guess that Elena had told him. After dinner, Bjorn asked me if we could walk together along the waterfront and asked Rolf to excuse us."

"Speaking of talking a walk, Dad," Peter said, putting one of his legs up on an empty grocery crate to stretch it.

"Hold on. I'm getting to how Kjell ended up as Bjorn. We found a bench overlooking the harbor. I told him that I was just happy to meet him, and that my interest was finding about my biological parents and how I came to be adopted. Bjorn sat for a while without saying anything and then, without looking at me, he said, 'Eric, as you have discovered, you are the son of Bjorn Svensson, but not my son. Your father died in Germany in 1941. In 1939, I was Kjell Hendrikson.'"

"So he admitted then that he wasn't really Bjorn Svensson," Peter said. "Kind of a confession to you."

"I suppose so," Eric replied. "Bjorn said that when the telegram arrived in Hamburg, announcing the sudden death of my grandfather, Erik Svensson, and requesting that Bjorn, the real Bjorn, return to Sweden, he was very distressed. It was not only because of the death of his father, but also at the prospect of returning to run Gevarfabrik, in which he had no interest."

Peter stopped pacing. "So they changed places." He looked down at his father who had seated himself again with his back to the piling. "Amazing! And it was Bjorn, not Kjell, who went to England to train for the resistance and got killed in Germany. That makes sense since Elena said he was the one who was so anti-Nazi."

"That's right. I called Elena after my meeting with Bjorn. We had a long conversation, and she filled in some details. She told me that it was when she found out that Bjorn, my real father, had been killed that she decided to ask the Frosts to adopt me."

"But how could Kjell and Bjorn make the switch work?" Peter asked.

"I guess, they looked enough alike physically," Eric said. "Bjorn told me even their landlady couldn't tell them apart."

"Okay ... and because Kjell had grown up in the Svensson household—like we heard last night—he probably knew a lot about the family."

"Also," Eric said, "Elena told me that Kjell was very entrepreneurial and seemed to have an instinct for making money. It was my father, the real Bjorn, who proposed the switch. Elena, Bjorn, and Kjell all discussed it and made a pact of secrecy.

"I'm not really sure why Elena didn't tell me the truth at first. I think, in a way, it was habit. She said it started with their agreement in Germany, which was very important then because Bjorn was in the resistance."

"And, I guess, eventually, it was a way for her to keep the sadness secret too after Bjorn was killed," Peter said.

Eric nodded. "Yes, I think you're right." He paused and then continued, "While we were sailing this week, Bjorn, Kjell-Bjorn, that is, told me they had imagined that the switch could somehow be a temporary thing. Someday, the war would be over, the real Bjorn would return to Sweden, and Elena would join him. Then they would find a way to resolve the exchange of identities. He admitted that it was probably a youthful fantasy."

"So what was all that about Kjell in the story that we heard from the so-called Bjorn last night at dinner?" Peter asked.

Eric stood up and flexed his back again. "On the boat this week, Bjorn prepared me for that. He said he wanted Anna to understand where he was coming from. I think he was planning to tell her the truth last night after we left them."

"I guess he was trying to justify himself, that is Kjell, in her eyes." Peter said. "It must have been a shock when he told her the rest of the story." That might explain why she seemed so distant this morning, he thought. "So we aren't really related to Bjorn or Anna because Bjorn is Kjell, not your father and not my grandfather. That kind of changes this whole movie, Dad. For both of us."

Chapter 34

PETER AND ERIC WALKED back to the field where the organized dancing had ended. Some children were still running around the maypole. The caller and the accordion lady with the instrument beside her were sitting down. They were drinking beer and bantering with people on surrounding blankets. Eric said he was ready to head back to Smavik and hoped Lars had returned for them.

Peter had more questions for his father, but it was time to take a break. He also wanted to think about Anna. What would he say to her? And was it a coincidence that she had been called away just after he and she found out about their real relationship or the absence of it? Had she somehow arranged it to avoid … avoid what?

Peter told his father that he wanted to stay on for a while and talk to Goran Lundskog, whom he had met at lunch. At least some discussion with a Swedish political science professor would qualify as a contribution to his assignment that had taken a distinct second place to his Swedish family connection in the last few days. Peter spotted Goran and went across the field to tell him that he would be back in a little while if he could make arrangements to get back to Smavik later in the evening.

Peter and Eric gathered up the blanket and cooler. The earlier breeze had disappeared, and it was quite hot away from the water. Peter and his father shared a beer as they walked back up the road carrying the cooler between them.

"Anna mentioned to me that her father had raised the issue of some kind of an agreement with you. I guess that's what he meant last night about finding a way to protect her."

"Yes, that was the next thing he brought up that night when we first met. He said we needed to come to an understanding. What was done was done; he had been Bjorn for most of his life. Whether it was right or not originally, it was now a fact. He explained that it would be very disruptive and hurtful, particularly for Anna, to have it all come out in public; the only people who knew were Elena, himself, and now me. Bjorn said that he only wanted to protect Anna. He wanted me to agree to a financial settlement and sign a document that would bind us to secrecy. Otherwise, he said, there could be years of fighting in the courts, and eventually, everyone would lose.

"I told Bjorn I wasn't interested in money. I was just interested in who my real father was. So why had I gone to all the trouble to compare the voice recordings? he wanted to know. I explained that it was just personal curiosity," Eric said.

"And professional. Right?"

"Well, sure ..." Eric looked slightly sheepish.

Peter grinned. "He probably thought you were going to blackmail him."

"He didn't say that exactly, but he certainly seemed suspicious. I told him I didn't feel entitled to any money and I thought Elena felt that way too. But I don't think he believed me. Bjorn insisted that we should agree in writing. I told him I guessed I would have to talk to a lawyer if I was going to sign something like that. So we agreed to meet the next afternoon at the house in Brewster.

"Maureen Darby was out of town, so I called Jed and filled him in on my conversation with Bjorn the evening before. Since he knew the story of the switch and my adoption, I thought he would be curious to meet Bjorn."

If he hadn't already, Peter thought.

"Jed said that he saw 'some issues' and agreed to come to the meeting. I did have some misgivings about asking him because Jed is such a nitpicker. I was afraid he wouldn't be satisfied with a two-line agreement saying I made no claims and I would keep everything secret."

"So what happened at the meeting?"

"There was some polite conversation about Sweden and Gevarfabrik. Bjorn asked Jed a lot of questions about his legal experience and if he was a member of the family. He seemed to think he had met Jed before. Jed said that was unlikely because his work in Sweden had involved minerals companies not arms manufacturers.

"Eventually, we got down to business, and Bjorn explained his view of the situation. Then Rolf produced a short document they said they would like to get my signature on."

"And Jed said he wanted to generate a thirty-page agreement to cover all contingencies?" Peter asked.

"No, actually Jed said his counsel to me would be not to sign anything at this point. He said that any agreement by me to be a party to the Kjell-Bjorn switch might be considered fraud. Jed didn't see any way to resolve the situation short of public admission by Bjorn and a good-faith effort by him or the courts in Sweden to find any rightful heirs and turn the assets of Gevarfabrik over to them. An alternative, he suggested, would be for Bjorn to provide some proof that my father had actually signed over his inheritance of Gevarfabrik to Kjell."

"Because if the real Bjorn hadn't done that, you as his child would inherit Gevarfabrik," Peter said.

"Yes. I guess that's what Jed had in mind. He even suggested that my father might have written something to Elena before he was killed confirming that I was his son and heir. Actually, I found out when I got here that I would be the only heir because the real Bjorn was an only child." Eric stopped and put down the chest. "Split another beer?"

As they resumed their walk back to the house on the inlet where they had arrived earlier, Eric continued, "When Jed explained his reasoning to Bjorn and Rolf, Bjorn seemed shocked. He told Jed that this was a family matter, that it was part of a completely voluntary agreement he had made with a friend in 1939 with Elena as a witness. Rolf suggested that even if there was anything wrong, the time had long passed for any action to be taken against Bjorn. That seemed reasonable to me, but Jed wasn't buying any of it. He said he didn't know how the Swedish courts would look at it. If I signed off on the switch, I could be liable for being part of a conspiracy with Bjorn to defraud other heirs and cover up a theft of identity. Jed seemed a little frustrated with my attitude, I'm afraid."

So Jed had been "the skunk at the lawn party," Peter thought, who prevented a quick agreement with his father. Of course it wasn't really a "family matter." As his father had just explained, they were not related to these "Svenssons."

"Anyway, things got patched up before Jed left," Eric went on. "Bjorn said he would have his Swedish lawyer get in touch with Jed through the corporate counsel for the U.S. subsidiary of Gevarfabrik, which is not far from the Cape in Middleboro. He hoped that together, they could work something out. Then Bjorn started talking to him about their boats and sailing in Sweden. And they found some common ground ... or water, as it were."

And then Jed disappears. A lucky break for Bjorn or something else? Peter wondered.

"After Jed left, I told Bjorn that I thought Jed was being a little extreme. I felt a little embarrassed for Bjorn. I told him I'd talk to my regular lawyer and see what she thought. See if we couldn't work something out. Bjorn seemed relieved. We talked a little about my trip to Sweden. Rolf suggested that it was too bad I was flying over on a commercial flight when I could go back with them the next day. Bjorn agreed and insisted that I join them. He said they could fly me home, too. And I could get credit for my ticket for another trip somewhere else.

"He said we could talk on the plane and would have time in Sweden to think about an agreement that would satisfy my American lawyer. That seemed reasonable. And I thought the idea of flying over to Europe in a private jet sounded pretty neat. So I packed up and took off in kind of a hurry the next morning, as you know. Rolf picked me up at the house Tuesday morning, and we met Bjorn at the plane.

I called Jed at his office from the airport and told him I was leaving for Sweden with Bjorn and Rolf, which led to our argument. I also left a message for Mrs. Knight about the cats, but I know she has trouble figuring out how to get her voice mail. So I'm glad you checked out things at the house."

There seemed to be more to Jed's involvement than his father was telling him. "Why did you send Jed the transcript of the recording?"

"After the meeting, he called me and said that there could be something in it that would be relevant to the agreement that Bjorn wanted to me to sign."

"Was there?" Peter asked.

"I didn't think so, but Jed insisted."

But it was the proof, along with the recording, that Bjorn wasn't Bjorn, he was Kjell, Peter thought. "So where do things stand now on the agreement?"

"Bjorn and I talked last weekend in Sundsvall and then on the boat. Rolf was also involved and interfaced with the company's law firm to come up with an agreement and look into the legal issues. I think one of their lawyers will be at the lodge in Lofsdalen next week to explain the agreement, which we'll send to Maureen Darby to get her input on. I know Bjorn is pretty anxious to get this settled."

Peter moved them over to the side of the road and put down the cooler. "Dad, you know, I think Jed's right. You shouldn't sign anything until you get information about Swedish laws and whether the switch between Bjorn and Kjell was legal. You need to get some advice from a Swedish lawyer."

Eric took a final gulp of his beer and put the empty bottle back in the chest. "Peter, look, I appreciate your input, but I do think this is really a family kind of thing and not that big a deal. We don't want to create a problem for Anna. Besides, I sure don't want to inherit a gun factory. Do you?"

Peter felt his frustration at his father's casual attitude building. "At least let's you and me go back to Stockholm on Monday and talk to an attorney there. Maybe even have our own lawyer in Lofsdalen."

"Look, you've met Bjorn and Anna. They're reasonable people. I think you're being like Jed, finding issues here where there really aren't any. And I told you, I won't sign anything until

Maureen Darby looks at it." Eric spoke the last sentence slightly more slowly than normal, which Peter recognized as a sure sign in his father of contained irritation.

"I hear you, Dad. But you don't mind if I find a lawyer in Stockholm on Monday?" Eric looked at Peter, blew out a breath, picked up one side of the cooler, and waited for Peter to pick up his side.

They reached the Karlssons' house on the inlet and walked down toward the dock. The cow had retreated to the middle of the field and ignored them. Two sailboats were still tied up at the dock, but Lars and the cabin cruiser were not there. As they were discussing what to do, one of the families they had been introduced to at lunch emerged from the Karlssons' house. They were just saying good-bye to their lunch hosts.

Eric asked if he could use the telephone to call Lars in Smavik. Mrs. Karlsson told him that Lars had been back and left an outboard motorboat for them with a chart to show the way back to Smavik. "It's not far and quite easy, really," she said.

Peter said that he could take his father back and return to Grenvik in the outboard. When the departing family overheard their conversation, they offered to take Eric back to Smavik, insisting it was not out of their way.

"And we'll talk about all this tomorrow, Peter," Eric said, stepping aboard the sailboat.

Chapter 35

PETER CHECKED THE OUTBOARD. It was a small aluminum whaler with a good-sized motor. A chart with the course marked on it was under a seat cushion.

As he walked up to the road that led to the field to meet Goran, Peter tried to sort out the thoughts that were tumbling around in his head. Anna kept coming up on top. Why did she have to get called away? Why couldn't it have been Rolf who had an emergency at Gevarfabrik? Would she go to Lofsdalen after she returned from her emergency call? Maybe he could get there on Tuesday after his meeting with Anders on Monday.

Did his father fully appreciate how anxious Bjorn, and probably Rolf, were about concluding an agreement to maintain the secret of the Bjorn-Kjell switch? Before Bjorn knew that his father had discovered the truth, Bjorn had been politely dismissive of his father's efforts to meet him. When he found out, he had jumped into his corporate jet and gone to the U.S. Then, Bjorn had flown his father back to Sweden and entertained him nonstop, going on two weeks. Bjorn clearly wanted to get his father to sign the agreement before he went back to the U.S. But how far would Bjorn and Rolf go to make sure that he did?

Peter decided he should convince his father not to go to Lofsdalen. He would talk to his father in the morning. They could tell Bjorn that they needed some time together and take the ferry back to Stockholm that evening or sooner. After all, with Anna gone, there wouldn't be much to do.

When would he see her again? Why hadn't he gotten her cell phone number when they were together? He replayed her odd behavior that morning. Maybe she just needed some time to think. As he reached the edge of the *Majstang* field, a disturbing thought crossed his mind. Had her response in Sundsvall to him just been part of Bjorn and Rolf's plan to persuade him and his father? Impossible, he thought, but the idea refused to go away completely. He kicked a small rock and sent it bounding up ahead of him. It passed close by Goran, who was sitting on a large boulder off the side of the road smoking a pipe.

"Gooaal!" Goran shouted cheerfully, imitating a soccer announcer.

"Oh, sorry. Did I hit you? My mind was off somewhere," Peter said, coming up to him. A few of the maypole participants still dotted the field behind him.

He reassured Peter he was okay and suggested that they go back to his house. "Will you take a light dinner with us?"

They walked a short distance down the road, past the little supermarket and the pier where the road turned and followed the shore. In a little way, they came up to a small two-story house. It was brick red with white shutters and a sharply pitched roof. It stood between the road and shore, surrounded by patches of wildflowers and grass. As they approached, two little girls about seven and ten years old ran out to greet them, wrapping themselves around Goran's legs and waist. They were dressed in native costumes with full skirts and dirndls over calico blouses. Peter noticed their olive skin and dark brown eyes and wondered if they were adopted.

"My girls," said Goran smiling broadly. They were introduced to Peter and each one shyly shook his hand. Goran's wife met them at the door. Like the girls, she was olive-skinned and had dark brown hair. Her outfit also matched the girls'. She introduced herself to Peter as Leyla. Her light accent was difficult to identify, but it was not Swedish. Her English also carried a British flavoring that Peter had found was common with many Europeans who spoke English. She said that dinner would be soup and some leftovers from her contribution to their earlier lunch.

"Leyla teaches sociology," Goran told Peter as they walked around the house to a deck overlooking the water. "We both have some personal as well as professional interest in neo-Nazis. Leyla is Turkish. And, you know, of course, that Turkish immigrants here have been victims of some ethnic violence attributed to neo-Nazis."

The three adults sat on the deck. A small cruising sailboat was tied up on the shore below the house. Peter asked if neo-Nazis were a focus of her work.

"No. I study extremist groups of all types. The neo-Nazis are just a manifestation of that type here in Sweden," Leyla replied.

The couple told Peter a little bit about themselves. They had met at the university in Lund as undergraduates. Leyla's father had originally come to Sweden with her family for a year when she was seventeen. Her father had been a guest lecturer at Lund. At the end of the year, she had decided to stay on and attend the university.

"Turkey will always be my home country, but I found the opportunities for women in Sweden very compelling. And so was Goran," she added smiling at him. "In the year that I was here with my family, I saw how different it was for girls and women. My family was sad that I didn't go back with them, but they understood. They visit us here in the summer."

Goran and Leyla had married after graduation and eventually settled in Lund. Their house on Grenvik had been built by Goran's great-grandfather. They came for a month every summer, alternating July and August with Goran's brother and his family.

When Leyla left to feed the girls, their conversation turned back to Goran's interest in the neo-Nazis. He described his perspective as a historian and a political scientist. "At the moment, I am looking at the connection between the neo-Nazis of today and the old Nazis and sympathizers of Nazism during the Second World War."

"Is there a connection?" Peter asked.

"A weak connection, I am finding. The original pro-Nazi people in the 1930s and 1940s were always a very small minority here. And now, of course, most have died or are too old to be very active."

"But wasn't the government of Sweden somewhat sympathetic to the Germans during the war?" Peter asked.

"Not really." Goran paused to relight his pipe. "Officially, Sweden was neutral. Ironically, both sides in the war took advantage of that. There were intelligence services of all the major powers here, and Sweden traded with both sides. Toward the end of the war, Sweden began to tilt toward the Allies and provided a safe passage for a number of victims of the Third Reich.

"Most Swedes were very anti-Nazi. In fact, it was difficult for the government, being a democracy, not to let the anti-Nazi feeling become too strong and give the Germans an excuse to reconsider their decision not to invade," Goran said.

"But some people obviously had no trouble selling war supplies and weapons to Germany and making money at it," Peter said.

Goran made an expression that crinkled his nose slightly, and he seemed to be searching for how to respond.

Peter decided Goran was probably too polite to be the first to bring up Bjorn's role as head of Gevarfabrik. "Yes, I know about Bjorn Svensson's role in that. Rolf was pretty clear when Anna and I toured the plant yesterday morning about how successful Gevarfabrik had been during the war."

"Ah yah," Goran said. "But like other businesses, he also supplied the Americans and the British, at least according to the official company history."

"But what about a connection between the skinheads and organized political parties now in Sweden? My research here last fall led me to believe there was a relationship with a number of older, more respectable-seeming individuals," Peter said.

"Possibly. But those connections—if they exist, at all— are quite well hidden. There are no clear links between any of the right-wing political parties and the neo-Nazis." Goran went on to explain that the ultra-right political parties in Sweden were a small minority that typically received less than two percent of the vote in national elections. The largest and most moderate group of ultra-nationalists were the Sweden Democrats who had recently received about one and a half percent of the vote. "Four percent of the vote nationally is required to gain a seat in parliament. The remainder of the far right wing is a small, fractured minority. I am certain that it includes some active supporters of the skinhead, white power, anti-immigrant violence. By contrast, the Sweden Democrats attempt to portray a more moderate, respectable face like their ideological cousins, the National Front of Jean-Marie Le Pen in France."

"And then there is the question I have been trying to answer. The neo-Nazi groups here seem to have some financial resources, more than seems reasonable from the kinds of jobs they hold," Peter said.

"Yes. I think they are receiving funds from outside sources, not just small donations by a few old sympathizers." Goran looked over Peter's shoulder. "Oh, it looks like we need to help Leyla with the supper preparations."

As he helped to set the table, Peter considered Goran's last remark. Given Bjorn's avowed fear of neo-Nazis, it wasn't likely that, even if he was an old Nazi sympathizer, he would be a source of funds. He distributed a collection of brightly colored plastic plates and glasses while Goran and Leyla brought out an assortment of cheeses, smoked fish, and bread along with several bottles of beer.

Before he sat down, Goran produced a bottle of Swedish *snaps* and three small glasses. "Our official drink for toasts," he said. Peter noticed the label *Aalborg Akvavit*. He remembered the power cruiser they had seen earlier in the day, which had been named the *AkvaVitt* with two "t's." He asked Goran what the difference was.

"Well, of course, *Akva* means 'water' and *vit* means 'life,' like the French for *snaps*, which is *Eau-de-vie*." But *vitt* means 'white.' So I suppose it means 'white water,' as we encounter in kayaking."

Leyla asked Peter about Boston and his writing for *VERITAS?*. In turn, Peter asked her about her work. Her major interest was in teaching, but her research interest was currently on what factors fueled extremism. "The skinheads have become identified with the neo-Nazis, although I don't think they all are. I think some are just rebellious young men who are attracted to the White Aryan Resistance movement, the '*Vitt Ariskt Motstånd*' or VAM, as we call it here in Sweden."

"'*Vitt*' as in '*AkvaVitt*'?" Peter asked.

"Correct," Goran replied. "Your ear for Swedish is quite good." Peter nodded, wishing that he'd been wrong.

Leyla went on, "Some young men are unhappy with their jobs or are without jobs. They believe that foreigners are responsible." Leyla went on to explain that Sweden had absorbed a large number of immigrants in the last fifty years creating a population that was now about 10 percent foreign-born and first-generation Swedish. In response to this demographic reality, the government was involved in a major effort to integrate the newcomers into Swedish society. However, she explained, it was a difficult task when the economy was not able to provide full employment or sustain a high level of social services. Bad feelings often arose when native Swedes imagined that immigrants were taking their jobs and costing the government too much money.

"But, it's one thing to understand the point of view of angry white power youths and another thing to feel afraid when they look at me and my children with hate in their eyes. I often feel uncomfortable just seeing them on the street." Leyla paused and pressed her lips together momentarily. "In fact, today at the maypole dancing, I saw two skinhead types and it was as though a dark cloud had suddenly appeared in front of the sun."

"Yes, I saw them too," Goran added. "I don't think I have ever seen them on Grenvik before, but then there are always a lot of visitors at Midsummer."

"I didn't see them. Where were they sitting?" Peter asked.

"They weren't really on the field. They were standing by the edge of the road watching, behind where you were sitting, Peter," Leyla said. "They stayed for a while and then left."

"I guess it just wasn't their scene," Peter said, trying to sound casual, but he felt a shiver ripple through his scalp as if a cold breeze had singled him out at the picnic table. Had they come in on the *AkvaVitt*?

They cleared the dishes, and Peter helped Goran and Leyla with the washing up. When Goran went to put the girls to bed, Peter asked Leyla about her childhood in Turkey. When

Goran returned, they talked about current politics in Sweden and in the United States.

Finally, Peter realized that it was actually getting a little dark. There was still light in the sky but the woods around the house had blurred into a gray curtain beyond the edge of the lawn. Peter and Goran exchanged contact information. They agreed to try to meet again before Peter returned to the States. Peter thanked Goran and Leyla for dinner and left to find his way back to the dock where the outboard was tied up.

He walked down the road past the ferry dock and the field where the maypole stood by itself in the half-light of the long evening. It was cool, and a light wind off the water rustled the leaves on the maypole. He heard music and the murmur of conversation from a house nearby where festivities were continuing. Further along, at a house back from the road, a string of lanterns outlined a terrace, on which a number of people were dancing to more modern music than he had heard in the afternoon. The road became quite dark as it passed through a section of tall pines. Peter hoped the skinheads that Leyla and Goran mentioned had left the island. Or were they among the number of young backpackers he had seen who were probably camping out in fields around the island?

As he neared the Karlssons' house by the dock, he saw only one light on and no sign of a continuing celebration. Peter walked quietly past the house onto the dock. The Svenssons' outboard was tied up at the far end. He climbed in and untied the lines. He pushed off and let the boat drift away from the dock, hoping the noise of the motor wouldn't wake anyone.

He looked at the chart and realized that borrowing a flashlight would have been useful even on this, the longest day of the year. It was a little too dark to make out the details on the map. He thought he remembered the course that had been marked out; it wasn't difficult. At the end of the inlet, bear a little to the right and head past the large island about half a mile away; leave that island on the left and a smaller one on the right. Beyond these islands, bear left across another half mile or so of open water to Smavik and Sodra Smavik. When he approached the channel separating Smavik and its sister island to the south, he should be able to see the light on the Svenssons' dock on the shore up to his left.

The outboard engine started on the first pull. Peter maneuvered past the stern of the Karlssons' sailboat and down the inlet. He was relieved to see that the *AkvaVitt* power cruiser was no longer tied up at the mouth of the inlet. When he reached the open water beyond the inlet, he brought the outboard around about thirty degrees to the right, roughly southeast, he guessed, and twisted the throttle handle on the motor. The outboard engine was relatively powerful for the little whaler. The sea was calm, and the outboard skimmed across the water toward the passage between large and small islands.

Soon, Peter was passing the large island on the left. He thought that he could see Smavik in the distance. Right on course, he thought. The large island's rocky shore to his left rose steeply into pine forests punctuated by an occasional cottage. The noise of the outboard seemed amplified by the echo off the shore. Peter relaxed the throttle thinking he might be disturbing people whose houses were close to the water. But even at a reduced speed, the engine noise seemed undiminished. Curious, Peter turned the throttle down to idle speed and then realized the motor noise was still very loud except that it seemed to have a deeper pitch.

Peter looked for another boat ahead and on the right. Then he turned and looked directly behind. About a quarter of a mile away, a large boat was outlined against the sky. It had no running lights. From its silhouette, it appeared to be a power cruiser.

The *AkvaVitt? Vitt* as in white power, not the whitecaps on waves? Were these the skinheads at the maypole dancing? An adrenaline rush of fear and anger erased the mellow mood of his evening with Goran and his family. How the hell had skinheads tracked him down here?

Chapter 36

AS HE PASSED THE end of the large island on his left, Peter looked across the open water toward the dark merged shorelines of Smavik and its companion Sodra Smavik. He twisted the throttle handle of the outboard motor and aimed for the point on Smavik where he thought the Svenssons' dock should be. No dock light was visible yet. The whaler skimmed across the dark, still water—fast but probably not fast enough to outrun the hulking power cruiser.

He turned back again, hoping to see that the *AkvaVitt* had taken a different course in the open water. No luck. It was following the whaler exactly in the middle of its wake; from the sound of its engines, it was trying to overtake his small boat at full throttle. The *AkvaVitt* was about a hundred yards behind him and gaining.

Peter remembered the channel between Smavik and Sodra Smavik. It was directly across from his current position and would be closer than the Svenssons' dock. If he could get in among the boats moored there, he might have some protection. In the channel, his small outboard should be able to evade the *AkvaVitt* and find a safe spot to land. He shifted his course about forty-five degrees to the right, aiming for the channel opening where he saw a notch in the islands' profile against the sky. He looked back at the power cruiser. He saw that he had gained a precious few seconds before its crew realized that he had turned. But the distance between them was closing rapidly. The channel between the islands was still about a quarter of a mile away. At this rate, the *AkvaVitt* would get to him before he got to the safety of the channel. His experience with powerboats was limited but he thought an unexpected maneuver might give him the time he needed.

Seconds went by. When the *AkvaVitt* was about twenty-five yards directly behind him, he pushed the throttle handle hard to the right and leaned left into the turn. The whaler responded well, and he carved a sharp turn nearly under the bow of the *AkvaVitt*. In a second, he was passing the left side of the larger boat.

He glanced up and saw the pilot of the cruiser was still looking straight ahead, probably wondering why he had lost sight of the outboard. There were two other crew members; the instrument lights from the cockpit glinted off their shaved heads. One of them saw him and shouted.

Peter's focus was on the substantial wake he was about to encounter just behind the large cruiser. He wanted to hit the wake at right angles but he saw his U-turn around the cruiser had been sharper than he had estimated.

He caught the wake at an angle that tipped the outboard as it leapt fully out of the water, its motor whining. In the fraction of the second that he was airborne, he shifted his weight hoping to land more nearly level. He overbalanced and when he landed, the outboard's left rail went underwater along with his arm up to his elbow. The boat righted itself but the water in it completely covered his feet.

He continued his turn, now behind the *AkvaVitt*, in the calm, foamy water between the wake waves of the cruiser. As he approached the second wake, a powerful light flashed out from the stern of the power cruiser, accompanied by two loud pops.

The bullets missed, but the light caught him, momentarily leaving him with a huge blue-white after-image. Forcing himself to ignore it, he eased the throttle slightly and hit the second wake at right angles.

The small outboard launched itself cleanly over the wave this time. It landed heavily but fully upright. Out of the corner of his eye, Peter saw the cruiser turning in a wide arc carrying it, at least temporarily, away from him.

With the throttle full on, he adjusted his course slightly for the channel opening. Looking back, he saw the cruiser had come around and was now about fifty yards behind him.

In the next few seconds, the *AkvaVitt* made up most of the distance between them. But suddenly, he was in the channel with boats moored all around him. He cut the throttle and dodged around a large sailboat taking his little outboard under its bow anchor line. Peter ducked but felt the rope brush the top of his head.

He looked for a good spot to land on the shore to his right. But he would have to beach the outboard and scramble up the smooth rock shore. During that time, he would make an easy target for whoever had been shooting at him from the cruiser. Moving in and out around the moored boats, keeping their large hulls between his outboard and the *AkvaVitt*, he seemed safe, at least temporarily.

The cruiser continued to track the whaler but stayed close to the shore of Smavik where there were fewer boats in the channel. It seemed to be waiting for an opportunity to catch him in open water again.

Further in, the channel narrowed and several boats that were moored there slowed the *AkvaVitt's* progress. Beyond that point, the channel widened again, but it was clear of boats, probably because the channel became too shallow, Peter assumed. He wondered if that would discourage his pursuers.

With a large sailboat shielding him from the power cruiser, which was a little behind and still on his left about thirty yards away, Peter gunned the outboard engine. He passed quickly by the last of the moored boats and out into the open water beyond.

He turned to see what the *AkvaVitt* would do. It was carefully threading its way between several boats in its path, still in pursuit. Looking ahead, Peter saw about seventy-five yards of open channel. Beyond it, he could just make out the narrow opening separating the two islands that marked the end of the channel.

He hoped that Anna had been right when she had said that it was too narrow for large boats and wrong when she said that she would not even try to squeeze through in an outboard. If he could make it through the gap out of reach of the *AkvaVitt*, he could land at the Pederssons' dock and make his way back to the Svenssons' house on foot.

Halfway across the section of open water, Peter looked back and saw that the *AkvaVitt* had cleared the boats in the middle of the channel and was again in full-throttle pursuit. Apparently, the channel was still deep enough to accommodate the power cruiser, or at least the skinheads thought so. The *AkvaVitt* was quickly closing on him, and the gap was still about thirty yards away. If the cruiser did not slow down, both boats would reach the narrow end of the channel at almost the same instant.

Instinctively, Peter put his head down to gain whatever reduction in wind resistance he could. The rocks and pines on the shores on either side raced by, growing closer as he approached the end of the channel. The deep throbbing of the *AkvaVitt* engines echoed off the shores in the channel, increasingly overpowering the buzz of his outboard engine.

Each second, Peter expected to hear the engines of the *AkvaVitt* suddenly strain as its propellers were reversed to stop it before it reached the gap. Was Anna too cautious? Had she exaggerated the narrowness and shallowness of the gap? Was it really deep and wide enough for the power cruiser? If so, his outboard would be crushed there, or in the open water just beyond.

The gap was now only yards away. On the left, the rock-walled shore of Smavik was almost vertical and ten feet high, at least; on the right, the rock-bound shore of Sodra Smavik sloped down into the gap, making it hard to judge its width in the twilight. But neither side offered an escape for Peter. He and the power cruiser were committed to the narrow passage. He held his breath.

Suddenly, he was in the gap. His shoulder brushed the rock wall on the left side and the outboard throttle arm jumped in his hand. A second later, before his mind had registered the significance of the bump, he heard a muffled thud from behind.

It was followed immediately by the screech of fiberglass and metal on rock.

Peter turned to look back and saw the *AkvaVitt* completely out of the water. It was on its side skidding up the rock slope above him on the right-hand side of the gap. Its underside was completely exposed, and its twin propellers were spinning furiously. One propeller dragging along the rock produced an angry trail of sparks and a grinding scream as the boat continued on its unnatural course up the smooth rock. At the top of the slope, it hit a large pine and bounced off with a crash that partially masked a human cry of pain.

As his outboard shot out into the open water beyond the gap, Peter watched in fascination as the huge powerboat slid past the gap high on the shore of Sodra Smavik and then down toward the water a few yards to his right. Just as it reached the shoreline, a fireball erupted from the hull. The carcass of the boat slid into the water and began to drift away from shore fully engulfed. Peter felt the heat from the flames on the side of his face and right arm.

With its engine still whining at full throttle, the outboard continued away from shore. Peter was not sure what to do: proceed to the Pederssons' dock or turn back to attempt some rescue. As he eased the throttle arm and pushed it away from him to begin a left turn back toward Smavik, he realized that neither choice was possible.

The small craft that had maneuvered so well just seconds before now was totally unresponsive. He turned up the throttle, and the engine revved up but to no effect. Then he remembered that the motor had struck something in the gap. He tipped up the engine to look at the propeller. In the light from the fire consuming the *AkvaVitt*, he could see that the propeller was badly mangled and remained motionless regardless of the engine's speed.

Chapter 37

THERE WERE NO OARS or anything else in the whaler that looked like they could be used as a paddle. The middle seat was firmly bolted down and offered no possibilities. Peter's mobile phone was sitting in its charger in his cabin.

He scanned the shore of Smavik and Sodra Smavik for a reaction to the sound of the crash or the light from the fire. The Pederssons' house was out of sight behind the other side of a bluff on the south shore of Smavik. The north shore of Sodra Smavik was heavily wooded. No houses were visible from the water.

The flaming hulk of the *AkvaVitt* was floating a few yards offshore. Except for the hiss and crackle of the flames, it was very still. There was no response on either shore to his shouting. After a while, he gave up his efforts to attract help and realized he was shaking.

After a few minutes, the fire in the hull of the power cruiser began to die down. It lay on its side smoking with no signs of life on it or in the water around it. Peter stared at it as he drifted away from the shore. Finally, the hull of the *AkvaVitt* slipped under the water, leaving only a small patch of burning fuel.

A light but persistent wind was blowing the whaler away from land. By the time he thought about swimming ashore, he was nearly a quarter of a mile from the islands, and he dismissed the idea. His father had always taught him to stay with the boat if it was still floating, upright or upside down. He knew eventually he would drift onto or, at least, close enough to one the archipelago's thirty thousand islands to get to shore.

For the time being, he was stuck alone on the water, but far happier than he had been a few minutes before. He remembered Anna's reference to the Norse sea god and decided that he owed Njord a Swedish toast next time he had glass of *Akvavit* in his hand. This was a problem that the wind and the currents, or a passing boat in the morning, would resolve. As his adrenalin level decreased and the outlines of the islands receded, Peter began to feel cold. The left sleeve of his shirt was wet and so were his running shoes from the water the boat had taken on earlier. His shorts were dry but offered little cover.

The top of a plastic jug that had been made into a bailer allowed him to get most of the water out of the bottom of the boat. There were two seat cushions that had remained reasonably dry. He put one on the bottom of the boat to sit on and the other against the stern seat. Lowering himself down onto the cushions and drawing his knees up, he tried to offer as little surface area to the breeze as possible. It wasn't comfortable, but it was tolerable.

He determined he would look up every few minutes to check his progress towards some landing. With his immediate situation stabilized, his mind turned back to the question he had asked himself earlier. How had the skinheads, neo-Nazis, or whoever they were found him? Was he spotted in Stockholm at the ferry and followed? Or had his connection with the Svenssons been discovered and used to find him? If Bjorn had been the target of the swastika-painting incident that Anna had described, then perhaps the neo-Nazis had been watching the house in Sundsvall and recognized him there. Was his presence on Smavik putting his father in danger too?

He looked out and noticed the sky was getting lighter in the northeast. He hunkered down again and closed his eyes.

* * *

What seemed like a short time later, he heard a voice; someone was speaking Swedish very nearby. He opened his eyes and realized it had suddenly become much lighter. There was land directly in front of him, just a few yards away. The voice had come from a swimmer who was treading water beside the boat. The swimmer was an older man and judging from his fleshy arms and face, heavyset. His gray hair was slicked down on his round head.

"Hello," Peter replied, looking out over the side of the boat. "Sorry, I don't speak Swedish."

"Are you American or Canadian?" the swimmer asked.

"American. I ..." Peter hesitated to explain how he had come to be in this situation. He decided to keep it simple. "I lost my propeller on the way back from Grenvik to Smavik last night."

"Ah, yah," responded the older man. "If you were Swedish, I would say when you came back to your wife last night, she said you were so drunk she wouldn't let you in and told you to sleep in the boat." He smiled broadly enjoying his joke at Peter's expense.

Peter tried to appreciate the older man's humor but explained that he was, in fact, a bit cold and needed some help to get back to Smavik. The older man introduced himself as Per Lindstrom and said he would be glad to help. He grabbed the rope from the bow that was trailing the water and towed Peter to the dock. Peter climbed out stiff with cold and from crouching in the boat. Peter's heavyset rescuer, who was well insulated for swimming in the Baltic, climbed onto the dock dripping but apparently comfortable in the cool morning air with only a towel around his thick neck.

"Will you take some breakfast with me?" Lindstrom offered.

Peter nodded gratefully and followed Lindstrom up the path to a small cottage. The cottage had a single large room that apparently served as kitchen, sitting room, bedroom, and office. A large desk dominated one side of the room. Piles of papers and books surrounded a laptop computer. Lindstrom explained that this was his "getaway" house, where "I can write without being interrupted, except for occasional shipwreck survivors," he said with a quick smile. Lindstrom didn't realize how close to the truth he was, Peter thought.

There was a fire in a small stove in the center of the room. Peter took advantage of the rack in front of it to dry his shirt and socks. Lindstrom put on a robe and offered Peter a blanket. Peter walked around in front of the stove trying to warm up and get the kinks out of his legs. "So what island is this? Is it far from Smavik?"

"No, not so far. Perhaps twenty minutes in your little boat. This is Viksholm Island, a bit east of Smavik," Lindstrom replied.

Peter explained that he was staying on Smavik with the Svenssons.

"Ah yah," Lindstrom exclaimed, looking serious.

Peter wasn't certain what Lindstrom's reaction meant but decided to provide a simple and not untruthful explanation. "Bjorn Svensson and my grandmother knew each other before World War II in Germany. She was studying there."

"I see, yes," Lindstrom said. "Does your grandmother live in Sweden?"

"No, in the U.S., and actually she has not seen Bjorn since before the war," Peter replied.

"Yes, okay. That was a long time ago." Lindstrom went back to the coffeepot that he had been filling. "So you are meeting him for the first time?"

"Yes. And his daughter, Anna," Peter said. "Do you know them?"

"No. Only what I read in the newspapers," Lindstrom replied. "But we need to discuss how to get you back to Smavik. I suppose you would like to call them. Unfortunately, I don't have a telephone here ... On purpose," he added.

Lindstrom suggested that they have a look at the boat after breakfast and see whether it could be fixed easily and then decide what to do. "And there's a telephone at the ferry dock where you can make a call."

For breakfast, he brought out cheese and bread along with some coffee and sweet rolls. It all tasted exceedingly good to Peter.

After breakfast, they went down to the dock to look at the outboard motor. The connection between the propeller and the drive shaft appeared to be broken. The propeller itself was intact but badly bent. Lindstrom suggested that they might be able to persuade his friend Eskil, who operated a small boat repair shop on the island, to fix it.

"On a Sunday morning, after Midsummer?" Peter asked, surprised.

"Oh, I think so. His wife died last year, and he's always happy to have visitors, especially ones who pay."

They removed the motor and carried it between them along a cart road from Lindstrom's cabin. "Eskil's shop is in the village, just a short walk," Lindstrom said cheerfully.

The road led through the woods and past an occasional field as it traced the shore of the island. After about half an hour, they arrived at the village. There was a ferry dock and a seasonal grocery store, which, according to Lindstrom, supported the summer population of about three hundred. The repair shop was just beyond the dock. There was a small boatyard and a workshop attached to the house. The doors to the workshop were open. From the clink of metal on metal, someone appeared to be working inside.

Lindstrom introduced Peter to his friend Eskil, a short stocky man with a ruddy complexion and a fringe of gray-black hair. His workshop was well lit and very tidy. He continued to work on a small outboard engine on a stand as they talked. Lindstrom spoke to him in Swedish and apparently explained something about Peter and the Svenssons. They examined Peter's outboard motor. Eskil agreed to see if he could fix it.

Peter left Per and Eskil talking and went to find the telephone to call the Svenssons. By this time, his father would certainly be concerned about him. He also wanted to call Claes to tell him about the *AkvaVitt*. The Swedish equivalent of the Coast Guard probably should be notified, but Claes could take care of that. He called directory assistance to get the Svenssons' number but found that it was not listed. There was also no telephone in the Pederssons' name.

His call to Claes was picked up by the answering machine. Peter left a brief message with the basic facts of the previous evening's incident and his current situation. He said he would call again when he got back to Stockholm Monday morning.

Peter rejoined Per Lindstrom and Eskil at the repair shop. Per translated for Peter. Eskil didn't have a replacement, but he said he could straighten out the propeller and replace the safety clutch in the drive shaft. That part had sheared when the outboard hit the rock in the gap. He said it would take him about an hour to fix it.

Lindstrom suggested that meanwhile, they have some coffee. They sat at a table on the dock in front of a small café. Peter asked Lindstrom about his writing.

Lindstrom smiled and seemed to consider his answer. "I write mystery sort of novels. I don't expect the Nobel Prize for literature but people seem to enjoy them."

"Anything translated into English?" Peter asked.

"Yes, most of my books, but they sell in England, not in America, so you probably would not have seen any."

Peter gathered that Lindstrom was quite a successful author commercially. Modesty seemed to be a common trait among the Swedes that Peter had met. Lindstrom asked Peter about his work. Peter described his work as an investigative journalist for *VERITAS?*.

Lindstrom said he had heard of the publication but was not familiar with it. "So you are here on vacation, Peter?" he asked, changing the subject.

Peter gave Per an abbreviated description of his two days in Sundsvall and his first experience at a maypole dance. "You said you knew about Bjorn Svensson from what you read in the newspapers. I'm curious. What do the Swedish newspapers say about him?"

Per looked slightly uncomfortable. "Oh, I should say what they always say about our successful industrialists. Praise from the conservative press and less positive things from the left-wing papers. But let's go back and see how Eskil is coming along with the outboard engine," he said, getting up from the table.

Eskil was just fitting the propeller back on the outboard motor's drive shaft when they arrived. It still looked very bent, but he assured Peter that it would get him back to Smavik. Eskil accepted the equivalent of about fifty dollars in *kronor* for his work.

By the time they reached Per's cabin and had the motor attached to the boat, it was just before noon. He declined Lindstrom's offer of lunch and thanked him for all his help. Lindstrom found a wax pencil and traced Peter's course on his chart back to Smavik. The day had turned out clear and warm.

After about fifteen minutes, Peter rounded a small island and saw Smavik and its sister island across a stretch of water. He set his course for the Pederssons' yellow house near the gap between the islands. As he approached the narrow gap between Smavik and Sodra Smavik, he could see no sign of the *AkvaVitt's* skid over the rocks on Sodra Smavik. Peter headed north following Smavik's shore past the Pederssons' dock. He was taking no chances with the gap and motored the long way around. After another few minutes, Peter turned into the little cove to tie up at the Svenssons' main dock. Anna's and Bjorn's sailboats were at the inner dock but blue covers had been put on their sails since the day before.

Peter made the outboard fast at the dock and walked up to the terrace in front of the main house. There was no one around. He noticed that the outdoor furniture had been covered. He knocked at the door of his father's cabin. There was no response, and the door was locked.

He turned, went to the door of the main house, and called out. There was a reply from the kitchen. It was Mrs. Pedersson.

"Mr. Frost, is that you?" She came out of the kitchen drying a pot. "Did you have a good time last night?" she asked in a pleasant but slightly reproving tone.

"Well, actually ..." Peter started to explain and then decided just to agree. "Yes, very good. Thanks. So where is everybody?"

"Oh, they left you a note. I think it's on your cabin door. They have gone to Lofsdalen in the mountains. They said they were leaving today because their plans had changed."

Chapter 38

"THEY LEFT? WHEN? WHAT time?" he asked Mrs. Pedersson. "Why?" He shook his head in surprise.

She provided a partial answer to his questions. "They departed in Mr. Rolf's plane about eleven o'clock. And Lars has taken the launch to Moja to pick up some supplies and leave his friend off at the ferry," she replied as if to explain the deserted compound. "But he will be back to take you into Stockholm."

"Christ," he swore under his breath. Bjorn and Rolf had spirited his father away. Again? He was angry at himself for not coming back with his father the previous night. Maybe he could have prevailed on him to go to Stockholm.

"Would you like me to prepare something for you to eat?" she asked pleasantly. "Or did you have some breakfast on Grenvik?"

Peter mumbled a "No thanks" to her offer and walked up to his cabin. It appeared from Mrs. Pedersson's remarks that the general assumption had been that he had stayed overnight on Grenvik.

When he reached his cabin, he found a handwritten note wedged in the door. It said:

Dear Peter,

I must apologize. Our plans have changed. We shall leave for Lofsdalen this morning. I understand that you have business in Stockholm on Monday. Please join us in Lofsdalen on Tuesday. There is a flight to Sveg at 7:30 PM from Arlanda Airport, SAS 533. Our driver will pick you up at Sveg Airport to take you to the lodge in Lofsdalen. Lars will take you back to Stockholm on his way to Lofsdalen this afternoon.

Cordially,

Rolf Stengren

Peter showered and changed clothes. He rolled up the shorts, shirt, and underwear he had been wearing and stuffed them into the bottom of his carry-on pack. As he reached in, he felt a piece of paper. He pulled it out and found it was a note in his father's handwriting.

Peter,

I hope you're OK. Rolf says you spent the night on Grenvik. He insists we have to leave and don't have time to wait for you. Says he has arranged for you to get there Tuesday. Not sure what's going on.

The note was unsigned. Peter wondered if his father had been interrupted in writing it by Rolf, telling him they had to leave immediately. It would be just like his father, Peter thought, to politely drop whatever he was doing to accommodate Rolf— and like Rolf, Peter thought, to expect him to. Why had Rolf said that he had spent the night on Grenvik? Was that just a guess meant to reassure his father so they wouldn't be held up leaving? A thought flashed through his mind: Maybe Rolf knew he wouldn't make it back from Grenvik, just like Jed had never made it to Nantucket. That seemed incredible. But even a slim possibility that it was true made Peter very uneasy.

Peter started to walk back to the main house to question Mrs. Pedersson about Rolf's assertion that he had spent the night on Grenvik, but he decided against it. His concerns about Rolf's intentions were multiplying rapidly. The idea of waiting for Lars, who had not left with the others for Lofsdalen, to take him to Stockholm was unappealing.

Suddenly, the thought that he hadn't been able to bring into focus came to him: Lars had also remained behind also two weeks ago when they left the U.S. in the Gevarfabrik jet. Lars had come to the U.S. with Bjorn and Rolf, his father had told him.

But Bill Reilly, quoting the manifest, had said that only his father, Bjorn, and Rolf had flown back to Sweden on the Gevarfabrik jet. Had Lars been left behind to deal with Jed? Despite the warmth of the sun on his back, Peter felt a cold chill.

Returning to Stockholm was a priority. The outboard that had eventually gotten him back from Grenvik could also get him to the ferry landing there now. He would simply retrace the route he had taken the night before. In addition, it was more or less in the opposite direction to Moja so he wouldn't accidentally meet Lars in the launch.

He returned to the cabin and collected his backpack. Mrs. Pedersson was not in sight, and he decided it was just as well to leave without alerting her.

Peter walked quickly down the path from the cabin and across the terrace to the dock. The outboard was tied up at the float where he had left it. There was a gas can for the outboard in a shed by the dock, and it was full. He headed out of the cove and west away from the Svenssons' dock toward Grenvik Island.

As he looked across to the opposite shore to set his course, he saw two boats coming toward him from his left at high speed. One of them appeared to be about the size of the Svenssons' cabin cruiser, the other was somewhat larger. He was on the verge of making a rapid turn back to Smavik when the larger boat turned north crossing about a hundred yards in front of him. It was clearly marked *Polis*. He relaxed and continued on course. The smaller boat, also marked *Polis*, passed to his left, heading for the channel between Smavik and Sodra Smavik. The first *Polis* boat disappeared around the northern tip of Smavik. He guessed they might be investigating the wreck of the *AkvaVitt* in response to the message he had left for Claes.

How would Claes react to his encounter with the power cruiser, the second incident involving skinheads? Would he suggest that Peter leave Sweden as soon as possible saying he couldn't ensure his safety? Probably. He would have to deal with that when he gave Claes a full briefing about the *AkvaVitt*. Another topic for discussion with Claes was Bjorn's identity switch in 1939. He was uncertain about disclosing that information. It was still not clear to Peter whether the switch represented anything illegal. Maybe Claes would have a clear answer. But more important, his father needed help in dealing with Bjorn and Rolf.

Peter made his way to Grenvik without difficulty. He spotted the inlet that led to the Karlssons' dock. From there, he skirted the island until he came around to the pier on the other side of the island where he and his father had sat the day before. He tied up the outboard and went into the grocery store to inquire about the ferry schedule. A round-faced woman in a white smock was energetically stocking bananas and oranges into bins from a crate on the floor. "Ah yah, on the wall there is the ferry schedule. You have just missed the two o'clock ferry. There is one at three and also at five today."

He went up the road to the bakery that he had seen the day before. He ordered coffee and a Swedish pastry with almonds and raisins and a sweet filling. He sat at one of the tables outside on the lawn. At another table, a young couple was engaged in a quiet, serious conversation, their hands clasped together as they looked at each other. Their large backpacks and attached sleeping bags lay alongside the table. His dinner with Anna and the touch of her hand came back to him.

Several other groups of low-budget weekenders occupied other tables and parts of the lawn. Apparently, they were also waiting for the three o'clock ferry. An older couple, who looked like they might be American or German, bicycled in and went into the bakery. No skinheads. It was a peaceful, pleasant afternoon away from Smavik. How had he and his father suddenly found themselves in a very unpleasant and perhaps dangerous situation? And where was Anna in all this? Nowhere, he hoped. He wondered again when he would see her.

He walked back to the ferry dock and used the public telephone to call Claes. He hung up when the answering machine picked up. A ferry, smaller than the *Cinderella*, arrived at three, crowded with returning passengers. All the seats on the outside deck were taken. Peter found a place on a bench in a corner in the main cabin. The timetable in the supermarket indicated the trip to Stockholm with its many stops would be about two and a half hours. Eventually, the gentle rolling of the boat and Peter's short, uncomfortable nap the previous night made him drowsy, and he closed his eyes.

He woke up with a start and saw that they were approaching Stockholm's outer harbor area. Large gas storage tanks and other industrial facilities were coming up on the right side of the waterway. He wondered what had awoken him, perhaps the bump of crossing the wake of another boat. Then he remembered the dream. He was with Anna in the launch except that the launch had a sail and looked like Anna's boat. They were sailing through a lot of small islands, and he was afraid they were going to bump into one. He was at the wheel, and Anna was watching him. He found that turning the wheel didn't seem to have much effect on the direction of the boat. As he tried to avoid hitting one of islands, he saw the boom swinging around in a dangerous jibe, and the boat lurched. That was when he had woken up. Peter looked out, but by then, they were well beyond any wake that they might have crossed.

In about fifteen minutes, they arrived at Stromkajen where he and Anna had boarded the ferry for Moja on Friday. Peter shuffled up the gangway and looked the length of the quay for skinheads. There were none in sight. He joined the crowds of returning weekenders on the wide sidewalk. The streets were filled with strollers, tourists and natives, in a holiday mood, enjoying the last evening of the Midsummer weekend. He wondered what the mood was in Lofsdalen and wherever Anna was somewhere in the far north of Sweden.

Chapter 39

THE ROUTE TO THE Sheraton Hotel from the quay took Peter past Strombron Bridge and along Stromgatan. Three blocks further on, he arrived at the hotel overlooking the Norrstrom toward Gamla Stan. It was convenient, a short walk to Central Station and shops in the center of Stockholm. Normally, he would have returned to the quieter, less touristy Wallin Hotel, but the Sheraton on a busy street seemed a safer, more public location.

When he approached the main entrance, a doorman offered to take his backpack. Peter waved him off and walked through the automatic doors. The large lobby was quiet. A long reception counter occupied a wall on the right; opposite the main doors at the back was a restaurant.

Peter checked in and found the elevators beyond the reception area. His room was in the front of the hotel overlooking Gamla Stan. He stretched out on the king-size bed and called Claes's office number. After several clicks and a couple of rings, Claes answered. Wind noise in the phone indicated he was outdoors.

"Peter, are you all right?"

"Yes, I'm ..."

"Are you still in the archipelago?" Claes interrupted.

"No. I'm calling from the Sheraton in Stockholm."

"Good. Please stay there in your room. I need to talk to you. I will be ..." Claes paused a moment. "... there in about one hour to see you. I will come to your room. Agreed?"

"Yes, sure but ..."

"Good. *Hejdå*." Claes hung up.

Despite the casual "Heydo" goodbye, the usual warmth in Claes's voice had been missing. Peter wondered if Claes had decided that he was more trouble than he was worth or that Claes could afford. Peter called the Wallin Hotel to see if any messages had been left for him since he checked out. Bill Reilly and Elena had each called and asked to be called back. A Mr. Anders had called several times but had not left a message.

"I spoke to him myself just about one hour ago. He was quite excited, I should say," the receptionist said.

"Like upset?"

"Yes, that is a better word," she replied.

Peter thanked her and hung up. He punched in Anders's number hoping there wasn't a problem with their meeting the next morning at the Vasa Museum. Peter counted five rings before an answering machine started. He began to leave the number of the Sheraton when Anders picked up.

"We need to meet tonight," Anders said, apparently recognizing Peter's voice. There was fresh desperation in his voice.

Peter hesitated. "No … that doesn't work for me. I want to meet tomorrow at the Vasa Museum at ten."

"No. It must be tonight, and I need money. I will explain. You are able to get money, yes?"

"Ah …" Peter began. Hearing the emotion in Anders's voice made him reluctant not to offer him something. "I could make a small down payment, tomorrow, maybe." He tried to remember how much he had in emergency travelers checks.

"Small?"

Peter guessed conservatively. "Maybe a few hundred dollars."

"More. I need more." Anders sounded pitiful.

"Let me see what I can do."

Anders made a guttural sound of disgust. "And more later, you must promise."

"I'll try."

"I must come to you tonight."

Peter looked at his watch. Claes would be there about seven, probably stay for an hour, maybe more. He was uncomfortable about Anders coming to the hotel, but it was probably more of a risk for Anders than for him, he decided. "Okay, make it about nine o'clock. I'm at the Sheraton on Tegelbacken. I'll be in the restaurant in the lobby."

"You will have the money." It was not a question. The line went dead. Fear seemed to be giving Anders an assertiveness that Peter had not seen before.

Peter hauled his backpack up onto the bed and found a side pocket. In it were dirty socks, below which were his passport and a couple books of American Express Travelers Cheques. He found a total of twelve hundred dollars. He returned to the reception counter and asked a tall, dark-haired clerk, whose nameplate read Gregor, about cashing the checks.

"Certainly, sir," he said in an accent that defied easy identification. "How much do you need?"

"Twelve hundred dollars," Peter said, instinctively lowering his voice despite the nearly deserted lobby.

Gregor drew himself up stiffly. His eyes scanned Peter's clothes down as far as the edge of the counter would allow. They took in his wrinkled shirt and blue jeans. "You know, sir, that the stores are closed this evening. Perhaps you would like to wait until tomorrow morning?"

"No, I wouldn't, Mr. Gregor," Peter said, looking into Gregor's eyes and carefully pronouncing his name.

Gregor's eyes narrowed slightly. "I will see if we have U.S. dollars in that amount. We have been very busy this Midsummer weekend," he said, trying to recoup a little lost dignity.

Peter returned to his room with twelve one-hundred-dollar bills in a hotel envelope. He called Elena. It would be a little after lunch on the East Coast.

"Oh, Peter, I tried your mobile number but there was no answer. I just wanted to know how you and your father were making out with ... Bjorn and all."

"Well, okay." Peter realized he hadn't really thought about what he was going to say to her or what he wanted to ask her. He didn't want to increase her anxiety, which he was now beginning to understand had been well founded. But he had some questions for her that might telegraph his own growing concerns. She waited for him to go on. "I know all about Bjorn and Kjell and the switch now." Peter heard his grandmother sigh.

"So you are with your father and he told you everything?" she asked.

"We were together on Smavik, the island that Bjorn owns. Over the weekend, he told me how he found out and that it was the real Bjorn Svensson, my grandfather, who was killed fighting the Nazis in Germany."

There was a long pause. "Yes, he was very brave to do that." Another pause. "And maybe foolish, too," Elena said with an edge in her voice.

"So did he ... my grandfather really know that he had a son before he died?"

"Oh yes. When he was in England training, I wrote to him and he wrote to me ... often, before your father was born and afterward. He was very pleased that Eric was named for his grandfather Erik." She was quiet again for a moment. "How is your father getting along with Kjell?"

Her use of Anna's father's real name was jarring and reinforced the reality of Peter's concerns about the agreement and his father's situation. He wondered what the real Bjorn would have wanted in this situation. Had his grandfather realized he might not return from Germany? Had he expected to leave his family's company to his friend Kjell or had he intended something for his son?

Peter responded to Elena's question. "Well, they spent a week sailing together. And I think they got along pretty well."

"Yes." Elena paused. "Yes, I always thought Kjell was quite charming when I knew him in Germany."

"Aunt Elena," Peter said reverting to his familiar name for her. "What do you think my real grandfather Bjorn wanted if, you know, he didn't make it?"

Elena did not respond.

"Look, the problem is that Bjorn, I mean Kjell, is trying to get Dad to sign an agreement that says the switch is okay. Dad will get some money, a sort of payoff, I guess. But it seems there could be some legal issues about inheritance and changing identities," Peter said, thinking about what his father had told him concerning Jed's objections.

Peter heard Elena sigh, but she said nothing. He continued, "Dad said that Uncle Jed believed that Bjorn might have written you and said—"

"Damn Jed!" she spit out.

Peter waited for her to say something more, but there was silence. "Aunt Elena?" he said. A moment later, there was a click, and the line went dead.

He was shocked at his grandmother's outburst. Her anger and uncharacteristic outburst suggested that Jed's involvement in the question of his father's Swedish parent went deeper than his father knew; it seemed to validate the existence of a document that might undercut Bjorn-Kjell's claims to Gevarfabrik; and it reinforced his fear that Jed's disappearance was the result of his discovering Anna's father's real identity.

Peter retrieved an orange juice from the minibar and turned on the television. There was a soccer game on, which he half-watched, thinking about Jed and what had gone on between him and Elena. It seemed certain now that the visit to Sundsvall, recorded in Jed's 1970 business diary, was not coincidental. Apparently, his grandmother Elena didn't appreciate Jed's interest, and that accounted for the tension that he had observed between them.

In less than the hour he had estimated, Claes arrived. He was wearing a windbreaker and an open-necked shirt. He looked tired and unusually serious. He looked Peter over as if to confirm that he was okay.

"Is it whiskey time?" Peter asked using one of Claes's favorite expressions.

"Unfortunately, I am still on duty," Claes responded. He sat in the desk chair, which he had turned backwards, and leaned forward on his elbows. "Please tell me about your activities since you left Stockholm last Wednesday, and then I would like to hear about what happened last night. I would like the details."

Peter sat on the edge of the bed and briefly described his trip to Sundsvall, his visit to the Svenssons' house, and an uncomplicated version of his meeting with Anna.

"I understand Anna Svensson is quite attractive and a very capable doctor," Claes said. Peter wondered if Claes had somehow read between the lines of his account. He went on to describe his tour of Gevarfabrik and finally his meeting with Bjorn Svensson on Smavik. Peter recounted Saturday's events up to his leaving Smavik in the outboard. He did not mention what his father had revealed to him about Bjorn Svensson's true identity. That would be a long discussion, and he knew Claes wanted to hear about the boat incident.

Peter said that he had seen the *AkvaVitt* in the inlet on Grenvik before lunch. He explained how he came to take the outboard back to Smavik about midnight. He described the boat chase into the channel between Smavik and Sodra Smavik. Claes smiled slightly and shook his head when Peter described his maneuver to gain time to get into the channel and then make it through the gap at the far end on the assumption that the *AkvaVitt* would not try.

"Are you certain that the power cruiser you saw in the inlet on Grenvik was the one that pursued you that night?" Claes made some notes in a small leather notebook that showed signs of long use.

"I can't be totally sure but it looked the same." He told Claes about Goran and his wife spotting the skinheads at the maypole dancing.

"Perhaps they were trying to accomplish what the gentlemen in Stockholm were unable to do," Claes said.

"But how would they know where I was going to be on Saturday night? A lucky guess?"

"No. Perhaps your friend Anders is the source. He may have told them you were staying at the Wallin Hotel and they read your father's note. Did you leave it in your room when you went to dinner?" Peter shrugged.

Claes went on, "After the power cruiser crashed, you said it sank quickly. Did you see anyone escape from it and swim away?"

"No. I watched. The water was pretty calm. I would have seen them."

Claes straightened up in his chair to stretch his shoulders and then resumed. "But do you think that anyone might have been thrown out when the *AkvaVitt* hit the rock?"

"And survived? It's possible, I guess, but I didn't see anybody. Wouldn't you have found them?"

"Probably. We sent two boats out this afternoon with divers. We found an oil slick and some debris floating in the water. The divers found the boat. The boat seems to match the one that was reported stolen this morning. You said there were three men. But, you see, we have only recovered two bodies from the water."

Claes stood up. "Well, okay. No more questions, Peter. But I'm afraid this further incident with the skinheads means that you must make plans to leave Sweden as soon as possible." Peter started to say something, but Claes held up a big, weathered hand. "You are clearly a target. We cannot protect you, and we do not want to use you as bait. So you—"

Peter interrupted. "There's something else I have to tell you about. I can't leave. There's a problem with my father."

Claes frowned, and one eyebrow moved higher than the other. "Your father? He should probably leave as well."

"Well, he can't leave right away. But that's not it." Claes continued to look skeptical but said nothing.

"You remember I told you about my Swedish grandfather?" Claes nodded. "Well, there is a legal question. Bjorn Svensson wants my father to sign an agreement accepting some money in return for ..." Peter wasn't sure how to put it. "... in return for giving up some other claims."

"Yes, I understand. I would think that was quite normal. Do you feel the amount offered is not enough?"

"No, no. That's not it. It's complicated." Peter got up and went to the windows looking across to Gamla Stan. "This is going to sound strange but Bjorn Svensson is actually someone else, not my father's father." Peter turned back from the window to look at Claes. "Before World War II, he changed identities with my real grandfather in Germany where they were both studying. The person that is now Bjorn Svensson was, or is, actually Kjell Somebody-or-other. And this person calling himself Bjorn Svensson has been running Gevarfabrik ever since."

Claes's eyes were wide open. But he shook his head slightly when Peter had finished. "That is quite an interesting story," he said slowly. "And ..."

"The real Bjorn Svensson was actually killed in Germany during the war. And the problem is that this Kjell wants my father to sign an agreement saying that his becoming Bjorn is okay. I don't think that's legal."

"Well, then your father shouldn't sign it," Claes said turning toward the door.

"But my father is under a lot of pressure from Bjorn and his CEO Rolf Stengren to sign. I need to go up to their lodge in Lofsdalen the day after tomorrow to make sure my father doesn't sign anything before he talks to a lawyer here."

"Lofsdalen, a very beautiful part of Sweden," Claes said in a tone that made Peter think that his mind was on something else. "With the mountains and lakes, good hunting and not many people." Claes looked at his watch. "Peter, I must leave now and return to my office. There is a report to be written on the *AkvaVitt*. I am sorry but as I said, you must agree to leave Sweden as soon as possible. I will book a flight to London for you and send an officer and a car to take you to the airport at nine o'clock tomorrow morning. You agree?"

Peter blew out a breath in frustration.

"Peter, I will take you at your word, but if you do not agree, I will have to place you under arrest. Is that clear?"

He wanted to argue but realized it would be pointless. "Yes, and yes, I agree."

Claes's expression softened. "Peter, there will be other times, I hope. We will find these gangsters who have been harassing you. Then it will be safe for you to return to Sweden, and we will have a whiskey." He smiled and shook Peter's hand. "Also give your father my telephone number. I will be glad to speak to him about this question of the agreement. Perhaps I can recommend a lawyer for him."

Chapter 40

AFTER CLAES LEFT, PETER ran through his inventory of four-letter words. He kicked the minibar hard enough to jar the door open and bruise his toe. He reached in and grabbed a beer. He went over to the window and took a long swallow, trying to decide what his options were.

Perhaps the information that Anders would trade for a thousand dollars would be worth something to Claes, enough to allow him to make some arrests and buy Peter some time in Sweden so he could untangle his father from the Bjorn-Kjell agreement mess—and see Anna again.

Peter finished the beer and went to the lobby. The reception clerk with the attitude was not at the counter. His place had been taken by an attractive woman with short dark hair and a Russian accent. She found him a booklet with a domestic flight schedule. He confirmed that there were daily flights at 7:30 AM and 5.00 PM to Sveg, which Peter's map had indicated was the nearest airport to Lofsdalen.

He crossed the lobby to the restaurant to wait for Anders. There were only a few diners, an older couple and two men at separate tables. Peter requested a booth in the back from which he could see the doors at the front of the lobby through the entrance of the restaurant.

At five minutes to nine, Anders appeared from the direction of the elevators. He was wearing sweatpants and a hooded sweatshirt, his uncombed red hair poking out from under a faded baseball cap. His face was covered with sweat. But not from running here, Peter thought.

Anders sat down across from Peter. "Do you have the money?" he asked without preamble. Peter nodded.

"How much do you have here, now?" Anders leaned forward. Peter smelled old cigarette smoke on his breath. "I need to leave Stockholm tonight to go to my sister's home."

Peter drew back slightly and spoke softly. "Will I be able to reach you?" Over Anders's shoulder, Peter saw a waiter looking at Anders with a slightly disdainful expression.

"I will send you an e-mail with instructions," Anders said, his eyes moving around the room. "Now where is the money that you promised?" he asked pushing his hand across the table toward Peter.

Peter partially withdrew the hotel envelope from his jacket pocket and then replaced it. "There's a thousand dollars; that's all I could get on short notice. What can you tell me?"

Anders's hand on the table moved slightly. "You will give me the envelope if I tell you?" It was more a plea than a question. "Yes."

Anders spoke quietly and quickly. "What happened on the bridge to you, those were our people, but they were paid to do it."

"Do what? Beat me up?"

"No. Take you somewhere."

"Like kidnap?"

"Yes."

"Why? Because of what I wrote?"

"No. Someone, I don't know, offered money for a 'special job,' they called it."

"Why? Who would …?"

"That is all I know. You must give me the money."

"You must have some idea."

"I overheard something but you must give me the money before …"

Peter removed the envelope again from his pocket and held it with both hands on the table. Anders's hand moved toward it. Peter moved it back slightly.

"It's something to do with your father."

"My father?"

Anders's hand shot across the table and grabbed the envelope. He was out of the booth before Peter could react.

Peter wrenched himself out of his seat and went after Anders. Halfway across the dining room, Anders pulled a chair over behind him. Peter hurdled it, but Anders turned and flipped a table over between himself and Peter. Silverware and dishes crashed to the floor. Off-balance from jumping over the chair, Peter fell over the table. He landed on his hands and face on the restaurant carpet. By the time he got free of the table and was on his feet, Anders was out of the restaurant. Peter dodged around a waiter who was looking at the overturned table with his mouth wide open. Outside the entrance to the restaurant, Peter ran toward the elevators. Both elevators were at the lobby level.

Next to the elevators, there was a door marked with an exit sign. Peter ran to it and opened it. But the stairwell behind it was empty and completely quiet. He went back into the lobby. Directly across from the reception desk, past the entrance to the restaurant, he saw a set of doors that opened onto a side street by the hotel. Peter sprinted across the lobby ignoring the stares of two American-looking tourists and the two male diners who had come to the entrance of the restaurant. The side street beyond the doors was deserted.

Peter went back to the restaurant, paid his bill, and apologized to the waiters. He assured them that he was not hurt and mumbled something about having inadvertently offended his highly emotional old friend.

In the elevator, Peter tried to absorb Anders's revelation. If someone wanted to kidnap him and it involved his father, it had to be about the agreement. Were Bjorn-Kjell and Rolf willing to hold him as ransom to get his father to sign the agreement? And if they were willing to do that, his concern about Jed's fate was certainly justified. And now, his father was in Lofsdalen, in the middle of nowhere, with Bjorn-Kjell and Rolf and Lars. The elevator dinged, and the door opened for Peter's floor.

In his room, Peter went to the phone to call Claes. Would the scraps of information that Anders had given him about the bridge incident and his father be enough to persuade Claes that the problem was not Peter's harassment by skinheads but something else? As he reached for the receiver, the telephone rang.

"Peter?" Elena's voice was clear and strong. "I'm sorry I hung up on you a little while ago. I was mad and a little frightened."

"Don't apologize, Aunt Elena. I—"

She cut him off. "No, I just always wanted Eric's life to be simple and my life too ... well, at least not to dwell on what might have been." There was a long pause. "But Bjorn was killed and that was the end of that."

But it wasn't, and now things weren't simple, Peter thought.

Elena sighed. "Now it's all come back, and I suppose I blame Jed for poking into it years ago and then getting involved again."

"But did Jed know?" Peter asked.

"Yes. Of course he's always known that I was your father's mother. He was eight years old when your father was born. He was very curious, asking questions about who your father's Swedish father was. At first, I couldn't say anything because your grandfather was in the resistance and especially because of who he was, and I had to say he had gone back to Sweden.

"Finally, one Christmas when we were all at your Frost grandparents', he was older, a teenager, then he really pestered me. In a weak moment, which I regret," Elena said, her voice hard, "I told him everything. I swore him to secrecy, but he never stopped being curious and trying to talk to me about it. He even visited Sundsvall and spoke to Bjorn. He pretended to be a writer and asked a lot of questions. And I think he encouraged your father to find out who Bjorn Svensson was."

"But it was Dad who analyzed the wire recording and discovered that Kjell on the recording had taken Bjorn's identity and kept it."

Elena was quiet. Finally, she spoke softly. "Yes, that's true. And now your uncle Jed is missing and maybe drowned ... I don't know. Perhaps I shouldn't have passed judgment so quickly. I'm just afraid now that no good will come of all this."

But the question of his grandfather's intentions was still unanswered. Now that Elena had gotten her anger out, maybe she would be willing to tell him. He decided to assume the answer and ask another question. "Aunt Elena, when Grandfather Bjorn wrote you about leaving Gevarfabrik to Dad, did he mention what Kjell would get?"

There was a long pause. When Elena spoke, she sounded very tired but firm. "Your grandfather Bjorn wrote me before he left England for Germany in 1941. I think he finally realized how dangerous it was going to be for him in Germany. His letter, which I kept, is sort of a will. It says that your father is his son and that he leaves Gevarfabrik and all his property to him with a small provision for Kjell. Kjell was to run Gevarfabrik until your father was old enough to decide what he wanted to do. Your grandfather says that Kjell agreed to this." Elena sighed, and when she spoke, her voice sounded very weak. Peter had difficulty hearing her. "I just never thought we would come to this point."

Chapter 41

ELENA'S INFORMATION CONFIRMED PETER'S fears about the situation he and his father faced. Peter did his best to reassure Elena that he would seek some professional legal help for them. He thought that legal help might include law enforcement, but he did not share that with Elena.

After he hung up, Peter considered going for a run to clear his mind and think through what to do next. But both Claes's admonition and his own concern that Anders might have revealed his presence in Stockholm militated against it. So he was stuck in his hotel room for the evening to figure something out.

His father was in trouble, for sure. How could what had started as a perfectly reasonable effort by his father to learn about and meet his biological father turned so ugly? And it was a lot uglier than his father realized. He opened the minibar and closed it without taking anything out. He walked to the window and looked over at Gamla Stan envying the tourists there whose biggest problem was choosing a restaurant for dinner.

He was pretty certain that he could not count on any help from Claes in getting his father away from Bjorn and Rolf and back from Lofsdalen. From Claes's perspective, the Bjorn-Kjell switch must have sounded pretty strange. And it would sound even stranger when Peter tried to connect it to the attacks on himself by neo-Nazis. The neo-Nazis had plenty of reason to harass him without being paid to do so by a well-known, presumably legitimate Swedish corporation. It did seem unlikely, but how else would Anders have known anything about his father?

Whatever. His priority now was to get his father away from Bjorn and Lofsdalen. That was not something he could do sitting in Stockholm, or worse, in London if he complied with Claes's order. He was not expected in Lofsdalen until Tuesday. That offered the possibility, at least, that he could get to the lodge the next day and find his father without running into serious interference. Anna wouldn't be there until Tuesday, she had said. But could she help them? Would she? That thought crossed his mind again. What had passed between them in Sundsvall just a few days before now seemed very remote.

Peter let out a long breath. He went back to the minibar. There were two small bottles of Chivas Regal, but drinking alone did not appeal to him. He took a Heineken and snapped the cap off. Beer was not drinking. As the Germans said, *"Bier ist Essen."* "Beer is food."

Should he call Claes and take one more shot at convincing him to let him stay in Sweden and maybe get his help in extricating his father from Lofsdalen? He would sleep on it and maybe call him in the morning. If he called now and Claes didn't agree, there would probably be an officer posted outside his hotel room until he was taken to the airport in the morning for the flight to London.

So the plan would be to catch the seven-thirty flight to Sveg and rent a car. Anna had described the location of the lodge in Lofsdalen on a steep hill overlooking a lake. There was a long driveway with several switchbacks that snaked up to it. He would figure something out when he got there.

With his early flight in mind, he decided to get some rest. He channel-surfed for a few minutes but found nothing of interest that was in English. He switched off the television and closed the shades as tightly as possible against the persistent evening sun.

As he began to drift toward sleep, his mind reran some of the events of the last two days. He considered the page that Anna had received and her announcement that she would need to leave for an emergency consultation. What a convenient coincidence for Bjorn and Rolf!

And Rolf, he thought. His potential effective inheritance of Gevarfabrik, based on his union with Anna and his role as the handpicked successor to Bjorn at Gevarfabrik, was threatened. What would he do to protect himself? Did Anna really know Rolf? He didn't think so.

His plan to go right to sleep was a nonstarter. It was after midnight. He turned on the television again and managed to find a British documentary. It was a detailed look at the mysteries of the pyramids. Eventually, despite the thoughts that had kept his brain in gear, the program was sufficiently distracting to take his mind away from Rolf and Bjorn, but boring enough to make him drowsy.

He woke up and found the television was still on. There was morning light in the gap between the curtains. The red numerals on the bedside clock radio showed 3:30. He got up and went into the bathroom to get a glass of water. He went back to bed, but at four o'clock, he was still awake. He knew his body needed more sleep, but his mind wanted to remain conscious, running scenarios for extracting his father from Lofsdalen without provoking a physical confrontation.

At forty thirty, he got up, drank a can of orange juice from the minibar, and dressed for a run. At that hour, the chances of encountering skinheads seemed low. Downstairs, he crossed the nearly empty lobby to the main entrance of the hotel. The desk clerk nodded to him. There was a man in one of the lobby armchairs reading a newspaper.

Outside the hotel at five o'clock in the morning, it was full daylight but Stockholm was still mostly asleep. A black Volvo sedan and its driver were waiting at the curb. Peter wondered if one of the two men, or perhaps both, were plainclothes policemen assigned to watch him. So much for trust, he thought. Or perhaps it was protection.

He shared the streets with a few early commuters, some walking and some in cars. His run took him from the hotel on Tegelbacken east to Drottninggatan. When Peter turned the corner into Drottninggatan, he saw several police cars along the left side of the street. Their blue and white lights were strobing continuously. Behind the police cars was an ambulance truck with its doors open. Three officers stood around a perimeter in front of a service alley. Peter stopped to join the group of people who were looking from across the street toward the alley that ran back in the direction of the hotel. Police and emergency medical personnel were clustered on one side of the alley.

In a couple of minutes, a rolling stretcher was brought inside the perimeter. In the brief moment when the stretcher was pulled upright and before a dark sheet was draped over it, Peter caught sight of a hooded sweatshirt and some red hair. Next to the stretcher, a woman in a blue uniform wearing latex gloves stooped and picked up a baseball cap.

Peter shuddered and looked around. The group of onlookers continued to peer down the alley. Peter edged past them and walked quickly up Drottninggatan to the end of the block. He turned left and sprinted back to the Sheraton.

The Volvo sedan was still parked in front of the hotel. Its driver was standing outside the car talking on a cell phone. When Peter looked at him, he looked away. In the lobby, the man with the newspaper was still reading but had moved to sit facing the entrance. He didn't look up as Peter crossed to the elevators. Just as the elevator doors were closing, Peter saw him put down the newspaper and pick up a cell phone.

In his room, Peter double-locked the door and drew a deep breath. Anders, poor bastard, his fear had been justified. He had probably been followed to the Sheraton and observed at their meeting in the restaurant. It was also likely that Anders's people—whoever they were—had a watcher at the hotel: either the man in the lobby or the one outside with the Volvo, so getting to Sveg meant dodging Anders's killers as well as any police surveillance and certainly leaving the hotel before Claes's officers arrived to escort him to his flight to London.

He dressed quickly and collected his backpack. In the lobby, he checked out, trying to look as though he suspected nothing. The man with the newspaper was still there. He paid his bill and noted that there were no additional restaurant charges for broken dishes. He asked the desk clerk to call a taxi for him. Peter waited in the lobby. In about three minutes, a Saab taxi appeared in front of the main door. Peter exited quickly and threw his backpack into the rear seat of the cab.

"Central Station, please," Peter said. The taxi driver looked surprised but said nothing. Within a block, the black Volvo appeared behind them. In another two blocks, they were at the station. The taxi driver executed a U-turn and pulled into the drop-off lanes in front of the station. Across the street, the black Volvo had stopped. A passenger that he had not seen in it got out and was crossing the street toward them.

Peter started to get out of the taxi. "Oh, wait, damn, I forgot something at the hotel. I have to go back."

"Ah yah, okay," the driver replied, pulling into the traffic.

The black Volvo's passenger was left in the middle of the street, looking confused. As Peter's taxi pulled away from the station, the black Volvo made a U-turn and picked up his passenger. It began to follow them again. Peter quietly withdrew a one thousand krona note from his wallet and put it under his backpack on the seat. He figured that something over a hundred dollars should compensate the taxi driver and increase the chances that he could eventually retrieve his backpack. He made a quick note of the cab's registration number on the hotel receipt.

When they arrived at the hotel, Peter said, "This may take me a few minutes. I'll pay for the waiting time, of course."

"Okay, you may take your time. I will have a smoke," the driver responded.

Peter exited the cab and brushed past the man with the newspaper who was outside the hotel. Inside, Peter took an elevator to the fifth floor. There, he exited and went to the stairwell. He ran down six flights past the lobby level to the parking garage. The garage was half filled with cars but otherwise seemed deserted. He crossed the floor quickly to the exit ramp and ran out onto the street, which led directly to Central Station. There was no sign of the black Volvo. Peter ran the three blocks to the station. He found a cab that had just dropped off a fare and directed the driver to Arlanda Airport. He watched the road behind them as they drove through the quiet streets north toward the highway. The expression "a clean getaway" jumped into his mind. He hoped it would be that easy in Lofsdalen.

Chapter 42

THE TAXI DROPPED PETER at Arlanda's Terminal Two for domestic flights. By the time he was seated in the departure lounge, it was seven o'clock, half an hour until his flight. He wanted to talk to Claes, but it was a gamble. If Claes knew he was going to Lofsdalen, he might alert the police at the airport in Sveg and try to stop him. If he didn't call Claes, he would be completely on his own no matter what happened in Lofsdalen.

At seven fifteen, his cell phone rang. There was no calling number on the display. If it was Claes, that would be a problem. As he thought about the odds and also considered the possibility that it might be his father, the phone rang twice more. He finally pressed the green answer button, but said nothing.

"Peter ... hello?"

He was relieved to recognize Bill Reilly's voice. "Bill? It must be nearly midnight for you."

"No, actually about one in the morning." He paused. "I've got some bad news for you. A couple of lobstermen found a body on the beach on Monomoy yesterday. ID on the body indicates it's your uncle."

Peter let out a sudden breath. "Drowned?"

"Yes. Plus other injuries."

"What kind of injuries?"

"Not self-inflicted. So I guess I didn't need your dad's help after all."

"Well ..." Peter began, thinking just the opposite.

"We also found his boat, the *Gaylord*, off Monomoy in about thirty feet of water. It was sitting upright with serious damage to one side."

"Like a collision?"

"Like a collision. And it matches damage to the *BlueFinn* charter boat. Could be some kind of accident," Reilly said. "Except of course for that bullet we found in the back of Captain BlueFinn's head."

And the likely explanation, Peter thought, is that someone chartered the *BlueFinn* to go after Jed. They took over the wheel and rammed the *Gaylord*. Then they got rid of the captain because he was a witness.

Peter looked at his watch. It was twenty past seven and a line had started to form by the check-in desk. "Bill, there's something you should know. I don't have time to give you all the details right now, but ..." What could he say quickly? "I think Jed met with some Gevarfabrik people from Sweden before he disappeared."

"Yeah?"

"And I think they could be responsible," Peter said.

Bill let out a whistling breath that came through the phone. "For Jed's death? But didn't you tell me one of these Swedes was ... what, your grandfather? What's going on?"

"It's complicated, and it's not good. Dad is with these guys up in the mountains now. I'm on my way up there to ... Look, I gotta go. I'll give you Claes Vikstrom's number. I have to make another call and get on a plane."

"Wait a minute. Screw the pla—"

Peter interrupted Reilly with Claes's contact information and disconnected. He punched Claes's office number into his phone as he started down the ramp to the plane. At this time in the morning, he should get Claes's voice mail, and if not, he could always hang up. It rang four times, and Claes's secretary's recorded voice offered short messages in Swedish and English. Peter spoke quickly. "The body in the alley off Drottninggatan is Anders, my informant. He came to me last night after you left. He told me about the business on the bridge ... they were there to kidnap me. Probably hold me hostage to get my father to sign the agreement that I told you about. Also, you can expect a call from Bill Reilly of the Massachusetts State Police about the death of my uncle, a lawyer in the States, who advised my father against signing the agreement. I think my dad needs some help at Bjorn Svensson's lodge in Lofsdalen. If there's anything you can do, I'd appreciate it."

According to the map in the airline magazine, Sveg was about two hundred miles northwest of Stockholm. Peter was grateful for the continental breakfast and strong Swedish coffee that was offered during the short flight. In about an hour, they began to descend past a thin layer of clouds, and a landscape of lakes and small mountains appeared.

There was a single car rental desk in the small, modern terminal building. Peter found himself third in line. By the time he reached the counter, he saw the tall blond agent give him a distressed look. "I'm afraid we have no more cars left," she said.

"Nothing?"

"Well, I believe we have a small panel van, but no passenger automobiles."

"I'll take it," Peter said.

"It is in our garage on the way into Sveg. I will call them and make sure it is still available." She confirmed it was and offered to drive Peter into Sveg to pick it up. "Since there's nothing I can do here now," she said giving Peter a warm smile. They took her dark blue Volvo cross-country wagon south through a small village near the airport. The garage was located just beyond the village. The panel van was white and needed washing. "Can you wait a few minutes while they clean the vehicle for you?"

"No. I'm sort of in a hurry. I'll take it just the way it is," Peter said. The agent completed the paperwork and gave Peter a map. Lofsdalen appeared to be about forty miles northwest of Sveg.

A short distance from the garage, he turned onto the main road. Within a couple of miles, he was in Sveg. The streets were wide, bordered by traditional-looking large wooden houses painted either in the usual bright brick red or mustard yellow. A river to Peter's left accompanied the road into the center of the town. There, he turned north and quickly left Sveg. There appeared to be only a single road in the direction of Lofsdalen, so that finding his way back to the airport would not be a problem.

For several miles beyond Sveg, the road skirted the northern shore of a large lake. Across the lake, there was a range of low mountains. The road passed through several small towns. The terrain was often marshy with occasional stands of tall pines. There were few cars on the road, and he drove faster than the van's small motor seemed to appreciate. A Mercedes and a Volvo sedan, also traveling toward Lofsdalen, flashed their lights at him as he blew by them. About ten miles from Sveg, two police cars approached him at high speed, but ignored his white van and continued toward Sveg

Beyond the lake, the road climbed gently. At a town called Linsell, Peter turned west onto a narrower road toward Lofsdalen. According to his map, his destination was about twenty-five miles farther. A few miles east of Lofsdalen, he began to watch for the turnoff on the right that led to a small settlement and beyond it to the Svenssons' mountain lodge. Anna had mentioned a large glacial erratic that marked the intersection with the main road.

When Peter began to see the ski chalets outside of Lofsdalen, he realized he had gone too far. He turned around and found the road to the lodge. It led through pine-covered, hilly terrain past several modest houses. From the stacks of firewood, he guessed they were year-round residences. After about a mile, a sign in Swedish and English warned off trespassers, and the hard paving on the road ended.

He continued through the woods. After a short way, just as the road began to climb again, a narrow cart track led off down to the left. On a tree next to it was a small faded sign that read, "*Båthus*." Probably the boathouse on the lake below the lodge that Anna mentioned, Peter thought. He turned onto the side road, thinking he would leave his vehicle out of sight of the road up to the lodge, which continued uphill.

The van bumped over potholes and ruts in the dirt track. After about a quarter of a mile, he had a glimpse of the lake ahead, shimmering behind the trees. Just in front of him, there was a deep puddle across the road. Rather than risk getting stuck, he turned the van around with some difficulty and left it facing back toward the lodge road.

He decided to avoid the boathouse and began to bushwhack his way up the hill. After a few minutes, he came to a steep embankment. He scrambled up the slope and onto a section of the driveway to the lodge, which appeared to be winding around the hill. Below and to his right, he saw a small stone cottage next to a sturdy wooden gate across the road. Inside the gate, the driveway was paved. It turned right, beginning a traverse up the hill. A hairpin turn brought it back to the point where he was standing.

He walked along the edge of the road toward the side of the hill facing the lake. Above him, there appeared to be a number of sections of the roadway, which wound around the small mountain to the lodge. The climb up the hill, through light forest growth and over several sections of the roadway, eventually brought him to a nearly vertical rock outcrop. It extended in both directions around the hill and appeared to be about fifteen feet high. But it was climbable, he thought.

In about ten minutes, after a couple of false starts, he found a route with sufficient hand- and toeholds up the rock face. At the top, he climbed out onto a section of the driveway just below the lodge. Peter noticed that reflectors had been nailed to the trees along the edge, but there was no guardrail. Above him, the hillside had been cleared of trees, probably to provide a view of the lake from the lodge, whose shingled roof he could just see over the hill. He walked a little farther up the slope until the second floor of the building was visible. A small balcony extended from a large dormer in the center of the lodge.

Peter skirted around to his right and climbed a few more yards up to the cover of a large stone garage below the house. From there, he could see the entire timber and stone structure, the Svenssons' impressive mountain retreat, which occupied the highest point of land. A small parking area between the lodge and the garage held a Land Rover, a Jaguar, and a gray Mercedes. Stairs from the parking area led up to a terrace overlooking the lake in front of the lodge.

There was no sign of activity. Peter moved from the side of the garage across the parking area to the lawn below the terrace. He crouched below the terrace in front of the lodge. From there, through a large picture window, he saw Bjorn and Rolf standing and his father sitting with his back to Peter. He quickly made his way back to the far side of the garage to think. Meanwhile, perhaps his father would come outside for some air or walk around the house by himself. Then, convincing his father to leave would be the next challenge.

Peter crouched by the garage watching the terrace and considering his options. He had been waiting about ten minutes when he heard steps on the parking area coming toward the garage. He turned to move back downhill and froze. Walking up the slope toward him was Lars with a semiautomatic handgun pointed directly at him.

Chapter 43

PETER STOOD UP SLOWLY. Lars put the handgun in his windbreaker pocket as he advanced toward Peter but the angle of his arm indicated that he had not lowered the weapon.

"Good morning, Peter," Lars said. "Vee didn't expect you until tomorrow." Peter thought he heard more than a hint of forced surprise in his statement. Peter did not reply. He turned as the person he had heard near the garage came up behind him.

"Peter, this is Axel. He works with me on security matters for Mr. Svensson. But perhaps you have already met, at least in passing," Lars said, throwing a half smile at the other man.

Axel was tall with dark hair drawn back into a short ponytail. A freshly stitched cut extended from the center of his forehead to his temple. He wore khaki pants and a tight black T-shirt, which showed off a good physique as well recent scratches and cuts on his arms. Probably the third man from the *Akvavit* that Claes had suggested had survived the crash, and perhaps Lars's friend that Mrs. Pedersson had mentioned, Peter thought.

Axel said nothing, but his eyes narrowed and his upper lip turned up slightly as he seemed to be evaluating Peter.

Peter turned back toward Lars. Well, on to Plan B, he decided. But he wasn't sure exactly what Plan B was. Lars motioned for him to follow Axel. They walked back to the parking area and up the stairs to the terrace. On the terrace, Axel opened a set of French doors into the room where Peter had seen his father with Bjorn and Rolf. Axel held the door for Peter and followed him inside. Lars did not come in.

His father stood up looking startled. His face was drawn, and he seemed nervous. "Peter, I thought …"

Bjorn also looked surprised, but Rolf smirked. Bjorn nodded to Peter but seemed distracted. Rolf looked directly at him but made no sign of greeting.

Eric was holding some papers in his hand. He grimaced slightly and spoke to Peter in a low voice, "I think we have a problem."

The discussion between Bjorn and Rolf and Eric was taking place in what appeared to be the main room of the lodge. It was large and comfortably furnished with couches and rocking chairs, but the atmosphere seemed anything but comfortable. Bjorn was standing, leaning forward and supporting himself on a large desk near the picture window. His face showed anxiety and anger. Rolf was on his left toward the back of the room. He was leaning against a large stone fireplace with his elbow on the mantelpiece. His eyes were half-lidded and the corners of his mouth turned down.

Eric turned to Bjorn. "I would like to speak to Peter privately. We can go out on the terrace."

"No," said Rolf drawing out the word for emphasis. "You have read the agreement. We have discussed it, and you understand it. It is time to sign it. We have had enough delay."

Peter wondered how Rolf was prepared to enforce his statement.

Eric looked at Bjorn. "I don't really understand the problem. I'm not planning to tell anyone about you and Bjorn changing identities in 1939, and I'm not claiming any inheritance. I've just been curious about my birth father," Eric said.

"Curious like your relative Mr. Jed Barlow?" Rolf said.

"Yes, he was interested, but I don't think he had any other motives," Eric responded.

Rolf looked at Bjorn with an expression that seemed to convey some meaning that caused Bjorn to look away quickly.

Eric sat down heavily. "Look, I think we can work something out. I just don't want to sign anything now, here. When I talked to Jed Tuesday morning, he told me whatever I did in Sweden, I shouldn't sign any agreement. I told him I would think about it and I have. Also, Peter told me the same thing after he knew the whole story."

"Rolf," Bjorn said quietly. "Maybe Peter can come to understand our position. Let us explain. And then I hope he can persuade his father why it is best for everyone if he signs the agreement."

"Yes," Rolf said. "Perhaps his experience as a journalist here has given him a more realistic understanding of the world."

"Experiences like getting mugged on the Strombron Bridge in Stockholm?" Peter said without thinking. Both his father and Bjorn turned to Peter.

"Peter, are you—" Eric began, looking shocked.

Rolf interrupted him, smirking at Peter. "Something that happened recently?"

Bjorn ignored Rolf's remark and spoke to Peter. "Sit down, please." He motioned him toward the couch facing the fireplace.

"Bjorn, we have been through this, and I can explain the issues to Peter." Eric turned as if to move toward the door to the terrace.

Rolf looked at Axel and nodded. Axel moved a step back so he stood in front of the French doors.

Bjorn repeated his request for Peter to sit down. "Will you have some coffee? Rolf, be so good as to get Peter a cup."

"No thanks," Peter said but sat on the edge of the couch while Eric remained standing. He tried to think.

Bjorn ignored Peter's response and motioned Rolf toward the coffee that had been set out on a large table in the back of the room. "Peter, I believe your father has explained the circumstances of my life and how I came to own Gevarfabrik. It all happened in good faith, many years ago when your, how-to-say, biological grandfather and I agreed that I would return in his place to Sweden after his father died. We decided that I would take over managing the business of Gevarfabrik while he would help to defeat the Germans."

Peter looked over at Bjorn. Bjorn didn't realize that he knew about the letter that Elena had from his grandfather, the real Bjorn. He wondered if Bjorn even remembered it—probably not, or Elena would have been in danger.

"Yah!" said Rolf, returning with the coffee. He handed Peter the cup and said, *"Varsågod"* with exaggerated intonation.

Bjorn looked at Rolf, clearly annoyed at his sarcasm. "Rolf, perhaps Peter will take some sugar in his coffee?" Bjorn said.

Peter put the coffee down on the low table in front of the couch and waved Rolf away.

"Bjorn," Eric said, returning to the discussion of the agreement. "Surely my father expected to return to Sweden eventually and reclaim his identity. And he expected to have my mother join him there when the war was over."

"Yes, of course, Eric. But we know that did not happen because ... your father did not survive the war."

"But does that change who inherits the property of the Svensson family?" Peter asked.

Eric looked at Peter questioningly. "That's really not the immediate issue. I am not trying to make any claim to the Svensson inheritance. But this document that Rolf is insisting on says that I agree that my father gave everything to ... to ..." Eric gestured to Bjorn. "To his friend. But as Jed pointed out, I have no firsthand knowledge of that. It could be fraud. Maybe there are Svensson cousins that should inherit something. This agreement also says that I will destroy the recording and transcripts."

"That's right, because without the recording, there's no way to prove that Bjorn here isn't really Bjorn Svensson, but with it, you can prove that Bjorn is really Kjell," Peter said.

"Enough," said Rolf, turning deliberately to a gun rack behind him to the right of the fireplace. He carefully lifted a rifle out, examined it, and then pretended to take aim at something on the balcony that ran around the edge of the room. He turned back to Peter and Eric. "You do not understand that Bjorn and I must insist that you sign this agreement." Then he pointed the rifle directly at Peter and said to Eric, "Hunting accidents, as Mr. Svensson knows, can occur even here in Sweden where we are very careful with weapons."

"Jesus," said Eric, staring at Bjorn.

Bjorn continued to look directly at Peter and said, "Eric, please sign the agreement; otherwise, this becomes very difficult."

Peter had to assume the rifle was loaded, and even if it wasn't, he had to assume Axel was armed. Obviously, any thought of leaving with his father in a straightforward way had been naïve at best. He saw his father look down at the agreement he was holding. "Dad, don't sign it," he said, reaching for his father's arm. "If you do, we'll both have hunting accidents," he added under his breath.

Eric looked confused. "But, Peter," he began and then stopped. His expression hardened, and he nodded.

Rolf moved closer to Peter, pointing the rifle at his legs. "Some hunting accidents can be very painful." At that moment, Rolf's mobile phone chirped. He motioned to Axel who moved across the room to him. Rolf carefully handed the rifle to Axel who kept it aimed at the lower part of Peter's body.

Rolf flipped open his phone. "Stengren." He paused. "Ah yah, Anna." Rolf spoke in Swedish but Peter thought he heard Rolf say something like "Where are ...?" Rolf did not seem pleased with her answer. Bjorn started to say something to Rolf. But Rolf ignored him and spoke rapidly in Swedish to Axel, pointing at Peter and Eric. He turned to Peter and Eric, "I will return very soon. I suggest you proceed with signing the agreement before I return. And I am sure that after Axel's experience Saturday night with you, Peter, that he will not hesitate to encourage you to cooperate." Rolf gave a hard glance at Bjorn and left the room.

Peter wondered if Anna had gotten away from her consulting early and was calling from somewhere between Sveg and Lofsdalen. Rolf was probably going to meet her and find some way to keep her away from the lodge. Perhaps if Anna were at the lodge, Bjorn at least, would not resort to violence. Anna might be able to make it possible for Peter and his father to leave safely. Unless ...? But he put that possibility out of his mind. Somehow, he needed to get to Anna before Rolf did and make sure that she came to the lodge.

Peter looked up at his father. "Dad, why don't you sit down and let me look at the agreement?" Peter hoped his feigned resignation to their situation was believable. Bjorn relaxed his grip on the edge of the desk slightly.

Eric looked surprised. "Peter, I don't want to sign this." But he followed Peter's lead and gave him the document, sitting next to him on the couch. Peter found a pen in his shirt pocket as though to make some notations.

Bjorn leaned forward. "Yes, Peter, please make your notes on this copy. We can print out another one for signing." He seemed greatly relieved.

Axel moved back toward the middle of the room and leaned against a large table. He continued to hold the rifle pointed toward Peter.

Peter paged through the document as though looking for a particular section. Then he made a notation on the edge of a page and bent towards his father to show it to him. The notation said, "Fake a heart attack."

A heavy door slammed somewhere in the house.

Eric stared at the page for a moment. Then he nodded and said, "Yes, I see." He took the document from Peter and pretended to read the page carefully. Then he started to cough and dropped the agreement. His hands moved to his chest, and he looked alarmed. He started to get up and then fell back on the couch and made some noises in his throat.

Peter felt grateful for the hours his father had spent in community theater. There was the sound of a car starting up in the driveway. Bjorn looked very concerned. He motioned to Axel who came forward hesitantly holding the rifle.

Peter turned to his father as though he was trying to help, but he kept his attention on Axel. Bjorn said something in Swedish, and Axel moved to hand him the rifle. As soon as Peter saw Bjorn begin to take the rifle, he leapt over the couch and bolted for the terrace door. He was outside before Axel and Bjorn could negotiate which of them should control the rifle.

Rolf's Jaguar was just disappearing around the side of the garage on the first loop of the driveway when Peter reached the edge of the terrace. He wasn't sure just how he was going to reach Anna before Rolf did. He needed some luck, like finding the keys in the Mercedes or the Land Rover.

From top of the steps down to the parking area, Peter could see over the driveway and through the trees all the way down the hill to the road by the gatehouse. As he started down the steps, he saw a car passing the gatehouse. He had to assume it was Anna. Remembering the loops and switchbacks the driveway made around the hill, he decided that he might be able to scramble down the steep hillside and intercept Anna on foot before Rolf could get to her in his car.

Peter sprinted across the parking area and through the low bushes above the upper loop of the roadway. The bushes were planted on the steep bank, which ended at the top of a high retaining wall. The roadway ran below the wall, about a fifteen-foot drop. If he jumped down, he could cross this first loop of the road before Rolf reached it, giving him more time to traverse the longer slope below it.

He eased himself over the rock wall aiming toward a spot just at the edge of the roadway that he hoped was relatively soft. Nearly at the bottom of the drop, his left foot caught a protruding rock and knocked him sideways. Peter landed on both feet but his left foot, screaming in pain, gave way. He rolled onto the center of the roadway. He heard Rolf's car, its tires squealing around the edge of the hill to his left. He rolled and scrambled frantically to the far side of the road, wedging himself under the bushes there—out of sight, he hoped. Rolf's gray Jaguar passed him, still accelerating in the short straight section before braking at the next curve around the hill.

Peter struggled to his feet. He ignored the pain in his left ankle and found he could put some weight on it. He pushed through the bushes toward the lower roadway, which was about sixty yards below. The hill was steep but in most places relatively smooth and grassy with occasional pine trees and boulders. Peter tried to run but lost his footing and fell. His shirt caught on a dead pine branch and ripped below the arm. He allowed himself to slide, got up, stumbled again, trying to stay upright and favoring his ankle.

Crossing another loop of the driveway, he looked down to his left and saw a blue Saab on the road below him, rounding the first switchback. By then, his ankle was numb. He felt as though he was running on a badly designed prosthetic foot. Despite his foot's refusal to obey simple commands, he managed to reach the lower roadway just as the car was approaching.

As he hobbled toward the car, out of breath and shedding pine needles and other bits of dirt, he had a moment of doubt. What if it was another one of Rolf's men? Maybe he should have stayed out of sight until he could see if it was Anna. But it was too late, he waved. The car slowed and stopped. It was Anna.

She looked surprised to see him but did not smile. "Peter, are you out for a run?" And then apparently noticing his torn shirt, she was suddenly concerned. "Did you fall? Are you all right?"

"Yes … no. I need to tell you something," he said. Peter opened the passenger door, trying to control his breathing.

Anna's face relaxed slightly into a more understanding expression. "I know, Peter. We will have time to talk about … but get in the car," she said, reaching across and putting her hand on Peter's arm.

"What?" he said briefly confused. "Yes, yes, but now there's something else." He forced himself to speak more slowly. "Rolf … Rolf is threatening … to kill us if we don't sign the agreement. He was holding a gun and—"

Anna cut him off, looking at him questioningly. "Rolf threatened you? Physically?" She paused, drawing a long breath. "There are some strange things … when I went to Lulea, no one at the hospital there knew why I had come."

"Maybe someone wanted you away from …"

At that moment, Rolf's Jaguar appeared on the road coming toward them. It stopped with a screech of rubber directly in front of Anna's car.

Rolf got out and walked up to her side of the car. "Anna …" he began and then saw Peter. "What is he doing in your car?"

Anna's eyes narrowed, but otherwise, her face showed no expression. "We were talking, Rolf. We will see you at the lodge in a little bit. I think we need to discuss what is going on."

Rolf gripped the edge of the window so hard that Peter could see his knuckles turn white, but he said nothing. Then, after a long moment, he said, "Very well, I will turn around and follow you up there."

Anna closed the window and turned to Peter. "I will drive slowly. Tell me what has happened."

Chapter 44

HOW COULD HE EXPLAIN quickly what was happening? "Look, this agreement they want my father to sign, he can't do it. He shouldn't." Peter paused. "We need advice from a lawyer, our own lawyer. It may be fraudulent … criminal. And …"

"Criminal?" Anna let out a breath, frowning. Driving slowly, she turned toward Peter. "You said that Rolf pointed a gun at you. Were you serious?"

Peter grasped Anna's arm. "Yes. He said something about a 'hunting accident.' Rolf and your father are determined to get my father to sign before he can leave."

Anna briefly squeezed her eyes shut, shaking her head.

"Can you talk to your father and get Rolf under control?"

Anna did not respond. She looked straight ahead and slowed the car as they approached the switchback on the lake side of the hill. Peter looked back; Rolf's Jaguar was inches from Anna's rear bumper. His thin face was set in an angry stare at Anna.

"I will talk to my father. And Rolf …" She began. "I have a problem with Rolf, but I do not believe he would do anything … violent."

"Well, he told your man Axel to hold us there with a rifle when he left to meet you," Peter responded. And there's more about Axel, he thought.

They came around the last turn and into the parking area. Anna pulled in front of the garage. Rolf parked directly behind them blocking her car. She seemed surprised but said nothing. They walked up the steps to the terrace and into the house in silence. Rolf followed Anna and Peter and kept his hands in the pockets of his leather jacket.

When they entered the room, Bjorn was still standing behind the desk. He looked tired and anxious. He smiled weakly at Anna who crossed the room and went to him. Eric was still sitting on the couch with the agreement document in his lap. Axel had retreated to the back of the room. He was standing holding the rifle trained on Eric. Peter moved next to the couch where his father sat. Rolf stood just inside the door.

Bjorn cleared his throat, but Anna was the first to speak. "Axel, please put that rifle away. Now."

Peter thought that this must be the same even, respect-commanding tone that she would use in a medical emergency with assisting physicians and nurses. Axel looked uncertainly at Rolf and then walked to the gun rack behind Bjorn where he latched the rifle into place. When Axel turned back, Rolf spoke to him, and he left the room.

Anna spoke again. "Father, I know how anxious you are about this agreement with Eric, but I understand from Peter that Eric needs to consult with his lawyer in the United States and perhaps with his own lawyer here in Sweden. Your becoming Bjorn Svensson, even so long ago, needs to be resolved carefully and legally. And without threats," she added, looking at Rolf.

"But, Anna, without Eric's agreement, we might lose Gevarfabrik and everything we have. This is for you. And Rolf," Bjorn said.

"And Rolf? I do not think so." Anna said, first turning to her father and then to Rolf. "My trip to Lulea appears to have been some attempt to get me away from here. There was no emergency, and no one had heard of the doctor who called me. Now I can see why. And I think I know who is responsible."

Eric cut in. "Anna, I've explained to your father that I am not asking for any inheritance or compensation, and I'm sure Peter feels the same way."

Bjorn sighed. "All right then, but how shall we leave it? That you will take the agreement with you and get approval from your lawyers?" Bjorn's resistance seemed to have collapsed. "I suppose we have no choice."

"No." Rolf barked from the other side of the room. "You old fool, Bjorn! I could see when I arrived in Smavik that you had given in to Mr. Frost and his late cousin, Mr. Barlow." He held a small semiautomatic that he aimed toward Peter and Eric.

"Rolf!" said Anna. "You cannot threaten people with guns. Also, this is a family issue, and after your trick on Saturday and your behavior now, I do not think you have any standing in this family. Nor will you in the future. In fact, your employment at Gevarfabrik will be over as soon as I am in control, or sooner, if I can persuade my father."

Rolf looked at Anna and spit out two words in Swedish that Peter assumed were seriously obscene from the momentary look of shock on her face. Bjorn staggered and began to say something to Rolf, but Rolf ignored him.

"Despite what you think about family," Rolf snorted derisively, "I have some rights which transcend yours ... as you know," he said glancing at Bjorn.

Anna looked at her father with a questioning expression. He said nothing, but his eyes were wide with fear. Peter sensed a new dimension to the tension in the room, and he was for the first time afraid that Anna could no longer offer a controlling influence.

"Anna, dear," Rolf sneered, "we have run out of time and patience. Your father has tried to kindly persuade Mr. Frost Sr. here to sign the agreement that confirmed your father's ownership of Gevarfabrik. But like most stupid Americans who are always calling their lawyers, he is wasting our time. He pretends to agree that he has no interest in the Svensson family assets."

Rolf's anger was evident, but it seemed fully under control and even pleasurable to him as he went on in perfect English. Peter sensed his rant was a prelude to violence. But Rolf was standing far enough away so that even if he became completely intoxicated by his venom, Peter did not think he would be able to reach him before Rolf could react.

"But that's true," Eric protested.

"And then what has your relative Barlow been up to all these years?" Rolf responded.

Rolf seemed to be enjoying the debate with his father, which allowed Peter to think that perhaps if he moved cautiously, he might be able to get close enough to Rolf to spring for his gun hand.

"Mr. Svensson has told me about Mr. Barlow's interest in this matter. I am sure it is to secure money for his American family," Rolf said.

"That's ridiculous," Eric said.

Peter turned to Anna. "Jed Barlow's body was found yesterday. He was murdered after Rolf and your father came to the U.S." He edged toward Rolf

"My God!" Eric said.

Anna's head jerked around toward Peter. "What are you saying?"

"Hah," Rolf uttered in a short laugh. "We left on Tuesday morning. We understand that he disappeared the next day."

"You and Bjorn and my father left but not Lars," Peter said. "And it was probably Lars who went through my father's workshop lab in the cellar looking for the wire recording that proves that Bjorn is really Kjell."

"Well, you will just have to discuss that with Lars. I'm sure he will be happy to talk to you," Rolf sneered and then turned to Anna. "These people are not what they seem. Eric has been charming your father with his work as a simple engineer and a sailing enthusiast. And he even needs his son, your new friend Peter, to seduce you with his heroic status as the exposer of neo-Nazis in Sweden."

Peter inched almost close enough to launch himself at Rolf.

"Rolf, you are a fool. You don't know what you are talking about. This has to stop," Anna said taking out her mobile phone.

Rolf went on, his eyes mainly on Anna but darting looks at Eric and Peter as he spoke. "Anna, what you do not realize is that there is a more serious problem than your father's changing places with the real Bjorn Svensson, Eric's father, and I will tell

you what it is so that you will understand why you cannot dismiss
me like a servant."

"Nay, nay, Rolf," Bjorn said hoarsely. He was shaking
and sat heavily in the chair behind the desk.

Rolf looked at him and gave a half laugh. He turned back
to Anna. "When I first went to work for your father as his
assistant, I found some old letters from the period of the Second
World War in his personal files. One of these was a letter of
thanks from the German ambassador to Sweden in 1941." He
paused and looked at Bjorn with a faint smile. "The letter
thanked your father for his help in the arrest of a Swedish citizen
working for British intelligence in Germany." He paused. "That
Swedish citizen was the real Bjorn Svensson, your father's dear
friend."

Eric turned back to face Bjorn. "Oh, God, I hope that's
not true."

"But it is … as our Mr. Barlow suspected. He was stupid
enough to threaten us when we talked to him alone."

Anna looked at her father hoping to see denial in his
expression. But his face was red and contorted in anger. His eyes
were fixed on Rolf.

"Blackmail? Is that it, Rolf?" Anna began to push
numbers on her mobile phone.

Rolf swung his arm around, pointing his weapon at Anna.

Peter yelled at Rolf, hoping to grab his attention, and
leapt toward him.

Rolf fired.

Peter heard Anna cry out as he reached Rolf and gripped
his arm. But Rolf's gun was between them, the hot barrel
pressing into Peter's stomach. Peter felt Rolf's arm tense and saw
his face relax into a leering grin of anticipation.

"Peter, you are—" Rolf began. He never finished the
sentence. There was a deafening explosion in the room. Rolf
jerked sideways and slammed against the wall. Blood streamed
from the side of his neck.

Peter turned and saw Bjorn carefully setting a large
handgun down on the desk in front of him. It was still smoking.
Eric moved to Anna, kneeling in front of her.

Anna was sitting on the floor clutching her left arm. "Eric, would you put your belt around my arm up here." She indicated her upper arm. "Peter, are you all right?" He nodded. "Can you help Rolf?"

Peter marveled that her doctor's instincts were intact even as she sat bleeding on the floor. He leaned down over Rolf who was completely still; his eyes were open but lifeless. Peter reached to feel for a pulse on his neck, but there was only a large hole there. Peter's hand was bloody as he drew it away.

Peter went over to Anna. "How is he?" she asked. Peter shook his head.

"My father had a large-caliber weapon," she said quietly.

Peter looked up to where Bjorn had been standing, but he was gone.

"Can you make that tighter, Eric. I'm still losing blood," Anna said.

"We need to get you to a hospital," Peter said. "Is there one closer than Sveg?"

"No, not really." Anna's voice trailed off. "I am feeling a little faint." She put her head down between her legs.

"Okay." Peter was on his feet. "Dad, use the phone here to call the police and see if they can send an emergency vehicle to meet us. I'll take Anna's car."

Peter helped Anna to her feet, and they walked out onto the terrace. He was unaware of any pain in his ankle but afraid for Anna that he might trip over it. They took the steps to the parking area carefully.

When they reached the Saab, Peter helped Anna into the front seat and attached her seat belt. The sleeve and left side of her yellow blouse were soaked with blood. He went to roll Rolf's Jaguar out of the way. As he reached the door, he felt a metal object in the back of his neck. In his peripheral vision, he recognized Axel's black T-shirt.

"Get into the back seat of the Saab." Axel prodded his neck painfully.

Peter saw no alternative. He hoped his father had managed to reach the police. But as he was getting into the car, he looked up to the lodge and saw his father being marched across the terrace by Lars.

When they came to the car, Anna said, "Lars, Rolf is dead. Whatever orders you and Axel have are canceled. You need to release us immediately."

Lars's eyes narrowed, and the corners of his mouth turned up in a grimacing smile. He said quietly, "There are others."

Lars had taken off his windbreaker, and Peter's eyes were drawn to his bare arms. Below the short sleeves of his dark green T-shirt, the neo-Nazi double "S" lightning bolts were tattooed on each stringy bicep. Anna's gaze also seemed drawn to the markings on Lars's arms.

Lars's smile increased fractionally when he saw them looking at his arms. "Peter, you vill please move to the driver's seat and put your hands on the vheel."

He prodded Eric into the back seat and then climbed in himself and sat behind Peter. "Please drive back down the roadway. Slowly. As you noticed on the vay up, there are places where the hill is very steep at the edge of the road." He directed Axel to move Rolf's Jaguar and follow them in the Land Rover.

Peter remembered Reilly telling him about a hostage situation in which the victim had managed to keep talking long enough for the perpetrator to become distracted and provide an escape opportunity. Peter didn't know what long enough might be, but at least he could try.

"Lars, do you know what happened to Jed Barlow?"

"Keep driving. Slowly," was the response.

Peter had a sudden inspiration. "Apparently his boat capsized but he managed to swim to an island and ..."

Lars cut him off with a harsh-sounding Swedish word and continued, "That's impossible. He vas dead vhen he fell off the boat."

"I guess he must have gotten hit pretty hard on the head by the boom."

"Yah," Lars blew out. "It vas a boom for sure vhen the *BlueFinn* and his sailboat had a little accident. Your Mr. Barlow vas standing on the deck vafing til us to stop vhen the big boom came." Lars's high-pitched laugh filled the car.

Peter looked back at his father in the rearview mirror. His jaw was clenched in anger. Peter was counting on him to contain himself.

Lars went on without further encouragement. "I thought that old Captain Haake vas so drunk he vouldn't mind if I steered the fishing boat but vhen vee boomed into Mr. Barlow's boat, the old man tried to get the vheel away from me. So I had to shoot him," Lars said, his voice rising. He jammed the automatic harder in to Peter's neck. "Okay, vee stop here now."

They had come around to the section of the driveway below the terrace and the lawn overlooking the lake. They were just above the spot where Peter had climbed up the nearly vertical rock face. He eased open the back door of the car still holding his gun to Peter's neck and called to Axel.

Peter looked in the rearview mirror, and saw Axel approaching the car with a large red plastic can. He was smiling as he opened the trunk. Almost immediately, there was a strong smell of gasoline in the car. Axel returned to the Land Rover and drew it up behind them.

When the Land Rover made contact with the Saab, Lars walked beside the car with his gun aimed at Peter's head. "Perhaps, you have guessed, Peter, that Axel is looking forward to returning your toast from Saturday night. He vas very fond of the *AkvaVitt*."

Peter made no comment and held his foot hard on the brake. He knew his options were limited. Eric could jump out but would probably be shot. Anna was near unconsciousness and could not get out by herself. If he got out, the car would offer no resistance and be quickly pushed over the edge of the road.

The Land Rover strained at the Saab, pushing it only a few feet. Peter turned the wheel away from the drop-off toward the inside of the hill. But because all the brakes were locked on, the steering had little effect. The Saab continued to shudder toward the lip of the roadway. Rubber from both vehicles protested against the pavement.

Lars became impatient at the progress and got into the Land Rover pushing Axel over to the passenger's side. He gave the gun to Axel who kept it pointed at the Saab. Lars backed the Land Rover up and then came toward the Saab at a better angle to roll it off the side of the road. When the Rover hit the Saab with a loud, jolting bang, Anna groaned softly and the smaller car rocked sideways.

Peter saw a slim opportunity in the Land Rover's new position. At this angle, the Saab was being pushed from the side and its resistance to moving forward was actually greater than before. The Land Rover's engine was revved up and whined with the effort, its wheels squealing on the asphalt. Peter allowed the Saab to be pushed just to the edge of the pavement. Then he suddenly released the brakes and simultaneously came down hard on the accelerator. With a scraping of metal on metal, the little car shot away from the Land Rover along the edge of the road.

The Land Rover, its wheels still spinning against the road and its motor turning over at full speed, immediately accelerated toward the edge of the road, all resistance to its movement having disappeared. Through the rearview mirror, Peter watched the Land Rover shoot over the edge of the road and disappear. There were sounds of branches breaking, followed by a loud crash and an explosion. Then it was strangely quiet as Peter brought the Saab to a stop in the middle of the roadway.

Eric jumped out of the car and opened Anna's door. She smiled weakly as Peter and his father helped her out. They hurriedly carried her away from the Saab just before flames burst from the trunk and quickly engulfed the small sedan.

Moving down the road away from the fire, they heard the sound of heavy vehicles coming up toward them. In moment, a black Land Rover appeared. It was clearly marked in large white letters: "POLIS."

Chapter 45

THE LAND ROVER STOPPED, and the doors opened. Four SWAT-team-clothed men carrying semiautomatic rifles jumped out. They were identified as SAPO, Swedish Security Police members, by the markings on their black vests. They took up defensive positions, scouting the sides of the road and the hill below the lodge.

As the police team moved cautiously toward Peter, Eric, and Anna, the sound of a shot from the direction of the lodge caused them to turn and crouch briefly. When they resumed their movement up the road, they pointed their weapons away from the three civilians.

They were quickly followed by a tall figure in a flak jacket that Peter immediately recognized as Claes. He hurried toward them. Seeing that Anna was injured, he spoke rapidly into his walkie-talkie. Within seconds, three medics carrying a stretcher appeared from one of several additional police vehicles that had come up behind the lead Land Rover.

"Miss, ah, Doctor Svensson, we will take you to the hospital in Sveg by helicopter. If necessary, we can take you to Stockholm," Claes said.

"I'm going along. Dad, can you explain what happened here and up there?" Peter said gesturing toward the lodge. Eric nodded.

"Okay. I am glad you and your father are all right. We will talk later." Claes smiled briefly but warmly. He addressed the medics in Swedish and then turned to Eric and introduced himself. "Will you stay with me while we sort this out?"

Peter traveled with Anna to the well-equipped clinic in Sveg. The wound in her arm was serious, but the small-caliber bullet had passed cleanly through the soft tissue. The doctors told them that her recovery should be complete. That night, he slept at the clinic on a couch in the lounge. Claes had sent word that a forensic team was on its way and that he and Eric would remain at the lodge.

The next morning, Claes came to the hospital. He told Peter he had some difficult news for Anna. Peter sat with Anna while Claes explained that they had found her father's body upstairs at the oak desk in his bedroom. He had shot himself with a small-caliber handgun. His death had been instantaneous. Anna received the news stoically, but she held Peter's hand as she read the note that her father had left.

Later in the morning, Anna was able to leave the clinic. She asked to return to the house in Sundsvall. Claes said he had numerous questions but that he could interview them all there. They flew by police helicopter to Sundsvall, touching down on the wide lawn beside the house.

In the afternoon while Claes and Anna spent some time in her father's study, Peter called Elena and gave her a very sanitized version of events.

"I'm so glad that you and your father are all right, but I'm very sorry to hear that Kjell has died. Please give my sympathy to his daughter." Elena paused. "Now, I have the idea that what happened is a little more complicated than you are telling me. So I'll look forward to you both coming up to see me so I can hear the rest of it."

Peter smiled. He should have known better than to try and blow smoke in his grandmother's ear. "Just a few more details," he said making no attempt to sound convincing.

Next he called the *VERITAS?* office and spoke to Gene. To avoid a long explanation by phone, he told him that they were going to have to rethink the follow-up article on neo-Nazis. "My informant died."

"Natural causes?"

Peter didn't reply.

"I see. So what's Plan B?"

"There isn't one, and also, I'm not sure exactly when I'll be back," Peter said.

"Well, let me know when you work out your schedule," Gene said. "And by the way, our CFO expects you to find a cheap ticket even if it's by way of Zagreb with a connection through Oklahoma City."

Peter started to offer a retort about the imaginary CFO, but Gene had hung up. He called Jill and endured several minutes of good-natured complaining about the extra work his drug decriminalization article had made for her. But he was able to get off the line by pleading a shortage of charge on his phone battery before she began questioning him about his personal life. There would be time for that.

Later, Eric joined Peter on the terrace. "You said something on the flight down here about a letter that Bjorn had sent to Elena after I was born."

"Yes. It's basically a will that leaves Gevarfabrik to you with something for Kjell, which I guess goes to Anna."

"I'm not about take everything away from Anna," Eric said.

"Of course, but I think she has some thoughts of her own about Gevarfabrik."

Eric shook his head and blew out a breath. "Lord, what would your mother say? And my knowledge of guns wouldn't fill up a three-by-five card. Anyway, Anna's father, whoever he was, did build up the business, and she certainly is entitled to a big part of it. I hope we can figure out what to do together about Gevarfabrik."

Later in the afternoon, Claes emerged from his meeting with Anna and gave Eric a sheet of paper. "Anna asked me to make a translation of this for you and Peter."

Eric read it and then handed it to Peter.

My Dear Anna,

Please know that I am very sorry for what I did many years ago. I have caused you much pain. But I ask you to hold a small amount of love for me in your heart.

Your loving father

Eric,

I understand that you may have only hate for me but please try not to make any difficulties for my Anna. She is not responsible for what I did to your father. And you must know that I did not intend your father's death. I only wanted to prevent him from returning to Sweden for a time. I was afraid then for myself, that if I refused to sell Gevarfabrik rifles to the Germans that I would be killed just as your grandfather Erik had been, by their agents here in Lofsdalen in 1939.

Kjell Hendrikson (signed)

Peter looked at Eric. Eric's lips were pressed together but twisted into an expression of doubt. "I'm still in shock that Kjell was even indirectly responsible for my father's death." He sighed. "But I guess it's possible that he didn't intend the consequences. Bjorn and Elena and Kjell were all pretty young back then. At that age, you don't always think things through."

"Well, you were right when you told me that Bjorn-Kjell was a complicated guy. More than you knew," Peter said.

"Yes, and what's strange and sad is that I really enjoyed the week I spent sailing with him. He shared some recollections of my father, the real Bjorn, with me. But I can't imagine how he could talk to me about him after what he had done."

"Maybe in some way, he was trying to make it up to you," Peter said.

"Could be. Also he wasn't pushing me on the agreement very hard. As he says, he was mainly concerned about Anna. I think that Rolf was almost completely in charge of Gevarfabrik. And he was putting Bjorn-Kjell under a lot of pressure. He must have called him on the boat ten times a day."

Peter stood up and carefully put a little weight on his bad ankle. "I need to get something from the fridge."

"Beer?"

"An icepack and a beer."

In the kitchen, Peter pulled two light beers from the refrigerator and retrieved a bag of ice from the freezer. "By the way, there's something I need to tell you," Peter said, turning to face his father.

Eric looked at him curiously then grinned. "You mean about you and Anna?"

Peter smiled slightly. "Ah, no, that's not what I meant." As they stood in the kitchen, Peter went on to give his father a scaled down version of the incidents on the bridge in Stockholm and the pursuit by the *AkvaVitt*. He explained that, based on what his informant had told him, Rolf had probably been behind the attacks by the skinheads. "Maybe to take me as a hostage in exchange for your signature on the agreement."

"Oh, Peter," Eric said. "My interest in finding my real father got Jed killed and almost got you killed too." He shook his head. "You took a big risk trying to get your old man out of trouble. And I owe you a big apology for not appreciating your warning about the agreement when we were on Grenvik," Eric said, putting his arm around Peter's shoulders as they walked back to the terrace. Peter warmly returned his father's gesture.

After they had installed themselves on the terrace again, Peter asked his father if he thought that Elena had ever considered telling him who his birth parents were before he asked.

"I don't think so," Eric replied.

"Maybe she was just sort of in denial," Peter suggested, thinking that was like something Jill would say. "Maybe it became easier for her to believe the fiction that they had created. So, just like Kjell, after a while, she tried to believe the switch was reality. And I guess she used the pact that she and Bjorn and Kjell had made in 1939 as a reason for not telling you the truth. Even if that was in conflict with Bjorn's letter."

Eric looked across the Sundsvall valley in the direction of the Sodra Berget Hotel. "But I wonder what she might have done if she had known that Kjell betrayed Bjorn to the Nazis? If we tell her, that could be quite a shock."

"Yes, that's a tough call," Peter said.

Before dinner, Eric went for a walk. Anna found Peter and told him she wanted to be with him. "But no talking," she said. "At least, not serious talk. We'll have time perhaps, just not today." Her eyes were sad, but her smile was warm as she leaned in to kiss him and accept an awkward embrace that spared her bandaged arm.

They went out on the terrace where Anna lay down on a lounge chair under a light blanket. Peter propped his foot up on the table. They talked about Anna's apartment in Stockholm overlooking the eastern end of Lake Malaren on Segelbatvagen.

"That sounded sort of like you said 'Sailboat Way,'" Peter said.

"I did. You'd like it," she replied.

Later, she dozed, and Peter read a Per Lindstrom mystery that she had brought back from England.

That evening after dinner, Anna went to bed early. Claes took the opportunity to speak to Peter and Eric. They sat in the living room drawing on a bottle of Scotch that Anna had produced earlier for Claes. "I must apologize again that we did not arrive at the lodge in time to give you more help." He paused. "But in the future, I hope you will try not to do the work of SAPO by yourself," he said with a crooked smile.

"I might not have come at all, but I received a report yesterday morning when I arrived at work. It provided the identification of the owner of the power cruiser *AkvaVitt* that pursued you. The owner was Axel Arvidsson whom you encountered at the lodge. He was employed on the security staff of Gevarfabrik, as was Lars."

Peter nodded. "From what Lars and Axel said yesterday and the cuts I saw on Axel's face, I think he was probably at the wheel of the *AkvaVitt* and was thrown clear when it crashed. Lars probably took him off the island on Sunday morning."

Claes sipped his Scotch carefully and looked at Peter. "I think that we have found information that will be useful for your writing for *VERITAS*?. Yesterday, when we searched the lodge, we found records and documents that confirm what Rolf Stengren revealed to you about Bjorn-Kjell's responsibility for the capture of Bjorn Svensson in 1941. And some of the papers provide an answer to the question you had posed about the funding of neo-Nazis in Sweden.

"Rolf was an active neo-Nazi sympathizer. That apparently began when he worked for a music company producing hatecore records—it's a small neo-Nazi industry here. We also think both attacks on Peter were Rolf's work, not Mr. Bjorn-Kjell's. When Rolf discovered the truth about Eric's father's death, he conceived the idea of blackmailing Bjorn-Kjell—as you found out. Bjorn-Kjell thought that Rolf was simply negotiating with the blackmailers for him. In fact, Rolf had initiated the blackmail that forced Bjorn-Kjell to pay out significant amounts of money from Gevarfabrik to a sort of coordinating group for the neo-Nazis."

Claes stopped to make a short Swedish toast to Peter. "My superior suggested that I offer SAPO's congratulations to you—informally, of course—for helping us to bring this all to light. Anyway, I think that you now have some of the information that you wanted about the funding of the neo-Nazis here in Sweden.

"And by the way, Eric, Gevarfabrik should become significantly more valuable now that none of its profits will be diverted to the neo-Nazis. However, the company may now have to pay more taxes."

Claes finished the last of his Scotch in his glass and looked at his watch. "Yah so, it is getting late. I have to be in Stockholm in the morning for a meeting with a friend of yours, Peter, a Lieutenant Bill Reilly."

"Ah yah," Peter said, thinking that he had gotten the intake of breath almost right.

"He called me this morning. I think we may be able to help him with his investigation. There seems to be an involvement with people in Gevarfabrik's American subsidiary. Apparently, with their help, Lars, as he boasted to you, was responsible for the death of Jed Barlow."

"I think Lars also went to Dad's house in Brewster to get the wire recording."

"Well, he wouldn't have found it," Eric said. "I was going to give it to Jed for safekeeping but I didn't want to mail it. I thought that there would be time the morning before I left, but Rolf came earlier than I expected."

"So what happened to it, Dad?"

"I kept it," he said, reaching into his pants pocket and producing a spool of wire about the size of a hockey puck.

Peter rolled his eyes. Claes looked amused but said, "Perhaps, Eric, you would entrust me with the recording, for the moment."

Claes put the wire spool in a small plastic bag. He slipped it into his briefcase and stood up. After a round of warm handshakes, he left Peter and Eric standing in the large foyer by the front door.

"So, Dad, when this is all sorted out, it looks like you're going to own a gun factory and be a serious weapons supplier," Peter said grinning.

"Well, right now, I'm going to bed, and I'm going to try not to think about it." He gave Peter a hug. "What about you?"

"I think I'm going to go up and check on Anna."

The End

Acknowledgments

Many people have generously offered their time in reading and providing thoughtful criticism as this work progressed. I am especially indebted to my wife, Kathy, for her loving support and practical help in all aspects of the creation of *Swedish Blood*. My good friend Mike Fosburg offered me inspiration and suggestions. My daughters, Lisa, Alyson, and Amanda, read drafts and offered their loving encouragement and thoughts. I am also indebted to my friend and high school English classmate, author Bill Tapply, for his wise and extensive critique of an early draft of this novel and to author and writing coach Sarah Lovett for her support and advice. The members of my Cambridge-based writing group (Kitty Beer, Marty Levin, Jeanne Harnois, Jackie Fenn and Paula de Fougerolles) have read this manuscript over several years in serialized form and provided me with the benefit of their talent and experience. My old friend Seelye Martin offered his encouragement, as did writer Ed Rosenfeld and journalist Sam Doran. I am grateful to Kate Mattes and author Gillian Gill for their wisdom in some of the practical areas of authorship. My thanks to friends and acquaintances in Sweden for many, very enjoyable and engaging times there over many years. The help of my family and friends has been invaluable, but any shortcomings in this novel are my responsibility alone.